A CROWN OF IRON & SILVER

SILVER

SOULBOUND III

HAILEY TURNER

Cover design by AngstyG LLC.
Professional Beta Reading by Leslie Copeland: lcopelandwrites@gmail.com
Edited by One Love Editing
Proofing by Lori Parks: lp.nerdproblems@gmail.com

Don't miss out on sneak peeks, exciting news, and more!
Sign up for Hailey Turner's newsletter
to stay up to date on her upcoming books.

To Lily Morton
For being an amazing friend while halfway across the world.
My days aren't complete until we've spoken.
Your support means everything to me, and I'm so glad I know you.

SPECIAL AGENT PATRICK COLLINS SLAMMED THE MUSTANG'S TRUNK closed, swearing when he almost dropped the umbrella and his grocery bags. Not that the umbrella was doing much good against the icy rain coming down sideways, driven by a strong wind. His damp clothes were getting wetter, and no amount of drying charms would fix that while he was outside.

"Fuck it," Patrick muttered.

He pushed his personal shields out of his skin, letting the invisible barrier of magic protect him from the rain while under the umbrella. Patrick sighed in relief at the momentary respite from the weather. At 2130, Patrick was cold, tired, and hungry after a long day working out of the Supernatural Operations Agency's field office. He'd stopped by Westside Market on the drive home to pick up the groceries he'd forgotten to get last night. He was too tired to cook tonight, but hopefully pizza was waiting for him at home.

Stepping onto the sidewalk, Patrick headed down the street toward the five-story brownstone apartment building he called home in Chelsea. He'd shared the top-floor apartment with

Jonothon de Vere since July. He'd never realized how nice it was to have someone to come home to until he'd moved in with Jono. All those years of returning to a quiet apartment or hotel room paled in comparison of being met at the door with a kiss.

Some of the buildings he passed had windows decorated with Christmas lights and cutouts of Santa Claus and reindeer on the inside. A few had their curtains parted enough he could see the decorated Christmas trees inside the apartments. Ever since Thanksgiving, more and more homes were starting to decorate for the holidays, but everyone lagged behind the touristy spots in the city.

Patrick couldn't wait to get home, eat, and crawl into his nice warm bed. His latest case had involved a group of kappas in the Hudson River hassling commuter ferries. He'd ended every work day for the past three soaked to the bone. Heat charms in his leather jacket aside, if some other creature took over the New York harbor during December, he was punting the job to someone else.

If he got sick, he was taking the rest of the month off and heading to Maui.

Patrick hefted the three reusable grocery bags in his right hand, ignoring the way the nylon handles dug into his palm. He needed to walk one block, and then he'd be home and warm.

When he was half a block away—so close, yet so far—recognition burned through Patrick's magic with the heated spark of werecreatures. He squinted through the rain at the group of people standing in front of his apartment building and scowled.

"Are you fucking kidding me right now?" Patrick groaned.

His semiautomatic HK USP 9mm tactical pistol was holstered on his right hip and the gods-given dagger was strapped to his right thigh. Even with his hands full, Patrick wasn't without a weapon.

Patrick pushed more of his magic out of his soul, letting it form a mageglobe near his left shoulder. The small sphere of raw magic hovered in the air and kept pace with him as he closed the distance between himself and the suddenly attentive group of werecreatures.

In August, Jono had declared his own god pack, separate from the New York City god pack run by Estelle Walker and Youssef Khan. That declaration had created a lot of tension between their newly formed god pack and most of the other packs in the city. More than once they'd been accosted around the one-block territory they claimed as theirs.

Patrick wasn't in the mood for another fight. He wanted to get inside where it was *warm*.

"You know, the last time some of you came sniffing around, Jono broke a dozen bones. When your kind tried that shit with me, they ended up in the hospital before getting a trip to Rikers for assaulting a federal agent. You really want that same trip?"

"We're not here to fight," the tall, willowy black woman retorted, not moving from her spot.

"We came to talk," the Mexican American man standing opposite of her added.

Maybe they had, but Patrick hadn't survived this long by taking people's word at face value. He didn't recognize them, and he didn't trust them.

"Talking usually happens at Tempest," Patrick said.

The bar that Jono managed catered to the werecreature community. It had seen a slowdown in business since they'd formed their pack but was in no danger of closing. No longer seen as neutral territory, Tempest was where those willing to risk Estelle and Youssef's wrath went for help.

"We went there first. Jono wasn't in."

Patrick eyed the six werecreatures huddled underneath umbrellas as he approached. Now that he was closer, he could see the wide space between them that only happened when more than one pack was in the same vicinity.

Patrick put the grocery bags on the wet ground and dug out his cell phone, never taking his eyes off the werecreatures.

"Yeah?" Jono's deep voice answered after the first ring, his English accent thick in Patrick's ear. "You almost home, mate?"

"Downstairs. Got some unwanted visitors."

Jono ended the call on his side of the line without saying a word, and Patrick put his phone away. None of the werecreatures had moved much, except maybe to huddle closer together under their umbrellas. The stormy weather was shitty, and it was cold, and Patrick really didn't want to deal with pack issues out on the street. He didn't want to deal with any of it right now, not after the day he'd had, but Patrick didn't really have a choice

Less than ten seconds later, Jono yanked open the building's front door and stepped into the storm. The long-sleeved gray Henley he wore was immediately soaked, as were his jeans. Patrick spared him a glance when he would've preferred to let his gaze linger. A wet Jono was always nice to look at, but keeping his eyes on the threat in front of them took priority.

"We're not here to fight," the woman repeated, raising a hand in a defensive manner.

"Neither are we," the man in the other pack said.

"Then why are you here?" Jono demanded, coming down the stoop, his wolf-bright blue eyes reflecting light from the nearby streetlamp.

The werecreatures glanced at each other uneasily. Before any of them could speak, a car braked to a stop in front of their building. Patrick mentally guided his mageglobe down to his hand, curling his fingers around it to keep his magic out of sight but still at the ready.

No one said a word as the driver opened his trunk from the inside of the car before getting out. Water fell off the brim of his cap that had the name of a delivery app company stamped across it. "Uh, did one of you order the extra-large pepperoni?"

"I did," Jono said.

Jono moved between the two packs to accept the pizza box from the driver. Patrick stared mournfully at the box Jono held and how quickly the cardboard was getting drenched.

"I'm getting cold pizza tonight, aren't I?" Patrick said.

Jono turned his back on the delivery driver in order to deal with the werecreatures who'd crossed into their territory uninvited. He waited until the guy drove off before saying, "Start talking."

The woman cleared her throat. "Our packs live in apartment buildings across the street from each other."

"They're not sharing the block how we agreed," the man said.

"You took over our north corner without *asking*."

Jono held up one hand, and they both clamped their mouths shut. "You shouldn't have come here. It's not safe for you."

The woman crossed her arms over her chest, the puffer coat she wore bunching at the elbows. The faux fur lining the hood was the same dark brown color as her skin. "We had no other choice because..."

Her voice trailed off, the silence that followed full of explanations Patrick didn't need to guess at. God packs existed to protect the packs within their territories. That meant being in the public eye so others could live in hiding, but it also meant mediating problems between the packs under their care.

Estelle and Youssef were fucking terrible at that.

Back in August, they'd discovered the god pack alphas were selling independent werecreatures to a drug cartel and the Manhattan Night Court when it had been ruled by Tremaine. That master vampire was dead now, killed by his sire. Patrick had ignored Lucien's dealings for months since the fight against Santa Muerte and Tremaine at Grand Central Terminal. He hadn't ignored the shitty way Estelle and Youssef ruled over the packs who called the five boroughs home.

When Jono was an independent, there were times other werecreatures would discreetly meet with him for advice. It should have been Estelle and Youssef they went to, and it said a lot about the situation in New York that they'd gone to Jono before he even had a pack.

If that's what this situation was about, Patrick knew they couldn't turn the werecreatures away no matter how badly he wanted to. This wasn't the first time since August they had been approached for advice rather than needing to defend their territory and status, but it was the first time it had happened at home.

Jono studied the werecreatures for a long few seconds before looking over at where Patrick stood. "Wade's here."

"He better not touch my pizza." Patrick bent over to grab the grocery bags. "I'll conduct hospitality if you really want to do it."

"Rather you get inside where it's warm. No sense in having a chat where everyone can hear." Jono nodded at the apartment building's door. "You lot, get moving."

The werecreatures let Jono go first to open the door and filed up after him. Patrick strengthened his personal shields and raised one between Jono and the two packs, not taking any chances. He knew Jono could take care of himself, but it made Patrick feel better about the situation.

He closed his umbrella and walked up after everyone else, keeping the mageglobe between himself and the last werecreature in the group. More than one of them looked over their shoulder at Patrick, the wariness in their eyes impossible to miss. No one said a word until Jono let everyone into their home and the heart of their territory. A wave of hot air greeted Patrick, and he sighed in relief as he nudged the door shut with his elbow. He extinguished the mageglobe with a thought.

"Did you bring snacks?"

Patrick looked over at where Wade Espinoza was sprawled on the couch, eyeing the grocery bags hopefully. The Christmas tree that Jono had insisted on buying and decorating stood in front of the windows overlooking the street. The glow from strings of colorful, blinking lights was reflected in Wade's brown eyes.

The eighteen-year-old fledgling fire dragon had filled out quite a bit since August when Patrick and Jono had rescued him from Tezcatlipoca, an Aztec god who owned the Omacatl Cartel. He was still lean though, courtesy of a high metabolism, and a walking bottomless pit for a stomach.

Technically, Wade was legally an adult, but mentally and emotionally he still needed a lot of support after what he'd been through. Wade had a lot of lingering issues that stemmed from being forced to fight to the death to stay alive since he was fourteen. That sort of trauma wasn't easily overcome without help.

Three months of biweekly therapy visits paid out of Patrick's own pocket had given Wade somewhere safe to channel his emotions over what he'd endured. Jono's paycheck covered most of the food for all of them even though Wade didn't live with them. Wade had put on weight and looked like a normal teenager these days rather than a starved, half-feral kid.

"Did you eat dinner?" Patrick asked.

"He ate," Jono said, going into the kitchen to put the pizza box on the counter. "Made him spag bol."

"Yeah, but I'm hungry again. You're out of snacks," Wade complained. "My cupboard here is empty."

"If you didn't devour a week's worth of snacks in a single day, maybe you'd have some left over." Patrick dug into one of the grocery bags and pulled out a box of Pop-Tarts, which he threw at Wade. "Don't touch my pizza."

Wade caught the box and tore into it, pulling out a packet of strawberry Pop-Tarts. He ripped it open and stuffed one into his mouth to take a bite, never taking his eyes off the werecreatures. "Wha's goin' on?"

"A headache," Patrick replied as he followed Jono into the kitchen.

Patrick set the wet grocery bags on the floor to deal with later. While Jono went to get everyone situated, Patrick grabbed six glasses from the cupboard and filled them with water. A couple of slices of white bread was all that was left in the bag on top of the refrigerator, but it was enough to parcel out into six pieces.

Patrick carried everything out to the dining table in two trips, lining up the glasses and dropping a piece of bread near each one. He gestured at the offering. "Be welcome."

The werecreatures didn't move, not until Jono cleared his throat. "We're not discussing anything until you lot accept hospitality. If you decline, you can leave."

The woman and man—alphas of their respective packs, Patrick assumed—stepped forward to pass out the glasses and bread to their people.

Hospitality greetings were binding welcomes that protected a person's hearth and home. Breaking the welcome meant the transgressor was never able to cross the threshold and enter the home again. Patrick could feel the threshold wrapped around the apartment react to the intent of the act, magic prickling against the shields he still had up. The werecreatures seemed oblivious to the subtle power.

"You got this?" Patrick asked Jono.

"Go eat your pizza, Pat."

Patrick retreated to the kitchen and popped open the pizza box. He half listened to the conversation happening in the other room, but most of his attention was on his dinner. The pizza was still warm, and Patrick chewed his way through two pieces before slowing down long enough to grab a plate. Piling two more slices onto it, he carried the plate out of the kitchen.

Wade had raised the volume on the television a little, attention focused on the hockey game. It must have been a West Coast game to be broadcasted so late.

"Did you finish your homework?" Patrick wanted to know.

"Yes," Wade said, eyes glued to the flat-screen television.

Jono paused in whatever he was discussing with the two packs and said, "Wade."

"What? I finished!"

Patrick snorted. "Finished putting the homework away or actually doing it?"

"It's an essay, and it's not due until next week."

"Do your homework," Patrick and Jono said in unison.

Wade scowled and reached for the remote to turn off the television. He dragged his backpack onto the couch with a loud, obnoxious sigh. Patrick rolled his eyes at the dramatics of it all.

Sage Beacot, the fourth member of their pack, had helped Wade enroll in the Manhattan Educational Opportunity Center out of the Borough of Manhattan Community College. They'd started him off in the Introduction to High School Equivalency course that would lead into the HSE Diploma course. Wade hadn't finished high school due to running away at the age of fourteen and being subsequently kidnapped. He was basically starting over from scratch, and they were all determined to support his efforts.

Even though he was a dragon, Wade still thought of himself as mostly human and wanted to do human things. Patrick and Jono had both agreed Wade was better off going to school than working a low-wage job or joining the military. Getting Wade to focus was easier on some days than on others. They had better luck if he was here visiting or sleeping over at their place rather than staying at his own apartment. He didn't live with them, because Patrick knew the importance of having your own space after surviving something that should have killed you.

The one-bedroom apartment Wade called home in the East Village wasn't technically part of their territory, but Patrick had made it clear that Wade was pack and under their protection. Marek Taylor, a tech billionaire who owned the PreterWorld social media company and was the United States' one true seer, had covered Wade's rent for a full year. It was one less thing Patrick had to worry about.

Taking another bite of pizza, Patrick wandered over to where Jono was huddled with the two packs at their dining table. The table was circular, but the two packs had still managed to stay separated around it. Jono sat on a chair between them, listening to their varied arguments about who owned what territory on a single street in the Bronx.

Territory in large metropolitan cities was almost always measured in blocks rather than square miles. Packs claimed territory through agreements or fights, allowing pass-through rights to other packs if the rivalry wasn't huge. Borders were expanded or lost one house at a time, and that seemed to be the case here, mostly perpetuated by a newly arrived independent werecreature renting a home on the corner. Which meant Marco's *Escorpión* pack had encroached on Letitia's Gold pack, and no one was happy.

"Asking the independent to give up their miniscule territory on the corner isn't an option. Have they ever gone before the other god pack about territory other than during the initial move into the Bronx?" Jono said.

"Not that I'm aware of," Letitia said.

"Fine. I'll take their territory into consideration even though they aren't represented here."

"If they want their territory, then they should be here. They aren't, so I don't see why they matter," Marco retorted.

Jono raised an eyebrow. "Did you ask them to come with you?"

The silence from both packs was indicative of a resounding *no*. Patrick finished his third slice of pizza. Before starting on his fourth, Patrick flicked his fingers over the wet Henley stretched across Jono's shoulders, sending a drying charm coursing through Jono's clothes. Steam puffed up from his clothes and shoes. Jono tilted his head toward Patrick in silent thanks.

Patrick didn't do the same for himself, because he had plans to shower with Jono the second everyone left.

"You came to me, not Estelle and Youssef," Jono pointed out. "My pack doesn't decide shit the way they do. Which means we're not going to deny someone their right to territory just because they aren't present and didn't know to *be* present. That's not a game we play."

"We?" Letitia asked carefully, gaze flickering Patrick's way.

"*We,*" Jono stated in a hard voice. "Patrick co-leads our pack. You have a problem with that, then the door is right behind you."

Patrick took another bite of his pizza and stared them down. The uncomfortable silence lasted a few more seconds before they went back to arguing their respective cases before Jono. Patrick finished his slice of pizza and was contemplating a fifth when his phone rang.

"Goddamn it," he muttered. He set the plate down and wiped his fingers clean on his jeans before pulling his phone out of his pocket to answer it. "Collins. Line and location are not secure."

"Make yourself secure," Special Agent in Charge Henry Ng replied.

Patrick headed for the master bedroom. He closed the door behind him and used his finger to write out a silence ward on the wood. He pushed his magic out of his tainted soul and into the ward, letting static fill the bedroom. The world went quiet around him. All the werecreatures in the other room wouldn't be able to hear the conversation he was about to have.

Wade could, because magic didn't work on dragons, but the teenager knew better than to talk about what he overheard around people who weren't pack.

"Secured, sir," Patrick said. "Is this about the kappas? I turned in my report."

"No. This is different. We got a report of a missing child."

"That's usually a police matter, not federal, unless it crosses state lines."

"It becomes ours when it's believed the child was replaced by a changeling."

Patrick banged his forehead lightly against the door a couple of times. Crossing the veil between worlds definitely put a case within federal jurisdiction. "Gods fucking damn it. I hate dealing with the fae. Are you sure?"

"The PCB forwarded the case at the couple's request. They want an agent to take their statement, and they want it done immediately."

"Tonight? Sir, if it's a changeling, the kid will still be there tomorrow morning."

"Tonight," Henry said firmly. "I know you just got off the clock, but I need you to take this case. The family involved is the Wisterias."

Patrick banged his forehead against the door one more time for good measure. "Well, fuck."

The Wisterias were a rich, powerful blueblood family of witches and warlocks, who had cornered the potions market during the Gilded Age. They considered their conservative family its own coven, who only admitted new members when those new people married into the family. The Wisterias were politically and magically well connected, having supported some of the more xenophobic policies and candidates the government had put forth over the years.

Patrick was not looking forward to dealing with them.

"What's the address?" he asked. Henry rattled it off and Patrick committed it to memory. "Let them know I'm on my way."

"They'll be informed."

Henry ended the call. Patrick sighed tiredly before dragging his hand over the sigil on the door to break up his magic. The silence ward faded away, sound returning to his ears. Patrick looked down at his damp clothes and scuffed combat boots and made a face. Not the sort of clothes he should probably meet the Wisterias in, but if he was going back into the storm tonight, he wasn't getting two outfits rained on.

Yanking open the bedroom door, Patrick headed back to the dining area, surprised to see the packs had disappeared. Jono still sat at the dining table, staring blankly at the opposite wall where they'd hung a watercolor print of the London skyline.

"Did they leave or are they coming back?" Patrick asked.

Jono blinked, looking over at him. "They're gone. They accepted my decision."

"Which was?"

"An equal reduction of territory on the street to compensate for the independent weregrizzly, and one pack dinner a month to work out a possible alliance between the three."

"Sounds fair."

"We'll see if they accept it or turn to Estelle and Youssef."

"If they came to you, I doubt they'll run to those two."

"Maybe. I think they're mine," Jono said slowly. "I think when I gave the order for Nicholas to change form in the challenge ring, those two alphas shifted as well. So maybe they'll abide."

"Yours, huh?" He hadn't been present that day in August when Jono had left to meet with the god pack alphas and came back having claimed Sage as part of their pack. He couldn't say he minded the results. "Then maybe you're right and they will listen."

Jono shrugged, getting to his feet. "What was your call about?"

Patrick sighed. "I have a case. I need to go interview someone."

"Right now? In this weather? Please tell me it's not those bloody water bastards again."

"The kappas? Nah, that case finished today. Something different. There's a missing child."

"If you're this busy when Gerard gets here, I don't know when you'll have the time to see him."

"I'll make time." Patrick smiled crookedly. "I have to, remember?"

Captain Gerard Breckenridge was Patrick's former commanding officer and leader of the Hellraisers, Patrick's old Special Forces team. It'd been over three years since Patrick last wore the Mage Corps uniform, but Gerard would never hold that against him.

Gerard and a couple other teammates Patrick had fought with were taking a few days out of their leave to come to New York. Part of that reason was to make good on a promise to have Patrick buy them all drinks and to check up on him. Mostly, they were coming to meet with him about the off-the-record mission General Noah Reed had assigned all of them. The three-star Army general—who was a fire dragon in human form—hadn't let Patrick's lack of uniform stop him from handing out orders and expecting to be obeyed.

The Morrígan's staff, once thought locked away in the United States' Repository in Area 51, had gone missing during the Thirty-Day War three and a half years ago—or so that was what Odin's ravens had led Patrick to believe. While gods were known to lie, Patrick knew in his gut they weren't lying about this.

An audit on the staff after Patrick's meeting with Reed in August proved it was missing. No one knew who had it. No one knew for certain who had stolen it in the first place, though most laid the blame on Ethan Greene and the Dominion Sect. Ethan's quest to claim a godhead had nearly destroyed Manhattan back in summer. His desire for power was a dangerous thing that Patrick was intimately familiar with.

All anyone knew was that the staff—and whatever magic a war goddess had bestowed upon it—could not end up in Ethan Greene's hands.

The Hellraisers had been tasked with finding the weapon, as had Special Agent Nadine Mulroney and several other small groups of federal agents within the Preternatural Intelligence Agency. Patrick's best friend had been read in on the mission before he had because Nadine was PIA.

Patrick didn't blame General Reed for keeping the SOA out of the loop despite equal control of the Repository shared between the two agencies and branch of military. SOA Director Setsuna Abuku was still trying to clean house at their agency.

At the end of the day, Ethan was his father, and Patrick had a soul debt owned by a different goddess that said this was his problem above all others who might lay claim to it.

Patrick was looking forward to seeing his old team again, he only wished it was under better circumstances.

"If you gotta leave, can I have the rest of your pizza?" Wade asked. "I'm hungry."

Patrick rolled his eyes. "You're always hungry."

Jono leaned down to kiss him, lips dry and warm against his own. "I'll wait up for you."

"I don't know how long this interview will take."

"Like I said." Jono nipped at his mouth, sending a shiver down Patrick's spine. "I'll wait up."

After months of coming home to Jono, it still felt like a revelation some days. Despite the soulbond tying them together, Patrick was learning to believe that Jono stayed not because he had to, but because he wanted to.

"See you later," Patrick said.

He left the apartment, only pausing long enough to retrieve his umbrella from the bin on the landing where they stored them. Walking down the stairs, Patrick headed back into the storm.

2

THE UPPER EAST SIDE MANSION PATRICK FOUND HIMSELF STANDING in front of in the downpour was guarded by gargoyles that moved over the façade of the building in a menacing manner. Patrick ignored the stone creatures and rang the doorbell again, counting the seconds between the flash of lightning in the sky and the thunder that inevitably followed.

The winter storm churning right on top of Manhattan came with a cold viciousness he would appreciate better if he were home. Even with his umbrella, shields, and heat charm filling his leather jacket, Patrick was still cold. He pressed the doorbell button again, unable to hear the sound through the silence ward sunk into the home's threshold.

"Come on, hurry up," Patrick muttered.

It took another minute before the door was opened by a woman in her midtwenties. She wore a long sweater with a thick turtleneck collar over skinny jeans tucked into knee-high fashionable riding boots. Her blonde hair was twisted into a low bun, and her brown eyes were red-rimmed.

"Mrs. Wisteria?" Patrick asked, not sure if he had the right woman as he lifted his badge. She didn't feel like a witch to his magic. "I'm Special Agent Patrick Collins with the SOA."

The woman shook her head, giving him a tremulous smile. "No, sorry. I'm the nanny. My name is Arianna. Mr. and Mrs. Wisteria are upstairs with the police. I can take you to them."

Patrick crossed the threshold, and Arianna gestured at the pile of bread and glass pitcher of room temperature water sitting on a side table. "Hospitality first. It's required by the family for all who enter."

Patrick went through the motions without a fuss, sensing the home's threshold settling once he'd partaken in the ceremony. After he finished, Arianna led him through a mansion that was less a home and more a museum, filled with expensive art and even more expensive artifacts of magic. The feel of witch magic was strong in the home, recognition flickering through Patrick's soul.

The magic lacked warmth, feeling cold and sterile to his senses —much like the couple he was introduced to in a nursery painted in soft yellow and pastel green. The colors couldn't warm the icy reception he was given.

Arianna made an immediate beeline for the crib where a baby close to a year old stood on surprisingly steady legs, tiny hands clutching at the wooden safety bars keeping her in one place. Patrick didn't have much familiarity with children, but he didn't think most babies had that sort of steadiness in their chubby little legs at this age.

She was Patrick's sort of pale but lacked the pinkish hue most redheads carried in their skin. Her skin was porcelain fair, with no freckles. Her hair was pitch-black, eyes a dark brown, the irises slightly too large to be normal, even for a baby.

She watched everything with an awareness that was unsettling. She carried no real resemblance to her parents, both of whom stood some distance away talking with a pair of detectives out of the NYPD's Preternatural Crimes Bureau. The handful of cases Patrick had partnered with the PCB on over the last few months usually came directly from Bureau Chief Giovanni Casale. Tonight felt as if Patrick was intruding more than usual.

Thomas Wisteria was tall and blond, looking every inch the businessman he was in the bespoke suit he wore. The arrogance he exuded was difficult to miss.

Margeaux Wisteria's brown hair fell in loose waves around her pretty face. She wore diamonds in her ears, and the stone on her engagement ring was so large it dipped to the side of her finger. The gold of her jewelry matched the small athame hooked to her designer leather belt. Margeaux's full mouth was curved in a frown, brown eyes focused on the detectives. Her gaze snapped to Patrick the moment he arrived though, and she stared at him with a modicum of distrust he chose to ignore.

Recognition pricked Patrick's magic, telling him Margeaux was the blood member of the Wisteria family. Patrick had his shields locked down tight, keeping his magic from seeping out. He knew he felt human to her own magic, and he wondered how that would color their interactions if she didn't recognize his name. Some old witch families considered themselves superior to mundane humans in every way that mattered.

Patrick couldn't remember if his mother's family had ever been that way. Clara Greene, née Patterson, had been born into the Salem Coven, expected to be their next high priestess. Only she'd been murdered by his father, and Patrick was assumed dead as well. In reality, he'd been living under a false identity that had kept him safe from Ethan and the Dominion Sect until the Thirty-Day War.

It was a false sense of safety and security. No matter the name Patrick went by, Persephone still owned his soul debt.

"Mr. and Mrs. Wisteria, I'm Special Agent Patrick Collins," Patrick said, flashing his badge at them before tucking it away in his back pocket.

Margeaux's gaze sharpened. "Are you the mage who was involved in the summer solstice mess?"

Patrick managed not to wince. "I'm not here about past cases, ma'am. You requested the SOA send someone to check on your child."

"She's not our child," Thomas said.

The taller detective turned to face Patrick. He was an older man, not someone Patrick had ever interacted with before. His younger partner was just as unfamiliar.

"They're saying the child is a changeling," one of the detectives said.

Patrick looked over at where Arianna was holding the baby in her arms, murmuring softly to her charge. The little girl had her head turned toward them, those large dark eyes staring at Patrick with an unblinking gaze.

"How about you walk me through your reasoning?" Patrick said to the Wisterias.

"Can't you read his notes?" Margeaux asked, gesturing at the detective.

"I need to make my own." He hadn't brought anything to write on, so Patrick pulled out his phone to access the recording app. "I'll take it from here, Detectives."

The man nodded, and Arianna moved to show him and his partner out.

"Leave it here," Thomas snapped.

Patrick bristled at the use of *it* but held his tongue. Arianna ducked her head, cheeks flushing with anger or embarrassment; Patrick couldn't tell.

"Of course, Mr. Wisteria," Arianna murmured.

She set the baby back into the crib, gently patting her head in a silent goodbye. Arianna left with the detectives. The little girl watched her leave but didn't make a sound.

"What's her name?" Patrick asked.

"Our nanny?" Thomas replied.

"Your daughter."

Both bristled at the suggestion the baby in the crib was theirs, but Patrick pretended not to notice.

"She's *not* our daughter," Margeaux said coolly.

Patrick hit the Record button on his app. "Then explain to me what happened. How old is she?"

"*Our* daughter would be the same age. Ten months, three weeks," Thomas said.

"When did you suspect she wasn't yours? Have you done a DNA test?"

"No. We don't need one. I know she isn't ours," Margeaux said. "I want our daughter found. Surely the SOA has fae contacts it can reach out to and demand the return of our child?"

"That would require going through diplomatic channels, ma'am. The fae are considered members of sovereign nations."

"Then maybe you should wake up a diplomat," Thomas snapped with all the expectation of being obeyed.

Patrick clenched his teeth for a second. *Rich people. So fucking demanding.*

"Overtures to the fae aren't done lightly. The SOA will need more than your word about the situation." Patrick raised a hand to forestall an angry tirade as Thomas opened his mouth. "That's the *law*. A Petition to Compel needs to be filed with the courts first before anything can be done. Have your lawyers started that process?"

"Our lawyers have been informed of the situation. My coven is helping to provide evidence," Margeaux said.

"That's a start. I'd like to examine your daughter's aura, if that's all right?"

"I don't appreciate your insistence on calling it our daughter," Thomas said coldly. "Genevieve is our daughter, not that creature."

"She's still a child. It's not her fault she's in this situation."

Patrick approached the crib and rested his hands on the railing, staring down at the changeling sitting amidst plush designer blankets. She looked up at him without making a sound, tiny hands clenched into fists atop her chubby thighs.

"Hi there," Patrick said softy. "I won't hurt you."

Only a quarter of the world's population carried magic in their souls, but every living creature had an aura, that extension of their soul. Those who came from the preternatural world or beyond the veil felt different to magic users. Patrick's magic hadn't recognized the child as anything but human when he first arrived, but he knew fae magic was insidious. Sometimes, you never knew they were there until it was too late.

Changelings were adept at pretending to be human, no matter their age.

Patrick reached for the baby, letting his fingers hover above her upturned head. He called up his magic, pushing it out of his soul and through his shields. He ignored the soft, disgusted sound Margeaux made behind him. Patrick knew his magic, damaged as it was, felt wrong to other magic users, and was part of the reason he'd never had a partner. Right now, he had a job to do, and no amount of attitude from the Wisterias would stop him from doing it.

Pale blue sparks flickered at his fingertips before gently falling like rain down on the baby. He blinked, eyes filling with the shine of the baby's aura—brighter than any human was capable of giving off.

Patrick swallowed, fighting the desire to look away. He pushed aside memories of August, when he'd been forced to take shine on order of a god to save a werecreature's life. In the end, he'd survived sexual assault perpetuated by a now deceased master vampire and death herself in the form of Santa Muerte, a Mexican folk goddess. The shine of a soul still left a bad taste in his mouth these days that always made him think of marigolds.

The baby's aura had a depth to it no human's ever would. It felt otherworldly to his senses, recognition difficult to pin down, but the difference was stark when one knew what to look for. Patrick made a fist, snuffing out his magic.

The baby never blinked.

He looked away from her in favor of studying the photographs artfully decorating the nursery walls—every single picture that of a newborn baby who wasn't sitting in the crib. Whatever glamour the changeling had carried over the weeks or months had slowly started to fade in this city of iron, stripping the changeling of an armor she still needed to survive.

Changelings were fae children swapped for human babies, usually within weeks of birth. Patrick had a feeling the Wisterias' daughter had been missing for months rather than days. Until the glamour started to really fade, this child had been loved by her parents, and now that love was gone.

The changeling unclenched her fists and raised her arms, reaching for him. Patrick hesitated before smoothing his hand over her head, pushing back some of her thick hair. It felt like the finest of silk beneath his hand.

"You're right. She isn't yours," Patrick said, not looking at the Wisterias.

"Then get it out of our house," Thomas ground out.

The baby's face screwed up, her lower lip trembling. Before she could get out her first cry, Arianna came hurrying back into the nursery. "Let me have her. She hasn't been fed yet."

Arianna had a bottle of milk in one hand, and Patrick got out of her way. Arianna deftly swooped the baby into her arms, cutting off the distressed cry before it fully formed with quiet, wordless shushing noises. Arianna bounced the baby in her arms as she fed her, holding her how any mother would.

Looking at them, all Patrick could think was that orphans weren't born, they were made, and that the changeling would be given up more times than she had been kept in her short life. Discarded by the fae who'd left her in the arms of a strange family, bound by glamour and destined to lose parental love in the face of cold reality.

No child of any species deserved that.

Patrick turned to face the Wisterias and opened his mouth to speak. "I can call—"

The nursery window *shattered* as if a bomb had gone off, the home's threshold buckling beneath the blow, but it didn't break. Glass exploded through the room, the lights above going out, and Patrick reacted without thinking. He ripped his shields out of his body, expanding them to engulf the people around him. Arianna screamed and hunched over the baby whose real name Patrick still didn't know.

The explosion allowed cold winter wind and rain to enter the home—but that wasn't the only thing that came inside.

The roar of the wind twisted into screams as a deep cold filled the nursery. Patrick conjured up a mageglobe in his left hand while yanking free his gods-given dagger with the other. His breath puffed white in the air from the cold, skin stinging from the supernatural chill.

Gliding into the nursery through the jagged hole in the building came the spirits of the restless dead.

Their forms flickered between the corporeal and ghostly, lightning outside backlighting the horde. Their faces were inhuman expressions of souls who only experienced an eternity of pain, while their hands resembled claws more than fingerbones. They were nightmarish and difficult to look at for long.

Shuffling around them were creatures more solid, more real, than the specters who came to haunt the home. Fat, with the bodies and legs of spiders that curved into human torsos. Genderless, with long black hair and mouths that opened on glistening, poisonous fangs, the creatures clattered forward along the floor and walls and ceiling.

Patrick's magic burned with a particular sensation that only meant fae to him.

"Wild Hunt," Patrick said. When that name got no reaction, he tried again. "Sluagh."

The dead and the creatures who guided them responded to being named with screams that made the nerves in Patrick's teeth tingle. Patrick strengthened his shields and pulled them in, forcing Thomas, Margeaux, and Arianna closer to his position. It meant giving up ground to the Sluagh, but it was less space overall that Patrick would have to defend. He was a combat mage; his affinity didn't lend itself toward defensive wards. Offensive spells were more his specialty.

One of the spider creatures came forward, its eight legs ending in hook claws making no noise on the wet carpet. Its eyes were an iridescent, sickly green, gaze focused not on Patrick, but on someone behind him—the changeling.

"Let them take it back!" Thomas shouted.

"Oh, fuck you, I'm not giving a baby up to the Sluagh," Patrick snapped.

The Sluagh screamed their defiance to those words, their ghostly hands clawing at his shields.

"*I cast you out.*"

The snarled words made the hairs on the back of Patrick's neck stand on end. He spared a glance over his shoulder, taking in the rigid way Margeaux stood, her eyes glittering with magic. Bright red blood slid down her arm from the long line she'd cut up her wrist using the sharp-looking athame. Her blood dripped onto the nursery floor, staining the cream-colored carpet.

The athame was made of gold, and it took the sacrifice offered under the Three-Fold Law as its due.

"*I cast you out.*"

The wind picked up, and the restless dead screamed to be heard over it. The Sluagh pressed in close around them, Patrick's shields burning bright in the dark nursery. The entire building began to hum as witch magic poured through its foundation. Patrick kept hold of his mageglobe, letting his magic spin against his palm without a spell to shape it. He knew better than to interrupt a casting by someone else in their hearth and home.

"*I cast you* out!"

The words came out on a scream that carried more than Margeaux's voice. The power of the Wisteria Coven sang through her words, a joining of witches and warlocks buried in the threshold that surrounded the family's home rising up to defend. The walls might be broken, but magic built and called by blood would always stand strong when a threshold sought to keep out unwanted guests.

Patrick's stomach twisted uncomfortably as the room seemed to fold in on itself at the edges. A ripple flowed through the Sluagh, their forms flickering in the glow of Patrick's magic. No matter a magic user's strength—from a witch to a mage and all the ranks in between—a threshold was never to be ignored, especially not one built by a coven.

The Sluagh was sucked out of the building through the hole they'd made, cast out by Margeaux's command. Lightning flashed outside, the thunder that followed in its wake so loud Patrick's ears popped. The sound the Sluagh made when they retreated through the storm made him want to cover his ears.

Cold wind blew rain into the nursery through the hole. Dark shapes crawled around the jagged edge of the building, and Patrick nearly killed a gargoyle or two with magic before recognition of their presence stayed his hand.

Sirens pierced the rumble of the storm, getting louder as the lights flickered, sputtering back on. Patrick waited a couple of seconds before he slowly retracted his shields, drawing them back into his bones. He turned to look at Margeaux, who now stood wrapped in her husband's arms. The wound on her arm still bled, and Thomas was murmuring about getting her a potion and poultice.

Behind them, Arianna knelt on the floor, white-faced and shaking, still holding the baby in her arms. The baby's large, dark eyes looked at Patrick with a quiet intensity no human child her age would ever carry.

"Get it out of my home," Margeaux said in a shaky voice, refusing to look at the daughter that wasn't hers.

Patrick thought about pointing out the threshold hadn't cast the baby girl out the way it'd done the Sluagh. He held his tongue instead, because that was an argument for when he wasn't acting in his capacity as a special agent for the SOA while handling a missing child case from a prominent witch family.

Moving past the couple, Patrick knelt beside Arianna and held his hands out to the baby girl. He didn't know what the Sluagh had wanted with the changeling, but until he knew why the Unseelie Court was after her, he would keep her safe.

"I'll take her now," Patrick said.

Arianna sniffled, her lower lip trembling as she stared at him. "It's not her fault."

"It never is."

The fae took human children and left their own behind for different reasons—a whim, a debt, or a nightmarish gift. For all the Wisteria family's money, Patrick knew it wouldn't buy them any peace.

Children lost to Tír na nÓg rarely returned to the mortal world. When they did, they never came home sane.

3

Jono frowned at the water he could hear bubbling away in the kettle on the hob, drumming his fingers against the kitchen counter. He'd gone to sleep alone after Patrick texted about the case interview going long and to go to bed without him. Jono had woken up without Patrick, and with no new texts. It was his least favorite way to start a morning. His own texts had gone unanswered, and the single call he'd made had gone to voicemail after three rings.

The silence worried him, but Jono knew better than to blow up Patrick's mobile for an answer. Besides, the soulbond was a quiet presence deep in his soul, which told Jono that Patrick wasn't in any danger. It wasn't like in August, when the sharp pull to find Patrick one night had been an almost painful need.

Coming back from that mess had taken time. Patrick had resorted to cigarettes for weeks after the assault he'd suffered through, drunk too much whiskey some nights, but he hadn't shied away from Jono's touch after they talked.

These days, Patrick had quit smoking completely, managed to only need a nicotine patch on his more stressful cases, and it took weeks for the whiskey bottle to run dry rather than days. He was still a work in progress—they both were—but they were getting better.

The kettle started to whistle, and Jono turned off the hob before pouring hot water over the tea bag in his mug. As he set the kettle aside, his preternatural hearing picked up the sound of voices and footsteps on the stairs several floors down. Jono left his tea on the counter to steep in favor of striding toward the front door to open it.

"Pat?" he called out.

"Yeah, not so loud. You'll wake her."

"Her?"

Jono took a deep breath, smelling Patrick's bitter scent, Sage's mix of desert and forest, and a strange one that reminded him of the time he'd gone into the Chislehurst Caves in Bromley as a teen. It hit his nose and the back of his throat like cold rock and chalky bone. He swallowed against the taste, committing it to memory despite how disagreeable it was. Individual scents were one thing Jono would never forget as a god pack alpha werewolf.

Fenrir wouldn't either.

Jono could sense his animal-god patron waking up deep inside his soul, the immortal curious in a way that Jono always found led to trouble. Moments later, Patrick rounded the fourth-floor landing below with Sage right behind him. Jono's gaze zeroed in on the small form Patrick carried in his arms, the blanket glowing at the edges with a heat charm hastily written into the cloth.

"I still think I should call my office," Sage said as she dumped her long umbrella in the bin on the landing outside their door once they made it up the stairs.

"I don't know what fae Court your bosses work for," Patrick retorted, keeping his voice low.

"Not the one that calls down the Sluagh."

"That's not saying much. Both Courts have their own kind of Wild Hunt."

"Which my bosses wouldn't let loose on New York City without a damn good reason, and the one riding the storm last night wasn't theirs."

"You sure about that? That storm could've hidden anything in the clouds. It hid the Sluagh, remember?"

Jono closed the door behind them, the flat a bit cooler now with some of the heat let out. "Wild Hunt?"

"Have you seen the morning news?" Sage asked. She dropped her Birkin bag on the dining room table before divesting herself of the ankle-length winter wool coat she wore.

"Just woke up." Jono watched as Patrick carefully laid a sleeping baby not even a year old on the sofa. "I thought you said the case was about a missing child? Did you find the sprog and steal it?"

"Someone was stolen, but not her." Patrick straightened up and turned to face them. He looked tired, green eyes red-rimmed from lack of sleep. "Tell me there's coffee."

"I made tea."

"Ugh. This is America. We threw your tea in the Boston Harbor for a reason."

"I'll make coffee," Wade said through a yawn as he stumbled out of the guest bedroom. His brown hair stuck up in different directions, and it looked as if he'd slept in his clothes rather than pajamas.

Sage crossed her slim arms over her chest, the large diamond engagement ring on her left ring finger glittering in the light. She wore a gray wool sheath dress with three-quarter-length sleeves and knee-high boots with high heels. Her boots put her at eye level with Patrick, though Jono was still taller than both of them. While Patrick looked knackered, Sage looked ready for a full day in court.

"We are not taking custody of a changeling. She is fae, and if the Sluagh are after her, then none of us are safe," Sage said.

"I hate dealing with the fae," Patrick muttered. "And I'm not arguing with you about that, because yeah, none of us are safe from the Sluagh."

He conjured up a mageglobe and the sphere flickered a bit from whatever spell he cast through it. The ball of magic floated closer to the baby, and she seemed to settle more deeply into sleep. Jono figured Patrick had cast a silence ward.

"One of you mind telling me what's going on?" Jono asked.

Patrick dragged both hands down his face. Jono knew he must have been up for over twenty-four hours now, and it showed. What little sleep Patrick had managed to get over the last few days dealing with the kappas didn't seem like it was enough. Jono wanted to put him to bed and follow him there.

"The family who reported their child missing had theirs replaced with a changeling whose glamour finally faded enough for them to realize she wasn't their beautiful baby girl," Patrick said.

"How long did that take?"

"I don't know, but I'd bet my next paycheck they were swapped a couple of weeks after the real Wisteria baby was born. It's easiest to do when they're both young."

"You said the home's threshold banished the Sluagh from the premises. So how did any fae get inside that home to make the switch?" Sage wanted to know.

Patrick shrugged. "Didn't have to happen at home. Could've happened outside somewhere. New York City has a hawthorn path in Central Park. Pretty sure lots of nannies for the rich walk kids in that park."

"Kids aren't animals, Patrick. They don't get walked."

Patrick waved off her words. "All I'm saying is that's how changelings usually come into this world. When babies are newborns. The glamour that changelings are wrapped in is supposed to make the families love them and not question any differences they might see."

"I'm guessing it didn't work this time because the family were magic users?" Jono asked.

Patrick groaned, knuckling at one eye. "The fae *had* to choose one of the most conservative witch families in the country to fuck with this time around. The Wisterias had their suspicions apparently, but the changeling's glamour was really good, I guess. Until this week."

"What changed?"

"Who the fuck knows? Fae magic is temperamental in big cities. The iron everywhere eats away at the foundation of whatever spells and wards are cast by them."

"Which is why I think we should bring her to my firm. Tiarnán would know how to keep her safe," Sage said.

"We're not taking her to your firm. I don't trust the fae, this is an SOA matter, and—" Patrick dug out his mobile to get the time. "—the DC agent who handles changeling cases should be here soon to take custody of the baby. She took the first flight out today, but morning rush hour in the rain is a headache."

Sage frowned. "You're not keeping the case?"

"I'm keeping the case. I'm not keeping her." Patrick jerked his thumb in the direction of the sofa with the sleeping baby on it. "Especially not with Sluagh on the hunt."

Wade came out of the kitchen carrying two mugs of coffee and Jono's mug of tea, with a silver foil packet of Pop-Tarts clenched between his teeth. Jono took his mug first and watched as Wade offered Patrick one of the other two.

"I put whiskey in it," Wade mumbled around the wrapper in his mouth.

"You're my favorite," Patrick said, taking the mug and downing half of it, wincing all the while.

"Should let it cool," Jono said.

"Cold coffee is disgusting."

"What does the media say about the case? I haven't seen the news yet."

Sage blew out a heavy breath. "Oh, this is a PR disaster for the fae. Missing child of an old coven witch family who are being targeted by the Sluagh? The story writes itself, to be honest. The press conference this morning was a slick piece of spin."

"Are they accusing every fae? That seems a bit overdone."

Patrick shrugged. "You can't paint a whole race of beings as monsters if you only pick and choose. The Wisterias and their attack-dog lawyers are going the xenophobic route because they can and because it works. Get out front with your story first and you get to control the narrative."

Jono knew that playbook all too well. It had been used against god pack werecreatures plenty of times in the past, and still was, because it worked. The only difference was people always saw werecreatures as monsters and romanticized the fae. Appearances were everything sometimes, and the fae were beautiful—when they wanted to be.

"So now it's your job to find the missing child?" Jono asked.

Patrick glared down at his coffee mug. "There's no finding and returning someone who's been taken by the fae."

"Why not?" Wade asked. He was on his second Pop-Tart from the packet he'd carried out of the kitchen. Jono made a mental note to check his snack cupboard. Patrick's grocery shopping last night had filled it up a little, but Wade was notorious for eating his way through any and all available snacks.

"I'd ask if you've read any stories about Tír na nÓg, but I'm sure the answer is no."

"Not much use for books in the fight ring," Wade shot back.

Patrick winced. "Sorry."

Wade shrugged in a sulky way, but since he didn't storm off, Jono figured he wasn't as mad as he pretended to be. Navigating Wade's teenage angst and trauma was a minefield some days, but Wade was getting better at realizing they were never going to intentionally hurt him.

"Buy me more Pop-Tarts and I'll forgive you."

Patrick turned to glare at him. "I brought home *four boxes* last night. Did you seriously eat all four?"

Wade looked smug as he opened his mouth and took a large bite of his latest snack, getting crumbs all over his T-shirt. "Yes."

"I'll order some more for delivery," Sage said, pulling out her mobile.

Wade took another bite. "Is this going to be a case you can't close?"

Patrick glanced over at the sleeping baby, and Jono followed his gaze. She hadn't moved, wrapped up tight in her blanket. "Probably. Time moves differently past the veil, and Tír na nÓg is no exception."

"Don't the fae come from Underhill?"

"Different names for the same place," Sage said, tapping away at her mobile. "I'm getting you strawberry and the S'mores one, Wade. Don't eat them all in one day this time. The Pop-Tarts will be here in a couple of hours. You can get them after school."

Jono stepped closer to Patrick and wrapped an arm around him from behind. He pressed a kiss to the top of Patrick's head. "You need to take a kip."

"I need to call Henry after the baby gets picked up," Patrick muttered.

"You're no good to him sleep deprived, Pat."

"I'm feeling that."

Before Jono could reply, Patrick's mobile started going off. Jono didn't let him go as he answered it, merely dialed up his hearing to listen in.

"Collins. Line and location are secure," Patrick said. Jono's mouth quirked a bit at that show of trust in their pack.

"I'm downstairs, but it's pouring and I can't see the sky. Let's get this transfer done quickly," a woman said in a crisp, no-nonsense voice.

"Sky?" Wade asked sotto voice.

"Sluagh hunt from on high. They ride storms," Sage replied quietly.

"I'll be right down," Patrick said. He ended the call and shoved his mobile back into his pocket. "Wade, get ready for school. Sage, can you drop him off after the agent leaves on your way to work?"

Sage sighed, clearly still not happy about the baby's status but no longer arguing. "Yes, that's not a problem."

Jono let Patrick go so he could scoop up the baby, his mage-globe disappearing as he did so. Jono followed him out of the flat but didn't leave the building when they made it to the ground floor. Patrick went outside alone in the rain, the changeling baby wrapped up in the blanket still, but now she was awake.

She stared at Jono over Patrick's shoulder, her dark gaze eerie in its intensity. Jono took a deep breath, scenting her all over again through the rain and city smells that poured inside before the door shut between them.

Definitely a fae child.

The agent getting out of a nondescript rental car on the street was petite and blonde. She opened a heavy black umbrella and met Patrick halfway, using it to shield them all from the pouring rain. Jono waited inside the front landing, peering out the side glass window. They got the baby strapped into the borrowed car seat and then spent five minutes chatting on the sidewalk before Patrick returned.

"Where is she taking the baby?" Jono asked once Patrick made it inside again and the agent had driven off.

"Safe house," Patrick said as he headed for the stairs that led back up to their flat. "The SOA runs a couple across the country for children who aren't human and come into the agency's care."

"Like the Academy you went to?"

"No, those are only for magic users."

"Why wouldn't you keep her with you?"

"Can't run a case if I'm babysitting. Besides, if the Sluagh are hunting her, then she needs to stay behind wards that will keep her safe. I can't provide her with that sort of protection."

They climbed back up to the fifth floor, finding Sage texting away on her mobile while Wade shoved his MacBook and textbooks into his backpack. Jono stopped by the thermostat and turned up the heat a bit, not liking the way Patrick looked chilled. Werecreatures all had higher body temperatures, and Wade was a fire dragon who never felt the cold these days. Patrick had been out in cold winter weather for days already. The least Jono could do was keep him warm.

"I'll let you know if anyone at my firm is affected by this mess," Sage said, glancing up.

Her brown-eyed gaze was steady as she looked at them, the firmness in her voice that of an attorney who never backed down from a challenge. Jono hadn't regretted making Sage his dire, and he knew he never would. Sage was the rock their pack needed—calm, cool, and collected in the face of any threat. She balanced Patrick's hotheadedness and self-sacrificing tendencies, and Jono's own questionable decisions when it came to keeping Patrick safe, better than anyone else he could think of.

Trust didn't come easy in any of their lives, but Jono knew his small four-person god pack was better than Estelle and Youssef's any day of the week.

"I need to call Henry," Patrick said.

Jono watched him grab his coffee mug and retreat to the master bedroom. Sage tucked her mobile away in her Birkin and pulled out her turquoise pendant necklace. The piece of jewelry was a small artifact filled with fae magic to hide her scent. She never wore it in their pack territory unless she was leaving, and the second she slipped it around her neck, she smelled human to Jono's nose.

"I'll see you tonight?" Sage said as she adjusted the platinum chain.

Jono nodded. "Yeah."

Friday nights at Tempest had turned into an unofficial therapy night for the few packs who still risked coming around. Estelle and Youssef hadn't been able to ban Jono from New York City, nor keep him from his job thanks to Marek's status as a seer that came with federal oversight, but they'd made it explicitly clear that Tempest was off-limits to all the packs.

If Emma Zhang and Leon Hernandez weren't multi-million-aires in their own right, the bar would've been struggling. It wasn't quite publicly known as a werecreature hangout, but the majority of its patrons definitely weren't mundane human. Over the past few months, werecreatures coming in for a drink had slowed to a trickle while others with ties to the preternatural world had taken up bar space when they stopped by at all.

Estelle had hinted she would lift her edict if Emma and Leon fired Jono. They had both dug their heels in deep behind Marek's order to keep Jono employed. Disobeying a seer went against the law, and the pair were happy to obey the government over the god pack in this instance.

As for Jono, he refused to be cowed. So long as his presence at the bar didn't hurt Emma's pack, he'd keep working for them.

"Can you drop me off at the bodega near campus?" Wade said as he stood. "I wanna get—"

"Snacks," Jono finished for him.

Sage chuckled as she headed for the door. "We know."

Wade made a face at them, scrunching up his nose. "Nothing wrong with snacks."

"There is when people think we don't feed you. Come on, let's go. Traffic is ugly and I have a ten-o'clock conference call I can't miss."

They left, and Jono retrieved his mug from the coffee table before heading for the master bedroom. He found Patrick seated on the bed, still talking on his mobile. He'd managed to remove his jacket, but that was as far as he got.

Jono set his mug on the nightstand, then knelt in front of

Patrick. He unlaced Patrick's boots and pulled them off, along with his damp socks, setting both aside. He stayed where he was, warm hands stroking Patrick's thighs while he listened in on the conversation.

"—open up diplomatic channels with the fae. I don't know how receptive the fae ambassadors in DC will be after that press conference," Patrick said.

"We'll get the State Department brought on board. You and I both know the family is asking for a miracle though," Henry said on the other side of the line.

Jono hadn't ever met the SAIC for the New York City field office, but Patrick seemed to work well under him. It was nothing like the tense relationship Patrick had with SOA Director Setsuna Abuku, the woman who'd become his guardian at a young age. Theirs was a fraught relationship Patrick rarely talked about.

"I know. I've got my interview notes, and I'll wait to hear from the State Department's representative. I have some contacts I can reach out to here in the city."

"I have a feeling this case is going to be front and center in the news for a while. If there's any chance we can get ahead of the story, we need to take it."

"I'll let our PR people handle that problem. Just keep me away from the cameras."

"That's getting harder to do these days."

Patrick made a face, settling his hand over Jono's and giving it a tired squeeze. "Yeah."

"Keep me updated, Collins."

"Yes, sir."

Patrick ended the call and dropped his mobile on the bed. He flopped backward with a heavy sigh and closed his eyes. "Wake me up for lunch."

Jono snorted as he stood and started to divest Patrick of his weapons and clothes. "Get under the covers."

"This is why you're my favorite," Patrick mumbled a few

minutes later once he'd been stripped to his underwear and was buried beneath their blankets.

"I won't tell Wade." Jono leaned over and kissed him on the forehead. "Sleep, love."

Patrick was dead to the world before Jono even left the bedroom.

4

Jono poured what was left of the open Tito's Vodka into the jigger, but it didn't come to the top. He poured the vodka into the shaker anyway before prying off the metal pourer and tossed the empty bottle in the recycling bin behind the bar. Grabbing a brand-new bottle of Tito's from the lower storage shelves behind him, he opened it up, popped the pourer in, and finished off the ounce with a little extra in the shaker.

He shook it, poured it, and finished prepping the greyhound drink before placing it in front of the witch who had ordered it. "There you go. Ten dollars. Do you want to open a tab or no?"

"I have cash," she said.

Jono took her money and handed back change, earning himself a couple of dollars in tips that he left on the bar counter; he'd retrieve it in a bit. Walking down the length of the bar, he picked up the bottle of cabernet sauvignon he'd left out and uncorked it, topping up Sage's glass where she sat.

Tempest was quiet tonight; it always was these days. More than half the people in the bar were human of some sort or another, while most of the rest were magic users. He could count the number of werecreatures on one hand, but none of those who'd stopped by had made it over to the bar for whatever advice they'd come looking to get from him.

"How was work?" Jono asked.

Sage shrugged, reaching for her wineglass. "Long. Busy. We had a lot of reporters calling today for a sound bite."

"Didn't give it to them, I take it?"

Sage rolled her eyes. "No comment is always going to be your best answer to the press, Jono."

He reached across the bar to tap the top edge of her mobile. "What are you reading?"

"An article about the mayor's evening news conference. Did you see it?"

"No television here, remember?"

Tempest had been designed more toward a cozy lounge-type bar than sports bar; music had been the first and only choice over any television. With the wood paneling used in its design both upstairs and in the downstairs event area, along with the old-style amber lighting, televisions would've messed with the atmosphere Emma and Leon had wanted.

Jono had worked in bars of various sorts for most of his adult life. With eyes like his, steady work was difficult to come by. Discrimination might be against the law in both countries he'd lived in, but people still committed it, especially against his kind. What jobs Jono could find over the years were usually given to him by someone with ties to the preternatural world, and most of those paid under the table in cash.

Marek had been the first and only one who'd promised him more than a job and kept that promise.

Sage tapped away at her mobile before turning it around, holding it horizontal rather than vertical for wide-screen viewing. Jono crossed his arms over his chest and stared at the screen. The volume was low to middling, but he didn't need her to turn up. Despite the music playing in the bar, he could hear it just fine.

The setup was a low stage, with dark blue curtains hanging behind it. Three flags were positioned in a cluster to the right of the podium: New York City, the State of New York, and the United States. Jono couldn't make out the full designs with the number of people standing on the stage.

The man who stood behind the podium was tall and broad-shouldered, wearing a nicely tailored wool suit with a plaid tie. Curly ginger hair more on the orange side of the color scale was trimmed short, as was his graying ginger beard. He was a handsome bloke, older though he was, but Jono had a soft spot for gingers.

Mayor Doyle Ferbenn had been elected as an Independent last year, and he'd handled the fallout from several of Patrick's cases rather well. In his late forties, unmarried, and having run a crowd-funded campaign, the mayor was an atypical politician in some ways. Standing before the crowd of reporters in City Hall's press room, surrounded by his aides, he gave off a competent air despite his novice political background.

"I'm here tonight to address the latest threat to our city. We New Yorkers have always prided ourselves on welcoming everyone from all walks of life, whether human or not. But we will always draw the line when any of our citizens are threatened. I ask that the fae who call our city home reach out to one of their own and stop the madness flying through our skies from stealing any more of our children," Mayor Doyle Ferbenn said in the video.

"You were right," Jono said. "PR disaster."

Sage smiled thinly. "I know how this game is played."

Jono watched the press conference for another minute or so before shaking his head. Sage flipped her mobile around and closed the article. The video cut out, and she put her mobile away in her Birkin.

"How's the wedding planning going?"

Sage's smile shifted into something softer. "Haven't decided on a dress designer yet, but we're thinking about the Rainbow Room at Rockefeller Center or the Plaza Hotel for the venue next year."

"Not in the Hamptons?"

"That's Tempest pack territory. We decided not to intrude there."

Marek was part of Emma's Tempest pack even if Sage no longer was. She would've been exiled back in August if Jono hadn't stepped up and claimed her as part of his nascent god pack at the time. She still lived with Marek, their engagement a promise to a lifelong commitment Estelle and Youssef couldn't ignore. Marriage was still seen as an acceptable form of contract in every way that mattered, despite the modern opinion that it wasn't needed which was creeping into their generation.

Sage was accepted into another pack's territory because if she wasn't, Marek would have thrown a fit, and the federal government would have paid the New York City god pack a visit. Considering their actions and inaction with the Night Courts this past year, Jono knew Estelle and Youssef weren't keen on any government agency coming around any more than they had to. They already had enough problems dealing with the case from August and the attentions of the DEA and SOA.

All their federal problems didn't even touch on what Lucien brought. The master vampire was the new ruler of the Manhattan Night Court and had been making his presence known to the packs in rather brutal ways at times. Quite a few pack alphas had come through the bar asking for help in regards to broken territory borders.

Jono's hands were tied there, which rankled. Until packs publicly aligned themselves with his god pack and broke from Estelle and Youssef's, until they started tithing him, he couldn't do anything, no matter how much he wanted to. Sage had been firm in her counsel regarding that situation. They couldn't give protection like that without receiving something in return. Giving general advice to help smaller packs keep the peace between themselves and hope to bring them into their fold was one thing. Negotiating with a Night Court was something entirely different.

Unlike Estelle and Youssef, Jono had no qualms about knocking on Lucien's door at Ginnungagap and arguing about territory. When the day came, Jono and Patrick would do what needed to be done for the packs under their protection. Until then, it was their own they had to look out for.

"How is your firm dealing with the media interest?" Jono asked, moving away from wedding talk.

Sage pursed her lips. "We've had to set up more security at the building because of what happened with the Wisteria matter."

"You'll tell me if things get worse."

"I will. Marek might see it first though."

"Is he coming out tonight?"

"They should all be here soon."

Jono nodded, looking forward to seeing Emma, Leon, and Marek. He'd cut back on his visits to their home over the last month or so, knowing they'd been put under watch by the other god pack. Despite Marek's rank as a seer, the protections his status came with didn't cover Emma's pack. She and Leon had already taken too many punishments over the past few months for transgressions both real and imagined. Jono refused to add to it.

Meeting at Tempest was the easiest answer to that problem. Emma and Leon owned the bar, and they weren't going to fire Jono no matter how many times Estelle demanded they do so.

A trio of guys in the far corner booth near the toilets laughed loudly before one got up and headed for the bar. Jono drifted toward the beers on tap. "Another round?"

"Yeah, same ones as before," the guy said.

Jono nodded and got to work pouring out three more beers. He passed them over one at a time before turning to add the drinks to the group's running tab. As he wrote out the drink totals on the slip of paper clipped to the credit card in question, a heartbeat cut through the noise of the music and quiet conversation as someone walked inside.

He turned his head and looked over at the entrance to the bar. With the lack of the old crowd in the way, it was easy to watch Nicholas Kavanaugh sidle up to the bar counter at the other end. The blond god pack werewolf was a couple of inches shorter than Jono, with bright amber eyes that denoted the god strain of the werevirus running through his veins.

After August, when Jono had put Nicholas on his knees in the challenge ring, forced him to shift, and made him show throat, Jono honestly thought the other man would lose his status as dire for the New York City god pack. Nicholas hadn't been seen again until sometime in September—after probably being punished severely for his failure.

Jono believed Estelle and Youssef had taken their anger out on the other man over the course of that time frame. Werecreatures healed fast, but several weeks was a long time to hurt. Normally, Jono would be bloody pissed about a situation like that, but Nicholas reaped what he sowed. Jono wasn't going to waste sympathy on an arsehole.

Jono was still surprised Nicholas had somehow kept his position as dire.

"Seems like you've had lousy business lately," Nicholas drawled.

"Not lousy enough to close, if that's what you were hoping," Sage said, her wine abandoned in favor of facing off with Nicholas.

Nicholas' gaze flicked around the bar, taking in those who were human and oblivious to their interaction, the magic users who were looking askance at them, and the werecreatures who had all stopped talking and sat tense in their seats. Jono could hear their hearts pounding in their chests from having been caught where they shouldn't be.

"Bar is open to anyone. Even you," Jono said as he headed toward Nicholas. "Doesn't mean you'll get a nice welcome."

Nicholas' smile was slight and condescending. "I'll take a beer."

"And I'll take your money first."

Capitalism at its finest meant money was exchanged for a pint before business was dealt with. Jono shoved the cash into the register before pouring Nicholas a beer and placing the drink in front of him. Jono braced his hands against the edge of the lower work counter where a couple of rows of clean glasses were stacked.

"What do you want?" Jono asked.

"You know the drill. This isn't the first time I've come around to check on you," Nicholas shot back.

Jono didn't blink, gaze boring into Nicholas'. "Still employed. Still not your business."

Nicholas gestured at the rest of the bar and the werecreatures seated within. "They are."

Heartbeats spiked in Jono's ears, and fear pushed through the embedded smell of alcohol in the bar.

"They've done nothing but come in out of the rain for a drink," Sage said, having moved from her first seat to take up one closer to Nicholas.

The empty barstool between them was an invisible wall Jono knew Sage would have no qualms about crossing if Nicholas forced her hand. Considering Sage was a master at manipulating words, he doubted Nicholas would get that far.

"The alphas gave an order. They expect to be obeyed." Nicholas raised his pint glass to his mouth and took a sip. "You've been getting visitors you shouldn't have."

Somehow, Jono didn't think Nicholas was talking about the ones in the bar. He kept his heartbeat steady and calm, letting nothing seep through his scent that would give away his true feelings.

"You think so?" Jono asked.

In response, Nicholas pulled out his mobile and tapped at the screen a few times before turning it so Jono could see. The picture was taken from inside a car, the pouring rain and water running down the windshield distorting the picture. He could still make out the figures on the sidewalk and the faint glow of Patrick's mageglobe in the photograph.

Jono hadn't smelled anything out of the ordinary the other night. Which meant whoever had taken the picture had been passing through or used an artifact to hide their presence on the street while keeping watch.

Jono kept a stranglehold on his anger at being spied on, refusing to give Nicholas the satisfaction of an emotional response.

"I'm certain the SOA will be thrilled to know you're threatening a witness vital to their investigation into your pack," Sage said. When Nicholas looked at her, she pointedly tapped the edge of her mobile where she had it balanced against the bar to record. "I'll be sure to pass the video along to Agent Collins."

Nicholas' eyes narrowed and his hand tightened around his mobile before he shoved it back into his pocket. "I didn't consent to be recorded."

"New York is a one-party consent state, and I'm sure Jono doesn't mind."

"Not at all," Jono replied easily enough.

"There we go." Sage tapped at the screen a couple of times before calmly placing her mobile aside and out of Nicholas' reach. "I've sent the video to Patrick."

Nicholas clenched his jaw, letting go of his pint glass. "You place too much assurance on his job to save you."

"You're only pissed because that's leverage you don't have," Jono said, giving him a sharp smile. He kept his teeth human-shaped, knowing the lack of fangs would tell Nicholas he didn't see the other man as a threat.

In the back of his mind, Fenrir stirred, a distant, prickly presence that Jono actively ignored.

"He won't stick around forever."

Jono barked out a laugh. "Bollocks. You don't know what the bloody hell you're on about."

Jono knew that wherever Patrick went, he would follow. They hadn't ever discussed that future possibility, and Jono half thought Patrick believed he wouldn't stick around. Patrick would be wrong, but that was a problem in a future Marek hadn't warned them about.

Right now, the gods wanted them in New York City, and that's where they were putting down roots. The soulbond might tie them together, but it wasn't the only reason Jono wanted Patrick, and it never would be.

"I've been sent to remind you that the packs in this city aren't yours."

Jono's mouth curved in a hard smile. "Yet. They aren't mine *yet.*"

"Is that a challenge?"

"I put you on your knees once before, mate. Made you show throat before your alphas. You want to go another round, name the time and place." Jono leaned forward, gaze never leaving Nicholas', picking out the anger in the other man's eyes—along with the subtle hint of fear. "You tell Estelle and Youssef that if they go after anyone for coming here or into my territory, then I'll consider it exactly what Sage suggested it is—evidence of intimidation the SOA and DEA lawyers would love to have."

"Pack law will always come first for us. That's something you've never figured out. That's why you were never wanted in London or here."

"Come back to me when you understand what the bloody fuck pack law actually *means,*" Jono snapped. "It sure as shit isn't selling those under your care to their deaths. It's about *protecting* them. Now get the fuck out the bar."

"I'm enjoying my drink."

Jono snatched the pint glass back before Nicholas could grab it and poured the beer out on the floor behind the bar. "Not anymore, you fucking twat."

Jono didn't care about the mess he'd made; mopping always happened after closing anyway. Nicholas shoved himself off the barstool, a mixture of irritation and anger crossing his face.

"New York isn't yours," Nicholas spat out.

Jono smiled so hard it hurt. "It will be."

The words were a promise, falling in the air between them like a weight. Fenrir pressed against Jono's thoughts, clawing at his soul in reaction to the claim Jono wanted—the territory he knew should belong to him.

As was their *right.*

Nicholas left the bar without a backward glance, but the tight, hunched curve of his shoulders was proof he didn't like not having eyes on Jono.

Sage drummed her fingers against the counter a couple of times before grabbing her mobile. "I'll let the ones who stopped by your place last night know what's going on."

Jono nodded, looking past her at the few faces turned their way, the mundane humans oblivious to what had just happened and the small group of witches gone back to ignoring them now that Nicholas was gone. The werecreatures looked like they wanted to be anywhere else but here, and Jono wished that wasn't the case. He still beckoned them over to the bar and started closing out tabs.

They couldn't leave quick enough, though the last one hesitated after taking back her credit card. She was a slight thing, of South Asian descent, her large brown eyes meeting Jono's over the bar.

"Do you mean it?" she asked quietly. "That you want New York?"

Jono nodded slowly. "Yeah."

She glanced over her shoulder at her drinking partner, a tall, African American bloke who stood close by with a protective stance. "We'll let our alpha know."

Jono didn't know what pack they belonged to, but it said something that even after Nicholas' threats, they were willing to think about a future not spent beneath Estelle and Youssef's vicious rules.

The pair left, and Jono let out a heavy sigh. He went to retrieve Sage's drink as she texted people. "One of these days, I'll have no recourse but to kill him."

"Nicholas is their dire. He knows the risk," Sage said.

Jono carried the wineglass back to her spot and set it within reach. "Do you?"

Sage looked up and blinked at him. "Yes. I'm not going anywhere, Jono."

Steadfast and sure, and willing to put her life on the line for his. Sage was everything one could want in a dire, Jono just didn't want to ever lose her.

He reached across the counter and she leaned closer, making it easier for Jono to drag his hand and wrist over her throat, scent-marking her.

A familiar trio of heartbeats echoed in his ears, getting louder. Jono looked over at the entrance to the bar, watching as Emma, Leon, and Marek came inside out of the rain.

"Was that Nicholas we saw leaving just now?" Emma demanded.

"I kicked him out," Jono said.

Leon helped Emma out of her heavy winter coat as Marek set aside their umbrellas. Leon raised an eyebrow. "He looked in one piece."

"Which is an absolute shame," Sage said.

Marek came over and gave her a kiss in greeting. "Hey."

Sage smiled at him. "Hey, yourself."

Jono took in his friends, always pleased when everyone could get together, despite the circumstances trying to keep them all apart. Straightening up, he turned and grabbed bottles off the shelves in preparation of making everyone their preferred drink.

Conversations about the New York City god pack always went down better with alcohol.

5

PATRICK RUBBED HIS GLOVED HANDS TOGETHER, ABSENTLY CASTING A warming charm into the fabric. His arms and torso were warm, courtesy of the charms embedded in his leather jacket. The black sweater he wore beneath it added an extra layer of warmth, but it was the rest of him that was cold as he waited outside the restaurant.

The storm that had churned over New York for the past few days seemed to have let up for early Sunday evening. The clouds hadn't disappeared, and the weather app on his phone said rain was due to return in a few hours. Having grown up in Salem for eight years before living in Washington, DC, Patrick was used to the cold; he just didn't like it.

Citizens across all five boroughs had called in Sluagh sightings to the authorities, but most of those had been tricks of the eye. That didn't mean the restless dead weren't galloping through the clouds up above, waiting to strike at the unsuspecting. The tightness in Patrick's shoulders hadn't eased since the moment he'd stepped outside the office earlier.

Squinting at the street, he eyed the cars and taxis driving past the restaurant with the hope that one of them held his old team-mates. The Horseshoe was a gastropub in the East Village known for its burgers and beers and had been the agreed-upon meeting place for dinner before Patrick took everyone back to Tempest for drinks with Jono and Emma's pack. The Horseshoe wasn't high-end by any means, and wouldn't dent his bank account too badly.

A taxi braked to a stop in front of the restaurant and two passengers got out. Patrick didn't fight the smile that tugged at his mouth.

"Fucking hell, Razzle Dazzle," Sergeant Keith Pearson said with a mad cackle as he skirted between two parked cars to grab Patrick into a back-slapping hug. "Here I thought you'd be in a damn suit. Aren't you G-men supposed to wear suits?"

"That's the FBI, Chatterbox," Patrick replied, pounding him on the back just as hard. "Good to see you."

Keith pulled back, giving Patrick that familiar toothy grin, brown eyes narrowed against the strong wind. The lower half of his face was less tanned than the rest of it, alluding to a thick beard having been recently shaved off. His brown hair was tucked under a beanie, the length a little longer than regulations allowed.

"Only me and Gerard could make it up. All the rest of the guys are taking a few days with their families before they come out to meet us."

Patrick arched an eyebrow at that little update, looking over Keith's shoulder at his old team captain. "By all, does Chatterbox mean Arthur and Darren, or your entire current team?"

Captain Gerard Breckenridge held up a white box with a sticker slapped on top that said *Sin & Cakes* in cursive script. "Entire current team. Figured I'd break that news to you with a care package."

Patrick elbowed Keith out of the way. "Are those from Sienna?"

"My girl flew out to meet us in DC. Apparently, she's got a baker friend who let her make a batch of Gold Rush cookies in their bakery. She said you had to share," Keith told him.

"Fuck you, she said no such thing." Patrick took the offered box with quick hands. "Thanks, Smooth Dog."

Gerard drew him into a hard hug, careful of the box of cookies baked with West Coast love. "You're a civilian now. Thought you'd forget about that name."

"Not even when I'm dead."

Patrick drew back, taking in his former captain. The half-fae officer looked mostly human if one ignored the gently tapered points of his ears peeking out from light brown hair and his other-worldly silver eyes. Gerard was the kind of handsome people always looked twice at, and then again for good measure. He was a beautiful man who could command a room simply by stepping inside it, and who had commanded their team with an iron will Patrick had been more than willing to be bound by when part of the Hellraisers.

"Your hair isn't regulation," Patrick mused. "Leave get granted that quick?"

"Something like that."

"Let's talk about it inside." Patrick deftly smacked Keith's hand away from the cookie box. "I will stab you with my dagger if you even try to eat one. You're married to Sienna. You can get cookies whenever you want."

"Bullshit. I can't get cookies in the field," Keith shot back.

"Inside," Gerard ordered firmly. "I need a beer that doesn't taste like piss water."

Keith elbowed Patrick in the ribs. "He's been in a mood since he took a satphone call a week and a half ago."

Patrick frowned as he shoved open the restaurant door. "You called me a week and a half ago about this visit."

Gerard grimaced. "Yeah. Beer first. Then we'll talk."

The hostess gave them a polite smile, grabbed a couple of menus after confirming their party number, and led them to a booth in the rear of the bar. Patrick was sweating by the time they reached the table. He wasn't the only one peeling out of his layers of outerwear before sitting down. Patrick let Gerard and Keith take the bench facing the front door, knowing they'd feel more comfortable with eyes on the exit.

Patrick skimmed the menu, picking out a burger, fries, and a Guinness to wash it all down with. The other two perused the menu quickly, with Keith making drooling sounds over every option that caught his eye.

"When was the last time you had decent food?" Patrick asked.

"DC the other day with Sienna. Smooth Dog here got roped into the dog and pony show with the brass. I don't know what they've been feeding him," Keith replied.

"Food that wasn't A-rations," Gerard said.

"That really isn't saying much."

The waitress came over to take their order, and Patrick wasn't at all surprised about the amount of food they collectively ordered. Three burgers with fries, two orders of wings, potato skins, chili cheese fries, and a salad, along with their beer.

"Since when the fuck do you eat salads?" Patrick asked, staring at Keith.

"Sienna was on him during our last leave about not eating his vegetables," Gerard said with a straight face.

"I'm going to take a picture of it, send it to her, and not eat it," Keith admitted.

Patrick snorted. "You're such a fucking child."

"Speaking of children," Gerard interrupted before they could devolve into name-calling, "You have a Sluagh problem, and I saw on the news a story about a changeling."

Patrick made a face and quickly wrote out a silence ward on the table. The sigil glowed pale blue before fading into the wood. The restaurant around them went quiet, people moving beyond the table as if they were in an old silent film.

"The Sluagh went after the baby the other night. I put her in the care of an SOA agent that specializes in changeling cases," Patrick said.

"How specialized is the agent?"

Movement out of the corner of his eye had Patrick pause as their drinks arrived. If the waitress was aware of the silence ward, she didn't say anything, and passed out their drinks before heading off to the next customer.

"The SOA has safe houses for unwanted changelings. The agent acts as a go-between," Patrick said once she was gone.

"Go-between? As in, the veil?" Keith asked. "Like Spencer?"

Patrick shook his head. "No, a regular liaison."

"Boring. Speaking of Dead Boy, have you heard from him lately?"

"He called the day after Halloween bitching about drunken teenagers summoning zombies in the Bay Area."

Spencer Bailey wasn't really dead, but like the rest of them, he'd been christened with a nickname their fellow soldiers had come up with for him in the field. Spencer hadn't been a Hellraiser, but he'd been assigned to their team from time to time on a temporary basis by the powers that be for missions that needed his particular skills. He'd been competent and trustworthy, and if he hadn't been so specialized, Gerard would've snatched him up in a heartbeat.

A year older than Patrick, Spencer was a soulbreaker mage, capable of exorcising demons from souls and putting the dead to rest, amongst other things. He couldn't raise the dead, but his magic had an affinity for death and was too close to necromancy for anyone in the government to be comfortable with. Spencer was alive today because someone had decided he could be useful.

Patrick and Spencer had gotten resentfully drunk together over their shared status of being *useful* a couple of years ago after they were discharged from the Mage Corps. Then they'd gone their separate ways, picked up by different federal agencies, though they still kept in touch.

"You should know he's been read into the mission," Gerard said.

Patrick took a sip of his beer. "Doesn't surprise me. He's PIA.

We got a missing ancient magical staff that can theoretically raise the dead. Stands to reason we'd need someone to put the dead to rest again."

"We still don't know where the Morrígan's staff is," Keith said.

"But we know where it's been. Why'd you request leave, Gerard?"

Gerard tilted his head to the side, silver-eyed gaze contemplative as he stared Patrick down. He waited until Patrick took a sip of beer before answering, because he was a little shit like that.

"My fiancée is missing."

Patrick inhaled his beer rather than swallowing it. Some came out his nose as he coughed to get air, struggling to clear his lungs. Keith got up and stepped around the table to oh so politely smack Patrick on the back with a heavy hand to help him breathe.

"Oh man, you should've warned me you were going to open with that, Gerard," Keith said with a weak chuckle. "I could've had my camera out. His expression was priceless."

Patrick batted Keith's arm away, still coughing, but not as bad. "I'm sorry. Your *what?*"

"Food's here" was Gerard's calm reply.

Patrick glared at him as their waitress arrived with their appetizers, putting the plates between them. Keith retook his seat as soon as she left and immediately grabbed a chicken wing, dunking it in blue cheese.

"No." Patrick pointed his finger at Gerard. "Talk first. Eat later."

Gerard raised an eyebrow and stabbed a potato skin with his fork. "Which one of us is paid to give orders?"

"I don't wear a uniform anymore. I'm no longer a Hellraiser, which means I'm not obligated to jump when you say how high."

"You'll always be a Hellraiser, Patrick. I don't let my people go unless I bury them."

"Well," Keith said after a long, uncomfortable pause. "That got fucking awkward."

Patrick rested his elbows on the table and dragged both hands through his hair. He linked his fingers together over the back of his neck and glared down at his empty plate, jaw working. "Who is your fiancée?"

"Órlaith. She's Ruadán's daughter with a mortal woman," Gerard said.

Patrick raised his head, grabbed his pint of Guinness, and chugged it until the glass was empty. He shoved it to the edge of the table, glaring at Gerard while he tried to slow down the pounding of his heart.

"Since when do you mingle with the Tuatha Dé Danann?" he demanded.

Gerard snagged another potato skin with his fork. He shrugged, the neutral expression on his face not giving anything away. Gerard hadn't ever been overly emotional, but Patrick had served under the other man and knew that just because Gerard didn't wear his heart on his sleeve didn't mean he wasn't hurting.

"I'm half-fae, even if none of them like to acknowledge me. I don't care for them. You know that."

Patrick did, but that didn't make this situation better. He knew Gerard's paperwork with the military listed him as four years older than Patrick's twenty-nine years, but that was for his identity this time around. Gerard was several hundred years old, the son of a mortal woman and a Seelie fae lord he'd never disclosed the identity of. All Patrick knew was that Gerard resented his father's absence in his life over the decades, and he'd spent more time in the mortal plane than in Tír na nÓg.

The fae were sticklers when it came to a person's rank. Fae earned their titles through blood, heroic deeds, magical strength, and promises made, kept, and broken. Half-blooded fae held lower status in both fae courts, and always would.

Gerard, it seemed, was an exception.

Patrick knew exceptions were never all that they seemed, and rarely ever good.

"Another beer?" their waitress asked when she sidled up to their table with their burgers.

"Yes," Patrick said. He needed at least one more to get through this conversation.

"You're looking a little pissed off," Keith said once she left. "Need a smoke break?"

"I don't smoke anymore."

Keith stared at Patrick, his burger lifted halfway to his mouth. "Excuse me?"

"Jono hates the smell, so I stopped."

Keith let out a long whistle. "Damn. Never thought I'd see the day you'd give up smoking."

"I'm learning better habits."

"You still go to therapy?" Gerard wanted to know.

Patrick nodded. "When I need to."

He was a veteran, and the Thirty-Day War had been shitty for all of them. Only Gerard, Keith, Arthur, and Darren had opted to stay in uniform and continue to fight, while Patrick had entered the civilian world, nursing wounds that still bled in different ways even these many years later. Patrick wasn't ashamed of his mental health needs, but his visits to group therapy or his therapist had lessened over the last six months since meeting Jono.

After destroying Tremaine's Night Court, when the sense memory of being held down on Santa Muerte's altar was too insidious to ignore, Patrick had reached out for help a little more often. The nightmares were ugly, but waking up with Jono by his side always made it easier to call his therapist. The support he'd received from everyone had gone a long way toward Patrick finding his balance again.

That didn't mean he'd forgotten what had happened to him. Patrick compartmentalized his life because he had to. Some days, ignoring that the assault had occurred was the easiest option. What he never ignored was Jono's presence in his life.

"You haven't said much about Jono," Gerard said.

"I'm not going to say anything incriminating on an unsecured line." Patrick took a bite of his hamburger, making sure to get a piece of the bacon he'd added on. "He's god pack."

And god-touched.

But that was a detail he wasn't about to disclose, no matter how much Patrick trusted his old team. That information was Jono's alone to reveal.

"Does the Old Man know?"

Patrick snorted, thinking about General Noah Reed. "Jono told the Old Man off when they first met."

Keith's eyebrows rose to his hairline. "And your boy survived that meeting?"

"Yes."

"Does Jono know about the Morrígan's staff?" Gerard asked.

"My entire pack does."

Gerard paused in picking up another fry, silver eyes narrowing. He shoved the fry into his mouth before leaning back and crossing his arms over his chest. "Your entire *pack*? Is this one of those things you didn't want to discuss on an unsecured line?"

"What do you think?"

"I thought the SOA wasn't ever going to give you a partner?" Keith asked, moving the chicken wings around on the plate to find the best one to eat. He had a habit of digging for the crispiest piece, and Patrick was glad to see that hadn't changed.

"They didn't. The gods gave me Jono."

Keith's head snapped up, mouth dropping open. "Oh, shit."

The team's survivors of the Thirty-Day War knew about Patrick's fucked-up family and ties to the gods. His secrets had been peeled open beneath the hot desert sun in the push to stop Ethan's sacrificial spell in Cairo, Egypt, three and a half years ago. There'd been no hiding from his past anymore at that point, nor hiding the soul debt that tied him to Persephone.

Patrick was the reason, after all, for the graves in Arlington of the Hellraisers who hadn't made it home.

Gerard and the rest of them knew the truth, because that was the least Patrick owed them after they lied for him to the brass at the end of that fight. Ethan was a known threat to national security and always would be. Patrick's identity as his son was tied up in the courts, and even the military wasn't privy to that information.

His team had helped keep his secrets, because that's what family did.

"Can you trust him?" Gerard asked.

"Yes," Patrick said.

"Are you sure?"

"Jono has watched my six since I met him. I trust him enough to sleep with him, and he hates the gods as much as I do."

Gerard dragged a hand down his face. "Patrick."

"What?" Patrick asked testily.

"You should've told me."

"Same way you told me about your engagement?"

"That's different."

"Is it? When did everyone else find out?"

"After his satphone call," Keith admitted.

Patrick felt marginally better that it wasn't months, only days, of him being out of the loop. It still served as a reminder that he was one of the last to know.

"Look," Gerard said, leaning forward again to rest his elbows on the table. His mouth ticked down in a faint frown, and Patrick didn't miss the way he suddenly looked *tired*. "I requested leave for a family emergency. That's what the Old Man is putting in my records. The team came with me because they don't go into the field without me, but that's not the entire reason why we were all wanted Stateside."

"The Morrígan's staff," Patrick said, then took another bite of his burger.

Before Gerard could reply, their waitress returned, depositing a second Guinness next to Patrick's plate and taking away his empty glass. Gerard took a moment to eat half his burger in a couple of large bites. Patrick jangled his right leg under the table as he waited Gerard out.

"The person responsible for the audit of the Morrígan's staff three years ago doesn't exist," Gerard said a few minutes later.

"On paper?"

"Anywhere," Keith said with a grimace. "Onsite records were wiped clean. Only evidence we had was on a server they couldn't access because it was located at the Pentagon, behind an air gap, encrypted every way you could think of, and received updates bimonthly through a physical courier escorted by Special Forces. The identity the audit person used at the time was false, and the picture doesn't match any facial recognition records in any national database."

"So, magic."

"Glamour," Gerard corrected.

"Same fucking difference." Patrick put what was left of his burger down, suddenly not hungry anymore. "You think the fae stole back the Morrígan's staff?"

"I think it's not that easy or clear-cut, because things never are when it comes to the fae or the Dominion Sect. We know Ethan wants the staff. We don't know why, and we don't know what bargains he's made to find it."

Patrick thought of Hades and the betrayals immortals inflicted within their own pantheons for the sake of power. He wouldn't put it past any of the fae to make deals with Ethan the same way Hades had.

"Where does Órlaith come in?"

"I don't know all the details, I only know the Spring Queen called her warriors home, and that is not a call I can ignore." Gerard grimaced. "I would never ignore it for Órlaith."

The words were said in a quiet, tired voice, and Patrick wondered about the faint bitterness and worry in Gerard's tone.

"Brigid ordered you back?" At Gerard's nod, Patrick frowned as he dredged up what he knew of the Tuatha Dé Danann. "She's the Dagda's daughter, isn't she?"

"Yes."

"Which means she's immortal."

"Yes."

"I hate dealing with the gods."

"Welcome to bitter, population Patrick," Keith mused.

Patrick flipped him off. "Fuck you."

"You said *I love you* wrong."

"Finish your food. There's a werewolf I want to meet," Gerard ordered before they could devolve into further insults.

"Ooh, shovel talk time," Keith said with a grin.

Patrick made a face and picked up his pint glass again. His stomach was a hard knot. It had nothing to do with the food, but with the messy situation staring them in the face. Chasing after the Morrígan's staff was one thing—dealing with a missing fae lady who happened to be his friend's fiancée was an entirely different level of fucked.

By silent agreement, they shelved talk of the mission for later and finished their meal while discussing the rest of the team and their families. Patrick got brought up to speed on the newest additions, including the sorcerer the US Department of the Preternatural had deigned to assign the Hellraisers after Patrick was discharged.

"Not up to your level magic-wise, but Desmond is still excellent at watching our six. He's good people," Keith said as he took over demolishing the chili cheese fries.

Patrick rubbed a finger against the condensation on the outside of his pint glass, thinking about the change in his magic with the soulbond. The damage to his soul and magic during the Thirty-Day War had been the main reason he'd left the Mage Corps. Now, thanks to the gods, he could tap ley lines again through Jono's soul. Very few were privy to that information, and even if he wanted to tell Gerard, Patrick couldn't risk it—both for his own safety and

Gerard's.

"I'm glad. You need a good magic user," Patrick said.

Patrick removed the silence ward around them and flagged down their waitress once everyone was done with their dinner. It didn't take long to pay, and Keith plunked down cash for a good tip. Patrick pulled on his jacket and gloves before shoving his wool beanie on his head. Sliding out of the booth, he was surprised to see a couple walk past, following the hostess, with what looked like snowflakes on their shoulders.

"Is it snowing?" Keith asked, sounding confused.

"It wasn't even raining when we arrived over an hour ago," Patrick replied.

Gerard shrugged into his heavy wool coat, frowning in the direction of the exit. "Let's get out of here."

"You think it's the Sluagh?"

"The Sluagh aren't the only ones who ride the storms."

Keith glanced at Patrick as they hurried toward the door. "Could it be a reactionary storm?"

Patrick shook his head. "There hasn't been a displacement of magic."

"Doesn't mean the weather hasn't been tampered with. The fae are capable of affecting the seasons, and that includes the weather," Gerard said.

"Fucking great."

They stepped outside into an icy cold wind, the temperature having plunged at least twenty degrees since the start of dinner. The night sky overhead was thick with dark clouds, and snow flurries spun through the air, drifting through the street.

Patrick blinked as a couple of snowflakes caught on his lashes. He wiped them away, staring at his gloved hand and the falling snow that settled on it.

"This isn't normal. The forecast called for rain, not snow tonight," Patrick said slowly.

"No shit? I'm fucking freezing," Keith grumbled.

Patrick reached out and snagged Keith's winter coat, pushing his magic into the cloth. The heat charm was easy to cast, filling Keith's outerwear with a warmth that wouldn't fade. Keith sighed and shoved his hands into his pockets.

"Thanks, Razzle Dazzle."

Gerard raised his arm and flagged down the first taxi he saw rather than opening up a ride-hailing app.

"Where to?" Gerard asked once they were inside the vehicle.

"Tempest," Patrick said, giving the driver the address.

6

"You sure it's all right if I leave early?" Natasha asked.

Jono looked up from wiping down the bar counter where their only customer of the night had sat before leaving. He gestured pointedly at the empty bar; even the event room downstairs was quiet to his ears beneath the music.

"Not like we have much of a crowd, and if you have finals to study for, I don't mind letting you go," Jono said.

Natasha's shoulders eased up a little. "Thanks. I appreciate it."

A werelynx, Natasha wasn't part of Emma's pack, though Emma had argued for her right to stay employed at Tempest through at least the end of the semester. Looking for a new job while juggling university would've been too stressful. Estelle and Youssef had eventually agreed, needing to at least appear like they cared about the packs they were supposed to protect.

Natasha retreated to the small back office to gather her things and clock out. She waved to Jono as she left, heading into a night that smelled more damp than usual. Jono took a deep breath as the swinging door blew a gust of air into the bar. He frowned, rubbing at his nose.

It smelled like snow.

Shaking his head, Jono started putting things to rights behind the counter, needing to keep busy. The bar being so empty was depressing, but there wasn't anything he could do about that. Sunday nights were always slow, but they'd become slower since werecreatures had been ordered to give Tempest a wide berth.

Considering who Jono was meeting for the first time tonight, maybe slow was better. Being introduced to Patrick's former commanding officer in a loud crowd would've made focusing on the bloke difficult when Jono needed to work. It wouldn't matter that Emma, Leon, and Marek would also be joining them and had given him the okay to take an extra-long break. Jono took pride in doing his job and not slacking off.

Jono's mobile buzzed in his back pocket as he took inventory of some of the bottles on the shelves. He pulled it out, seeing a notification for a text message from Patrick. He unlocked his mobile in order to read it.

ON THE WAY. IT'S SNOWING. NOT NORMAL.

Jono frowned at that warning, glancing over at the closed door again. It hadn't even been raining when he opened the bar a couple of hours ago.

Jono texted back a response. WHAT DO YOU MEAN BY NOT NORMAL?

WE THINK IT'S MAGICALLY CREATED.

Jono grimaced. "Brilliant."

He was about to text back when the door to the bar was pushed open and a stunningly beautiful woman stepped inside. Jono straightened up, nostrils flaring as he took in her scent—something almost rancid that seemed out of place with her appearance.

In the back of his mind, Fenrir stirred.

Jono took that warning for what it was.

The woman unwrapped her scarf from around her neck, a bit of snow falling off her shoulders as she did so. "Getting cold out there."

Her Irish accent was familiar enough to Jono's ears, and it made him think wistfully of the city he'd left behind. New York City had the same sort of madcap bustle, just not quite the same mix of accents he'd lived amongst in London for most of his life. Jono put his mobile back in his pocket and gave her a friendly enough smile.

"So I hear. What can I get you?"

Shrugging out of her coat, the woman came over to the bar and slung her things over an empty stool before taking a seat. She was gorgeous in a model kind of way: tall, thin, fashionably dressed, with brilliant blue eyes and thick blonde hair tied back in a trendy braid. Her clothes were fashion forward and not office wear, the silk blouse she wore too thin for the December chill.

She had all the appearance of a hip New Yorker, but Jono didn't trust her for a second.

"Slow night?" the woman asked.

"Is it just you?" Jono wanted to know, figuring the answer to her question was obvious in the empty bar.

She smiled at him, the rose pink of her mouth parting around even white teeth. "Just me. Saw you were open and thought I'd get a drink to warm me up before I venture home in the snow."

"How bad is it out there?"

"Oh, just little flurries right now, but I think it might get worse." She tilted her head, looking up at him through her long eyelashes. "You won't close early, will you?"

Flirting came with the job, but Jono preferred when it didn't come from some creature playing at being human. Besides, the only person he was interested in for the rest of his life was shorter than her, a ginger, and constantly getting into fights.

"Nah, love. We don't close for a bit of snow. What can I get you?"

"Something sweet."

Jono was used to men and women coyly letting him decide their drinks over the years. When he was younger, he'd taken quite a few blokes home with him after closing if he liked their taste in alcohol and how they looked. They were usually the ones who didn't care about his eyes and what the color meant, though occasionally Jono would fuck someone who only wanted him because he was a werecreature. These days, the only man in his bed was Patrick, and he preferred it that way.

Jono set about mixing up an appletini, never completely turning his back on the woman. She didn't smell like magic beneath the corpse scent that lingered around her—but that could always be because he didn't recognize her kind of magic.

Fae, Fenrir growled in the back of his mind.

Jono wasn't surprised by that, considering what had attacked Patrick at the Wisteria home. The fae's mastery of glamour was well recorded in history.

He set the empty shaker down on the work counter, fingers trailing against the edge where the trigger command for the defensive wards set into the bar's wall had been burned into wood. Marek had gotten the federal government to pay for a mage to set strong defensive wards that anyone—even a mundane human— could trigger.

Jono knew they wouldn't be enough against a soultaker, but Patrick had assured him the wards were strong enough to defend against a lot of threats, including the fae.

"Here you go," Jono said, setting the drink down in front of her. She passed over a credit card, and Jono glanced at the name on it. He didn't believe for a moment it was hers. "Do you want to open a tab?"

She picked up her glass and took a delicate sip of the sweet drink. "Why not?"

Jono half turned to deposit her credit card by the register and was about to go back to cleaning when the door to the bar was pushed open again. Five werecreatures entered, their bright amber eyes reflecting the low light of the bar with a metallic glint.

Jono was familiar with only one of them. The New York City

god pack counted forty-seven members, a dozen less than the London god pack. They ranged in age, though all were werewolves. Estelle was a known purist that way and had exiled those who weren't werewolves from the pack when she took over.

Theodore Davis was low in the ranks, a bruiser whose face looked like someone had disagreed with his features in a fight before he was infected with the werevirus, and the only recourse was modifying them with a punch. Pity that's how he always looked—as ugly on the outside as he was on the inside.

Jono looked from the woman at the bar still sipping her drink to the werecreatures he doubted were there to check up on him like Nicholas.

This is going to get messy.

"You blokes here to drink?" Jono asked, watching as the five fanned out across the bar.

"Now why would we spend our hard-earned money at a place like this?" Theodore said.

Jono stared him down, noting the not so subtle shift of muscle beneath the other man's dark clothing and the gloves he wore. Theodore hadn't bothered with a winter coat, and neither had his fellow pack members. Their clothing looked old and worn—perfect for losing when one shifted form.

"Hey, lady," the only woman in Theodore's group said. "You should leave."

The woman sighed and set down her drink. "I detest when food thinks it has the right to give me orders."

Her words sent ice cascading down Jono's spine. Theodore's expression became uneasy. Jono took a step away from her, his back to the bar and its shelves full of liquor bottles. He flexed his hands, bones and muscles shifting to allow claws to form at the tips of his fingers in lieu of fingernails.

Jono split his attention between the two sets of adversaries, weighing his options. She watched him move with eyes that were no longer blue but a discomforting iridescent green. As he watched, her blonde hair lost its luster, the pale color disappearing into oily black strands that grew and grew until they tangled around her rapidly growing body.

Her glamour melted away, leaving behind something bitter, ugly, and unkind.

A spindly torso replaced her curves, rising up from a fat spider's body covered in bristly hair. Eight spider legs extended outward from the bulbous arachnid body while human hands clawed at the wooden counter. Standing as tall as he was, with dark gray skin that faded to black spider legs, the only bit of brightness on it was its eyes.

Its hair moved on its own accord, lifting and sliding all around its body. Jono ducked when a heavy lock of hair cut through where he'd been standing, slamming through liquor bottles on a shelf behind him. Alcohol and glass shards exploded around him, drenching Jono in rum and vodka.

More of its hair lashed out at the other werecreatures in the bar. Theodore missed being stabbed through the chest by vaulting over the bar to duck behind the work area where Jono was. Trapped between the two, Jono focused on the more immediate threat.

"You have something of ours," the fae hissed, its hair a writhing, living thing around its body. "You smell like it."

"Fuck off," Jono said as he reached up and slammed his hand against the edge of the bar—right over the command trigger. "And get the *fuck* out."

The intent was all in the feeling and directed at the threat. The magic burned his hand, but Jono didn't pull away. When he was younger, he would have, but being with Patrick had taught him that magic wasn't always bad.

The protective wards flared around the bar, the walls burning with them. The fae shrieked with fury, lifting two front legs and slamming their hooked ends into the wooden counter, as if that would keep it from being tossed out.

Tempest was a public space; no threshold encircled it. The magic embedded in its walls filled the space, focusing on the threat Jono wanted dealt with first. A noise Jono felt more than heard filled the air, and the fae was lifted off the floor and carried out of the bar by magical means. The door crumpled when it hit, breaking apart from the weight of the fae.

Jono had kept his eyes on the fae's exit to ensure it left—and it cost him.

Theodore slammed into him, leading with a silver serrated knife that buried itself to the hilt in Jono's stomach before he could twist out of the way. Agony he remembered from summer when he was trapped beneath Ethan's hands and magic and silver stakes burned through his nerves as he landed on the rubber mats that covered the floor.

Theodore loomed over him, a snarl on his ugly face as he dug the knife deeper. Blood slid up Jono's throat, making him gag.

"New York isn't yours," Theodore growled.

Jono headbutted him right between the eyes, feeling the cartilage in Theodore's nose crunch from the blow. "Tell your alphas to quit being bloody cowards and fucking fight me themselves, you arsehole."

Theodore howled at the hit, blood spattering over Jono's face. The heat in his skin was like acid, spreading from the knife in his gut through the rest of his body. Jono flipped Theodore off him, grimacing as the silver knife cut deeper with the motion.

Jono struggled to one knee, fumbling for the knife as Theodore got to his feet. Jono ground his teeth against the agony in his body that stemmed from the toxic weapon. He managed to get his hand around the handle of the knife and yank it free, but the burns on his skin and the stab wound wouldn't immediately heal. The absence of the silver blade didn't stop the spread of the reaction—a churning nausea that left Jono light-headed in the worst way, the taste of metal filling his mouth, biting and sharp.

Blood flowed down the front of his body, staining his shirt and jeans. Jono pressed one hand to the hole in his gut and raised his head. Swallowing blood, he glared at the werewolf who jumped onto the counter, fully shifted, their monstrous body blocking out some of the light.

"I just fucking cleaned that," Jono snarled.

Out of the corner of his eye, he saw Theodore's body writhing through a shift. Five against one wasn't great odds, and Jono had a moment of regret for kicking the fae out so quickly. He could've used it as a distraction.

Let me out, Fenrir howled in the back of his mind.

You'll kill them. We're not ready for a war.

But they were ready to fight.

The poison running through his veins interfered with his ability to shift, dulling his reflexes. All werecreatures were severely —sometimes deathly—allergic to silver. It impeded healing and shifting, making it impossible to recover from silver-inflicted wounds right away.

Lucky for him, he had an animal-god patron who could force his body into shifting.

It wasn't like summer, with the silver stakes driven through his shoulders that Ethan had ensured never left his body. The sickening nausea and blood loss wasn't as bad this time around. Jono let Fenrir's presence seep through his mind, drawing strength from the god. The howling in his mind drowned out the snarls around him as Fenrir clawed at his soul.

The god's presence was like fire in his veins, different than the burn of silver that stole Jono's concentration. The blood loss and open wound took second place as Jono struggled to rein in the god who wanted *out.*

Who wanted *blood.*

No, Jono ordered, digging in his metaphorical heels even as his body began to break apart. *They're mine.*

The pain from the shift that Fenrir forced him into was incandescent agony for the length of a single breath. Then Jono's nerves stopped talking to each other. While Jono couldn't feel pain, he could feel pressure—the snapping of his bones that vibrated deep inside his ears, the way his spine bent and broke into a different curve, and the tearing of his skin worse than the silver knife. His vision wavered, sliding into new colors and a different depth perception. Fur forced its way through new skin, the itch it brought heralding the return of sensation.

Jono could shift in less than a minute when pressed, but Fenrir had reduced it to mere seconds. The force of the god's power rushed through him, burning out his body's reaction to the lingering silver toxicity.

He lunged upward at the werewolf diving for him, catching the other one in the soft belly with his teeth. Jono clamped down and wrenched his head to the side. The werewolf's agonized howl broke off as flesh tore between Jono's fangs, the rush of blood coating his tongue and thick in his mouth. Jono kicked out with his hind feet, catching Theodore midlunge in the underside of his jaw and chest, claws cutting deep.

Jono was larger than the others in his werewolf form, and werecreatures as a whole were larger than their counterparts in nature. Which meant the work area of the bar got an utter *thrashing* as bodies knocked over glasses, alcohol bottles shattered from flailing limbs, and the shelves and mini refrigerator took a beating.

That's coming out of my paycheck.

Jono launched himself over the bar, landing on top of a werewolf and causing them both to roll with his momentum. Jono clamped his jaw on the back of their neck and raked his claws over their body. The high-pitched snarl they let out was filled with pain, and Jono had to fight Fenrir for control of his jaws.

Kill for me, Fenrir said.

The desire to kill in the midst of a fight was difficult to push back against, but Jono stubbornly refused to give in to what the god wanted.

We don't need that sort of attention right now.

As much as Jono wanted to break the werewolf's neck, he knew murder outside the challenge ring was usually frowned upon in the public eye, even if he was the aggrieved party here. So instead of murder, he went for maiming.

Jono unclenched his jaw and kicked the werecreature away from him with enough force to send them sliding to the rear of the bar, leaving a streak of blood behind on the floor. Jono rolled to all four feet, crouching low as he took in the rest of his adversaries.

Theodore had made it back over the bar, his fur damp in places from alcohol and blood. Two werewolves flanked him, while a third had planted themselves between Jono and the only way out of the bar. His nostrils flared, taking in their scents as he shifted his weight on his paws.

Jono could handle all five on his own—it would just cost him in blood and pain, and ruin the bar. Using the protective wards on Theodore and the others wasn't an option unless he shifted back to human. Jono knew Patrick was on his way, but Jono didn't know when the mage would make it to Tempest, or when Emma and the others would arrive.

But he knew what he'd thrown out of the bar, and if the fae was still out there, Jono was about to offer it dinner.

With a deep snarl, Jono lunged for the door, hitting the werewolf in his way head-on. Claws skittered on the floor around him as the others moved to cut him off and pull him back, but Jono wouldn't be deterred. He sank his fangs into the side of the werewolf's face, grating over bone and popping an eyeball. They lashed out, howling painfully. Their claws caught Jono in the side, the skin beneath his thick fur opening up.

Jono forced the other werewolf down and released their bleeding—but already healing—skull from between his teeth. He stepped on their body with enough force to break bone as he lunged for the entrance. The door was set up to open inward, and his only recourse was to break it down with the force of his momentum.

Also coming out of my bloody paycheck.

Wood splintered around him as Jono barreled outside, the icy, wintery cold a shock to the system. His nostrils flared as his paws sank into a thin layer of snow that covered the sidewalk and parked cars along the street. That in itself was an anomaly after days of rain. It shouldn't have snowed this much in such a short amount of time—not unless something supernatural had caused it.

Tempest was located in Alphabet City, a block away from Tompkins Square Park on Avenue B. The neighborhood was trending more upscale, a mix of residential flats in old and new buildings sharing space with bars and small restaurants. Sunday nights were still moderately busy, even in the middle of winter, but Jono doubted the bar's neighbors wanted this sort of excitement coming around.

Jono put his back to the street, paws skidding over the snowy sidewalk as Theodore and the others exited the bar at a dead run. Jono snarled a warning, the deep sound echoing around them— and was answered by something else.

Jono leaped to the side, missing getting hit by the silvery bits of spiderweb that splattered in the snow where he'd been standing. Jono tilted his head upward, seeing the fae from before crawling down the side of the building. The others looked up as well and tried to scatter, but one wasn't quick enough.

The fae opened its mouth wide and spat out a sticky mess of spiderweb that caught one of the werewolves in the side, pulling them to the ground. One of their packmates tried to pull them free, but the werewolf was stuck. The fae dropped down the building faster, its clawed spider legs making a clacking noise against the structure.

As much as Jono wanted to keep an eye on the fae, Theodore made that difficult. The werewolf abandoned his fellow packmates in favor of trying to corner Jono. Fighting like this in the middle of a public street was usually frowned upon by god packs the world over. The challenge ring existed for a reason.

If Theodore was willing to act so openly, then he was doing so with the blessing of his god pack alphas.

Jono dug his claws into the sidewalk, trying to get traction against the slippery snow as he reared up on his hind legs. Theodore slammed into him, but Jono was the one in control. Bigger and heavier than Theodore, with more years behind him in fights like this, Jono twisted his body and drove them both to the ground. He sank his teeth into Theodore's chest and jerked his head to the side as he leaped out of the way.

Flesh tore, and Theodore's howl of pain was loud in Jono's ears. Fur and skin filled his mouth; he spat the chunk of flesh out, licking blood off his fangs. He turned to keep an eye on the fae and the rest of the god pack members, not wanting to be boxed in.

Around them, the cars on the road were honking their horns, and people were actually getting out of their vehicles. Jono tensed, his fur bristling as every instinct he had suddenly told him to *run*.

Fenrir wouldn't let him.

The fae scuttling down the building froze, one of its thin human arms extended toward the werewolf trapped on the snowy sidewalk. Up above, lightning flashed in the sky, illuminating the dark, low-hanging clouds—and the Wild Hunt riding the storm.

The baying of hounds echoed in the night as the streetlights sputtered and died around them. Jono's wolf eyes compensated for the low illumination. Theodore and his packmates left their trapped member behind in their frantic need to escape. Jono let them go without a fight, knowing this was something they couldn't outrun.

People on the street abandoned their cars when they realized New York traffic wouldn't move fast enough to save their lives. People screamed as they ran, struggling not to slide and fall in the rising wind and blustery snow that heralded the arrival of something dangerous and old.

Ghostly horses and stags led by a pack of hounds with fiery red eyes dropped from the sky, gliding between buildings and over cars. They glowed with an inner light that burned Jono's eyes, but he couldn't look away.

The lead rider's face was covered in a leather mask, the tanned hide painted with blue sigils that made no sense to Jono. The leather tunic she wore couldn't hide the mutilated flesh of her body. The horse she rode was more bone than flesh, the ghostly image of its former body flickering with every stride the undead beast took. Behind her rode others, undead hunters claimed over the years for a Wild Hunt.

"Ble mae hi? Gallwn ei weld yn eich enaid," the ghostly woman said.

Jono wasn't fluent in Welsh, but Fenrir translated it to English in his mind. *Where is she? We can see her in your soul.*

He didn't know what the rider was on about with that demand.

The fae on the building shrieked in rage at a Wild Hunt it didn't belong to and had no hope of defeating by itself. Jono ducked his head, ears twitching as the howling picked up, the Wild Hunt overtaking everyone on the street. The fae tried to escape by crawling toward the roof of the building but was picked off by a pair of ghostly riders that speared it through its human torso and arachnid body. Its dying shriek was cut off when the riders tore it in half as they flew away.

A swarm of black hounds surrounded Jono, their red eyes burning like fire as they darted forward and back, taunting him. Jono lashed out with his front claws, slicing through solid flesh and grating against rib bones. He'd expected an ethereal body, not something solid, but Jono wasted no time in digging his claws deeper and bringing that hound to the ground.

Around him, the Wild Hunt picked people off the streets, their victims kicking and screaming as they were unwillingly claimed by the fae. Theodore and his packmates, despite their preternatural speed, couldn't outrun a Wild Hunt that could chase someone to the ends of the earth and beyond.

The werewolves were hassled and herded by black hounds before being gathered up in golden nets by riders on ghostly horses. Their protesting howls cut through the air, different from the hounds, and Jono snarled in response. He snapped at the black hounds that pressed in close, watching as the lead rider approached. She didn't speak, but she didn't have to—it was as if she could stare right into Jono's soul.

He didn't like that one bit, the sensation too close to what Ethan had put him through in June.

More riders approached, one carrying a golden net that made Jono's lips peel back from his fangs and had Fenrir fighting for control.

Give me your body, Fenrir demanded.

Jono hesitated, but before he could decide something so monumental, a familiar voice cut through the howls and screams filling the air.

"Get the *fuck* away from him."

Patrick's furious yell sent relief coursing through Jono's veins. Something streaked through the air to land in front of Jono's paws, forcing the lead rider to pull up short behind the circle of black hounds.

The spear was sleek, the pole made out of bone and topped with a long notched blade that embedded itself in the sidewalk. The black hounds scuttled backward, sliding between the legs of half a dozen ghostly horses, whining in distress. The fae around him froze, horses shying away from the weapon.

"He is not yours to take," someone else called out. "This isn't your home, Wild Hunt."

The lead rider's gaze dropped to the spear, and her eyes narrowed. She clenched her fingers tight around the reins in her hands before yanking on them. Her horse twisted to the side and vaulted over a hound before launching itself into the sky.

By an unspoken order, the Wild Hunt followed its leader into the storm, taking those they had captured on an endless ride. The ghostly illumination went with them, leaving the street in darkness for a few seconds. Then the streetlamps flickered back on, snow still falling on the eerily quiet street. Jono turned his head to see Patrick racing down the sidewalk toward him, followed by two men he recognized from pictures he'd seen on Patrick's mobile.

The taller man yanked the spear out of the sidewalk using only one arm. He spun it around with an unconscious ease, letting the intricately metal-capped end rest against the ground.

Jono stayed put as Patrick skidded to a halt beside him, boots sliding over the slippery sidewalk. Jono leaned into him, helping him stay upright. Patrick sank both hands into Jono's thick fur, bending down a little to look Jono in the eye. He didn't have to move far; Jono's werewolf form was large enough that Patrick could climb onto his back and ride him like a horse if the need was great enough.

"You all right?" Patrick asked in a tight voice.

Jono gape-grinned at him and couldn't resist licking Patrick's face. Patrick spluttered, using his jacket to wipe the wetness off his cheek.

"Hey!" someone yelled from farther down the street. "Who's paying the fare?"

Jono huffed out a snort.

Bloody taxi drivers.

7

"I understand the commissioner isn't happy, but it's not like I have control over the fae," Patrick said flatly.

Bureau Chief Giovanni Casale of the NYPD's Preternatural Crime Bureau crossed his arms over his chest and glared at Patrick. His winter jacket had an image of an NYPD badge screen printed on the left side over his heart. Casale's graying black hair was hidden beneath a wool beanie with NYPD stitched on the folded cuff. Patrick could sense the heat charms embedded in every piece of clothing Casale wore. Angelina Casale took great care in keeping her husband safe however she could.

"This mess on top of the missing Wisteria child isn't doing the fae any favors," Casale said.

Patrick looked down the street at where NYPD officers and CSU were finishing up collecting evidence of the frigid crime scene. Tow trucks were on hand to clear the abandoned vehicles. Officers had a long night ahead trying to match whoever owned the vehicles to the people the Wild Hunt had taken and then notifying the families of the missing.

"The SOA is handling the missing child case as the agency sees fit. As for the fae, that's better handled through the State Department. You should tell the commissioner that."

"These are innocent people who are now gone, Collins. You and I both know recovering them will be next to impossible."

Patrick grimaced. "I know. The SOA is working on it."

Casale's eyes narrowed. "Are you taking lead?"

"For now, but missing children aren't my specialty. The Wisteria case will most likely get transferred to a different agent in the long run."

"What about the Sluagh and the Wild Hunt?"

"I'm working on that problem. I'll keep you updated if I'm able to."

"Better than you have been, I hope. I don't like finding out about werecreature territory fights months after they've been going on. Especially ones that involve god packs."

"What makes you think I knew about that?"

Casale pointedly looked over Patrick's shoulder at the damaged entrance to Tempest and the space beyond where everyone else was holed up. "What makes you think I'm stupid?"

Patrick figured ignoring that question was his best option. "Anything else?"

"You should warn the owners that we're getting complaints about what goes on in the bar."

"Tell the people complaining the bar is cursed."

"And listen to the owners bitch about their property values going down?"

"Like you take those calls."

"My detectives do, and then *I* hear about it." Casale stepped back, pointing a gloved finger at Patrick. "I mean it. Keep me updated."

The Wisteria case was the SOA's problem now, not the PCB's. Still, Patrick wanted to keep a good relationship with the NYPD, so he'd honor Casale's request if the opportunity came up.

Patrick retreated into the bar, eyeing the pieces of what

remained of the door around the entranceway. He touched a hand to the doorframe and cast a shield to help keep out the cold and any unwanted visitors, along with a silence ward that encircled the bar with static.

"Someone in the pack is bringing over a sheet of plywood as soon as the police and media clear out. We'll get a temporary door put up tonight and go buy a new one tomorrow," Emma said from her spot behind the bar.

Leon stood beside her with a broom in hand, sweeping up the broken glass. Sage and Marek had finished piling up the broken barstools and damaged tables for a junk haul and were assessing the rest of the bar furniture for damage.

Jono sat on a barstool, wearing a pair of spare sweats taken from the employees-only room. Emma always had spare clothing stashed away in her pack's cars, homes, and places of work for unexpected shifts. Gerard stood a couple of feet away from Jono, his spear long since vanished from his hands to keep police from asking questions about it when they took his statement. Keith stood beside him, holding Patrick's box of cookies and surreptitiously trying to lift the lid and steal one.

"Those are mine," Patrick reminded him.

"I'm checking to make sure there's no damage," Keith replied blithely.

"Hands off," Gerard ordered.

Keith grumbled but obeyed, closing the box and setting it on the bar counter. Patrick walked over to Jono, eyeing the red slash of bruised skin over his abdomen. He pressed his hand against the shadow of a wound, fingers stroking over hard, defined muscle and warm skin. Jono still smelled a little like alcohol, though he'd cleaned the stickiness off his skin with a spare towel.

"Who the fuck got you with the silver knife?" he asked.

Jono settled his hand over Patrick's, flattening it against his abdomen. "Theodore and some others. The Wild Hunt took the lot, so we don't have to worry about them anymore."

Patrick made a face, annoyed that he couldn't track the fuckers down and give them a piece of his mind using his dagger.

"Ooh, murder face," Keith said with a low whistle. "Who's this Theodore that pissed you off?"

"Probably dead. It's his alphas I have a problem with," Patrick replied.

"You know what happened tonight is more of a challenge than Nicholas' visit was," Sage warned.

Jono grimaced. "I'm aware of that."

"God pack infighting?" Gerard asked.

"Eh." Patrick raised his other hand and made a seesaw motion with it. "More like we're a god pack and the one already here took offense to that."

Gerard stared at him. "Please tell me you're joking."

"Okay. I'm joking."

Jono snorted and pulled his hand away. Patrick reluctantly stepped back so Jono could stand up. He watched as Jono walked over to Gerard, sizing the other man up with a frank gaze before extending his hand.

"Jonothon de Vere, god pack alpha of New York City," he said. "You can call me Jono."

Gerard took his hand without hesitation. "Captain Gerard Breckenridge. Gerard is fine. Are you the one who watched Patrick's six back in June?"

"Everyone here did."

Gerard nodded, his mouth quirking at the corner as he let go of Jono's hand. "How many heart attacks has he given you?"

Jono rolled his eyes. "Too many. Could do without even one."

"I am right here," Patrick retorted.

"No one cares, Razzle Dazzle," Keith said.

Jono turned around and gave Patrick a questioning look. "Razzle Dazzle?"

Keith wiggled his fingers. "Because magic."

"Shut the fuck up, Chatterbox," Patrick said.

Keith grinned at him, unrepentant in the face of Patrick's prickliness. It was almost like old times in the field, the bickering and jokes that had gotten them through each day, because gallows humor was the only way to pass the time on the front lines.

Jono nodded over at where Sage was lifting a table with one hand to check for damage underneath. "Sage Beacot, my dire. There's one more of our pack, but he's home tonight."

"I texted Wade and told him to stay put," Sage said over her shoulder.

"Hopefully he listens," Patrick said, shoving his hands into the pockets of his leather jacket. "We still need to figure out how we're going to deal with Estelle and Youssef."

"I take it they're the other god pack alphas?" Gerard asked.

"Yeah. Tonight isn't the first time they've hassled us, but it's the most overt."

"Will they even know Theodore and the others are gone?"

Patrick shared a look with Jono. "Probably not for at least a few days if they don't report back. It'll be interesting to see if Estelle and Youssef file a missing person report."

Jono dragged a hand through his hair. "We'll have to inform them when I ring Estelle and accuse them of condoning the attack."

"They'll deny it and turn Theodore and the others being taken by the Wild Hunt on you," Sage said.

"They sound like such nice people." Keith looked at Patrick. "Why aren't they dead yet?"

"Because it looks bad when a federal agent gets involved in pack politics," Patrick retorted. "Also, the paperwork is a bitch."

Keith gestured pointedly at Jono. "You're already involved with Mr. Tall Dark and Abs-tastic over here. Give me a better excuse."

"There's four of us, almost fifty or so of them, and they still have packs loyal to them in the five boroughs. I could challenge them, but the space to do so is in their territory, and I don't trust their concept of following pack law," Jono said.

Patrick reached between Gerard and Jono to pick up the weapon in question that had wounded Jono. The knife was heavy in his hand, the balance off, but he doubted Theodore had cared about that. "They came with the intent to kill you. Keith is right. That's not something we can ignore."

Gerard held out his hand. "Let me see."

Patrick passed the knife over. "It's not an artifact."

Gerard took it, flipping the blade around in his hand with an expertise that came from decades of practice. "The knife itself is poorly designed, but it's coated in silver."

"Still got the job done of getting buried in Jono's gut," Marek said as he came over, dusting off his hands. "Lucky it wasn't your heart."

"Wouldn't have even happened if the Sluagh hadn't sent one of theirs in for a drink," Jono said. He frowned, shaking his head. "The one in the bar said I had something of theirs, that I smelled like it. The rider of the Wild Hunt said they were looking for a girl."

"You don't smell any different," Leon told him.

"We had a changeling in the flat."

Patrick made a face. "Your aura isn't carrying anything but your soul. I'd know if something had changed."

"Fae can mark you in ways you might not notice, Patrick," Gerard said slowly. "Your magic isn't like ours."

"I hate to say it, but maybe you should take a few nights off, Jono," Emma said as she lifted a rubber mat off the floor and carried it out from behind the bar. "Figure out what's going on with the fae first."

Jono frowned. "Em."

Patrick settled his hand against Jono's lower back in a gesture of support. "She's right."

Jono glared at him, wolf-bright eyes narrowing. "I can do my bloody job."

"Not saying you can't. But Estelle and Youssef are gunning for it along with your life, and your job is what anchors your work visa. You lose that, and it's going to make it harder for you to stay here."

"That's what a green card marriage is for. You two could fake it," Wade said as he walked into the bar and right through Patrick's shields as if they didn't exist. "I smell cookies."

"I told you to stay home," Sage said, frowning at him.

"Patrick," Gerard said, staring at Wade.

Patrick scowled at the last member of their pack who was not where he should be. "What are you doing here?"

"Where is your coat?" Jono demanded.

"Patrick," Gerard said again, but Patrick needed to deal with some teenage rebellion first before he listened to his old captain.

"You were told to stay where you were," Patrick said. "The Wild Hunt and the Sluagh are flying around in the sky and you're out there without any of us knowing where you are?"

Wade blinked at them before scowling and crossing his arms over his chest. He wasn't dressed for the weather at all—a T-shirt and jeans weren't appropriate winter wear in Patrick's book—not that the cold seemed to bother him. Patrick made a mental note to have a talk with Wade about remembering to keep up his human habits so that people didn't get suspicious.

"You said Jono got hurt and everyone is here. I'm pack. I didn't want to be left out," Wade argued.

"*Patrick.*"

Gerard's voice cut through the bar with a depth Patrick remembered from the battlefield. He instinctively hunched his shoulders before turning to face Gerard, who wasn't looking at Patrick but at Wade, as if he knew exactly what Wade was beneath his human skin. Whatever trick General Noah Reed had shown Wade back in August to help hide his dragon soul, it apparently wasn't enough to hide from the fae, or even a half-fae.

"That's Wade," Patrick said into the silence.

Gerard slanted him a *look*. "That's not all he is."

"Yeah."

"Well, I don't know what he is other than too young to be in a bar," Keith said. "How did you get past the police, kid?"

"Casale let me through, and don't call me kid," Wade retorted.

Jono crossed his arms over his chest. "You're grounded."

"What? Why? You can't ground me! I live on my own!"

"We pay your rent, and you're grounded because you didn't listen to an order from your dire. An order that was given to keep you *safe*."

Wade glared at Jono, anger in every line of his body. "You can't ground me. I'm eighteen."

"You're pack, and I bloody well *am* grounding you. The only place you're going is to school, and you're staying with Sage for the next week. No television, no internet, and your mobile's data will be cut off. You can make calls, and that's it."

"That's not *fair*."

"Then maybe next time you'll listen when we give an order regarding your safety."

"So, what? You're leaving me behind?"

"We aren't leaving you behind. Get that thought out of your head," Patrick said. "None of us are traveling alone from here on out, not after what Estelle and Youssef did tonight. We don't want you to get hurt."

Wade rolled his eyes. "Like they can hurt me. I'm not a werecreature."

"What are you?" Keith asked.

"He's a fire dragon," Sage replied. "Fledgling, to be precise."

Keith whistled again. "What the fuck have you been up to, Patrick?"

Before Patrick could figure out how to respond to that, Wade stalked toward them, paused long enough to swipe the box of cookies off the bar, and headed for the far back booth that had escaped damage during the fight.

"Those are mine," Patrick said.

"Fuck you" was Wade's angry response, the words muffled around a cookie already stuffed in his mouth.

Jono dragged a hand down his face. "Bloody hell."

"I think I need a debrief on the last year of your life, Patrick," Gerard said.

"You know, this was not how I thought our reunion would go," Patrick replied.

Leon held up a bottle of scotch, one of the few that had survived the fight. "Would alcohol make it better?"

As tempting as the offer was, all Patrick had to do was look at the bruising across Jono's abdomen and shake his head. "I've already had two beers tonight. I don't want to be drunk if I have to fight."

"I'll take a drink," Gerard said, turning toward the bar. "The gods only know I didn't get any in the field to soothe my nerves when Patrick pulled his usual stupid stunts."

"Had a tendency to go off half-cocked on his own, did he?" Jono asked.

"Oh, he's done that to you, too? Have a drink with me. We can commiserate on his self-sacrificing tendencies."

"You two should never have been allowed to meet," Patrick said.

Gerard ignored Patrick and took the glass Leon handed him. "If you have a Wild Hunt problem, then you need all the help you can get."

"I have my pack, but I don't know if Emma's should get involved." Patrick raised a hand to forestall her argument as she opened her mouth. "You know I trust you, Emma. But the harassment happening to you, your pack, and those who come to the bar can't be ignored. The god pack went after Jono tonight with the intent to kill. I don't want to be responsible for the death of anyone who belongs to you."

"You might not have a say in that," Marek said slowly as he

wrapped his arms around Sage's waist and rested his chin on top of her head.

Patrick stared into Marek's hazel eyes, wondering which fate was looking back at him. He couldn't ask, because that wasn't his secret to give up to people who weren't in the know, even if Patrick trusted them.

Marek made the choice for him.

"Your old teammates should know I'm a seer," Marek said.

Keith perked up at that. "Seriously? Like, some full-on oracle shit and not that fake palm-reading stuff? Man, I was gonna buy some lottery tickets—"

"No," Gerard said, cutting him off. "No lottery for you."

Patrick cleared his throat, glancing over at Gerard and Keith. "Everyone here knows about Ethan."

All the humor left Keith's eyes, the seriousness that replaced it comforting in a way. Gerard straightened up, his narrow-eyed gaze sweeping over everyone in the bar as if he were taking their measure all over again.

"If they know about Ethan, what else do they know?" Gerard asked.

"That the gods like to fuck with my life, and that's about it."

Emma's pack didn't know about the Morrígan's staff. Knowledge of the staff and the joint task force assigned to find it was highly classified. Patrick's pack knew because Jono and Wade had been there when General Reed briefed Patrick in August. They'd brought Sage up to speed in a private meeting afterward, and Patrick had no doubt she'd kept quiet about his mission. She might be engaged to Marek, but she no longer belonged to Emma's Tempest pack. Her loyalty belonged to them now.

Gerard nodded slowly. "All right. I'm glad you've got people you can trust watching your six when we aren't around. If we need backup—"

"You call me," Emma interrupted, giving Jono a fierce look. "I don't care what problems it will create with Estelle and Youssef. You know where I stand. Where my pack stands—with you."

Jono's jaw worked before he let out a thick sigh. "Em..."

"New York is our home, too. Don't forget that. Whatever is going on with the fae, it impacts us as well."

Patrick stepped closer, grabbing Jono's hand and giving it a comforting squeeze. "We'll figure it out."

Jono squeezed back. "Let's finish cleaning up and go home."

That was a plan Patrick could get behind.

PATRICK PUSHED OPEN the front door and ushered Jono inside. While Patrick knew Jono's core body temperature ran hotter than a human's, he'd still walked barefoot and shirtless through the snow after Sage dropped them off at the townhouse.

"Need a shower?" Patrick asked.

"Going to rinse off my feet," Jono said, his jaw popping with a yawn.

Patrick followed him into the bathroom attached to their master bedroom. He leaned against the doorframe, keeping an eye on Jono and watching as the taller man stripped out of the borrowed pants and stepped naked into the tub.

Patrick raked his gaze over Jono's body as he turned on the faucet and stuck his feet beneath the warm water to rinse off what muck the doormat hadn't scraped off. The play of muscles over his abdomen drew Patrick's eyes to the bruising that still marred his skin. It had faded a little, but wounds received from silver didn't heal quickly.

He clenched his jaw at the reminder of the attack. Patrick wanted to skin the werecreatures alive for what they'd done. He didn't like it when Jono got hurt.

"You hungry?" Patrick asked when Jono finished and stepped out of the tub.

"Knackered," Jono admitted.

Patrick let his gaze travel from Jono's feet, up his long legs, to his stupidly muscular torso, finally meeting wolf-bright eyes that never looked away. Patrick extended his hand, wriggling his fingers. Jono didn't hesitate to reach for him. His grip was warm and steady, and Patrick ran his thumb over Jono's knuckles.

"Come on. Let's go to bed."

Patrick led him back into their bedroom, ignoring Jono's huff of laughter when Patrick pushed him onto the bed. He shrugged out of his own jacket and stripped out of his sweater, tossing it aside. His dog tags were warm from body heat, even if he couldn't feel where they rested on his scarred chest.

Jono watched Patrick undress the rest of the way, methodically getting rid of his weapons and clothes. He crawled onto the bed, pushing at Jono's shoulders until he was lying down, with Patrick straddling his hips. Long fingers curled around his dog tags, tugging at the chain to pull him into a kiss that went from lazy to deep in the span of seconds.

Warm hands gripped Patrick's hips, thumbs pressing against bone. Patrick bit down gently on Jono's bottom lip before pulling away, dragging his mouth over the stubble along Jono's jaw, to his throat.

"They drew first blood, and I don't like that it was yours," Patrick murmured against the skin stretched taut over Jono's pulse.

He could feel it when Jono swallowed, and he tried his hardest to suck a bruise against Jono's throat.

"Better mine than yours."

"Fuck that."

Patrick continued kissing his way down Jono's body, licking over his collarbone and tasting the barest hint of sweat. Jono's hands skimmed up Patrick's ribs as he shifted lower, sealing his mouth over an already hard nipple. He sucked at it, head rising with the deep inhale of Jono's chest beneath his mouth.

He nipped at the hard nub before moving on, dragging his tongue over the sharp definition of Jono's abs. There wasn't an ounce of wasted flesh on the man, and Patrick was very appreciative of that fact. He was less appreciative of the bruise, the skin there hot even against his lips.

Patrick measured the wound with soft kisses, staring at Jono through his lashes as he did so. Jono had one arm tucked behind his head, the other stretched out so he could stroke Patrick's forearm. His cock was solid and warm where it pressed against Patrick's body, the interest impossible to ignore.

So Patrick didn't.

Patrick licked his way to Jono's cock, breathing him in. Jono bent his legs, feet flat on the bed, giving Patrick room. He tugged at Jono's balls as he sucked the sensitive head into his mouth, swirling his tongue over it. Jono's groan filled the bedroom as Patrick eased his mouth down Jono's cock, taking him in slow, lazy swallows.

"Fuck," Jono breathed, his hand coming up to touch the side of Patrick's face. "Love the way you look with my cock in your mouth."

The cock in question was growing hard against Patrick's tongue, in his throat, the thickness something he enjoyed. Patrick hummed around Jono's cock, enjoying the way Jono swore at the sound. Patrick's own cock was growing heavy between his legs, a gentle build of desire that had him rolling his hips against the bed every now and then, looking for friction.

Patrick pulled back a little, breathing through his nose as he did so, getting a lungful of Jono's musky scent. He wrapped a hand around the base of Jono's cock, giving it a squeeze. Jono's cock twitched at the pressure, the head bumping against the back of Patrick's throat. He pulled off all the way, licking his way back to Jono's balls. He tongued at the soft skin between them, tugging on one with his free hand.

Jono's thighs pressed against his shoulders, hips canting upward. "Bloody tease."

"You say that like it's a bad thing." Patrick propped his chin on Jono's thigh, casually stroking his cock. "How do you want to come? In my mouth? On my face?"

The way Jono's eyes darkened told Patrick either option was good. Jono reached for him, tracing his mouth with a careful finger. "Rather come in you."

It was Patrick's turn to groan at that, shivering at the possessive look on Jono's face. "Sure. Like I'd say no to that."

Patrick didn't protest when Jono half sat up, reaching for him. Patrick was dragged up Jono's body until he was lying on the other man, within easy kissing reach. He framed Jono's face with one hand, mapping out his mouth with an eager tongue. He heard the pillow rustle, then the sound of the lube bottle opening up.

Patrick moaned into Jono's mouth at the finger that pressed inside him, hips twitching away from the intrusion before pushing back against it. Jono fingered him the same way Patrick had sucked his cock—slow and easy, with a loving attention to detail that left him gasping and wanting more.

He panted against Jono's mouth, trying to breathe as Jono worked his way up to three fingers, stroking Patrick deep inside. He clutched at Jono's shoulders, rocking back against the fingers stretching him.

"You want me to ride you?" Patrick asked.

"Don't want you to do all the work."

Patrick nipped at his bottom lip. "Getting fucked by you is never work. Pretty sure it's the opposite of work."

Jono laughed before rolling Patrick onto his side until they fit together, back to front. He sucked in a breath as Jono hooked a hand behind his left knee and pulled his leg up, opening him up. Patrick turned his head, peering up at Jono as he propped himself up on one elbow.

He nearly swallowed his tongue when Jono pushed inside him

with a long, slow thrust that sent heat zipping up his spine. Jono never looked away as he pulled out and thrust back in again, still keeping to the same deliberate pace. Patrick hooked his hand over Jono's hip, fingers scraping against skin at the flex of Jono's body on the next thrust.

Patrick tipped his head back, letting out a gasp that Jono kissed away. He took his own cock in hand, stroking it in time to Jono's thrusts. Their bodies were pressed so close together there wasn't room for air as Jono fucked him with a single-minded focus that left Patrick breathless. The slow pace never picked up, the drag of Jono's cock inside him like exquisite torture that never let up.

Moments like this—where everything was warm and intense, and the world was kept at bay by Jono's touch—left words stuck in Patrick's throat he always managed to swallow back. One day, he knew, they would slip out.

"Jono," Patrick moaned, squeezing his eyes shut on a particularly deep thrust.

"Want you to come," Jono murmured into his ear. "You can do that for me, can't you, love? Come on my cock. I want to feel you, Pat."

Patrick never liked to give in to anything without a fight, but Jono made it easy—he always did. Patrick came with a cry, with Jono buried deep inside him, as he shook through his release. Jono gripped him tighter, body a rigid line behind Patrick as he rocked deep inside him with infinite patience.

Patrick turned his head into the pillow, breathing harshly, eyes squeezed shut against the spots still dancing across his vision. Jono moved against him, his thick cock sliding in and out of Patrick's body until his nerves seemed fried. Right when it was hitting the edge of *too much*, Jono stiffened against him, coming with several deep, grinding thrusts that made Patrick almost bite his tongue.

He could feel some of Jono's cum leaking out between his thighs. They never used condoms because the werevirus wasn't a disease Patrick could catch, and Jono had a thing about making Patrick smell like him.

After a moment, Jono gently guided Patrick's leg back down to the bed, breathing heavily against the curve of his shoulder. He didn't move to pull out, staying buried inside Patrick.

"They'll have to try a lot harder to kill me, you know that, right?" Jono said quietly as he flattened his hand over Patrick's chest.

"Gonna have to go through me first," Patrick muttered, still not opening his eyes. He half-heartedly clenched down on Jono's spent cock, earning him a press of teeth to his shoulder.

It felt like a promise.

8

"Park there," Patrick said, pointing at a spot in front of a mansion that happened to be empty due to the fire hydrant at the curb.

"You want me to get bloody towed while I wait for you?" Jono asked in an aggravated voice, but he still parked where Patrick wanted.

"The Mustang has government plates."

"Yeah, but I don't have a badge."

"I shouldn't be long." Patrick leaned across the console for a kiss Jono couldn't deny him. "If anyone asks, tell them you're waiting to pick me up for lunch."

"It'd be more like brunch at this hour."

Patrick rolled his eyes as he pulled on his gloves. "Are you still hungry? You had breakfast."

"I *made* breakfast."

"See if Wade left any snacks in the back seat."

"Wade leaves wrappers, not food." Jono turned off the engine and took the keys out of the ignition, not really bothered by the cold and the snow outside. "Go work. I'll be here if you need me."

Patrick nodded and got out. A blast of cold air snaked its way inside before the door shut, leaving Jono alone in the car. He craned his head around and watched Patrick cross the street once a car had passed. The Wisteria family lived in a posh neighborhood that Jono felt utterly out of place in.

The Wisterias' home currently had scaffolding set up in front of the building for repairing the hole in their nursery. The gargoyles were all perched on the wooden platforms, keeping watch over the damage. Jono eyed the area curiously. He'd done some construction jobs in his youth and figured the hole was halfway to being patched, which was incredible, considering the weather.

"Money talks," Jono muttered to himself.

He was still annoyed about his forced time off, even though it came with pay. Jono would rather be working and fairly earning his paycheck. He pulled out his mobile and queued up a show to watch while waiting for Patrick to return. Jono didn't know how long this meeting would last, but he honestly thought it would be longer than ten minutes.

Patrick returned in five.

"That was quick," Jono said when Patrick yanked open the front passenger-side door again.

Patrick scowled as he climbed back inside. "They refused me entry."

"Why?"

"I didn't get a straight answer out of their maid, but I'm going with pissed I treated the changeling like a person and I haven't found their kid yet." Patrick slammed the door hard enough he made the car shake. "Fuck. Henry's not going to like this."

Jono shoved the keys back into the ignition and started the engine, pulling back onto East Seventy-Fifth Street. The narrow one-way street was lined on either side with trees whose branches were bare and heavy with snow.

"Need to go by the office?"

Patrick shook his head. "No, I can work from home on my laptop. I can take my DC conference calls there."

"Who do you need to talk to in DC? The director?"

"Agent Bryce. She's the one who took custody of the changeling."

Jono nodded and reached the corner as the light turned green. He turned right onto Madison Avenue and saw the arsehole who barreled through the intersection and clipped the Mustang on the front left corner at the last second. Jono couldn't jerk the steering wheel to the right to get out of the way because there were pedestrians on the sidewalk.

He hit the brakes instead and snapped his arm out to brace Patrick as the impact reverberated through the Mustang. The airbags didn't deploy, which told Jono the damage was probably minor, but that didn't change the fact the driver of the other vehicle had run a red light.

Jono looked at Patrick, foot still firmly on the brake. "You all right?"

Patrick nodded jerkily, his pistol in hand when it hadn't been seconds ago and a mageglobe clenched in the other. He let out a harsh breath. "Yeah. Fuck. Thought it was an ambush."

Jono pulled over to the side of the street, out of the way of the crosswalk. He yanked up the emergency brake and got out of the car. The streets in this neighborhood had been plowed last night and salted; the driver couldn't blame the snow for his shitty driving. Jono scowled at the Rolls-Royce Phantom limousine idling in the next lane over up ahead with its hazard lights on. Strangely enough, the limo didn't look like it had taken any damage at all.

"Fucking rich wanker," Jono said.

"Look on the bright side. At least they'll have insurance," Patrick replied as he got out.

Jono eyed the damage over the left front wheel on the Mustang. The metal there was crunched and the paint horrendously scratched, but the wheel looked okay. It would still need to be taken in and fixed, and the axle alignment checked.

"Hey," Jono yelled as he approached the limo. "What the bloody *fuck* do you think you're doing? Your light was red, arsehole."

The side passenger door opened up and a tall, lithe woman in an ankle-length wool coat with fur trim got out. Jono paused midstride, taking in her scent. Even without the strangely floral scent emanating from her, he'd have been hard-pressed to ignore her fae heritage upon first look. Her impossibly beautiful face was dominated by pale pink eyes, while her dark green hair was twisted back in a half dozen intricate braids. Her delicate ears were adorned with tiny hoops of gold that went from lobe to sharply pointed tip.

"Apologies for the damage to your car. Our metalsmith will be happy to fix it while we give you a ride home," the fae woman said, her Irish accent a subtle hint in her voice.

Her voice was familiar to Jono only because he'd heard it on the other side of the mobile whenever he had to speak with Sage's managing partner about her absences due to pack business. He'd never met the woman, and this wasn't how he'd thought they'd be formally introduced.

"Deirdre?" Jono asked, unable to keep the wariness out of his voice.

The fae attorney gave him a slight smile as a stocky, barrel-chested man no taller than four feet got out of the limo. His wrinkled face was walnut brown, eyes the color of earth even though his hair and beard were the color of dirty snow. Unlike Deirdre, the dwarf wore grease-stained coveralls and didn't look like he belonged in that limo at all.

"Dinnae worry. I'll take good care of yuir car," the dwarf said in a deep voice, his accent that of the Old Country more than Deirdre's.

"I'm not giving you my car," Patrick said.

The dwarf smiled, the wrinkles deepening in his face. "Never asked ye fer it."

"I am sorry that we must meet under these circumstances, but the situation could not be helped." Deirdre gestured with one leather-gloved hand at the open limo door. "My lord wishes to speak with you, alphas of the New York City god pack."

The title made Jono clench his fist, because it wasn't a title they publicly called themselves—yet. Jono glanced at Patrick, then around them at the people who were walking and driving past as if they weren't standing in the middle of the street having a chat.

"Your doing?" Jono asked Patrick.

Patrick shook his head. "No."

Jono looked at Deirdre again, meeting her gaze and not backing down. "You lot set your Wild Hunt on me last night."

"We had no say in what happened last night. Please join us. Allow my lord a chance to explain," Deirdre said.

Patrick stepped closer, his arm brushing against Jono's. "I think we're gonna have to take that ride."

The dwarf walked forward, thrusting one large hand at them. "Your keys."

"Just so we're clear, I'm still not giving my car to you."

Jono let Patrick set the terms even as he handed over the keys. The dwarf ignored them as he retreated to the damaged Mustang and got behind the wheel, starting the engine. Deirdre stepped aside, gesturing once again at the limo. Patrick eyed her warily, his mageglobe gone but magic sparking at his fingertips. He climbed inside the limo without further argument.

Jono could do nothing but follow him.

Inside, four posh, tan leather seats faced each other, two on each side. The partition was drawn up between where they sat and the driver up front. Deirdre deftly climbed inside and closed the limo door behind her, taking a seat beside a Seelie *duine sídhe* fae lord that reeked of magic—a fae lord Jono recognized from August.

"You were at the Crimson Diamond," Jono said as the limo pulled forward with a smoothness he'd have appreciated better if it didn't feel like they'd been kidnapped.

The fae lord wore a bespoke charcoal three-piece suit. Silver hair fell to his shoulders, and his violet-eyed gaze held secrets Jono had no desire to share. A gold-tipped wooden cane rested at an angle against the opposite car door. The hand that gripped it was wrapped in silver filigree plates and links that arched over every knuckle and over the back to connect to a silver cuff. Gemstones adorned the larger plates, flashing in the light. Jono could practically taste the metal, making him wish he had some iron at hand.

"For a mediation, which you interrupted," the fae lord said, his Irish accent thicker than Deirdre's, but not by much, an echo of Ireland from long ago in his words.

Jono refused to apologize for their role in taking down Tremaine's Night Court and handing it over to Lucien. He took the fae lord's measure, aware that no name had been offered, but Jono remembered who Sage had wanted them to speak with.

"Tiarnán, is it? Could've rang us rather than run us off the road."

"An unfortunate necessity, Jonothon."

"This feels a little too mafia for my liking. What do you want?" Patrick said.

Tiarnán didn't seem put off by Patrick's direct demand. Beside him, Deirdre kept her mouth shut and her hands clasped together on her lap, but her attention never wavered.

"The Wild Hunt is not commanded by the Spring Queen. It is guided by a different hand. We had nothing to do with the ones who tried to claim you for eternity last night."

"If that's your version of an apology, it sucks."

"It is the truth."

"What are they after?" Jono asked. He figured it was the changeling, but Jono wasn't going to let on that they knew. It was information he refused to give up for free. Not to the fae.

Tiarnán hit a button on the console between his and Deirdre's seats. A light lit up, and the small speaker there crackled to life. "Take the long way."

"Yes, my lord," a male voice responded.

Tiarnán met Jono's gaze without blinking. "The Spring Queen has called her warriors home. It is a summoning that is not undertaken lightly."

Patrick went still, but he was shielded so tightly Jono couldn't get anything off him save his heartbeat—and that was as calm as the eye of a hurricane.

"If you need Sage to take on a few extra cases at work to cover your schedule, she's who you should be chatting with, not me," Jono said.

"I did speak with her. She counseled that your pack would be more amenable to my request than the one we initially reached out to."

Jono's eyes narrowed. "You went to Estelle and Youssef."

"They espouse themselves as the alphas of the New York City god pack, with all that rank applies. Yet they seemed reluctant to meet with us."

"They're being investigated for their role in selling werecreatures to Tremaine and the Omacatl Cartel. I'm not surprised they don't want to get involved with anyone else right now, not when they have the federal government interested in every single one of their dealings as alphas," Patrick said.

"Which leaves me calling upon your pack."

"I already have one case concerning the fae on my desk. I don't need another."

Tiarnán hummed thoughtfully. "The changeling."

"Not your business unless the kid is from your Seelie Court."

"I do not deal with changelings. They come from all the lands of Tír na nÓg, not this island I have called home for centuries."

"What did you ask Estelle and Youssef to help you with?" Jono wanted to know.

"The Summer Lady was taken from the heart of the Seelie Court by Dominion Sect mercenaries nearly two weeks ago. She is missing, and we asked for the god pack's help in finding her."

Jono clenched his teeth, his stomach churning at the mention of the Dominion Sect. "They said no?"

Tiarnán's smile was as cold as the winter wind outside the limo. "They declined to give us aid, a decision we will always remember."

"I get it, mate. You have a hard time understanding what no means." Jono held up a hand before Tiarnán could respond. "Not saying no, but I'm not saying yes. All I've heard is talk about a missing person. That's not enough for us to agree to anything."

Jono half wished they had Sage with them to help navigate this word dance with the fae, but he thought maybe Tiarnán had orchestrated this conversation to spare her an uncomfortable situation—or to give them an advantage. Sage was pack, but she was also an attorney at Gentry & Thyme. The last thing Jono wanted was to put her job at risk.

"You were both in the middle of what happened here in June, and from what I hear, you took down Tremaine's Night Court."

Jono shared a look with Patrick. "Don't know what you're on about, mate."

"I understand deniability for the courts, but your reputation is beginning to precede you in the preternatural world." Tiarnán's eyes darted from Jono to Patrick, then back again. "You are god pack, Jonothon. But you do not hold this city."

"Yet," Patrick replied in a low voice. "I'm still not hearing an offer."

Outside the window, buildings were replaced by a low rock wall covered in scrubby bushes as the driver turned onto the Seventy-Ninth Street Transverse. Memories of nearly being sacrificed in Central Park were still hard to forget these many months after. Jono shoved them aside, dispassionately taking in what he could see of the winter scenery around them.

Trees and bushes were bare across the landscape, the snow sticking to the ground and branches, creating a blanket of white that looked inviting. Appearances could be deceiving though, and Jono was done with playing games.

"We won't help for free," Jono said.

"Money will not be an issue," Tiarnán replied.

"I don't want your money."

Tiarnán tapped a finger against his cane, the silver links and plates on the jeweled hand adornment clinking together. It sounded like bells.

"Status, then. I can give you that."

"It will mean war, my lord," Deirdre said, finally speaking up.

"I am aware of what my favor will cost this city." Tiarnán tipped his head in Jono's direction. "I am prepared to pay it so long as you bring our Lady home, Jonothon."

"And if we don't?" Patrick asked.

"Then when Estelle and Youssef ask for an audience as the New York City god pack, I will greet them as such."

Legitimacy was a tempting offer, one Jono knew they couldn't pass up, but the fae never offered something without a price. A bargain was never exactly what it seemed when one made deals with the fae. Jono said nothing as the limo drove across Central Park, the quiet in the vehicle tense between everyone as he weighed his options.

"Do you speak for all your people?" Jono finally asked.

"I speak for the fae of the Seelie Court, for the *daoine sídhe* who bend knee to the Spring Queen. I do not speak for the Unseelie fae, nor for their Queen of Air and Darkness."

Half the fae was better than none. Jono had worked with less over the years when it came to carving out space for himself in cities that never wanted him.

"She called her warriors home. Does she think they won't be enough?"

"The mortal plane belongs to humans now, and we do not

know it as we once did when it was ours. Our dealings with the Dominion Sect over the decades have been few and far between. Yours is more recent."

"You mean August."

"I mean the Thirty-Day War." Tiarnán turned his attention to Patrick, his expression giving nothing away. "The fight during summer solstice damaged the nexus and ley lines beneath New York City, but did not destroy them. We have experienced that sort of damage once before when it rippled out from Cairo."

Patrick's voice, when he spoke, was devoid of all emotion. "You think because I'm a veteran and fought in that war, I know how to deal with the Dominion Sect?"

"Is that not the case?"

Jono wondered what the fae knew about the gods and the soul debt that bound Patrick to doing their bidding, if they knew anything at all. Information was a currency the fae traded in more than gold. He wished, in that moment, the fae were paupers.

"Fuck you," Patrick spat out.

Deirdre shot him a displeased look, but Jono knew that would never be enough to shut Patrick up. Patrick's temper being what it was, Jono sought to head off the explosion. The limo was too small of a space to have that sort of row.

"You agree that my pack is the rightful god pack to New York City, and we'll work on finding your Lady. If we fail to bring her back home, you owe us nothing, and we owe you nothing in return," Jono said.

Patrick's mouth twitched at the corners into a scowl. "And you don't hold it against us if we fail."

Tiarnán held Jono's gaze before leaning forward to extend his hand, his left one bare of silver adornments. "A bargain made will be a bargain kept."

Jono shook on it, because it would've been rude not to. Tiarnán's hand was cool against his, but the strength in the fae's grip reminded Jono of his own. Fae might look beautiful, but they were deadly in their own way.

"You have yourself a deal." Jono let go and leaned back in the soft leather seat. "Now, if you're going to use us to further your own reputation, best tell us what you know about how your Lady went missing."

Tiarnán smiled slowly, seemingly amused at Jono's unsubtle accusation. "What makes you think I would withhold information?"

"Fae," Jono scoffed.

Tiarnán chuckled. "A mutual partnership is beneficial to us both in a situation like this. Personal gain is secondary to the goal."

"Keep telling yourself that," Patrick muttered.

"Withholding information helps no one, least of all who we are trying to find. The Dominion Sect stole our Summer Lady from within the boundaries of our territory. Magic got them in and out."

"Wouldn't all of your guards have sensed human magic? The base structure is completely different from your own."

"The magic they used was not theirs, but fae."

"You think you have a traitor in your midst?"

"Some believe so. I am more apt to believe the Queen of Air and Darkness gave them aid of some sort." Tiarnán nodded at Deirdre. "Show them."

Deirdre pulled a compact mirror out of the purse nestled between her feet. She flicked the compact open with her thumb, and the soft glow that emanated from it told Jono it wasn't used for makeup. She passed it over to Patrick, who took it and angled the compact so both he and Jono could look into the beveled crystal set inside.

"Scrying crystal," Patrick said with a soft whistle. "These go for a fortune on the black market."

"No stealing," Jono said.

"I'm not Wade."

Fog filtered over the crystal before clearing. The figures on horseback trotted down a forest path that looked like no forest Jono had ever seen. The colors of the leaves and flowers on either side of the path were more vibrant than anything found on Earth. The view bounced around, the shakiness caused by the horse the rider who carried the receiving scrying crystal rode.

Jono could see three riders who were decked out in armor that wouldn't look out of place in a museum dedicated to medieval knights. Only the armor design was far more intricate than what humans had worn in the past, interspaced with leather tunics and pants of an unknown uniform. The clothing and armor all had sigils painted on them that reminded him of the ones the Wild Hunt's lead rider had carried.

The guards escorted a slim young lady riding a large stag instead of a horse. She looked completely out of place in modern-day clothing against the strange, ethereal scenery. Her thick red-orange hair was tied back in a braid that reached her waist. She looked over her shoulder at her rearguards, mouth opening to ask a question.

The words never came.

What looked like black lightning cut between trees to slam into all four guards, throwing them off their horses. The scenery spun, treetops and the sky creating a sickening blur of color across the crystal. When the motion stopped, all Jono could make out was dirt and the body of a dead horse.

"I wouldn't, my dear," someone warned beyond the scope of the scrying crystal's visual range, their voice making Patrick tense up. It took a moment for Jono to remember the bloke, because he'd been at Ethan's mercy more than Zachary Myers' last summer.

"Don't call me *dear.*"

A pair of feet clad in combat boots filled the view before the heavy butt of a rifle slammed down on the crystal and everything went dark. Fog filled the scrying crystal before the moment caught in time started up again.

Patrick closed the compact and handed it back to Deirdre, face devoid of all emotion. "I know who took her."

Tiarnán blinked at him, the only hint of surprise Jono could parse from his body language. "That is unexpected."

"I'd know Zachary Myers' voice anywhere. He's Ethan Greene's right-hand acolyte."

Deirdre paused in putting the compact away in her purse. She glanced up through her lashes at them, but the look wasn't flirtatious in any way. "What does the Dominion Sect want with the Summer Lady?"

"Aside from the obvious?" Patrick leaned back in his seat, jaw tight. "Your Summer Lady is immortal, isn't she?"

Tiarnán nodded slowly. "She is."

"Which means she carries a godhead."

Jono swore. "It always comes back to that, doesn't it? Ethan wanting a bloody godhead."

"Mortals cannot carry a godhead," Tiarnán said.

Patrick's expression never changed. "Sure."

"Why would Ethan work with the Unseelie Court?" Jono asked.

"Same reason he works with Hades." Patrick gave a stiff shrug. "Power."

Jono knew it was more than that, but he wasn't about to give up that information. It wasn't his story to tell, and he knew better than to give the fae more than they asked for. Partners or not, the fae weren't to be trusted.

Tiarnán shared a look with Deirdre before focusing on Patrick. "Tell me about Zachary Myers."

"He's a mage who practices blood magic. He's been working with Ethan for years."

"You have fought him before?"

"Unfortunately."

"Then you know what to expect."

Patrick snorted. "About as well as anyone was able to predict the Thirty-Day War. We said we'd try our best to find your

Summer Lady. Me knowing who took her for sure doesn't really change the playing field, because we need to figure out how to find her. Ethan and his mercenaries have spent the past two decades on the run. Finding them is a challenge for intelligence agencies. It's going to be worse for us."

"You made a promise."

"Yeah, we did," Jono said. "We promised we'd try."

The rest of the drive home was made in tense silence, all of Jono's questions for Patrick tumbling through his mind, unwilling to speak them within hearing distance of the fae. Tiarnán seemed content to let the silence settle, but his demeanor changed once they finally pulled up in front of the Chelsea townhouse some time later.

Two men stood on the pavement in front of the stoop. Jono immediately recognized Gerard and Keith, and it seemed Tiarnán did as well judging by the faint widening of his eyes. The limo pulled to a smooth stop, and Patrick shoved open the door before Deirdre could reach for it. Jono followed him out, nodding at Gerard.

The Mustang braked to a halt behind the limo, and the dwarf got out. Patrick went to inspect the vehicle, muttering under his breath about magic and the car's paint job. Jono stepped out of the way as first Deirdre, then Tiarnán, exited the limo.

"Lord of Ivy and Gold," Gerard said in a tone of voice Jono was familiar with from Patrick. It was very much a *fuck you*, only with different syllables.

"You two know each other?" Patrick asked from the driver's side of the Mustang.

"I was not aware you knew—" Tiarnán began.

Gerard cut him off. "It's not your business how I know Patrick."

Tiarnán swept his gaze over everyone before turning to duck back into the limo. "Sage is excused from her casework until further notice. I hope you keep our bargain, Jonothon."

"Not one to break my word," Jono replied.

Tiarnán said nothing to that, merely let Deirdre join him in the limo and close the door. The dwarf took the front passenger-side seat, and once his door was shut, the driver pulled away. Jono watched them leave until the limo turned the corner and disappeared from sight.

"Do I want to know what you two were doing with that asshole?" Gerard asked with a frown.

"Politics."

"Dog and pony shows are a bitch," Keith said with a knowing nod. "It's freezing. How about we yell at each other upstairs?"

"How about everyone get in the car and we head over to Marek's place?" Patrick countered.

Jono nodded and walked back to the Mustang. This wasn't a conversation they needed to have out in the open where anyone could hear it.

9

"WHERE'S MAREK?" PATRICK DEMANDED AS HE STEPPED INSIDE THE apartment. The mansion the Tempest pack lived in on the Upper East Side was split up into a couple different apartments, but Marek's was the one they always hung out in.

"Nice to see you, too," Emma said, rolling her eyes.

Patrick paused long enough to take off his shoes so he didn't track snow and dirt into the home. Wade was on the couch in flannel pants and a T-shirt, holding a plate piled high with cinnamon rolls. He crammed one into his mouth and said something that Patrick couldn't understand.

"No one is going to take that plate away, so slow down and chew," Jono admonished.

"It looks like he has enough to share," Keith said.

Wade flipped them off and took another big bite. Patrick flopped down on the couch beside him and conjured up a mageglobe. He cast a silence ward, filling the breadth of the apartment with static.

After a moment, Wade offered him the plate of cinnamon rolls. "Sorry I ate your cookies last night."

Patrick snagged a cinnamon roll and took a bite. "Don't worry about it."

Jono made his way to the kitchen to grab some coffee. Leon was cooking a late breakfast, and the smell of chorizo and eggs made Patrick's stomach growl.

"I'll make more eggs," Leon said.

Emma had disappeared, most likely to get Marek and Sage. Patrick caught Gerard's eye and waved at the love seat. "Take a seat."

They'd argued on the drive over about Patrick and Jono making a bargain with the fae, but Patrick viewed the agreement as necessary. That still didn't mean Gerard approved, and his old captain still seemed unhappy about it.

"You could have said you were already working on finding Órlaith instead of taking up with Tiarnán," Gerard said.

"We need the clout. If the fae are willing to view our god pack as the only legitimate god pack in New York, then it's not something we could pass up."

"It's not that simple."

Patrick took another bite of the cinnamon roll. "I know it's not. We did our best to deny them as much wiggle room as possible and left ourselves an out. Bargain is null and void if we don't save your fiancée."

"You talked with Tiarnán?" Sage said as she came down the stairs with Marek trailing behind her.

"Your boss said you're on leave while we deal with this," Jono said.

Sage made a face. "I have a hearing this week."

"Better ring him and figure out who will cover for you."

Patrick shoved the rest of the cinnamon roll into his mouth and chewed quickly. Emma reached over the couch between him and Wade, a mug of coffee in her hand, which he happily took.

The coffee was hot, flavored with hazelnut creamer. Patrick gulped down a mouthful before speaking. "Deirdre had a scrying crystal that had a memory recording embedded in it. The scene showed Órlaith being escorted home in Tír na nÓg right before they were attacked. The person who spoke before she was taken was Zachary Myers."

Gerard's swearing overrode Keith's, which was saying something. Gerard got to his feet and started to pace, mouth a hard line. A warm hand settled on Patrick's shoulder, and he tipped his head back to look up at Jono.

"Thought it was him," Jono said in a low voice. "I remember his voice from June."

The same way Patrick knew Jono had remembered the mayor's aide who had been present during his torture at Ethan's hands and during the fight at the Crimson Diamond in August. Scent and memory were intertwined, even more so for a werecreature, whose enhanced senses meant forgetting was near impossible.

Some nights, when the nightmares came, Patrick wished he could give that to Jono.

Patrick reached up to interlace their fingers together. "We're dealing with the Dominion Sect more directly than we did back in August. I need to know if you've seen anything, Marek."

Marek sighed. "I still have visions, but anything that concerns you directly draws a blank. You know that. The future is too fucked where you're concerned."

"They wouldn't have stayed in Tír na nÓg. They'd have left with her for the mortal plane," Gerard said.

"A world with billions of people in it for them to go to ground. Those aren't good odds," Keith said.

"There has to be a way to track her. What good is magic if—" Jono began.

"We got company," Wade cut in, craning his head around to look out the window at the view of a snow-covered Central Park. "Your favorite people just arrived."

"Who?" Leon asked as he came into the living area balancing four plates in his hands piled high with food.

Wade sank back into the couch, chewing on his bottom lip. "Estelle and Youssef. I can hear them."

"Motherfucker." Leon sighed irritably as Sage helped him put the plates on the coffee table. "What a way to ruin breakfast."

"I'm going to shoot them," Patrick decided.

"Don't get blood on my floors," Emma ordered everyone as she headed for the front door. "If Estelle and Youssef are here, they're here for us, not you. I'll go meet them downstairs."

Patrick snuffed out his mageglobe and got to his feet. The silence ward faded away, allowing Estelle and her pack to hear everyone's heartbeats. He doubted it would change her approach. She was here for a reason, and he knew it wasn't to bring an early Christmas present.

Jono walked around the couch and faced the front door. Patrick went to stand beside him, intent on showcasing a united front. Wade stayed where he was on the couch while Sage left Marek's side to plant herself to Jono's right. She gave them both a grim smile before straightening her shoulders and putting on an air of disinterest.

Emma finally arrived with Estelle and Youssef. Behind them walked Nicholas. Patrick eyed the trio of uninvited guests, curious about the lack of backup.

"They leave people outside?" Patrick asked no one in particular.

"A few," Jono said.

"If they touch my car, I'm gonna arrest them."

"Still overprotective about your stuff, are you?" Keith called out. "Glad to see that hasn't changed."

"I've gotten better about sharing, but not when it concerns territory."

Estelle's bright amber eyes narrowed at the sight of everyone before her gaze settled on Jono. Emma took a step forward to go join Leon but was abruptly yanked back to Estelle's side. Estelle's grip on her arm looked hard enough to bruise, judging by the way her skin went white from pressure beneath Estelle's fingers.

"That's really not the way to treat the lady of the home," Gerard said.

Estelle ignored him, which Patrick knew was the fastest way to get on Gerard's shit list. "You were given an order, Emma."

"How about I give you one?" Patrick said. "You're interfering in SOA business. Get the fuck out."

"Interesting how that always seems to be your excuse when we find you with the Tempest pack," Youssef replied.

"Interesting how you set your wolves on me. Couldn't stomach doing your own dirty work? Or is it you couldn't risk showing your hand to the feds? Bit late for that, innit?" Jono shot back.

Estelle smiled coldly. "I don't know what you're talking about."

Jono snorted. "Of course you don't. Nicholas didn't stop by to intimidate some bar customers the other night. I suppose those five empty spots in your pack where Theodore and his lot used to fill will be ignored at the next alphas' meeting, won't they?"

Estelle and Youssef said nothing to that, their body language never changing. Patrick wondered what the werecreatures on their side of the divide were getting off the three. Whatever it was, they weren't happy.

Patrick didn't like how Estelle hadn't let Emma go. Neither did Leon, but the other man hadn't moved a muscle save to clench his hands into fists. Emma had her gaze locked on her partner, never blinking. Whatever silent communication they were having kept Leon from arguing.

"Looks like you brought people to fight, not to talk," Keith drawled from his spot on the love seat. He'd kicked one foot up on the coffee table, casually using the flat edge of his Ka-Bar to scratch at the side of his head. "That seems a little unfair. Also, you're interrupting a meeting. Rude."

"Another friend of yours, Patrick?" Youssef asked.

"It's Agent Collins. I didn't give you permission to use my name," Patrick retorted.

"The lady is attending to her pack needs while we are here. You should let her go so she can continue to do so," Gerard said, staring Estelle and Youssef down as he moved to a position that gave him more maneuverability.

"I don't take orders from mundane humans," Estelle said derisively.

Which meant Gerard was leaning hard into his human half. It was a trick that didn't require shields, not the way Patrick needed them. Gerard could pass as human with a twist of low-grade glamour if one ignored his eyes and ears. Patrick thought it odd Estelle hadn't noticed, but she seemed a little distracted. Clearly, she hadn't expected so many people to be here when she dropped by.

Gerard smiled, the one that had always made Patrick wish he could hide in a bunker on the field. Patrick looked over at Keith and raised an eyebrow. Keith raised both of his and silently mouthed, clear enough for Patrick to read his lips, *Fire in the hole.*

Wade looked at Keith, then at Patrick, and sank farther into the couch. He crammed the last cinnamon roll into his mouth and tried his best to blend into the background, all the while chewing furiously.

"I'm Captain Gerard Breckenridge, of the United States Department of the Preternatural, here on orders of the military to speak with the government-sanctioned seer Marek Taylor. The security clearance required for this meeting means you're going to let Ms. Zhang go and get the fuck out before I throw you out," Gerard said icily.

Patrick's skin crawled from the subtle power emanating from Gerard now that he'd unleashed a bit of temper. Usually, his old captain was the epitome of calm, but there were moments—few and far between—where rage was all Gerard knew.

Everything always ended so messily when that happened.

"Emma said we weren't allowed to get blood on the floor," Patrick said, forcing his tone light.

Gerard tipped his head in Patrick's direction in silent acknowledgement of that reminder, but he only had eyes for the god pack. "Let her go. I won't ask again."

Maybe it was their standing through the government, or the fact that Gerard wasn't completely human and it showed now that he let it, but Estelle listened for once. It was a concession Patrick added to their small column of wins since June.

Estelle unwrapped her fingers from around Emma's arm one at a time, revealing bruised skin beneath. The bruises immediately started to fade. Emma held her head up high as she walked back to Leon's side. He pulled her close, wrapping his arm around her and glaring at a spot over Estelle's shoulder.

"I don't like the games you play," Jono said in a low voice as he walked past Gerard to approach the other pack. "Never have, never will. Your missing pack members were arseholes, but they still deserved a better alpha than you."

"If you harmed them, then we will consider that a declaration of war," Estelle said.

Jono came to a stop an arm's length away from her and crossed his arms over his chest. "Against the fae? Best of luck with that. The Sluagh took them. You aren't getting them back. You should be used to that by now. You've always been one to throw away your people like they were rubbish."

Youssef took a threatening step forward but didn't get any farther than that as Patrick conjured up a mageglobe between him and Jono, filling it with raw magic. Youssef pulled up short, eyeing Patrick's magic with a disgusted look on his face. Patrick knew his magic, corrupted as it was, wasn't easy to be around. Right now, he considered that side effect a plus.

"The government considers your actions today, as well as the actions of your dire the other night and your pack members last night, interference. The video Sage took has already been handed over to my supervisor. Think real hard about how you want to play this, Youssef," Patrick said.

Youssef's amber-eyed gaze snapped from Jono to Patrick. His

lips curled, revealing sharp fangs. "Jonothon can't hide behind you and your badge forever."

"That goes double for the Tempest pack," Estelle said.

Jono smiled, showing all teeth, and Patrick hoped he wasn't going to do anything that would require bail money or staining Emma's hardwood floors and rugs.

"You've fucked with Emma's pack enough. Next time, grow a fucking pair and come at me on your own. Or are you too scared that you'll lose?" Jono asked.

Estelle lifted her chin. "You wouldn't survive a challenge against me."

"I put your dire on his knees. I have to wonder how many people who were there that day wished it had been you."

Estelle lunged at Jono quicker than Patrick could raise a shield between them, furious preternatural speed beating the silent, half-formed command trigger running through his mind.

It couldn't beat Gerard's spear.

The weapon cut through the air so quickly that Estelle was forced to do some rather ungainly midair twisting that had her landing on her back. Youssef was by her side in an instant, the both of them staring at the weapon lodged in the floor mere inches from Estelle's head. Nicholas had his claws out, but the icy fury on Gerard's face made him freeze where he stood.

"Well, at least it's not blood," Wade muttered from the couch.

Patrick choked back a laugh, but Keith didn't even bother to try. His cackle filled the living area of the apartment as Gerard stalked over to retrieve his spear. Jono stayed where he was, staring down the god pack through the shield Patrick had erected between the two sides.

Gerard yanked the spear out of the floor, the wooden hole tearing even more as he did so. He spun it with the casual ease of a man who knew how to use a weapon of war.

"Jono gave you an order. In my line of work, when your superiors issue one, you get a fucking move on," Gerard said into the tense silence.

"Jonothon will never be my superior," Estelle growled as Youssef helped her to her feet.

"You sure about that?" Patrick asked.

The look Estelle shot him would've flayed him to the bone if she had a shred of magic in her soul and knew how to use it.

"We'll escort you out," Sage said, stepping up to the line they'd formed between the other god pack and Emma's Tempest pack. "On the government's orders, of course."

Nicholas moved to guide Youssef and Estelle to the door but was violently shrugged off. That little hint of discord within their pack made Patrick smirk. He didn't stop smirking for the entire time it took to kick the three out of the mansion.

Outside, snow was falling, the wind a sharp, icy thing that cut beneath Patrick's leather jacket. Despite the heat charms, Patrick shivered from the cold and hoped he wasn't getting sick.

"Whatever game you think you're playing, you're going to lose," Youssef said as they walked toward the pair of SUVs idling on the street.

"Doubtful," Jono replied. "Next time you have something to say to me, say it to my face."

"Is that a challenge?"

"It's not murder if it's a challenge. Best remember that."

It never was inside the ring. Patrick knew that from previous cases and from the stories Jono had told him. You could do anything you wanted to a werecreature who issued a challenge inside the ring and the law would never consider it murder. The preternatural world had its own laws never written to code, but they were still valid, still enforced, still allowed.

The modern world was still old in some ways—in the way blood was spilled, the way people were buried, the way they prayed to a god for absolution.

Sometimes the old ways were the only path forward.

Patrick watched the other god pack leave, not blinking until the taillights disappeared around the corner. Everything running through his mind stayed there until they were back upstairs behind closed doors and another silence ward that he cast with such force it made his fingertips go numb. As soon as the static faded away, Emma rounded on Jono.

"I am *done* showing throat to those fuckers," she ground out.

Jono looked at her with a calmness in his wolf-bright eyes that didn't match the tension in his jaw. "Em—"

"*No.*" Emma made a slashing gesture with her hand, her fingernails sharp like claws. "They aren't worth my pack's association, and I refuse to be loyal to them any longer."

Emma grabbed Leon's hand and together they put themselves before Jono, going down on their knees and angling their heads to show their throats.

"You're better than those bastards, Jono. You always have been," Leon said into the quiet that had settled over everyone.

"We aren't a big enough god pack. I can't keep you safe," Jono said.

Emma shook her head. "You've done more to keep some of us safe than they have for the entire time they've led the god pack here. Kennedy and the others wouldn't be alive today without you."

Patrick thought about the woman they'd saved from Tremaine back in August, not sure if being severely traumatized was better than being dead. But she and the few other survivors were safe, living in a home together in upstate New York that Marek had bought for them after discussing options with Jono. The SOA and DEA sent agents around once a week to check up on them. It wasn't quite witness protection, but they were away from the city they couldn't stay in any longer.

Healing wasn't easy, wasn't always linear, and sometimes leaving everything behind was the only way to start over.

Patrick nudged Jono in the side. "If we find the Summer Lady, then we'll have the acknowledgment of the fae that we're the only legitimate god pack in New York City. Estelle and Youssef lost whatever agreements they had with the Night Courts, but I'm sure we can work something out with Lucien."

"You aren't making any more bargains with that arsehole," Jono retorted.

"What bargains?" Gerard asked sharply.

Patrick winced and waved off the question, holding out no hope that Gerard would forget about it. Patrick watched Jono lean down and drag his wrists over Emma and Leon's throats, his fingers curving around the back of their necks. Jono closed his eyes, taking a deep breath, his entire body stiffening. Emma and Leon jerked in his grip, but Jono didn't let them go far. He held them steady as he did whatever it was god pack alphas did when taking on the loyalty of a new pack.

Patrick would never know that feeling, would never know what put that look of wonder in Jono's eyes when they opened again. But he was fiercely glad that Jono was getting the opportunity to experience it now, to know what it was like to finally lead how he should.

"I take on responsibility of your Tempest pack," Jono said, his voice deep with a promise Patrick knew he would never knowingly break.

Emma and Leon breathed in tandem, sharing in the give-and-take between them. Jono lifted his hands away from their throats and turned each one over so his palms were raised to the ceiling, offering the pair help up. Emma and Leon gripped his hands, and he hauled them to their feet with easy strength.

"Thank you," Emma said, a lightness to her tone and body Patrick hadn't ever witnessed before.

"They'll know you've left their protection once someone catches your scent."

"That won't matter. If I need to get a protective order from the courts to keep them away from our territory, I will," Marek promised.

"I'll get it filed for you," Sage said.

"It's great that you guys smell different now, but you're out of Pop-Tarts," Wade called out from the kitchen.

"Did you not just eat a dozen cinnamon rolls?" Patrick demanded.

"No, because you ate one. It's not a dozen if one ended up in your stomach."

Patrick made a face. "You can snack later, Wade. We need to get going."

"What's the plan?" Keith asked.

Patrick turned to face Gerard. "We can't wait on the rest of the Hellraisers. We need to go to Tír na nÓg today."

"The Hellraisers can be wheels up in less than an hour and here by tonight. We should wait," Gerard replied.

"Still not fast enough. If we're going to find your fiancée, then we need more information, and I don't trust Tiarnán to give it to us straight."

"Not trusting a fae. Shocking," Keith muttered. "Present company excluded, sir."

Jono held up a hand. "Hold on a moment. Fiancée?"

Gerard tapped the heel of his spear against the hardwood floor, the sound like soft bells ringing in Patrick's ears. The spear disappeared before the sound faded. "I'll pay for the damage to your floor, Ms. Zhang."

"Don't worry about it. We can afford to fix it. And call me Emma," she said.

"You shouldn't give your name so freely to my kind."

"You're Patrick's captain. I trust his judgment."

"Hey, now," Marek joked, which Patrick couldn't even be mad about.

Emma shot Patrick a tired smile. "When it comes to the few people he considers friends."

Jono frowned at Patrick. "How long have you known the Summer Lady is Gerard's fiancée?"

"Since last night at dinner. I was going to tell you when we got to the bar, but I was a little distracted by the Wild Hunt trying to take you for a ride. I'm the only one who gets to do that," Patrick said.

Wade made a gagging sound as he came back from the kitchen, carrying a bottle of hot sauce for his eggs. "Gross."

Everyone ignored him.

"Are you *sidhe*?" Sage asked slowly, staring at Gerard.

"I am of the Tuatha Dé Danann, for all that it's worth something to be called such in this day and age," Gerard said.

It wasn't a straight answer, but Patrick shook his head at Sage when she would've pushed for more. "Leave it, Sage."

Gerard crossed his arms over his chest. "We really should wait for the rest of the team."

"You can, but there's a hawthorn path in Central Park that I'm planning on taking a walk down. If I have to get Tiarnán to come open it for me, I will. I can tell whoever we meet on the other side of the veil that you sent us, but I'd rather you be there with us, Gerard."

"I haven't missed your impulsiveness at all."

"Look, we need answers. Who better to give it to us than Brigid herself? Besides, you said it yourself. She called her warriors home, and that includes you. Waiting any longer isn't going to change what you'll face over there."

Gerard's jaw tightened before he let out a heavy sigh. "If I told you no, you'd still go, wouldn't you?"

"I don't wear a uniform anymore."

"That's a yes," Jono told Gerard.

Gerard snorted. "I know."

"I thought you couldn't cross the veil? That it took too much power and you'd need a bunch of sacrifices to do it?" Leon asked.

"The fae are more tied to the mortal plane than others. The

roots of the Otherworld have burrowed into this one for centuries, and human memory won't let that connection die."

"Like Yggdrasil," Patrick said, thinking of the Norse world tree.

Gerard nodded. "Yes. We are remembered better than others. There are paths to Tír na nÓg that are always open to the fae, you just need to know where to find them."

"Do you want us to go with you?" Emma asked.

Patrick shook his head. "No. Time moves differently past the veil. Minutes there are hours here. Marek should probably get you guys that protective order just in case. I don't know how long we'll be gone."

"I'll have Tiarnán draw it up and get it filed today," Sage said, already pulling out her cell phone.

"The Hellraisers can be here tonight. We have a sorcerer on the team who can stay with your pack for extra protection, Emma," Gerard offered.

"We have space for a few extra people. We can cover the hotel costs for the ones we can't house," Emma said.

"And food, if Wade doesn't eat it all," Leon added.

"Hey," Wade mumbled around a mouthful of chorizo and eggs. He'd claimed one of the plates on the coffee table as his and was already halfway done with it. "I'm going with them."

"You're still grounded," Jono said.

"But you said pack needed to stick together."

Patrick dug out his cell phone and dialed a number he knew by heart. He let it ring three times before hanging up. He repeated that two more times, waited for thirty seconds, then called one more time. Setsuna answered almost immediately.

"Line and location are secure," Patrick said.

"I hope you're calling with news about the missing Wisteria child," SOA Director Setsuna Abuku said.

"We'd have more luck winning the lottery every day for a year than finding their daughter."

"That's not a conclusion their lawyers will accept."

"Shame. Listen, I'm going across the veil with my old captain. The Dominion Sect kidnapped the Summer Lady, and we need to find her."

"The Wisteria child should be your focus, Patrick."

"I'll ask about her for you when we cross over if you want, but if the State Department can't get answers out of the fae, I don't know how you think I will."

Setsuna sighed irritably, but Patrick didn't really care that he was making her job harder. Their personal and professional relationship, already strained over the years, had only gotten worse since Patrick first set foot in New York City.

Persephone might have tricked him into a soul debt in order to save his life as a kid, but Setsuna had been the one who'd taken it upon herself to hide him and raise him from a distance. A name change, boarding school at an Academy, and intermittent checkups didn't necessarily equate to a familial relationship. Setsuna was his boss, and she'd been his guardian, but that didn't mean he trusted her.

"Have the Wild Hunt and the Sluagh been dealt with?"

"No."

"I'll inform SAIC Ng that you're following a lead and are going off the grid and he needs to assign someone to the fae issue in your absence. Don't spend long past the veil, Patrick."

"I'm hoping we'll only be gone for a couple of days. I'll call you when I get back."

Patrick ended the call and shoved his phone back into his pocket. He looked over at Gerard, who was still on the phone calling his team. Gerard flashed him a thumbs-up, and Patrick nodded.

"Hey, Razzle Dazzle. If we're going past the veil, I'm not going without a weapon. Tell me you have something I can borrow," Keith said.

The only physical weapons Patrick had were his semiautomatic HK USP 9mm tactical pistol and his dagger, neither of which he could give up. Requisitioning extra weapons from the SOA would take too long and involve way too much paperwork.

"No, but I know a guy."

Whether or not Lucien would be willing to help them out was the million-dollar question.

Gerard twisted around in the front passenger seat so he could glare at where Patrick sat in the back of the Mustang with Keith. Jono glanced at Patrick in the rearview mirror, the other man having crossed his arms defensively over his chest.

"I didn't have a choice, okay?" Patrick said.

"There is always a choice with that asshole—you shoot him in the heart and cut off his head, or you set him on fire."

Jono nodded agreement. "Yeah, mate. What Gerard said."

Patrick glared at him. "I don't know why I thought you two meeting would be a good idea."

"Why? Because we won't let you sod off and do something stupid?"

"We're already doing something stupid by asking Lucien for help. I'm going to need a shower afterward to feel better about myself," Keith said.

"I thought you lot fought with him in the Thirty-Day War?"

"Yeah, but that doesn't mean we had to *like* it."

"Lucien's Night Court was an ally during the Thirty-Day War

that everyone likes to forget about. Being an ally doesn't mean we liked working with the asshole. The undead can't feed off the dead, and that's all the food they'd have left if the Dominion Sect succeeded in releasing the hells into our world. Demons don't make good meals, so the mother of all vampires told her children to fight with us," Patrick said.

Jono took a breath but couldn't get a read on Patrick's scent. He knew Ashanti was a sore subject for the other man, and Patrick's guilt over her death had never left him.

"It'd be nice if the dead stayed dead," Keith said wistfully.

"If that were the case, I might actually get a vacation."

Jono turned down the street that Ginnungagap was located on, slowing his speed. Rather than park on the street, he drove into the alleyway next to the warehouse turned nightclub. A motor-cycle was parked near the side-door entrance up ahead. Jono braked to a halt behind it and turned off the engine.

Everyone got out, the cold smacking Jono in the face. Gerard's scowl hadn't disappeared, and only got deeper when the side entrance opened soundlessly on oiled hinges. Carmen lounged in the doorway in her true form, the curled horns of her kind spiraling back over her skull. Her leather pants and jacket didn't look warm enough for the weather, and Jono could smell the sexual desire emanating from her like perfume that all succubi exuded. It never did anything to him thanks to the buffer Fenrir provided, but he worried about the others.

"Carmen," Gerard bit out.

"Captain," Carmen practically purred. "I'd say it's a pleasure to see you again, but it's not."

Patrick made a face, gesturing at both Keith and Gerard with one hand, his fingertips glowing with magic. Jono stopped being able to smell everyone between one breath and the next. The only thing he got was the scent of garbage from the dumpster down the way.

"Cut it out, Carmen. Is he here?" Patrick said.

Carmen tilted her head to the side, her long black curls spilling over one slim shoulder. "My master will listen to what you have to say, but it will cost you."

"We can pay it," Jono said.

Tithes from packs were what kept god packs afloat, along with leases to housing and land that passed down from one set of alphas to another. Jono's god pack was starting out with nothing, but Marek had already promised to bankroll their needs in conjunction with the tithes Emma's Tempest pack would give them. As the creator and majority owner of the social media site PreterWorld, Marek had money to spare, and then some.

Carmen shoved the door open wider and sauntered into the depths of Ginnungagap. Gerard approached the entrance and stepped inside, his entire body tensing as he crossed over the threshold.

"Patrick," Gerard ground out.

"Yeah, I know. It's fucking weird, but it hasn't hurt us so far," Patrick said as he stepped inside.

Weird was an understatement. Stepping inside Ginnungagap always set Jono's teeth on edge. Whatever lived in the walls of the space—primordial void or something worse—sometimes seemed as if it had a mind of its own. Even Fenrir's presence in his soul wasn't enough to kill all of Jono's worry. How people danced the night away here was beyond him.

Once Jono entered the club, the city noise beyond the walls was muffled to a point even he had to strain to hear it. He blinked, eyes easily adjusting to the interior brightness.

Last time he'd been inside Ginnungagap, construction had still been ongoing. Now, the club was fully finished, and the area they entered was a dimly lit corridor that led to a couple of toilets. They walked single file down the corridor and came out into the rest of the club space.

With the lights on, Ginnungagap was thrown into high relief. A well-stocked bar lined the opposite wall, and the dance floor took up half the rear area, while lounges and low leather seats took up space with tables closer to the front of the building. The dance floor extended beneath the mezzanine where a small stage for DJs was built into the rear wall.

Carmen headed for the stairs on the other side of the club that led up to the mezzanine. They followed after her, climbing to a VIP level that contained a smaller bar but more comfortable seating.

Lucien sat on the bar itself, casually flipping a switchblade between the fingers of one hand. His motorcycle helmet rested on the bar counter beside him, along with his leather jacket. His dark brown hair was free of product and a little messy from the helmet. Pale, even beneath the bright halogen lights used to illuminate the club after hours, Lucien's black eyes were the only hint to what gave him his daywalker status.

As a direct descendant of Ashanti, the mother of all vampires, Lucien was more powerful than most other vampires still walking the Earth. Ruthless, murderous, and never one to put down roots for long, Lucien had taken over the Manhattan Night Court out of revenge. He stayed out of a promise to Ashanti.

Jono's lip curled at the sight of the master vampire. Jono hated Lucien, but what he hated more right now was the fact they'd come to the bastard for help.

Patrick had been right, though Jono wished he weren't. In a pinch, when one needed illegal black-market weapons, Lucien was your go-to bloke.

"Halfling," Lucien bit out.

"Fuck-face," Gerard replied with an amount of viciousness that Jono approved of.

"Heard you can't do your job properly."

"Come closer and I'll show you how wrong you are."

"We're here to buy weapons, not murder each other," Patrick said.

"I won't mind a bit of murder. My money is on Gerard," Jono replied.

Patrick scowled at him. "You're not helping."

Jono shrugged, never taking his eyes off Lucien. "Like Patrick said, we're here to buy weapons. Unless you're incapable of providing what we need?"

Lucien's mouth curled up at one corner, a flash of jagged fangs revealed between his lips. "You couldn't afford my prices."

"Name it."

"Who's paying?"

"We are," Patrick said, jerking his thumb at Jono. "As god pack."

Lucien slid off the bar counter and strode their way. "That's new. Finally giving in to the beast that owns you?"

Jono didn't blink as Lucien came right up to him, refusing to give ground. He was taller than Lucien, but their strength was fairly equal, and their speed was a draw split by milliseconds. Jono wouldn't mind sinking his teeth in the bastard's throat and tearing it out, but that wouldn't get them what they needed.

"Weapons," Jono said flatly. "Whatever they need, for your usual amount. Marek will pay it."

"Getting the seer to do your dirty work for you? Great way to start off your tithing system."

"It's a favor," Patrick ground out. "Kind of like the promise you made to Ashanti."

Lucien's black eyes slid his way and Jono tensed, not liking the anger creeping into the master vampire's gaze. He shifted on his feet, edging between the two, managing to refocus Lucien's attention on him.

"Do not speak my mother's name," Lucien hissed.

"You want us gone? Then name your price. We're after the Dominion Sect, and you know what that means. You want to keep feeding off humans, then you best make a choice," Jono said.

The undead still needed to feed, and they couldn't feed off the dead, only the living. Ethan's desire to turn himself into a god would ruin the world, and vampires wouldn't necessarily survive the change in status quo.

"The enemy of my enemy is useful," Carmen said as she went behind the bar and hefted up a heavy-looking storage case.

"That's not how the saying goes," Keith said as he and Gerard went to inspect the merchandise.

"Ten thousand," Lucien said.

"For the entire lot?" Jono asked.

"For each piece they buy. Bullets included."

"That's—" Patrick started to protest.

Jono raised a hand, cutting him off. He never looked away from Lucien's face. "Done. What's the routing number?"

Lucien rattled it off before saying, "Next time, it'll cost you more."

"Figured giving you the Manhattan Night Court would be interest enough."

"You'll pay whatever I say you'll pay if you want what I have to offer."

Patrick looked like he wanted to throttle Lucien as he pressed his mobile to his ear. "Yeah, I got the routing number for the wire transfer. He likes offshore accounts. Hopefully your bank won't flag anything."

Jono dialed up his hearing so he could listen to the conversation.

"It'll be fine. Tell me the amount when you're ready," Marek said on the other side of the line.

Jono grabbed Patrick's free hand and pulled him out of reach of Lucien, pushing Patrick ahead of him as he deliberately turned his back on Lucien. At the bar, Gerard and Keith had settled on a pair of long guns that made Patrick whistle appreciatively.

"Nice," he said. "FN SCAR-H?"

Gerard nodded and angled one of the weapons toward them. Scratched on the metal were symbols Jono didn't understand. "Warded."

Patrick reached out and dragged a finger over the barrel of the weapon. The symbols glowed with a faint light at his touch.

"Military grade. Magic feels like it was set by a witch. Weapon won't jam."

"The serial numbers are all filed off, so I'm going with stolen," Keith said.

Gerard shook his head. "We don't have to pay for these."

"You aren't walking out of Ginnungagap with them if you don't," Carmen said.

Gerard ignored her. "It's not worth owing him, Patrick."

"I have a lot of practice with owing people shit. This is a transaction, plain and simple." Patrick nodded at what was on display. "Pick your weapon, sir."

"We get something out of it as well, aside from what you lot are outfitting yourselves with," Jono said.

Keith snorted. "An empty bank account?"

Jono looked over his shoulder at where Lucien stood, watching them. "Validation."

Lucien never made bargains with anyone, never gave loyalty that wasn't coerced. Lucien's grudging willingness to supply their god pack with weapons was more than Estelle and Youssef would ever get out of the master vampire. That it came because of a promise to a long-dead goddess didn't change the outcome.

They'd pay, but so would Lucien, in a way.

In the end, Gerard and Keith chose their weapons, and the final total made Patrick wince. He still passed it along to Marek.

"Because I always like funding terrorism," Marek muttered over the line. "All right, money is sent."

Lucien stared at his mobile, and a few seconds later, he nodded. "Money's been transferred."

Carmen unzipped a black duffel bag and started filling it with their purchases, the sultry smirk on her face full of mockery. "Pleasure doing business, boys. Until next time."

As much as Jono wanted to deny they'd be back, he knew he'd be lying if he did.

"MY SNEAKERS ARE GETTING RUINED," Wade whined. "Whose idea was this? Because it sucks."

"You had the option to stay home," Jono reminded him.

"No. The pack is going, so I'm going."

The stubborn look in Wade's brown eyes was marred by the pout on his face as he stared down at where his new Nike sneakers sank into the snow that covered the path they walked on. Noon on a weekday in Central Park, even in winter, usually still had people around: joggers, the homeless, hot dog carts. Today, their group seemed to be the only ones in the entire park.

"You'll live," Patrick said.

"My sneakers won't."

Jono snorted and shared an exasperated, if fond, look with Patrick. They'd given Wade the option to stay with Emma's pack while they crossed the veil, but the teen had adamantly refused. They were all big on letting Wade make his own choices, and Patrick especially was careful about not trying to influence his decisions. Patrick had done that in August and still carried some lingering guilt over it, even though Wade had been integral in that fight against Tremaine's Night Court.

"So where is the hawthorn path?" Sage wanted to know.

"Past Bethesda Fountain up ahead and across Bow Bridge. It's in the copse of trees on that side of the Lake," Gerard said.

"Your bosses ever take you out here for a picnic in some faerie ring?" Keith asked.

Sage rolled her eyes. "I work for them—that doesn't mean I completely trust them. If they ever asked me to cross the veil, I'd say no."

"Speaking of food, nobody eat or drink anything offered to us when we get to Tír na nÓg. Goes double for you, Wade," Patrick said.

"What if I'm hungry?" Wade asked.

"Then you ignore your growling stomach until we get back here. Fae offerings aren't to be trusted."

Wade patted at the pockets of his winter coat Jono had made sure he'd worn before leaving Marek's flat. "Hope I brought enough snacks. Someone's gonna water the Christmas tree while we're gone, right?"

"He's going to eat you out of house and home," Gerard said with a faint chuckle.

"The Tempest pack tithes will more than cover our living costs and keeping Wade fed. Ten percent from them is quite a hefty amount. Estelle and Youssef will be hurting without their money. And yes, Wade, Emma will take care of the Christmas tree," Sage said.

Jono rubbed at his chest, taking a deep breath. The cold air burned his lungs but couldn't burn out the lingering scent-memory of what taking on Emma's pack had felt like. His soul had cracked open when he'd touched them, their individual scents and the pack scent they carried transferring to his awareness. Jono would know their scents until the day he died or they left him, whichever came first.

"Here's hoping Em and the others will be safe while we're gone," Jono said.

"Tiarnán will file the protective order."

"Not sure that will be enough."

Gerard looked over his shoulder at Jono, the duffel bag carrying the weapons hanging from one shoulder. "My Hellraisers won't let anything happen to them."

Jono nodded slowly, believing in that promise because he knew Patrick did.

Terrace Drive curved slightly up ahead, leading into Bethesda Terrace. In the summer, when Central Park was thick with greenery, it was difficult to see it until one was upon it. In winter, most of the trees were barren, their spindly branches lined with white snow. The pathway they walked on hadn't been cleared by the city yet. Most people weren't venturing outside unless they absolutely had to. A citywide curfew hadn't been called yet, but Jono figured it was only a matter of time.

Jono's gaze was drawn to the sky and the dark gray clouds hanging low over the city. The chill in the air was icy, and the weather was below freezing, even in the middle of the day. While the weather wasn't the start of a reactionary storm, it was still a threat they had to be careful about.

They came around the bend, the view of Bethesda Terrace now unobstructed by trees. Buildings in the distance rose above Central Park's tree line, reminding Jono that for all the hint of a forest the trees provided, it was an illusion.

The fountain on the lower level that was the centerpiece of Bethesda Terrace had been turned off for the winter. The large basin was full of snow, and the statue's angel wings were lined with it as well. Beyond the open area was the Lake, the water near the shoreline iced over.

Jono squinted against the glare of weak sunlight reflecting up from all the snow as everyone sidled up to the terrace railing. Gerard pointed at the Lake and the swath of bare trees and wintery shrubs that covered the park to the east of it.

"The hawthorn path is in there. We'll need to cross Bow Bridge to get to it," he said.

"Weird that people don't stumble across it every day," Keith mused.

"You need a fae to open the way, and they need to be of decent magical strength."

"Does that mean you're a mage like Patrick?" Wade asked.

Gerard shook his head. "No. We don't classify our magic the way humans do. Besides, my magic is only good on the battlefield, and I don't like to use it around civilians."

"Smooth Dog didn't come to the military through the Mage Corps," Patrick said.

Gerard rolled his eyes at the nickname, but the smile on his face was fond. "Let's move out."

They trudged over to the left-hand staircase and maneuvered down the snowy steps to the lower terrace. The only sound around them was everyone's feet crunching through snow and the distant hum of street traffic Jono could make out if he dialed his hearing up a little. He was on edge out in the open like this. It didn't help that no one else was around. The only heartbeats Jono could hear came from their group.

They exited Bethesda Terrace for the path that led to Bow Bridge, a popular tourist spot for pictures. It used to be on Jono's jogging path when he'd go for a run on his days off, but he still had bad memories about Central Park. He'd switched up his jogging to other parts of the city until the weather became too wet for a comfortable run.

Patrick adjusted his stride to fall back beside Jono, who was taking up the rear of their little group. Jono reached out to hold Patrick's gloved hand.

"Okay with being out here?" Patrick asked.

"I'm all right, love," Jono promised, wondering if some of his unease was coming through the soulbond.

"You know, you still haven't told me what you want for Christmas."

"I have you. I don't need anything else."

"Okay, see, you get me every day. That's not special."

"Beg to differ, mate."

Patrick shook his head, but the smile he shot Jono told him the exasperation was feigned. "Seriously, what do you want?"

"Doesn't matter. You can get me anything and I'll like it. Didn't have a proper Christmas for years before coming to New York."

The old ache tied to memories of his family wasn't as strong these days. Jono had grown up on a council estate in North

London, but his family had wanted nothing to do with him since being infected by the werevirus from a bad blood transfusion after a car accident. No family and no pack meant the holidays were just another day until he'd immigrated to the States.

Emma and her pack had rekindled his love for Christmas, if only because it brought everyone together. This year was the first time Jono was spending it with someone he was starting to fall in love with. Patrick, for all his stubborn prickliness and hard edges, was someone Jono knew in his heart he could never let go of, soul-bond or not.

"I'm shit at picking out gifts. Can't you give me a hint?"

"Patrick got us socks one time," Keith said from up ahead. "The entire team. Socks. You don't want that, Jono."

"You bitched about trench foot for so long I thought you would've appreciated the socks."

The laughter from the group was almost loud enough to drown out the distant echo of a scream—almost, but not quite.

Jono's head snapped back, and he blinked a drifting snowflake out of his eye. The clouds above seemed to get darker as he looked, appearing hazy from falling snow. The wind picked up, stronger and faster than before. Trees swayed around them from the force, snow falling off of branches and landing on the ground with dull *whumps*.

"Something's coming," Jono said, tugging Patrick forward.

"I hear it, too," Sage said grimly.

"Let's go," Gerard ordered.

"Which one of the damned things is it?" Patrick wanted to know as he yanked his hand out of Jono's grip to keep his balance as he ran.

"They sound like the fae from the bar," Jono said.

Patrick swore. "Fucking Sluagh. We need to cross Bow Bridge before they reach us. There's no coverage there, and it goes over the Lake. None of us need to fall into water in the middle of a fight and get hypothermia."

"This is a shitty Christmas vacation," Keith said.

"Shut up and run, Chatterbox."

They ran, snow churning underfoot and in the sky above them. Jono watched as Gerard unzipped the duffel bag he carried with one hand, holding it open and to the side for Keith to get at. They never broke stride, working with a seamlessness that was impressive. Keith pulled out both of the weapons, waited for Gerard to drop the duffel bag, then tossed him the second rifle. Their extra ammunition was already clipped to their belts.

They handled the weapons with an ease that reminded Jono of Patrick's skill with a gun when the need arose. At the moment, Patrick had opted to go with his magic over his own weapons. Three pale blue mageglobes flickered with raw magic where they hovered at shoulder height, keeping pace as he ran.

Jono couldn't feel the burn in his soul that meant Patrick had tapped a ley line through the soulbond. Since August, Jono had worked with Patrick to overcome his guilt about being able to access his full magical reach again through Jono's soul. Whether it was Fenrir's presence or something else the gods had carved into his soul during June, Jono was now a breakwater of sorts for Patrick.

The scars in Patrick's own soul made it impossible for him to channel external magic, but being bound to Jono gave him back that ability. The process was painful to a certain extent for Jono, but pain was something he'd long been able to work through and ignore.

Jono caught Patrick's eye as they ran, giving him a nod that Patrick returned. If it came down to it, Patrick would use the soulbond to hopefully even the odds.

They passed snow-covered benches that lined the path, the bare trees on the gentle sloping hill off to the side swaying in the sudden headwind they were running against. Patrick and Keith seemed the most affected by it due to their lack of preternatural strength. Gerard kept pace with Keith, and Jono kept pace with

Patrick. Sage and Wade ran between them, with Wade occasionally looking over his shoulder at what chased them.

"Eyes forward," Patrick yelled. "Let me worry about your six."

Wade followed the order with a scared look in his eyes, head snapping back around. He stumbled, but Sage was there to keep him upright. Jono could hear Wade's heart beating faster than everyone else's, and hoped it wasn't a precursor to him shifting mass into his dragon form. Even as he watched, a hint of red scales crept up the back of Wade's neck, and Jono swore.

Patrick put on a burst of speed to reach Wade. "Keep it together, Wade. We're right here with you."

Jono chanced a look over his shoulder, unsurprised to see a writhing mass of undead spirits breaking free from the clouds above. "We got company."

"Bridge is up ahead," Gerard shouted.

Patrick flicked his fingers at a mageglobe, the sphere of magic expanding at his touch to cover them all in a maneuverable shield. The world became faintly blue tinged, but the color change didn't matter when it was the shield that kept them from being skewered by the spears that clattered overhead and fell to the ground outside the shield's radius as they ran.

"Are you gonna shoot them?" Wade yelled.

"Not until we get behind some cover," Keith replied.

The path straightened out a little, Bow Bridge coming into view. The picturesque cast-iron bridge was covered in snow, the planters on the railings piled high with mounds of it. The water on the Lake churned from the wind as they hit the start of the bridge. The sound of their footsteps changed now that they were running above water.

The screaming of the Sluagh got closer.

"My shields won't be enough if they do a sustained attack," Patrick said, his breath puffing out in small clouds as he ran.

"Get past the bridge and head east. We'll buy you some time," Gerard said.

"Spelled bullets won't do much good against the dead, and we can't cross the veil without you."

Gerard made a gesture with his free hand that Jono didn't understand, but which made Patrick nod. When Patrick started to slow his stride, Jono cut his pace, refusing to leave him. When they made it to the center of Bow Bridge, Patrick skidded to a stop and spun on his feet, raising his arms to the sky.

"Need me?" Jono asked tightly as he also slid to a halt in the snow while everyone else kept running.

"Not yet."

The shield disappeared, the world returning to wintery gray. Above them, the Sluagh was a dark, roiling horde against the clouds—spirits and fae beasts who held allegiance to the Unseelie Court. Their twisted forms were nightmarish to look upon, but Jono kept looking, because that's where the threat was.

The mageglobe spinning between Patrick's hands shot up like a rocket, streaking through the sky. The Sluagh split apart to avoid a direct hit, the spirits and creatures writhing in the sky—and then getting blown apart in a messy explosion of magic that turned the snow black with blood.

The Sluagh screamed at a decibel that made Jono's ears ring. He dialed down his hearing to near-human levels, but that was only marginally better.

"That's one way to make a mess and piss them off," Jono said, grabbing Patrick by the arm.

"Won't hold them off for long."

Patrick stumbled at the speed Jono ran at, but Jono kept him upright and didn't let him go until they were off the bridge. Gerard and Keith had their weapons pointed at the sky, covering their retreat, but the pair swiftly turned around once Jono and Patrick made it back onto solid land.

"Head for the trees!" Gerard yelled.

Everyone made sure to keep to the pace that Patrick and Keith ran at, unwilling to leave their human members behind. Patrick raised another shield around them just in time to save the group from getting pinned beneath messy, sticky spiderwebs that clung to the shield.

"Shit," Patrick said, making a sharp motion with his hand.

The shield cracked open down the center and peeled apart, taking the spiderwebs with it. A second layer had already been erected, and Jono watched as Patrick shrank it down as much as he could to make them a smaller target. It wasn't a smooth transition —defense wasn't Patrick's strong suit—but it held.

They followed Gerard off the path and into the cluster of barren trees and winter shrubs that lined the Lake where they were at. The Sluagh shrieked above them, the sound of their wailing close in a way that made the hair stand up on the back of Jono's neck.

"What the fuck is *that*?" Wade exclaimed.

Jono looked ahead as they dodged around trees. Bright lights sparkled in the air ahead, and the trees around them started to fill with mist. Strange plants started to push through snow, forming a path.

"Almost there," Gerard yelled.

The Sluagh screamed their displeasure and broke through the branches, sending clumps of snow falling all around them. The sky above was blotted out by bodies and spirits, Patrick's shield flickering from the weight of the Sluagh.

Patrick flicked his fingers at his remaining mageglobe, the sphere pulsing with magic. "Gerard, we need to—"

Whatever Patrick was going to say, he never got the chance to form the words.

The ground heaved beneath their feet as tree roots shot up from the frozen dirt. One wrapped itself around Jono's ankle and yanked him to the ground. Jono went down hard, managing not to impale himself on a root out of sheer luck. He turned his head in time to see Patrick get tossed into a tree and pinned there by a spider fae that could've been the twin from the one in the bar.

The shield above them splintered and disintegrated, and Jono's heart beat hard in his chest.

"Patrick!" Jono yelled.

He knew Patrick wasn't all that great with defensive wards, but the shield had buckled quicker than Jono was used to it happening.

"I got him!" Wade yelled, sounding frantic.

The ground heaved again, and Jono reared back, slamming his elbow into the face of a spider fae who'd dropped down out of the sky half on top of him. Bone crunched under his elbow, and Jono twisted around on the ground to slam his boot into the fae's arachnid belly. The skin there was soft, not remotely protected, and the force of his kick put his leg up to midcalf into the fae's body.

Brackish blood poured out of the fae's human mouth, staining Jono's shirt and jacket. He wrenched his foot free and grabbed the fae by its throat, tossing it aside. Jono got to his feet, claws curving away from his fingers. He kept his balance against the roiling ground below while the Sluagh screamed around them.

The mist got thicker, the barren trees around them fading into older ones that carried strangely colored leaves on their branches instead of snow. A flurry of color swirled around them on a burst of wind that smelled of spring, some sticking to the blood on Jono's hands—petals, not snow.

He couldn't see Patrick.

"Get down!" Gerard bellowed.

Jono obeyed instantly, because that tone of voice was the same sort Patrick used whenever they were in a fight and he was about to make something explode.

A storm of arrows cut through the air where he'd just been standing, slicing into what remained of the Sluagh. The screams this time were like a death knell, piercing the air loud enough to send birds flying into the sky, calling out a warning as they did so. Jono gritted his teeth against the sound, still frantically trying to get eyes on Patrick.

The Sluagh faded away into a darker mist that was overtaken by the one surrounding them. The trees solidified around them, leaves a deep teal green, with magenta-colored blossoms. The hawthorn trees interspersed between others were the same size and shape as on the mortal plane, but their coloring was eerie and unreal beyond the veil. The strange mist drifted around white-barked trunks, obscuring the deeper parts of the forest. Jono scrambled to his feet and opened his mouth—

And hunched over as something *snapped* in his chest.

He would've fallen to his knees if Sage hadn't gotten her shoulder underneath him and kept him upright, grip tight with worry.

"Jono, what's wrong?" she asked.

He sucked in a breath that tasted like flowers he'd never smelled before, the soulbond burning in his soul. All Jono wanted to do was chase after Patrick, but he couldn't get his bearings. He couldn't tell if Patrick was alive or dead, and that scared him more than he was willing to admit, so used to being able to feel where Patrick was through the soulbond. But here past the veil, whatever magic lived in this place was interfering in a way Jono didn't care for.

Jono steeled himself against the ache, not wanting to worry Sage any more than he already had, but it was difficult to do with the way his heart pounded in his chest.

"Patrick's gone," Jono said, the words like acid on his tongue.

"*Shit.*"

The sound of hooves thudding against the ground made them look over at a path cutting through the strange trees that hadn't been there before. Fae in armor he'd seen before in the scrying crystal cantered their way on ethereal-looking horses. Gerard and Keith picked themselves off the ground, and that's when Jono realized they were missing more than Patrick.

"Where's Wade?" he asked, hands tightening into fists.

Sage stiffened, her eyes darting from side to side as she craned her head around. "I don't see him."

The lead rider pulled up short, the horse planting its feet hard against the dirt in front of their broken group. The rider stared at them with golden eyes, half her face covered by an intricate gold mask that connected to a helmet adorned with filigree in the same design of thorny roses.

"My Lord Cú Chulainn, the Spring Queen bids we escort you home," the rider said in a melodious voice.

"Cuckoo *what?*" Keith demanded, staring at Gerard in shock.

And *oh*, that was a revelation Jono knew would gut Patrick if he were still there to witness it.

PATRICK HIT THE TREE HARD ENOUGH TO DRIVE THE AIR OUT OF HIS lungs, pain radiating through his back. He slid down to the cold ground, fighting for breath.

Next time, I need to remember to shield the ground.

He hadn't expected the attack to come from below, and Patrick would kick himself later for that, as soon as he could breathe again. A blur of movement had him bringing up his arm, magic sparking at his fingertips. His concentration broke when the spider fae grabbed him by the throat and pinned him against the tree. Patrick's head spun from the hit, and all he could make out was the iridescent green of the fae's eyes as he struggled to get air into his lungs.

"Patrick!" Wade frantically yelled.

Patrick yanked free his dagger and stabbed the fae in the side of its human torso. Skin gave easily beneath the matte-black blade, the smell of burning flesh reaching Patrick's nose. The fae screamed, its fingers loosening from around his throat as it jerked away, sliding off the blade. Blood dripped down his hand, making his grip slick. The fae stumbled backward on its spider legs before being wrenched around and tossed aside by Wade. Patrick stared up into Wade's wide, frightened eyes, trying to get his bearings.

He drew in breath, trying to keep his heartbeat steady. Worse than the newly acquired bruises and aches was the realization that while he could feel the soulbond, he couldn't sense Jono.

"I don't see the others," Wade said, a tremor in his voice.

Patrick coughed, using the tree to drag himself back to his feet. Red scales had crawled up Wade's neck, curling over his jaw, a sign of his fear and lack of control. Wade could maintain his human shape as if it were instinctual, but he had a difficult time doing so when panicked fear was all his brain could process. It hadn't happened often since August, and they were still helping him work on his control.

Patrick shifted position to stand in front of Wade, putting himself between the teen and the Sluagh still circling them. Heavenly magic trailed through the air after his dagger as Patrick raised the blade between himself and the Sluagh. His leather jacket was pulled back against his shoulders a little as Wade clenched his hands around the charmed material.

"Don't shift," Patrick said. His voice came out a little rough, and he coughed to clear it. "I'm not going anywhere."

Wade's grip tightened even more. Patrick held himself still when Wade pressed his forehead to the back of Patrick's shoulder, trembling hard.

Should've left him with Emma's pack.

Too late for regrets now.

Patrick expanded his shields to encase Wade, wincing at the dull throb in his head as he did so. He conjured up a mageglobe, filling it with a strike spell, the command trigger a half-formed whisper in the back of his mind. Around them, the trees had changed to a barren ghostly forest that wasn't part of Central Park. Snow covered everything, from the dirt they stood on to the gnarled trees that seemed to move of their own accord.

The thick mist couldn't hide the Sluagh as the Unseelie fae

surrounded them. The Sluagh held their position, and Patrick didn't like what that meant at all. He sank his fingers into the mageglobe, adrenaline coursing through his veins.

"If you think we cannot counter the spell you are about to cast, then you would be wrong. Tír na nÓg is not kind to those who harm its children."

The voice had an accent that reminded Patrick of the people who lived in the Gaeltacht regions of Ireland, where the old ways were still practiced. He'd done a joint mission there with the *Sciathán Fiannóglaigh an Airm* once before during his early days with the Hellraisers. It had given Patrick a healthy dose of wariness when it came to dealing with the fae of either Court.

"If you think I won't try, then you don't know me," Patrick ground out.

The Sluagh parted, restless dead and solidly alive fae stepping aside to allow a tall figure to walk forward. The Unseelie *duine sídhe* fae was lean beneath the black leather and gray steel armor he wore that Patrick could only wish was made out of iron. His long white hair was paler than his skin, while his eyes were the color of a storm on the horizon. The fae carried a halberd in one hand etched with symbols Patrick couldn't read. They glowed softly through the mist, the feel of fae magic grating against his shields.

The mist rolled behind the Sluagh, drifting around large shadows that solidified into creatures standing at least eight feet in height. Huge, broad-shouldered, and carrying the stench of old blood with them, the group of Unseelie fae made a half circle around the one with the halberd, their own battle-axes nearly as tall as Patrick.

Their green-brown skin was as wrinkled as a walnut. Their faces were square in shape, with large hooked noses and lipless mouths. Deep-set eyes were pitch-black, no sclera showing at all. Shoulder-length black hair shimmered a dark blue green, like an oil slick on water.

Every last one of them wore a red cap that fit snug to their heads, the fabric of the headpiece lifting away into a long, curved point weighed down by a skull. Blood smeared over skin where the red cap's tight brim dug into their heads, dampening their hair with the ever-present blood in the fabric.

Patrick's grip tightened on his dagger, his heart pounding in his chest. Red Caps were some of his least favorite fae to deal with.

The fae with the halberd raised his free hand and gestured at the Sluagh. The screams that pierced the air as the restless dead scattered by silent command made Patrick wince. It didn't make him feel as if the odds had gotten any better.

"Draw down your magic," the fae said.

"And if I don't?" Patrick shot back.

"You are far past the veil, and there is no one here who will aid you."

"He's got me," Wade said, sounding a little nervous but never letting Patrick go.

The fae smiled, the coldness in his stormy eyes making Patrick tense. "You are not enough in our home."

Patrick rather thought Wade could be, but he didn't want to test the teen's limits. Wade had done enough fighting in his short life. If Patrick could spare him any more, he would, even when the teen was willing.

The mist rolled again as more Red Caps appeared, coming out from the tree line to surround them. Patrick eyed the new reinforcements, counting up the enemy and coming away with the uneasy knowledge he wouldn't be able to take them all down. Even if by some out-there chance he did, there was no leaving Tír na nÓg without help from the fae to open the hawthorn path. He doubted the Unseelie fae lord standing in front of them would do it even under duress.

They were *stuck* here, beyond the veil, in the hands of the Unseelie Court.

If Patrick were alone, he might be tempted to test out how

badly Persephone wanted him kept alive by trying to fight the Red Caps. Wade's rapid, scared breathing behind him killed that idea. Right now, his first priority had to be Wade.

As much as Patrick was worried about the others, he couldn't focus on them. Patrick didn't know where Jono and the rest had gone, but he hoped they'd made it to the Seelie Court. One of them needed to get information about Órlaith so they could stop the Dominion Sect and get her back.

The fae lord took a step forward, raising the heavy halberd in his hands. "Draw down your magic."

Patrick flexed his fingers before finally doing as ordered, pulling his magic back into his soul. Taking a deep breath, Patrick locked down his personal shields as tight as they would go, his bones aching from them. He didn't lower his dagger.

"Hand over your artifact," the fae demanded.

"Come and take it," Patrick said, tightening his grip.

It came out as a threat, and the fae took it as one. Roots shot up from the earth, wrapping around Patrick's wrists and ankles. Patrick was yanked to the ground and would've caught himself with his face if Wade hadn't wrapped his arms around Patrick's waist and refused to let go.

The tension in his spine was so sharp it made every vertebrae hurt, as if it were going to snap in half. The delicate bones in his wrists grated together, rough roots scraping over his skin. Patrick's hand spasmed, fingers forced apart, and the dagger fell from his grip. Wade was quick to snatch it out of reach of a tree root, holding it tight without getting burned, which was a miracle in itself. Patrick knew how dangerous the dagger could be for those with ties to the preternatural world. It seemed Wade's immunity to magic included weapons forged by gods.

Good to know.

Wade slashed at the roots with the dagger, the blade slicing through them like butter. The roots around Patrick's ankles spasmed as if in pain before releasing him to disappear back into the ground. Patrick shoved himself upright, ignoring the ache in his joints and rib cage. Wade hung off him like a limpet, still clutching the dagger.

"I'm keeping the dagger," Wade announced in a firm, if slightly higher-pitched voice. Patrick side-eyed him, noticing that his eyes were no longer brown, but gold with reptilian slits.

The fae stared at him, eyes narrowing, and Patrick wondered if he knew what Wade really was the same way Gerard had. He thought that might be the case when no one rushed them to fight Wade for the weapon. Maybe the fae could see auras of those with a preternatural bent better than a human could.

"If the blade finds its way into the mage's hands, I will cut them off," the fae promised.

Wade said nothing to that, which Patrick was grateful for. He rather liked having all his body parts attached.

The fae closed the distance between them, booted feet crunching over the snow. He was tall, taller than Jono, and Patrick had to tilt his head back to look him in the eye. Patrick refused to give ground to the fae, no matter how badly Wade trembled against him. That was a show of weakness they couldn't afford.

Patrick tensed when the fae reached for him, having a split-second flashback to Tremaine and Tezcatlipoca in the Crimson Diamond. Then his brain caught up to the fact it was Wade behind him, and the fae didn't touch him beyond what it took to remove his pistol from the holster on his hip. Patrick let him, because he could lose a gun so long as he still had his dagger—even if he had no idea what Wade had done with it.

The fae clenched his hand around the pistol, his strength enough to crunch the metal into a shape that had no hope of firing off a bullet. He dropped the broken pistol to the ground and kicked it aside.

"That was my favorite gun," Patrick said. It was his only gun at the moment, and if he didn't think using his magic would get them instantly murdered, he'd go for a spell right now.

Except he kind of liked living, and Patrick knew Jono would kill him if he died.

"The Sluagh say you smell of the girl," the fae said.

"I don't know what you're talking about."

The fae's gauntleted hand slammed against the side of Patrick's face, snapping his head around hard enough to make his ears ring. Bruising heat coursed through his jaw, blood filling his mouth from where he'd bitten through his tongue. Patrick spat out blood and wiped a trickle off his split lip with the back of his hand.

"Queen Medb is expecting you, Patrick."

The winter cold had nothing on the ice that poured down his spine. "I never gave you my name. Get it out of your mouth."

The fae's smile was thin and mocking. "There is no secret the Queen of Air and Darkness does not know, and that includes names."

Patrick had to wonder if they knew his real name, the one he'd been born with, and whether Medb had learned it when he was born or if Ethan had told her. Both possibilities made him want to drink until he could forget.

"Yeah, well, I don't know yours."

The fae didn't offer it up, not that Patrick expected him to. Tonguing at his teeth to make sure they were all accounted for, if a little loose in spots, Patrick spat out some more blood right between the fae's feet.

"Your hospitality is shit," Patrick said, slurring the words a little.

The fae pulled a pair of silver and onyx bracelets from the leather handbag hanging from his belt. They pulsated with a sickly feel of magic, feeling like salt in a wound the way it grated against Patrick's shields.

"Your hands, or your companion will be a guest here, always," the fae said.

"Patrick, don't," Wade said, his grip tightening on Patrick's arm. "I can fight them."

Patrick glanced over his shoulder at Wade, not seeing the dagger anywhere. Patrick wasn't about to ask where it'd gone, trusting in Wade's thieving ways to keep it safe when he couldn't. Wade, for all the stubborn clenching of his jaw, still looked like a scared kid in Patrick's eyes.

"You shouldn't have to," Patrick told him, in as kind a voice he could manage while backed into a proverbial corner by the enemy.

Patrick extended his hands, even though he didn't want to. The fae snapped the silver and onyx bracelets around Patrick's wrists and—

He went numb.

Foreign magic sank into his skin, down to his bones and soul, fighting against the shields Persephone had layered into his body over the years. Patrick drew a breath that tasted of metal but nothing else. The world dulled around him, sound an echo in his ears rather than all encompassing. The winter chill lessened to something he didn't think much about, which Patrick knew was dangerous, but he couldn't find it in him to care.

He couldn't reach his magic.

The binding was subtle in its makeup, sinister in its application, and Patrick had to force down his fear. He shoved it down deep, relying on old SERE training to find his balance again in the face of a crippling situation. He needed to not panic, because his life wasn't the only one on the line.

The bracelets shrank down until they sat flush against his wrist before twisting and moving up his forearms as if they were vines. Patrick's hands spasmed when a hundred tiny needles pricked his skin at the exact same time. He scratched at the twists of silver and specks of onyx, but they couldn't be dislodged.

"You smell different," Wade said, his voice no louder than a whisper in Patrick's ears. He had a feeling that wasn't really the case.

"Magic," Patrick muttered, struggling to concentrate against a sudden creeping exhaustion that weighed him down. "Not mine."

"Yeah, I can smell *that*." Wade tugged at Patrick's arm. "What if I eat them?"

"The Red Caps will probably give you indigestion. Remember what I said about food offered by the fae and not eating it?"

Wade grumbled something Patrick couldn't make out. Most of his attention was focused on the fae lord who had bound Patrick's magic. Concentrating was going to be a problem. Having to work harder to hear and see everything around him was going to give Patrick a headache before too long.

The fae lord turned on his heel and walked away. "Bring them."

Several Red Caps stepped forward with a menacing look on their ugly faces, hefting their axes in big, scarred hands. Wade's grip tightened painfully on Patrick's arm. Patrick didn't say anything. He merely pulled Wade forward, their feet crunching through the snow as the Red Caps surrounded them, with the fae lord leading the way.

Patrick pressed a hand to his chest, fingers rubbing against the wool of his sweater. He could barely feel it, and his arms seemed weighed down by the silver and onyx bracelets that had effectively muzzled his magic. The exhaustion weighing down his body was as much a kind of shackle as the bracelets.

Patrick knew it was all in his head, that the fae magic embedded in the bracelets was causing the muffled dullness between his brain and body, and the rest of the world, but that didn't make it any easier to accept.

He hated not being able to react to a threat in a quick manner, and that was the corner he was backed into.

They were marched down the snowy path for an indeterminate amount of time. Patrick could barely make out the gray sky above through the twisted branches of trees growing close together. He could hear the Sluagh even if he couldn't see them. The restless dead soared somewhere above in the clouds that blocked out the sunlight.

Wade walked close beside him, his arm constantly brushing

Patrick's in a self-soothing sort of way. Patrick didn't mind, preferring to have Wade within arm's reach. He might not have his magic, and his dagger might not be immediately available, but he'd be damned if he let something happen to Wade on his watch.

The only other sound in the cold, heavy quiet that filled the strange forest was everyone's breathing and the thud of feet sinking into snow. Patrick didn't bother to try to track where they were going—this was Tír na nÓg, after all.

Underhill.

Annwn.

All the old names for this land beyond the veil crossed Patrick's mind, but no matter the name it carried, the Otherworld was home to the fae of both Courts. It would always be dangerous.

The trees thinned out after a while. In the distance, large branches of a single tree rose into the sky, empty of leaves. The path widened, eventually merging into a meadow where nothing grew, and in the center was a massive dead tree that could've rivaled a skyscraper in height.

Patrick thought the white of the ground in the meadow was snow until he stepped on it and his boots crunched over bone. He looked down, seeing white bone dust drift across his black combat boots. Walking over the dead sent a shiver down Patrick's spine.

"Gross," Wade said. "Not a hoard I'd ever choose."

"Do I need to inspect your apartment when we get home?" Patrick asked.

Wade slanted Patrick a look, chewing on his bottom lip. "No?"

Patrick made a mental note to do just that—because they were leaving Tír na nÓg before too much time passed them by on the mortal plane. He had to believe that.

Up ahead, the tree bark looked as if it moved, until Patrick realized creatures clung to the dead tree. The closer they got, the clearer they became. Long limbs, thin torsos, with hooked claws for fingers, the goblins clung to the dead tree like monkeys, watching them as they approached.

The Red Caps moved into marching lines on either side of them, with the fae lord taking point. No one spoke, and Patrick kept his eyes on the crack in the tree up ahead. The darkness was made of shadows that seemed to move, and not from a trick of the light. The tree might be dead, but something lived inside it.

Wade leaned in close, nearly tripping over a femur bone as he did so. "Are you sure you don't want me to eat them?"

"No eating the enemy."

Besides, Patrick wanted to know why Medb hadn't simply ordered them killed on sight. In his experience, it was never a good thing when the gods wanted you kept alive.

Patrick reached for Wade, taking the teen's hand in his own gloved one. He didn't want to risk being separated where they were going. Wade seemed to settle slightly at the touch, his fingers grasping at Patrick's and not letting go.

"I need you to do what I tell you to, okay?" Patrick asked, forcing the words out around a numb tongue.

Wade nodded, nothing sulky or reluctant in the gesture at all. Patrick breathed a quiet sigh of relief. They wanted Wade to have his independence, but he still needed to be looked after, whether he liked it or not. At eighteen, he was still emotionally younger than that, the trauma he'd been through coloring a lot of his choices and actions. Therapy helped, but so did having control of his own life, and Patrick didn't want to take that away from him completely. In a situation like this though, he needed to.

The crack in the dead, ancient tree was the height of a three-story building, and as wide as a large house. The goblins on its trunk and branches scuttled about; Patrick's skin crawled from their unceasing attention.

The sound of a bird cawing in the distance made Patrick look up at the sky. He could see the clouds easier now, the Sluagh circling overhead like the start of a tornado. Flying lazily between the treetops at the edge of the meadow and the low-hanging clouds were two small specks that winged ever closer.

The birds cawed again, the sound echoing strangely in the air. It reminded Patrick of the ravens perched atop Grand Central Terminal back in August. He narrowed his eyes, trying to get a better look, but everything was a little blurry in the distance due to the binding.

The Sluagh screamed a warning, the restless dead that made up their ranks flying toward the ravens.

"This is not their home," the fae lord said to the goblins as he stepped into the depths of the dead tree. "Keep them away."

Patrick didn't think the fae was talking about them. He managed one last look at the ravens flying through the air before a Red Cap shoved the flat of his war axe against his back, shoving Patrick forward.

"Move," the Red Cap growled.

They moved, stepping into a darkness that seemed all-encompassing. Patrick couldn't see what was right in front of him, though that didn't last long. The blade on the fae lord's halberd started to glow with a dull yellow light. He banged the butt of the pole weapon against the ground three times, the sound echoing in the dark around them.

Slowly, pinpricks of light started to form, the glow a soft bioluminescence rather than fire. The interior walls of the dead tree became streaked with light in various blues and white that moved. It took a moment for Patrick's eyes to adjust before he realized that the lights were soft bulges on the backs of giant beetles the size of his head, their hard-shelled wings spread to reveal their own light source.

They crawled around the sides of the tree and the dirt floor overrun with roots. In the center, carved stone blocks had been adhered together to form pillars that extended into walls which connected to the tree. Hanging between them was a set of double doors made entirely out of bones and eyes that blinked against the light. The lock was set inside what looked like a mouth full of teeth.

Patrick watched as the bones shifted on the doors, pulling the mouth higher until it sat at the fae lord's head height. Patrick didn't think the door was alive like a human was, but he couldn't tell what sort of magic powered it, not with his own bound.

"I think it's unfair you won't let me eat them and that thing is gonna eat us," Wade muttered.

Patrick squeezed his hands. "It's not going to eat us."

He hoped.

The fae lord stepped up to the door and leaned forward. The mouth moved a little against the bones, and Patrick tried not to think about what was happening. A few seconds later, the fae lord stepped back, half turning to address the Red Caps. Wade made a gagging sound, and Patrick couldn't blame him.

Tentacles curled out from between the fae's lips, moving in the air. As they watched, the fae sucked them back inside his mouth, but Patrick was never going to get that sight out of his brain.

"Guard the entrance," the fae lord ordered.

The Red Caps turned and headed for the crack in the tree to stand guard outside in the meadow. Patrick didn't move, not even when the bone doors opened, the mouth still moving even as it was split apart. The fae spun the halberd in his hands, pointing the blade at them.

"Move, or I will make you move."

Patrick figured that would consist of a lot of spilled blood, so he gripped Wade's hand hard and walked through the open doors.

On the other side was a stone corridor lit by will-o'-the-wisps that hovered in the air above them. The light followed them down the sharply sloping corridor that led underground. Patrick bit the inside of his cheek, using the pain to remind himself that this wasn't New York, and there were no vampires here.

He half thought about sneaking his dagger back from Wade, but his reaction times were shit at the moment. Patrick set aside his desire for murder in favor of surviving another hour.

They walked until they came out on a rocky terrace that overlooked a vast cavern. The air didn't smell much better. Beams of weak sunlight filtered down through the huge underground space from holes up above, revealing stalagmites and moss-covered boulders rising out of a subterranean lake. The terrace they were on connected to a granite pathway that led down to the cave floor.

If they weren't being held prisoner, Patrick might think the place was beautiful, but he knew the fae of either court were never all that they seemed.

Something splashed down below in the lake water, a large shadow coming to the surface before disappearing again. Patrick thought they were being watched, but he couldn't pinpoint from where.

"You go first," the fae lord said.

Patrick tugged Wade after him, not liking having the enemy at his back but unable to do anything about it. He wished they had more light to see where they were going, but the will-o'-the-wisps had floated closer to the roof of the cavern rather than the floor. Rocks rolled beneath his boots a couple of times on the trek down, but Patrick managed to keep his balance. They made it to the floor of the cavern, and the fae lord took the lead again, striding toward the single row of rocks that spanned the length of the lake.

The spine of something too large to be a fish rolled above the surface near a clutch of stalagmites in the center of the dark water before disappearing back into the watery depths. The fae paid the creature no mind, and Patrick wished he could do the same.

"If it eats me, I'm biting my way out of its stomach," Wade whispered.

"Stay close," Patrick told him.

They followed the fae onto that stone pathway, and Patrick had to let Wade's hand go in order to traverse the lake. Some of the stones were close together, others required a bit of a jump, and Patrick knew that if they fell into the water, they'd be dinner for what lived in the lake. With his magic bound, it took all of Patrick's concentration to make it across. Once or twice he nearly lost his balance, arms windmilling until Wade steadied him.

When they made it to the other side, Patrick let out a harsh breath of relief, unsurprised when Wade immediately latched onto his hand again. Wade stayed close as they walked deeper into the cavern, the path snaking underground, past stalagmites, pillars of quartz crystal, and sheared smooth granite cave walls until they reached a tunnel.

This one seemed carved out of quartz crystal, their reflections in the walls distorted shadows. In the far distance, a pinprick of light grew and grew until it became a way out. The tunnel opened onto a bridge built of stone that connected the cave system they'd traversed to a castle built atop a lone mesa rising from a foggy canyon. Patrick couldn't see the bottom and wasn't sure he wanted to.

The bridge they walked on wasn't the only one connected to the castle from some distant point. There were other bridges, with distant figures heading toward the place that housed the Unseelie Court.

Something heaved itself up from the cliffside, the creature bigger than the Red Caps. It wore no clothing, its skin pebbled like rocks, with bits of moss pressed into the creases of its elbows and over its skull in lieu of hair. It carried a club made from a downed tree, which it slammed down between them and the bridge. The earth shook beneath their feet, and Patrick hoped they weren't all about to go crashing down into the canyon.

"Who dares to pass?" the troll asked in a deep voice. Its breath smelled of dead things, and its teeth looked rotten in its mouth.

The fae lord pointed his halberd at the troll. "You know me and the favor I carry."

The troll grunted, raising its club, its earth-dark eyes staring at Patrick. "Proceed."

"Okay, I wouldn't eat him. I'd get food poisoning," Wade whispered.

Patrick pulled him forward after the fae lord, the bridge covered in a light dusting of snow. The wind that blew through the canyon was ice-cold, howling around them. It made Patrick wish he still had his beanie, but he'd lost it during the fight. Even the heat charms in his leather jacket weren't quite enough to counter the cold in Tír na nÓg.

The castle loomed up ahead, made of black stone, carved granite, and bone. The troll on the other side raised its head to peer at them over the railings of the bridge but otherwise didn't challenge them. The double doors that led into the castle were like the ones in the tree—made of bones and blinking eyes, with a mouth that needed to be kissed to grant passage. The fae lord did so willingly, and the doors opened.

They stepped inside, the chill of winter following them into the castle. Strange fae watched them as they walked: hags with feet damp from river water, goblins with twisted limbs, and gnomes with mouths full of sharp teeth. Creatures Patrick couldn't see scuttled in the shadows, while the distant wail of banshees echoed through the castle. Here and there were fae in the shape of the one who escorted them through the castle: tall and beautiful in a cold, empty way.

They were led to the throne room of the Unseelie Court, where weak sunlight shone down through a glass dome ceiling. The floor was made of onyx, rising up into a dais that cradled a throne. The throne itself was carved from a barren tree whose roots spread across the dais, clinging to the edges. Thorny vines twisted over the armrests and the high back of the throne, their thorns red with blood.

The heart of the Unseelie Court was its queen, and Medb was terrifyingly beautiful.

She wore a patchwork dress made out of the skin of dead enemies, each piece sewn together with silver thread. Her own skin was as pale as the snow falling outside, making her dark eyes look like black holes in her face. Her ash-colored hair fell across her shoulders in thick waves, held in place by a crown made out of fingerbones. Around her slender throat was a string of eyes—different shapes, sizes, and colors—that moved out of sync with each other, looking at everything and nothing all at once.

Everyone back on the mortal plane believed the fae—especially the *daoine sídhe* of either Court—were the epitome of beauty. In reality, the fae were made of half-truths masquerading as lies, though they would never admit it.

The fae lord came to a stop and banged the metal-capped end of his halberd against the floor, the sound echoing loudly in the throne room.

"I bring you the mortal you requested, my queen," the fae lord said.

The Queen of Air and Darkness smiled in a way that made Patrick want to hide, preferably in a place where the nightmares couldn't find him.

"Such a gift you have given me, Cairbre," Medb said, her voice smooth like honey on a poisonous tongue. "Ethan's firstborn son."

"Man, your dad sucks," Wade said.

Patrick choked on a weak laugh, refusing to flinch beneath Medb's gaze. "Yeah."

Even across the veil, Patrick couldn't escape his father's messes.

"I'M TIRED OF WAITING," JONO SAID.

He stared at the cherry-red double door carved with animal reliefs and what he would call Celtic knotwork, but didn't know what the fae referred to it as. The entrance to what he assumed was a throne room of some type had been closed to them ever since their arrival at the palace built out of stone and living trees in a strangely colored forest.

Two armored fae carrying spears that smelled of magic to his nose guarded the entrance. Jono figured he could take them.

"I would advise not rushing the door," Sage said.

"And I would advise they open it before I tear it down."

They'd been waiting in the antechamber for what seemed like hours, their weapons having been confiscated, though the fae had left everyone their mobiles. That was time wasted when he could've been searching for Patrick. The soulbond was muted in his soul, giving up no hint of Patrick's whereabouts. Jono wasn't sure if it was due to them being past the veil, or something worse. Having to sit here and wait wasn't doing his temper any good.

"Right. We're going to have that chat," Jono decided.

He strode toward the doors, unsurprised when the guards crossed their spears to block his way. Jono bared his teeth at them, fangs pricking his lips.

"You have not been summoned," one of the guards said.

"We've been sitting on our arses out here long enough. Your queen will see me."

The fae guard to his right stared at him through a gilded mask that connected to a helmet. His shoulder-length hair was poppy-colored, while his eyes were the color of amber.

"You will stand down."

"Sure thing, mate."

Jono grabbed both spears and wrenched them out of the guards' hands. He tossed the weapons behind him, out of reach, and ducked under the blade of a short sword that sought to take off his head. The blade bit into the wooden door, and Jono lashed out with one foot, catching the guard on his left in the stomach.

The fae was knocked backward into the wall, the stone there cracking from the impact. Jono jumped clear of the back slice from the short sword, using preternatural speed to get beneath the other fae's arm to grab him by the throat. His fingers dented the metal collar protecting the fae's throat.

"Uh, I don't think killing the guy will help us get an audience," Keith said.

Fenrir bit at Jono's mind, scratching at his soul. Rather than fight the god, Jono let him in, just enough that his senses ratcheted up higher than they ever had before outside summer solstice.

The fae's eyes widened behind his mask, stiffening in Jono's grip. Magic coiled in his right hand, but Jono had learned a thing or two about magic since meeting Patrick. He slammed the guard's head against the door, denting the metal and knocking the fae unconscious.

"This was *not* the first impression we wanted to give them," Sage hissed when she came up to his side.

"I don't care," Jono replied.

Soft giggles from the ceiling made them look up. Pixies darted above them, making lazy loop patterns in the air, their wings glowing softly.

"Welcome, wolf," they singsonged. "Oh, welcome, Vánagandr."

Jono growled, the sound coming from his throat, but the resonance was all Fenrir. The immortal didn't seem to care for one of his names on their tongues.

"Vana what now?" Keith said.

Sage stared at Jono with narrowed eyes, her mouth twisted into a frown. "Jono? Why did they call you that?"

He didn't answer her. Fenrir clawed at his mind as he gripped the rose-gold handles of the doors and shoved them open. He put all his strength behind the push, ignoring the way the metal burned his hands with magic. Fenrir made it so that it didn't hurt, and the burns would heal in moments anyway.

The doors slammed open, the noise they made when they hit the wall loud enough to cause all conversation in the throne room to stop. A sea of faces turned to look at them. The *daoine sídhe* of the Seelie Court carried a beauty that didn't catch Jono's eyes at all.

The pixies flew through the air in front of him, diving down to help part the crowd, their dragonfly- and butterfly-like wings fluttering rapidly. The fae stepped aside, eyeing him with collective disdain as Jono passed. A ring of guards encircled the dais with its throne, blocking his way. Arrayed behind them was a group of fae dressed far more grandly than anyone else in the room save their queen.

Gerard—or Cú Chulainn, if that's what he wanted to go by—was the odd bloke out where he stood off to the side of that posh group, glaring at Jono with a resigned look on his face. He hadn't changed into any fancy robes or armor, still wearing the clothes he'd put on that morning.

"You couldn't have waited a little longer?" Gerard asked.

"Not in the mood to wait. We've spent too long here past the veil, and I need to find Patrick and Wade," Jono retorted.

He kept walking, smelling the shield he couldn't see that stood against the spear tips pointed at him from the guards. Fenrir howled in his mind, blocking out all sound for a second or two. Jono flexed his hands, claws cutting through skin, and he knew he'd have no trouble getting through that shield.

Fae magic would not stand against a god's wrath.

Brigid must have known that, for the Spring Queen stood from her golden throne and lifted one slim hand at the warriors who guarded her.

"Let them pass," Brigid ordered in a melodious voice.

Her accent reminded Jono of Ireland, but it wasn't quite what he was used to—older, different, but still similar enough for him to recognize the cadence.

The fae guards didn't hesitate to obey, though the high-ranking warriors behind them were reluctant to move. As one, the guards shifted ranks, providing space for Jono, Sage, and Keith to pass through. He refused to go around the *daoine sídhe* who remained in his way, shouldering them aside when they wouldn't move.

Once he reached the bottom of the flower-covered dais, Jono planted his feet wide and stared up at the ruler of the Seelie Court, refusing to bow his head.

Brigid's hair was the color of the sun at dawn, with licks of living fire burning at the tips of the long red curls. Her eyes were the dark blue of water in a well, deep and fathomless, full of power Jono only ever saw in the eyes of other immortals. She stood tall, dressed in a flowing green gown cinched in at the waist with a belt made of gold chain. A cape made out of flower blossoms cascaded down her back and pooled at her feet, carrying the scent of spring. A crown of hawthorn flowers woven through a twisted filigree of silver and gold encircled her head, the white blossoms bright against her hair.

Jono smiled, revealing sharp fangs, and let his soul crack open.

Fenrir poured through Jono's mind, his body, stealing all the breath in his lungs and filling up his soul. This time, Jono didn't fight it. All of Jono's senses became heightened, his thoughts weighed down by Fenrir's power. The god stared through his eyes at the immortal burning like fire before them.

"Cousin," Jono said, Fenrir's voice coming past his lips as a growl more reminiscent of teeth scraping against bone, his own accent gone. "It has been an age."

"Fenrir Lokisson," Brigid said, her voice like the crackle of fire in Jono's ears now. "You have not granted patronage in centuries. What brings you to my Court uninvited?"

"Ah, but we were invited. On the word of Cú Chulainn no less."

"Cú Chulainn has spent too long in the mortal world. Hospitality is not served through lies."

"There is no lie when none has been spoken. The halfling knew not of my patronage." Fenrir spread Jono's hands, mouth twisting into a smile Jono knew wasn't his. "We fight on the same side, cousin. Against an enemy who has wronged us. Would you deny me and mine an audience merely because anger clouds your judgment?"

Brigid stepped down from the dais, a figure of fire and power in Jono's eyes. She reached the floor to stand in front of him, as tall as he was, with a fierceness in her ancient eyes he would always be wary of.

"My granddaughter is missing, she who is the last remembrance I have of Ruadán. What do you hide from me where she is concerned?"

"Nothing. I know not where she is hidden."

"Yet you are here."

"This one who carries me is bound to the one Persephone owns. That one crossed the veil with Cú Chulainn because there is a soul debt he must pay. We followed. We always will."

"I know of whom you speak. I bled for the blade we all forged for him. He is not here."

"Not in your Court, no."

Brigid's eyes narrowed, her beautiful face like stone. "Medb has sent no messenger with demands."

"Do you think she who holds another's throne would be so kind as to give you a warning?"

To that, Brigid said nothing, and the quiet in the throne room was heavy in Jono's ears.

"The Sluagh and Wild Hunt wreak havoc in the mortal world. We lose time arguing here. Grant us passage through the hawthorn paths. Open the crossroads to us."

"And what do you expect in return?"

Fenrir's smile deepened, fangs catching at Jono's lips. *"You have already promised to fight. Your blood in the dagger was binding. I ask for nothing that you have not already given."*

"My warriors are enough without your interference."

"If that were true, then the Summer Lady would have been found by now."

"You *dare* insult me in my hearth and home?"

"Your warriors are long absent from the mortal plane. Few of your daoine sídhe *choose to reside in the iron cities that burn you. Those who do, they understand what is at risk better than your people who hide beyond the veil here in the Otherworld. Your Lord of Ivy and Gold understood that when he bargained with this one."*

"Tiarnán offered something he had no right to give."

"But he gave it, along with his word. A bargain made is a bargain kept, cousin."

Brigid stepped closer until she stood nose to nose with Jono and the god who inhabited his skin. She burned before him, heat from her body and soul scorching him like fire. Fenrir never closed Jono's eyes.

"The crossroads will find you. Do not enter my Court as you are without invitation again."

Fenrir said nothing to that demand, merely relinquished Jono's body and mind, burrowing deep into his soul again. Jono staggered backward, nearly losing his footing. He would have, if Gerard hadn't steadied him.

Jono shook his head, ears ringing, but that only made the

sudden headache worse. He winced and tilted his head back, his nerves feeling rawer than if he'd gone through a shift.

"Odin's wolf will burn out your soul. It is always the case for those who carry his favor," Brigid said.

Jono tipped his head back down, staring at the goddess before him with human eyes once again. She no longer burned like the sun in his eyesight.

"He chose me. I never went looking for him," Jono said.

"It is the ones who are looking who will never find the favor they yearn for." Brigid turned her head slightly to pin Gerard with her steely regard. "Órlaith chose you over all others I brought before her, Cú Chulainn. Find her, or Tír na nÓg will never welcome you home again."

Gerard bowed low to his queen and goddess. "By your will, my queen."

Gerard grabbed Jono's arm with a bruising grip, dragging him away from the dais. It took a few seconds for Jono to get his feet underneath him. By then, Sage and Keith had both joined them, the four of them marching out of the throne room and into the antechamber, where the guards from earlier had been replaced with new ones.

Gerard led them back the way they'd come, through wood and glass corridors, stairs made out of roots and stone, and rooms draped in flowers. The fae they came across on their way out stepped aside, gazes never leaving their small group. Jono steeled himself against the sensation of being watched, hoping it would disappear once they were outside.

They were given back their weapons at the entrance to the palace by a pair of dwarves. Gerard and Keith rearmed themselves, slinging the strap of their rifles over their shoulders.

"Interesting make, these are," one of the dwarves said.

"Humans may not be good at a lot of things, but they excel in warfare. I am glad you kept these safe," Gerard replied.

It wasn't thanks of any sort, because the fae considered thanks an insult. That, at least, Jono remembered. The dwarves bowed their heads and stepped aside.

"Good hunting, my lord," the other dwarf said.

They all stepped through the grand, carved wooden doors that were easily two stories high. In the garden courtyard outside, the fae astride giant stags who guarded the entrance hadn't moved. The palace itself sat atop a large hill, the path back to the forest easy to follow. The *caw* of birds in the sky above had Jono looking up, squinting against the bright sun. Two ravens glided through the air, circling them. Fenrir growled irritably in his mind.

Annoyances. Always, the god grumbled.

The names came to Jono through Fenrir, and he wondered what Huginn and Muninn were doing past the veil in a world that wasn't their pantheon's home. They belonged to Odin, after all.

"Does Patrick know what you carry in your soul?" Gerard asked, breaking the tense silence that had fallen upon them all after leaving the throne room of the Seelie Court.

"He knows," Jono replied. "He's going to be right pissed about you though."

Gerard's mouth twisted as he stared straight ahead as they walked. "It was never my intention to mislead anyone."

"Yeah, fuck that. You misled *all* of us," Keith said angrily from behind them. "I don't even know what to call you."

"I've always been Gerard to you. I gave you that name, Keith. We fae don't give out names lightly."

"Yeah, but you never gave us your *real* one. You're supposed to be our captain, but apparently, you're a god. What the fuck are we supposed to think about something like this?"

Gerard said nothing to that accusation, walking beside Jono with a forced-calm expression on his face.

"How long have you carried Fenrir in your soul, Jono?" Sage asked, her voice flat and nearly emotionless.

Jono could still smell her anger though, the scent of it sharp in his nose. She'd left her pendant back home before heading out with them, and her scent was a tangle of emotions between them. He knew this was an issue that was going to possibly strain some of his friendships.

"He's always been there, ever since the accident," Jono said slowly.

"Then why didn't you *tell* us? Why didn't you trust us?"

Jono made a face she couldn't see, grinding his teeth together. The pressure did nothing for the headache that still hadn't gone away. If this was how Marek felt every time the Norns spoke through him, no wonder he always wanted to lie down for a kip afterward.

"I do trust you, Sage."

"Clearly you don't if you and Patrick kept this a secret. You've had a god riding your soul for years. You could've challenged Estelle and Youssef well before now."

"I was never in a position to do so, even with Fenrir. Even now, we aren't there yet."

"You think we aren't? When is enough going to be enough? When do you get to decide that?"

"When it won't get all of us killed."

"Gods complicate things. They aren't always the answer," Gerard said.

"You're one to talk, Mr. Oh By The Way I'm Immortal," Keith said snidely.

Gerard sighed. "Technically, I'm half-mortal, Keith."

"The myths don't see it that way, and you've been worshipped as a god. You still have a godhead, like your fiancée," Sage pointed out. "Maybe you shouldn't be the one going after Ethan to get her back."

"I'll risk it."

"Better have a good bunker handy once we tell Patrick what you are," Keith snapped.

Gerard's jaw tightened, but he said nothing in response to that remark.

Their strides ate up ground until they were walking down a path lined by ancient trees, thick branches arching overhead and forming a living tunnel. Sunlight peeked through the gold-green leaves, tiny sunbeams highlighting strange plants around them. Pixies fluttered through the trees, fighting over nectar from flower blossoms with brilliantly plumed birds. Jono could no longer see Odin's ravens flying overhead, but he had a feeling they were still there.

The summer heat faded after a while, coinciding with an uptick in mist, the same sort that had rolled over the hawthorn path when they were separated hours earlier.

"We're approaching the crossroads," Gerard warned.

"What are they?" Sage wanted to know.

"A place in the hawthorn paths that leads to either Court. I was taking us to the Seelie Court as we came out of the veil when we were ambushed earlier."

High above, the ravens Jono couldn't see cawed a warning that made him rock to a stop. "Something's out there."

Gerard made a grabbing motion at the air, and his spear snapped into his hand out of nowhere. He hefted it in both hands, spinning it until the blade pointed in front of them.

"Spriggan," Gerard said after a moment. "Show yourself."

A tree down the way moved—then Jono realized it wasn't the tree moving, but a creature that looked like one. Its elongated body was made of tree bark, with branches sprouting from its head, each one covered in tiny leaves. Its eyes were like knotholes that didn't blink. When it smiled, its teeth were made of stone.

The spriggan bowed, the twigs that made up its fingers curling with the motion. "Cú Chulainn, I bid thee well."

"Who sent you?" Gerard demanded.

"Who sends anyone to anywhere?"

"I'm not in the mood for riddles, spriggan."

Jono flexed his hand, claws cutting through his skin. "Neither am I."

The spriggan walked forward in a gangly way, its long limbs giving it an almost swaying motion. "Peace, peace, Cú Chulainn. I come with an invitation."

"Whose?"

The spriggan spread its hands, smiling in a way that wasn't friendly at all. "Why, the queen's of course."

Jono and Gerard shared a look, both of them knowing the spriggan didn't mean Brigid.

Gerard spun his spear around, digging the metal-shod end of it into the earth. "Take us to her."

The spriggan beckoned at them, cackling all the while. "By all means. Follow me."

13

"I'M HUNGRY," WADE SAID.

Patrick didn't open his eyes. "Eat a protein bar."

"I did."

"Eat another one."

"I don't have any more." The sound of plates clinking together reached Patrick's ear, though he had to strain through the cottony feeling in his head to hear it. "Can't I have one of these things that looks like an apple?"

Patrick opened his eyes and turned his head, squinting at where Wade stood by the table in their tower room. The table was piled high with fruit he didn't recognize and slices of meat he had no idea what animal—if it *was* an animal—it came from. A pitcher of water and a decanter of wine sat in the center of the table.

Patrick ran his dry tongue against his teeth, mouth parched. "No eating or drinking anything the fae offer us."

Wade looked at him askance. "Is it an offering if it's just sitting here?"

"You've been spending too much time with Sage. Yes, it's still food given by the fae. Do you want to be stuck here for decades because you ate a fruit when you shouldn't have?"

"Like they could keep me."

"You didn't want to be kept before by Tezcatlipoca, and he still managed it," Patrick reminded Wade as gently as he could. "Medb is a goddess the same way Tezcatlipoca was a god. Don't eat the food, Wade."

Wade sighed loudly, but he stepped away from the table, which was all Patrick cared about. They'd been immediately imprisoned after being presented to Medb, who hadn't done much more than look at them before ordering them locked up.

Patrick closed his eyes again, too tired to do much more than shift his position on the chair that was the only piece of furniture in the room aside from the table. It was hard as a rock, but large enough that Patrick could sit with his legs slung over one of the arms while he leaned his aching head against the backrest.

The binding the bracelets had wrapped around him felt as if it was draining him of his magic when he knew that wasn't the case. It wasn't like when his magic was being eaten by a soultaker. This was more like it was shoved in a box, out of reach, while his strength was sucked dry.

Patrick was *tired*, and forced exhaustion was an insidious type of jail he'd break out of if he could. He scratched at the skin around the onyx and silver bracelets. The metal was warm—not enough to burn him, but enough for him to always know they were there. As if he needed a reminder when he couldn't reach his magic.

"Hey." A finger poked his cheek. "You awake?"

Patrick raised a hand and clumsily batted at Wade. "Yeah. I'm awake."

"You were snoring."

"I was not."

"Yes, you were."

Patrick rubbed at his face, dragging his eyes open with effort. "What do you want?"

Wade peered down at him and blinked a couple of times. "I think I hear Jono."

A jolt of adrenaline shot through Patrick's veins, giving him enough energy to sit up and swing his legs around. "What?"

Wade tipped his head to the side, nose wrinkling as he concentrated. "Pretty sure it's him. He's the only one I know who uses *fucking wanker* like it's going out of style when he's really angry and telling someone off."

Patrick stared at him. "You can hear him through magic and however many stone floors there are between us?"

"Yes?"

"Remind me to never have sex with Jono when you're crashing at our home."

Wade made a face. "*Gross.*"

Patrick still didn't know if Wade's abhorrence of intimacy was due to having experienced it negatively while enslaved by Tezcatlipoca, but he wasn't going to ever force Wade to talk about it. He only hoped the teen talked about it with his therapist.

"I can't hear a fucking thing. I thought they warded the room for silence?"

Wade shrugged. "Probably? Doesn't work on me."

If Patrick's brain didn't feel as if it had molasses running through his thoughts, he would've remembered that. "Shit. Okay. Can you tell if anyone is standing guard outside?"

"In the stairwell? No."

"Think you can open the door?"

Wade rolled his eyes. "Probably? You want me to break it down? I'd offer to pick the lock, but no way in hell am I kissing a door like that other guy with the tentacle mouth to get us out of here."

Patrick pinched his nose, trying to get his brain to work better. "You pick locks?"

"Pickpocket, remember? Locks are easy."

"If you get arrested for breaking and entering at any point going forward, I'm letting you sit in jail for a day to think about what you've done before I come get you."

"Jono would bail me out within an hour."

"Then he'll be sleeping on the couch. Break down the door, but try to be quiet about it."

Patrick pushed himself to his feet as Wade went to deal with the door. He wasn't sure if Wade could break them out of their tower prison, but anything was worth a shot at this point. Wade ran his hands over the wooden door, tapping his fingers in areas, before he braced his shoulder against the side the hinges were located on.

"Usually people go for the lock," Patrick said.

Wade made a face, gesturing at the lock and knob that didn't have a normal keyhole. "I think I saw a tongue. Fuck no am I getting up close and personal with it."

Wade shifted his weight, pressed one hand against the smooth wood, then rammed his shoulder against the door. Patrick wasn't expecting much to happen, so when the door ripped off the hinges and fell onto the landing with a loud bang, Wade on top of it, he winced.

"That was not quiet."

Wade shoved himself to his feet, a hint of red scales curling over his jaw. "Yeah, but we're free."

Patrick shook his head as he walked out of the room. "Your definition of free is very different than mine. Someone will have heard that."

Wade pouted. "But I got us out!"

Patrick patted him on the shoulder. "Yeah. You did good. Now let's see if we can't find Jono before the fae find us."

Patrick put those odds at *terrible* for them, but he didn't say as much to Wade. Mostly because the damn bracelets were messing with his magic, and his reaction time was for shit.

"Where's my dagger?" Patrick asked as they started down the winding staircase. Patrick needed to keep one hand on the wall to maintain his balance.

Wade had taken point, and he looked over his shoulder at Patrick. "It's, uh, hidden?"

"Wade."

"I didn't want them to take it, so I put it where the rest of me is."

Patrick blinked, because that sounded like mass shifting, and he knew dragons shifted differently than every other preternatural creature. "Come again?"

"It's safe, I promise."

"Tricky, tricky," something hissed from far below. "You aren't allowed to leave unless we let you."

Wade froze on the next step down, and Patrick ran into him. Wade barely moved from the impact, keeping them both upright. "Um. I guess they heard us."

Patrick carefully maneuvered down the steps until he stood in front of Wade. He wasn't in any capacity to really fight, but it was his job to protect Wade.

"Patrick," Wade said.

"Stay calm. Don't shift. We're in a tower. You'll bring it down on top of us if you do, so I *really* need you to not shift, okay?"

"Okay."

Patrick had to strain to hear what was coming up to meet them. He didn't fully hear it through the cottony feeling in his head until he saw the shadow stretching up the curved wall below. Patrick recognized the half-human, half-spider creature that came into view from that night in the Wisterias' nursery.

The fae grinned at them, spider legs clacking against the stairs. "The queen demands an audience."

"You know what? I think I'd rather stay in the room," Wade said slowly.

The fae opened its mouth wide, and Patrick tensed. He couldn't move fast enough to dodge the stream of spiderweb the fae spit out of its mouth. The sticky strands hit him smack in the chest, and Patrick was yanked down the stairs. He managed not to break his face by sheer luck, skidding down the stone steps and feeling every last one of them until he came to a stop against the fae's spider legs.

Before the fae could grab him, Wade was there, cutting the spider webbing with Patrick's dagger. The matte-black blade caused the fae to rear back, hissing frantically, all eight of its legs clattering on the steps. The dagger's magic never rose to the surface, and Patrick reached for it before he thought better of it. Then he yanked his hand back once he realized what he was doing.

Wade tried to hand it to him anyway. "Here."

Patrick shook his head, wincing at the soreness in his body. "No. Keep it until we're out of here."

"But—"

"Cairbre promised he'd cut off my hands if I held my dagger while we're here. Fae don't make promises lightly. I need you to keep it safe for now."

Wade scowled stubbornly, still brandishing the dagger at the fae farther down the stairs. Patrick got to his feet slowly, wincing at the bruising he knew was coming up on his body, even if he could barely feel it. Wade steadied him when he was finally upright, the both of them standing behind Patrick's dagger.

From down below, heavy, thudding footsteps vibrated through the stone. Wade's hand wavered, but he never dropped the dagger. "Patrick?"

"Don't fight, no matter what happens," Patrick said.

The smell of something rotten drifted up the tower stairs. Patrick swallowed against the smell, knowing it had to be bad if it smelled awful through the binding wrapped around him. Wade gagged, sounding as if he was about to puke.

The fae skittered up the wall, its eight legs clinging to the stone. It scuttled back out of sight, laughing at them, strands of spiderweb trailing from its mouth. The creature that took its place blocked the light from below. Being hunched over couldn't hide the ogre's height. It was taller than the Red Caps that had brought them to the palace, but that was where the similarities ended.

The ogre's shoulders were so broad they nearly touched the wall on either side of the tower stairs. It was barefoot, the pants it wore held in place by a thick leather belt that carried two wickedly sharp knives. Barrel-chested, with skin a muddy ochre, its chest was riddled with scars, and its flat, misshapen face wasn't much better.

Three eyes sat above its squashed nose. Each one sat at a different height on its skull, each a different color and blinking out of sync. Its teeth, when it smiled, were rotten, and its tongue was just as black. Its breath reminded Patrick of decomposing bodies.

"Okay, I'm not hungry anymore," Wade said.

"The queen wants to see you," the ogre growled in a deep voice.

Before Patrick could respond, the ogre grabbed him by the arm, moving quicker than he thought something that size could. The grip was like a vise, pressure bruising, and Patrick was yanked down the steps.

"Hey!" Wade shouted. "Let him go!"

Patrick banged his knee against the edge of a step, swearing when skin split and blood started trickling down his shin beneath his torn jeans. The ogre twisted around in the tight space, taking Patrick with him. Patrick managed to get his feet underneath him and staggered after the ogre at a pace he could barely keep up with through the fog in his brain.

When he would've lost his balance again, Wade grabbed him by the back of his leather jacket, keeping him upright. The ogre didn't stop, merely continued down the twisting stairs. Patrick did his best not to fall again and kept shooting Wade warning glances when it looked like the teen was contemplating where best to try to punch the ogre.

"No," he finally hissed. "Don't do anything stupid, Wade."

The stubborn look in Wade's eyes told Patrick the teen wanted to do exactly that, but he listened, for once, or seemed to.

The spider fae was waiting for them at the bottom of the tower. The ogre shoved open the heavy door, and the other fae skittered out of the way. It clattered down the cavernous hall they'd entered, eight legs clicking against the stone floor. Patrick's arm felt as if it were going to be wrenched from the socket from the way the ogre held him. Pain seeped through the muffled haze surrounding him, and he grimaced.

Patrick's gaze darted around the palace halls they were escorted down. Not that he thought they had a chance in hell of getting out on their own.

However long later, the ogre turned a corner and they entered a hallway he remembered from before. The doors at the far end were already open, and beside him, Wade perked up.

"That's *definitely* Jono," Wade said.

"Great," Patrick muttered.

They entered the throne room, the place lit by what looked like ice-white ball lightning that crackled on metal sconces. The glass dome above only showed a cloudy, starless night sky, and Patrick knew that wasn't good. Too much time they couldn't afford to lose had passed back on the mortal plane if it was night here already.

"Patrick."

Jono's voice cut through the fog in his brain like nothing else could. Patrick tore his gaze away from the glass dome to stare at where Jono, Sage, Gerard, and Keith stood before Medb's throne. As relieved as he was to see everyone, Patrick really only had eyes for Jono.

Something eased inside him, a tension he'd carried since the Sluagh appeared over Central Park fading away. There was a beat where his heart used to be that grew louder as he met Jono's gaze. For the first time in hours, it felt as if Patrick could breathe again now that Jono was here.

Jono took a determined step forward. The fae guards moved to block his way, spears crossing in front of him. Jono rocked to a halt, wolf-bright eyes blazing with anger. He looked one thought away from murder, and as much as Patrick wanted Jono by his side, he knew they couldn't afford to piss off Medb any more than they already had.

"It's okay. Just stay there, Jono," Patrick said.

Jono glared at him, as if silently arguing with that fact.

Patrick glanced around the throne room, seeing it had been cleared of everyone but Medb's most loyal fae and enough guards to skewer them all on pole weapons a couple of times over.

The ogre's grip shifted, and Patrick found himself being flung forward in the direction of the throne. He crashed to the onyx floor, managing to not hit face-first by virtue of Wade catching him by the shoulder before that happened.

"Thanks," Patrick muttered.

"He smells wrong," Jono said, looking at Patrick over the crossed spears of two Unseelie fae guards who had stopped him from moving closer. "What did you do to him?"

"You do not give the orders here, wolf," Medb said from her throne.

Patrick looked away from Jono to stare at Medb. The Queen of Air and Darkness sat tall on her throne, still in the patchwork dress of skin from earlier. She wasn't looking at him, but at Jono, the smile on her face promising nothing good.

Wade helped Patrick to his feet as the ogre took up position behind them, a deterrent to their friends from trying to get closer. Jono still sized the ogre up in a way Patrick knew was him looking to start a fight.

"We came to bargain in good faith," Gerard said.

"You lie as well as any of us, Cú Chulainn."

"Fae don't lie."

The name didn't click for Patrick—not immediately. It took another couple of seconds before his fogged-up brain made the connection, and when it did, his stomach knotted up hard in his gut.

"Cú Chulainn," Patrick repeated, the name foreign on his tongue in a way that hurt. Names were guarded zealously by the fae, but some were known to all because of the history their myths lived in. And Patrick—he knew the legends that were half-forgotten, but still real.

"I *told* you he'd be pissed," Keith said.

"Now is not the fucking time, Keith," Gerard snapped.

"What," Patrick said with numb lips, "the fuck. Gerard, what—"

Patrick nearly bit through his tongue at the burning shock that coursed through his nerves from where the bracelets were embedded in his skin. The silver grew warm, the heat of it rapidly turning painful. Patrick shoved up the sleeves of his sweater and jacket and tried to claw the bracelets off, but the metal wouldn't move.

"*Stop,*" Gerard said in a tight voice. "Your Majesty, please. Let him go."

"These two entered my lands uninvited, so I took them. I can do what I like with them," Medb said.

"They were invited by me."

"Your word carries naught the weight it once did. If that were the case, Tír na nÓg would have guided you to my sister at the crossroads, not to me."

"The Sluagh ambushed us."

Patrick ground his teeth against the burning pain in his arms, still trying to claw at the metal. Wade grabbed his hands, easily pulling them away from bleeding, burning skin. The hot ache of deeply bruised muscles in his left arm made Patrick grimace as he tried to pull free, but Wade wouldn't budge.

"Your Majesty, my pack and I came here to bargain," Sage said, her voice firm and unwavering in the face of Patrick's obvious agony. "Surely there is something you want from us."

"I have what I need to ensure Ethan's obedience," Medb said, gesturing casually in Patrick's direction.

Patrick *laughed*, the pain not enough to steal his breath completely. He raised his head, breathing through clenched teeth. "I'm a worthless payment for an immortal, if that's what you're hoping for. Ethan won't trade me for a godhead he already holds."

He swallowed against the bile rising in his throat, willing the nausea away. Jono stared at him with unblinking, wolf-bright eyes before half turning to look at Medb but still keeping Patrick within sight.

"You helped the Dominion Sect steal the Summer Lady, but they haven't brought her to you yet. That's why you want to keep Patrick," Jono said. "You want to trade him. Fuck that."

Medb stood in a fluid motion, her long, ash-colored hair swinging around her face. Something thin and long, like an insect leg, curved around her head from behind her, pulling her hair back over her shoulder before disappearing. The fingerbone crown never moved as she took the obsidian stairs down to meet them.

Medb's guards moved to flank her, but it was Cairbre who offered her his hand. She took it, allowing him to escort her to where Gerard and the others stood, surrounded by the enemy. Medb was as tall as Jono, but neither looked impressed with each other. Gerard took a step forward, never letting go of his spear.

Patrick still hadn't fully wrapped his slow brain around the truth—that Gerard had pretended to be less than he was for so many years. That the gods had once again fucked with Patrick's life in a way that hurt more than anything else in recent memory. Betrayal was always a cold, deep wound that took years to heal, and he wasn't ready to bleed that deep again.

"Ethan won't give up Órlaith for Patrick," Gerard said.

"I made a bargain with Ethan through his emissary, but the Dominion Sect has failed to follow through. Perhaps I should offer you the same bargain in order to get what I want," Medb said, her bloodred lips twitching into a smile as cold as winter's kiss.

"You expect us to believe you'd keep your word?" Jono asked derisively. "Patrick's life isn't yours to use as a bargaining chip."

"I think you will waste time you do not have searching for the Morrígan's staff when I can give you what you want." Medb raised her hand to touch Gerard's face, but he leaned away from her. "For a price, of course. Our kind do nothing for free."

"You took the staff?" Patrick asked slowly, not sure he believed her.

Fae spoke in half-truths one syllable removed from a lie. He couldn't discount what Gerard had told him about the person who'd stolen it from the Repository though—the one who'd done it with fae magic. Patrick was beginning to think they hadn't been human at all.

"The staff belongs to our war goddess. It never should have found its way into human hands."

"And you think it's better served in yours?" Gerard wanted to know. "It doesn't belong to you, Medb."

"I am willing to give it up for a price if you bring me the Summer Lady as Ethan should have."

And there was the catch. A goddess' ancient weapon in exchange for the life of an immortal—for what reason, Patrick didn't know, he just knew it wasn't good.

Patrick glanced at Gerard—Cú Chulainn—and wondered what he would do. They needed to find the Morrígan's staff before Ethan did, but if the cost was Gerard's fiancée, Patrick wasn't sure Gerard could pay it.

Wade's stomach growled loudly, the sound causing everyone to look at him. He made a face. "Everyone wants this staff, and all I want is some snacks."

"Later," Patrick muttered.

Medb returned her piercing attention to Gerard. "What will it be, Cú Chulainn? The staff you so desperately seek, or your Summer Lady?"

"The mission we were given applies to all of us. I'll need Patrick and Wade to come back with me," Gerard said after a long, fraught silence.

"My bargain does not include them."

"You stole them because you thought Patrick would be leverage for you against Ethan. He isn't. Patrick is worthless to you, and if you keep him here, you will have to deal with Persephone. She owns his soul debt. Not you."

Medb's dark eyes narrowed, the only hint of her annoyance Patrick could see. "She would not dare come to Tír na nÓg."

"Odin's ravens fly through our skies. They are always watching, no matter the realm. The All-Father holds alliances with the Greek gods and none with you. Odin will tell Persephone where Patrick is, and her wrath is worse than it ever has been since she lost Macaria."

"Then it will be war, if that is what our cousins wish," Medb hissed.

Gerard straightened up. "War is already here. You aid it with this bargain you offer. If you want me to bring you the Summer Lady in exchange for the Morrígan's staff, I will need Patrick and his magic to help me locate Ethan."

Medb studied him through narrowed eyes, Cairbre a silent presence beside her. Then her gaze shifted to Patrick, her attention a heavy thing. The pain in his arms abruptly eased, the sudden absence of it making him choke on a gasp. Patrick flexed his hands as the silver and onyx bracelets seemed to liquify back into their original form, splitting open on a seam that hadn't been there before and falling to the floor. Startled, Wade let his hands go.

The binding peeled itself out of Patrick's soul, falling away. The rush of his magic reconnecting to his mind made Patrick sway a little on his feet. Wade steadied him with a careful hand before kicking the bracelets far away from them. The wool of Patrick's sweater rubbed painfully against the burns on his arms, but he forced himself to ignore the irritation.

"If you fail to bring me the Summer Lady by winter solstice, then the mage is forfeit," Medb said.

"Like to see you try to take him," Jono growled.

"Jono," Sage warned.

Medb never looked away from Patrick. "Do we have an accord, Cú Chulainn? Your lover in exchange for the Morrígan's staff and this one's freedom?"

Part of Patrick didn't want Gerard to say yes, because Órlaith didn't deserve whatever Medb had planned for her. The rest of him was too angry to care.

"What about me?" Wade asked.

"She can't hold you, no matter what bargains she makes," Patrick said, testing the words and hoping he spoke the truth.

Medb let go of Cairbre's arm and walked toward Patrick, her guards parting smoothly to let her pass. Wade's eyes widened, but before he could panic, Patrick put himself between the teen and the immortal headed their way.

"Uh, if she can't keep me, does that mean I can eat this apple-looking fruit?"

Patrick rolled his eyes but didn't turn around. "Wade."

The sound of the teenager taking a bite out of something with a lot of crunch came from behind him. "What?"

"You're grounded."

"I'm already grounded."

"Then you're grounded more."

Medb offered Wade a smile Patrick would never trust as she came to a stop before them. "You can stay, if you like, dragon kin. The Unseelie Court would never turn you away."

"Wade has a pack," Patrick told her. "Ours."

"Human lives are worthless to one as long-lived as the fledgling will be."

Patrick never took his eyes off Medb, the queen's smile full of secrets he knew he wouldn't like. "Doesn't fucking matter. Wade belongs with us."

"Such loyalty. A pity it is wasted." Medb looked over her shoulder at Gerard, her hair swinging around her thin body as she did so, moving as if it were alive with things Patrick couldn't see. "Well, Cú Chulainn? Have you decided?"

"We have an accord," Gerard said in a grim voice as he rapped the butt of his spear against the onyx floor.

The heavy electric feel in the air shifted to something lighter. A promise had been witnessed, and once again, Patrick was a bargaining chip. At least this time, he was able to leave on his own two feet.

Medb returned to her throne carved from the dead tree, with its bloody, thorny vines that moved to accommodate her. She studied them from her seat on high before nodding at Gerard.

"The crossroads will find you," Medb said.

Jono pushed past the guards blocking his way with a snarl, striding over to Patrick. He immediately dragged both hands and wrists over the sides of Patrick's neck, scent-marking him, before framing his face.

"Let's get you home, yeah?" Jono said in a low, angry voice.

Patrick nodded, taking a steadying breath. He refused to look at Gerard as the others came closer. "Yeah."

Home sounded great, for however long they could stay there before needing to cross the veil again.

"This tastes like an orange," Wade said, taking another bite of the half-eaten, dark purple fruit in his hand.

"So, so grounded," Patrick muttered.

14

They walked through the veil, pulling free of the clinging mist that marked the separation between worlds. They arrived in a copse of snow-covered trees, night having fallen on the city when they'd previously left it with the sun high in the sky. Crossing through the veil from Tír na nÓg back to the mortal plane made Jono's stomach churn for a couple of seconds before everything settled. The winter chill was colder than he remembered, the icy wind making him shiver unexpectedly. Jono wondered how much time they'd lost while past the veil.

The distant sound of cars was abruptly overtaken by the beeps of everyone's mobiles connecting to the nearest tower. Jono pulled his out, unwilling to remove his left arm from where he'd draped it over Patrick's shoulders. In the light from all their screens, Jono could see everyone's breath puffing in the air as they all took stock of messages and voicemails coming through.

"It's December *sixteenth?*" Wade exclaimed. "We weren't even gone an entire day!"

"Time runs slower past the veil in Tír na nÓg. It's normal that we lost about a week on the mortal plane for the amount of time we were beyond the veil." Gerard scowled down at his mobile. "We only have five days left until winter solstice. That's not enough time."

"Oh man, I'm going to have to retake my class, won't I?"

"Let's head back to my place. Your team is probably there, Gerard," Sage said.

"Is that what we're calling you now?" Keith asked, the bitterness in his voice seeping through his scent.

Gerard stared at him, brow furrowing. "Keith. I'm still who I said I was."

"If you think you can order me to shut up about this, then you're wrong. The rest of the team deserves to know, right, Patrick?"

Patrick's shoulders tightened beneath Jono's arm. "I'm not talking about this right now."

"But you—"

"I said I'm not fucking talking about it!" Patrick yelled.

His voice echoed in the cold night air, the silence that followed tense and smelling of bitter anger to Jono's nose. Gerard's mouth was pressed into a tight line, eyes on Patrick, who wouldn't look at him. Jono gently ran his hand up and down what he could reach of Patrick's upper arm.

"Let's get somewhere warm and get you seen to, yeah?" Jono said to him.

"I'll call Victoria and see if she's available," Sage said.

"I've got a med-kit back home. I'll deal with my wounds there," Patrick told her.

"Patrick—"

"Go home, Sage. Take Wade with you. I'll see you in the morning."

"Patrick," Gerard said, stepping closer.

Patrick shrugged out from beneath Jono's arm and deliberately turned his back on Gerard, walking away from them all. Jono watched him go for a second before looking over at Sage.

"Send Victoria to our flat if she's available," Jono said.

Sage nodded. "Will do."

"Here," Wade said, holding out Patrick's dagger. "He should probably take this back."

Jono accepted the weapon, wondering why Wade had it in the first place, but wasn't going to waste time asking. Instead, Jono went after Patrick, the other man using the flashlight on his mobile to light the way rather than magic. That told Jono more than anything else Patrick wasn't in the right headspace after what he'd gone through.

Jono reached for Patrick's hand and gently took it, mindful of the injuries on his wrist and forearm. He could smell blood and the particular scent of burnt flesh that made him absolutely furious. Fenrir had been willing to reveal himself to Brigid, but not to Medb, no matter how loudly Jono had argued in that dark throne room.

He took a deep breath, evening out his senses but keeping them dialed high. Who knew what was riding through the clouds above them as they walked through Central Park at night. Jono wasn't about to leave Patrick unguarded.

"I have your dagger," Jono said.

Patrick nodded, stopping only long enough for Jono to slip the weapon back into its sheath on his right thigh before starting down the path again.

Patrick's flashlight absolutely ruined Jono's night vision, but he compensated just fine. He got them out of Central Park by way of Bow Bridge and the snowy paths that put them out onto Central Park West via Terrace Drive.

The traffic on the snow-plowed streets wasn't as heavy as Jono was used to at this time of night. A passing bus was half as full as it normally would be, and he frowned as he noticed they seemed to be the only pedestrians on the street. New York was the city that never slept, but it seemed downright comatose right now.

Patrick already had his mobile in hand, ride-share app open

and route selected. A few minutes later a car pulled up, and Jono kept his too-distinctive eyes averted and half-closed until they were in the back seat. He made sure to sit behind the driver, knowing most people didn't care for a god pack werewolf in such close proximity.

"Didn't think I'd get any rides tonight," the driver said as he pulled into the street. "Curfew has been bad for business."

"Curfew?" Patrick asked.

"You a tourist or something? Must be if you're out at night. The fae keep snatching people off the street. Whole city isn't supposed to be outside after dark, but this is New York. Gotta hustle for that cash, and no curfew is gonna stop us."

Patrick glanced at Jono, expression unreadable. "They never stopped hunting."

"Can't worry about that right now," Jono said.

The rest of the drive home was made in silence. Their driver dropped them off out front and sped off before they even made it to the sidewalk. Jono crunched his way through snow, the stoop at least having been shoveled clear by someone. He pulled his keys out of his pocket and let them inside the building, the air marginally warmer on the landing, but not by much.

Jono led the way upstairs, letting them into the flat at the top. Patrick touched the wards on the doorframe as he passed, magic flickering at his fingertips.

"I'll turn on the heat," Jono said.

The flat was cold from their weeklong absence while across the veil, though the Christmas tree looked alive. He turned the heat as high as it would go, listening as the vents rattled from the blowing air. Their building wasn't warmed by steam heat, though Jono thought they would've come home to a warmer flat if they had a radiator.

His mobile buzzed in his pocket. Pulling it out, Jono unlocked it and read Sage's text: VICTORIA IS ON HER WAY OVER.

Patrick was in the kitchen, having poured himself a glass of water and was chugging it like he was in a timed contest. Jono frowned at him. "Go slow. When was the last time you drank something?"

"Before we left for Central Park. I didn't eat or drink anything they offered," Patrick said.

Jono opened up Wade's snack cupboard and pulled out a chocolate protein bar. He ripped it open and handed it to Patrick. "Eat."

He watched Patrick with a critical eye as the mage ate that protein bar and another one before finishing up a third glass of water. He seemed to be favoring his left arm, and Jono didn't like that.

"Come on, let's get you sorted."

Jono led Patrick to their bedroom, where he carefully divested the other man of his jacket and sweater. Jono hissed angrily as deep bruises in the shape of large fingers were revealed on Patrick's left arm. What looked like bright red, first-degree burns twisted around Patrick's wrists and forearms, edged with deep scratches from where he'd tried to claw them off.

"Should've ripped their throats out," Jono said as he guided Patrick to the master bathroom.

"That's not good diplomacy."

"Fuck diplomacy." Jono gently pushed Patrick down onto the edge of the bathtub before pulling the med-kit out from beneath the sink. "Victoria is on the way over."

Patrick pressed a hand against the scars on his bare chest, absently scratching the skin there. "I need a shirt."

Jono got him a shirt and some Tylenol. Patrick stayed where he was, looking exhausted and hurt in a way that went deeper than the physical. Jono knelt before him, resting both hands on Patrick's thighs. He looked up into Patrick's green eyes, wishing he could wipe away the pain in them.

Patrick pressed his hand against Jono's cheek, thumb settling against the corner of Jono's mouth. Jono turned his head enough so that he could kiss the pad of it gently.

"Tell me what happened in the Seelie Court," Patrick said.

So Jono did, not leaving anything out, because they'd long since stopped keeping secrets from each other.

"Sage is pissed at me for not telling her about Fenrir," Jono admitted when he finished.

"I know that feeling."

Jono lifted a hand, stroking his fingers over Patrick's cheek. "I'm sorry, love."

Patrick looked away, jaw tightening. "You aren't the one who lied to me."

"I can still be sorry you're hurting."

Patrick sighed tiredly, leaning forward to rest his forehead against Jono's. "Yeah."

Jono didn't close his eyes, content to let Patrick lean on him for however long he needed.

"THANKS, VICTORIA," Jono said as he escorted her to the front door of the flat.

Victoria Alvarez nodded, pulling on her gloves before wrapping a scarf around her neck. "He can take the bandages off in the morning. The burns should be healed by then."

Victoria was an RN witch at Mount Sinai and Marek's personal on-call nurse for the migraines his visions gave him. She was also, apparently, now the on-call nurse for Jono's god pack, a fact she'd disclosed upon her arrival half an hour prior.

Jono had called Emma while Victoria dealt with Patrick's burns, getting up to speed as best he could on what had happened during the time they'd been gone. Word had gotten out about Emma's Tempest pack changing loyalties, which would need to be dealt with, but not right now. Jono had a voicemail from

Estelle sitting on his phone that he wasn't in the mood to listen to yet.

"Text me when you get back to work. I want to know you got there safely."

"I will."

Jono handed her a couple of twenties. "For the wait time of your taxi, and your ride back. You can bill me for your services later."

"I can cover my ride."

"You shouldn't have to since we pulled you away from work. Please, take it."

Victoria gave in with good grace, pocketed the cash, and left with a casual wave goodbye. Jono locked the door behind her and turned the lights off on his way back to the bedroom.

Patrick had gotten out of his boots and was sitting on the bed, staring at his mobile. A beep indicated a text had come through. Judging by Patrick's scowl, it wasn't one he cared for.

"Gerard?" Jono asked.

"I think you mean Cú Chulainn."

The anger in his words, in his scent, was overridden by the sharp bitterness of betrayal that Jono could practically taste. Jono approached the bed and gently pried the mobile out of Patrick's hand, setting it aside on the nightstand next to his dagger and the dog tags that Jono hadn't ever seen Patrick without.

Jono touched them, the flat metal cool beneath his fingertips. "What do you want to do?"

Patrick scratched at the skin close to the edges of the bandages wrapped around his wrists and forearms. The bruises Patrick had apparently gotten from an ogre had already shrunk some, courtesy of the potion he'd taken. They'd be gone by morning, but they still looked painful.

"I want you to fuck me," Patrick said.

While normally Jono had no qualms about a request like that, he worried about the reasoning behind it, about the way, when he kissed Patrick, it wasn't easy at all. Patrick kissed Jono angrily, almost viciously, and Jono let him for the few seconds it took to realize what Patrick was after.

Jono tangled his fingers in Patrick's hair, giving it a gentle tug even as he nipped at Patrick's bottom lip. "No, love. Not like this."

"Jono—"

"I said no. We aren't bringing this into our bed."

This being the burning, bristling anger and need to lash out coiled in Patrick's body. Jono remembered that same feeling from years ago, a half-forgotten bruise in his memories when his family had kicked him out of their home in the council estate in North London after he got infected by the werevirus. He'd been a teenager back then, thrown out on the streets, nursing that feeling of betrayal and unwantedness for years.

Family, he knew, always inflicted the deepest wounds.

Jono grabbed the hem of Patrick's T-shirt in both hands, skimming it upward. His fingers brushed over more bruises, and Jono was careful about pulling the material over Patrick's raised arms, not letting it catch on the bandages.

He got them both undressed, leaving their clothes on the floor in favor of helping Patrick forget. Jono gently guided Patrick farther onto the bed, kissing him all the way. When Patrick would've wrapped his arms around Jono's neck, he pulled them away, gently pressing Patrick's hands down onto the mattress.

"Don't want you to undo Victoria's hard work," Jono murmured, lips grazing against the shell of Patrick's ear. "Keep them here for me and don't move."

Patrick flexed his fingers against Jono's, tilting his head back. "Okay."

The word came out grudgingly, the tightness in his body still coming from anger. Jono wasn't about to let that continue.

Jono pressed a kiss against the pulse in Patrick's throat, breathing in the scent of him—bitter, like it always was because of his magic, but mixed with the pack scent Jono had pressed into his skin earlier. Jono licked at the taste of him, teeth gently catching against skin when Patrick took in a deep breath, throat working as he swallowed. The soulbond thrummed between them, Jono's awareness of it no longer blocked by fae magic. It hadn't been broken, but being separated past the veil hadn't been easy to compensate for.

Jono shifted down the bed, dragging his hands down Patrick's torso as he did so. He grabbed Patrick by the hips, holding him still. Jono licked Patrick's cock from root to tip, suckling at the crown. Patrick jerked at the touch, legs pressing against Jono's shoulders. He wasn't hard, not yet, but Jono knew how best to change that.

He swallowed Patrick's cock, sucking at it hard enough to make Patrick gasp. Jono pulled back slowly, scraping his teeth carefully against warm, sensitive skin as he did so. Patrick tried to arch upward, fighting against Jono's grip, but unable to really move. Jono pulled his mouth free, arching an eyebrow at Patrick and the hand reaching for him.

"What did I say?" Jono said.

Patrick rolled his eyes, but the faint flush that came to his cheeks had less to do with anger and more to do with arousal, which was all Jono cared about. "Don't move my hands, but touching you isn't going to dislodge the bandages."

"That's not the point." Jono gripped Patrick's cock at the base with one hand, making it easier to lick at the tip and tongue the slit there. "Lie back and let me take care of you."

Jono sucked Patrick's cock back into his mouth, intent on making him feel good. Which was easy for him, because giving Patrick pleasure was something Jono enjoyed. He liked the sounds Patrick made, the way he shivered at Jono's touch. Even better was the way his scent changed into that heady thickness that came with sex and arousal and *want*.

The anger bled away beneath Jono's mouth as Patrick's cock hardened against his tongue. Patrick's scent lost the sharpness of hurt he'd carried with him out of Tír na nÓg, and Jono hummed in satisfaction. The vibration had Patrick trying to buck beneath his mouth, but Jono kept him still.

Jono lavished attention on Patrick as if they had all the time in the world to stay like this when he knew that wasn't true. That didn't stop him from getting Patrick fully hard before finally taking his mouth away. Jono used his hands to spread Patrick's legs wider, tilting his hips up higher.

"You're driving me crazy," Patrick muttered, voice hitching in his throat.

"Don't see how that's a bad thing," Jono replied right before dragging his tongue from the sensitive skin behind Patrick's balls down to his furled hole.

Patrick swore at the first lick over his entrance, legs going tense against Jono's body. Jono did it again before gently sucking at his taint, teeth catching on the rim of his hole. The full-body shiver that racked Patrick made Jono smirk before he pressed the tip of his tongue against Patrick's hole and worked it inside. He opened Patrick up with his mouth, then his fingers, gently forcing Patrick's body to make room.

Jono only stopped when he felt fingers in his hair, Patrick's breathing loud in his ears. Jono lifted his head, catching Patrick's hand in his as he did so.

"Thought I told you to be still?" Jono said.

"You make that impossible."

Jono sat up and leaned over to grab the lube from the night-stand drawer. He slicked up his fingers and pushed two into Patrick without waiting, listening to the choked-off sound Patrick let out.

"You were saying?"

"I was saying you should fuck me."

The words came out on a gasp, and Jono smiled lazily down at Patrick, teasing him with quick strokes against his prostate.

Patrick pushed back against the touch, head tipped back as he moaned.

"Not what it sounded like," Jono said, pulling his fingers free.

Before Patrick could protest, Jono guided his cock to Patrick's hole, pushing through the lingering tightness to sink inside him without stopping. Jono leaned over Patrick, pressing both of Patrick's hands against the mattress as he slid into that tight heat. Patrick arched against him, moaning as Jono filled him up, entire body shuddering. Jono dug his knees into the bed and pushed in as deep as he could, Patrick's body opening up to make room for his thick cock.

Jono let his mouth hover over Patrick's, breathing him in. "I won't let the fae keep you, because you belong to me. That bitch can't have you, Pat."

Patrick's mouth parted, but whatever he was going to say got replaced by a wordless cry as Jono pulled out and thrust back in with enough strength to push Patrick up the bed. Jono held Patrick down by his hands, keeping him there as he stole a kiss. The next thrust was just as hard, giving Patrick a bit of the roughness he'd wanted at the beginning, but without the anger and searing betrayal.

"Don't stop," Patrick said against his mouth, breath coming quick.

Jono didn't; he kept fucking him with quick, hard thrusts that shook the bed and had Patrick searching out his mouth with a desperation Jono wanted to smooth away.

Sweat slid down Jono's back, the warm air in the room nothing close to the clenching heat of Patrick's body. Patrick writhed beneath him, working to meet every thrust, his skin flushed red, a thin circle of green around black in his eyes. He smelled like sex and need and *want*, a heady mix that Jono couldn't get enough of.

"Jono—"

His name on Patrick's lips was like a prayer almost. Jono let go of one of Patrick's hands to reach between them and stroke his cock. Patrick came on the second stroke, back arching as Jono pounded into him, trying to breathe through it. Jono kissed him, mouth catching on the corner of his lips first before slotting properly together. Jono swallowed Patrick's cry and the gasp that followed it, fucking him through his orgasm.

Jono came with a shout moments later, burrowing his face against Patrick's throat as his hips stuttered through his own release. He ground deep into Patrick, chasing the last shreds of that white-lightning feeling pricking through his nerves.

He lay on top of Patrick, both of them breathing heavily as they came down from a sex high Jono didn't want to give up. Pulling out, Jono rolled onto his back, letting Patrick sprawl on his chest. Jono stroked his hand down Patrick's sweaty back a few times before moving lower so he could slip a finger back inside Patrick's loose, wet hole.

Patrick shivered against him but didn't protest, merely settled into the cradle of Jono's hips. Their cum was drying between them, sticky on their skin, but Jono wasn't in any hurry to move and clean them up.

"You're allowed to be angry and hurt," Jono said quietly, holding Patrick close. "Just don't push me away."

Patrick pressed his fingers against the skin over Jono's heart before flattening out his hand. "I won't."

And that—that was progress. It was growth, because Jono knew even two months ago Patrick would've hesitated before agreeing to something like this, and it would've been a lie. But his heartbeat was steady in Jono's ears, truth seeping through the scent of sex hanging heavy in the bedroom.

This was trust, and Jono would do his damnedest to be worthy of it.

15

"WE MADE A BARGAIN WITH MEDB, AND WE HAVE UNTIL WINTER solstice to complete it," Patrick announced.

Tiarnán paused in writing on his legal pad, looking up as Patrick and Jono entered the main conference room of Gentry & Thyme. "That was unwise."

"I've made worse decisions."

Jono snorted softly from behind him. "No need to be proud about that."

Tiarnán leaned back in the leather seat, staring at them. "What was the bargain?"

"That's between us and Medb. We're here to find out what's been going on with the Wild Hunt and the Sluagh while we were past the veil."

Patrick wasn't about to disclose what they'd bargained for with Medb. Finding the Morrígan's staff was critical, but he had a feeling Tiarnán wouldn't appreciate that retrieving it would come at the price of his Summer Lady. Not that Patrick had any plans to give her—or himself—over to Medb.

Tiarnán set down his pen and got to his feet, reaching for his gold-tipped wooden cane as he did so. Tiarnán was impeccably dressed, and no one would mistake him for human, despite the trappings of a human-style law firm around them. Patrick eyed the wooden cane he held, wondering if it was a weapon or an artifact along the lines that Setsuna carried.

He wasn't going to ask and looked up to meet Tiarnán's violet-eyed gaze. This conversation could've been done by phone, but Patrick had wanted to see if Jono could get anything by way of smell off the fae lord.

"Secrets are unbecoming of the bargain we made," Tiarnán said.

"You breathe secrets, mate," Jono retorted.

Patrick crossed his arms over his chest, the motion easier after waking up with healed bruises and mostly healed burns. Victoria's potion and poultices had worked wonders, but they hadn't fixed everything. Only time and rest could do that.

"If you're not going to help, that's going to keep you out of favor with Brigid," Patrick said.

It was a wild guess that maybe struck home, and maybe didn't. Tiarnán was too long-lived to give away anything by way of expression of body language. Patrick hoped something closer to the truth came through his scent for Jono to get.

"Our bargain is not Brigid's concern," Tiarnán said.

"Isn't it?"

"It is our duty as *daoine sídhe* to keep our children safe. I do my duty here, on the mortal plane, because it would be remiss of me not to."

"That's not an answer."

"It is all you are getting."

Patrick shrugged. "Brigid didn't seem happy you'd offered us an alliance."

"I will honor it in her name."

Patrick wondered if the promise was meant as an insult or not. You never knew with the fae.

"What about the Wild Hunt and the Sluagh? They're still

pulling people off the streets. How often did it happen while we were gone?" Jono asked.

Tiarnán turned his head to look out the wall of windows that oversaw the Manhattan street below and the tall building across from them. Patrick couldn't hear the sound of traffic through the silence ward wrapped around the conference room, but he knew it was the usual rush-hour mess on a Friday morning.

"Often enough," Tiarnán said slowly.

"Your queen could earn some PR points by calling them off."

"Brigid does not control either. If she did, they would not be hunting here."

"But they are, and both are after someone. We just don't know who."

"Their target may not necessarily be the same one."

"The Sluagh went after the changeling. The Wild Hunt?" Patrick shrugged, looking over at Jono. "You said the lead rider was a woman looking for a girl."

Tiarnán frowned. "You must be mistaken. The Wild Hunt does not have a female leader. It is not their role."

"Way to discriminate. Don't ever say that around Sage."

"The lead rider was a woman. Dead, but a woman, and the rest of the Wild Hunt followed her orders," Jono said.

"You misunderstand me. The Wild Hunt is led by a god, and Gwyn ap Nudd would never relinquish his position to another."

Patrick shared a look with Jono, shoving down the spark of hot anger that cut through him. His ability to leash his anger was shit after yesterday—last week—however fucking long time had passed since he'd learned of Gerard's betrayal. Learning yet more gods were circling was enough to make him need a drink, preferably several.

"What would make him give up leading the Wild Hunt?" Patrick asked.

Tiarnán gripped the knob of his cane with both hands, looking old rather than timeless for a single second, all it took for Patrick to blink.

"Nothing," Tiarnán said. "The Wild Hunt has always belonged to him. It did before this land was stolen, and it will be long after it falls. Death has existed always, and so has he."

Patrick shook his head and turned on his feet. "Death needs to fuck off in all its many aspects."

Patrick left the conference room, ignoring the curious stares from some of the other fae they passed on their way out. He hadn't thought they'd get the answers they needed out of Tiarnán, but at least they'd gotten something. The bargain between them only counted for so much, but he'd take the hint and the warning Tiarnán had offered for what they were.

"I don't think he cares for Brigid," Jono said on the elevator ride back down to the lobby.

Patrick would've banged the back of his head against the wood paneling of the elevator car, except Jono casually grabbed him by the jacket and hauled him close. Patrick rocked forward onto the balls of his feet, letting Jono steal a kiss.

Jono let go of the leather and smoothed it out. "Off to Em's?"

"Yeah."

Today was December seventeenth. They had four days left to find Órlaith before winter solstice rolled around. Winter solstice would hit on December twenty-first, but all the back-and-forth across the veil was cutting into their search time. Patrick honestly didn't know where to start except for the one place he didn't want to.

Turned out, he didn't get a choice.

They stepped out of the elevator and turned toward the exit. The second Patrick got eyes on who stood between them and the guarded glass doors to the building, he rocked to a halt, causing Jono to nearly run into him. Jono grabbed him by the shoulder and gently steered him forward so they weren't in the way of anyone else coming off the elevator.

"Can't ignore him forever," Jono said quietly.

"If we didn't have a mission, you bet your fucking ass I could," Patrick muttered.

The simmering anger he'd let go of last night beneath Jono's touch came roaring back in full force, making his hands shake. Patrick clenched them into fists as they headed to where Gerard waited in the lobby, dressed for winter but carrying himself as if he were waiting for a war to start.

He wouldn't be wrong.

"We need to talk," Gerard said in a quiet, tired voice once Patrick stood in front of him.

"Not here," Patrick retorted.

"I wasn't going to suggest here. The Lord of Ivy and Gold knows every word spoken within these walls."

Gerard turned on his heel, heading for the exit, acting as if he fully expected Patrick to follow him. Patrick was angry enough—and petty enough right now—that he half thought about heading for the door that led to the parking garage even though they hadn't driven here. They'd left their car at Emma's while past the veil to avoid street cleaning tickets.

Jono shook his head, and Patrick knew he wouldn't be allowed to ignore this situation.

They stepped outside into the cold winter air, gray slush shifting around Patrick's boots. The snow plows had come through last night despite the curfew, and the streets downtown were cleared, but small snow piles had built up along the curb. The sidewalk looked icy, and no one was moving very quickly.

Patrick tugged his beanie down over his ears and squinted against the cold wind that made his lungs hurt. He should've worn a scarf. Gerard hailed a taxi, the yellow vehicle pulling over and turning the light off on its sign to indicate the driver now had passengers.

Jono and Patrick climbed into the back seat while Gerard took the front, telling the driver "Rockefeller Center."

Nobody talked on the drive uptown; the only sound in the taxi was the radio, tuned to a Spanish station. Patrick stared out the window, gaze catching on passing cars and the people hurrying down the sidewalks. He leaned his head against the glass window, peering up at what he could see of the cloudy sky above. Snow wasn't falling, but that didn't mean it wouldn't start.

Rockefeller eventually came into view, and the taxi driver pulled over to let them out. Gerard paid in cash before shutting the door and meeting them on the sidewalk. Patrick watched the taxi drive away rather than look Gerard in the eye.

"Why here?" Jono asked.

"Because we won't be as noticed in a crowd," Gerard said.

"You mean there's less chance of me murdering you without witnesses," Patrick snapped.

Patrick turned his back on Gerard and walked toward the railing that overlooked the ice-skating rink on the lower level. The famous Christmas tree's lights glowed a deep red, and ice-skaters were already on the rink. The city curfew apparently only applied at night, because trying to get millions of people to stay home behind thresholds during the day was pretty impossible.

People had lives they had to live, after all. Some days, Patrick wished someone else would live his for him.

Patrick was left alone for a few minutes until Gerard and Jono came over to where he stood, cups of coffee from the coffee stand down the way in their hands. Jono handed Patrick a to-go cup and he grabbed it, taking a sip. The coffee was bitter and over-roasted, but warm, and he drank half of it down before Gerard finally spoke up.

"Can you ward us?" Gerard asked.

It wasn't an order, when it so easily could have been. Patrick scowled but conjured up a mageglobe anyway. He filled it with a silence ward, allowing a bubble of static to engulf them, the white noise blocking out the city around them. He guided the tiny sphere between two railings, letting it hover there mostly out of sight.

"I'm sorry," Gerard said.

"Fuck you," Patrick said through clenched teeth.

"I deserve that."

Patrick reached out and shoved Gerard as hard as he could, making the other man rock on his feet. He turned to face his old captain, mouth opened to yell, but the words were all jumbled in his brain and on his tongue.

"*Fuck* you," Patrick said again, because it was worth repeating.

Gerard's silver eyes brimmed with more emotion than Patrick had ever seen at once, but that didn't make him feel better. That didn't make this fucked-up situation easier to deal with.

"I'm *sorry*, Patrick. I never meant to hurt you."

Patrick shoved Gerard again, keeping hold of his coffee cup because it was the only thing stopping him from punching Gerard like he deserved.

His coffee—even the shitty brew Jono had bought him—deserved more than that.

He deserved more than that.

"You know about me—or you knew about me," Patrick spat out. "You're a fucking *god*. A fucking *immortal*. You know how I feel about them—you—*fuck!*"

Gerard's mouth twisted. "I know."

Patrick let go of his coffee cup where it sat on the railing to shove Gerard with both hands, putting all his strength behind the push. "Fucking *why*? Why did you lie to me?"

Gerard caught himself as he stumbled backward. He reached for Patrick, but his hand stopped halfway before clenching into a fist and dropping down to his side. "I never lied, but we all have secrets to keep."

"Don't you fucking dare turn this on me. My identity is tied up in the courts. I'm bound by laws and a soul debt, while you're bound by *nothing*."

"Nothing but my word," Gerard said quietly.

Patrick glared at him, trying his hardest to ignore his watering eyes. He'd blame the sting of wetness on the wind. "Your word is shit, Gerard. Or should I call you Cú Chulainn now?"

"Every name I go by is a true name for me. I'll answer to whatever name you call me."

"Asshole?"

Gerard rubbed at his forehead with gloved fingers. "Would it make you feel better to call me that from here on out?"

"A bottle of Macallan would make me feel better so I could drown myself in it."

"Patrick," Jono said quietly.

Patrick ignored him, still glaring at Gerard. "Did you know? About me, specifically? All this time I thought you were my friend while being my captain, but you're just another fucking god who *used* me—"

"I never bled for your dagger," Gerard cut in, jaw tight as he stared at Patrick without blinking. "It was forged without me because I didn't *know*. If Brigid called me to the Seelie Court to bleed for the gods of heaven, I never heard her summons."

"You heard her when she called about Órlaith."

"Because Órlaith is my fiancée."

Patrick's lip curled, biting around the shape of words he knew would hurt. "Not your first."

Gerard didn't move, didn't speak, not for a long few minutes. Patrick stood in front of his old captain and refused to move, because he'd done all the running he could when he was younger, and he knew it wouldn't get him anywhere.

It never did.

"Aífe and I...we lost too much when we walked this earth as we once were," Gerard said slowly, the words heavy and tired-sounding. "I killed my son, and a marriage can't outlast that. Ireland was never home after I buried Connla, so I left it for Tír na nÓg when the Otherworld would have me while I grieved. But grief can't sustain a man or a god, Patrick. Not forever. When I returned to the mortal plane, the Great Famine had taken root, and nothing I did could save the few who prayed to me still. So, I left. I boarded a ship and came here, to America, where NINA signs dictated my prospects until the Civil War arrived."

Gerard lapsed into silence, his gaze distant, as if he were looking at something else that wasn't New York now, but New York then. Patrick waited Gerard out, chewing on his bottom lip, because he wanted answers and he wasn't hearing any yet.

"I was made for war. I was trained for it, and I lived it for the Union during that time on a battlefield full of iron. But there was so much death during those years that even a god could tire of it. When the Civil War ended, I fled west, then north, and lost myself until Scáthach found me again."

"I know your story. I know what was written about you," Patrick said.

Gerard blinked, coming back to himself. "You don't know the truth that's sustained me. That was never written for the masses. My old teacher had Órlaith with her when they found me in Montana decades after the Civil War. The first time I laid eyes on Órlaith, I knew she could be my home the way Ireland used to be."

"You bargained her away for the Morrígan's staff. You bargained my life as well."

"I said I would *bring* Órlaith to Medb. I never said I would hand her over."

Jono snorted from behind Patrick. "That's some shaky word game you're playing, mate."

"I have never considered this a game." Gerard's gaze moved from Jono back to Patrick. "Your life was never a game to me, Patrick."

Patrick's fingers twitched, and he wished Keith were there so he could steal a cigarette. "Sure seems like it from where I stand."

"I would sooner give up my godhead than see harm come to Órlaith. She taught me that life was worth living when I didn't care about anything except the drink in my hand. I love her the way I should have loved Aífe, and I learned that on my own. There are no stories about us, because we never gathered worshippers to pray for us. We never needed that when we had each other."

"You love her. That's fucking great. What about me? When I was assigned to the Hellraisers, did you know about me? About my soul debt?" Patrick forced out between clenched teeth, the words like knives in his throat.

Gerard shook his head, never looking away. "No. I haven't lived in the Seelie Court for centuries. I knew nothing about what Persephone had done to you. I wasn't looking out for you because of the gods, but because you were assigned to my team, and General Reed asked me to. I think maybe he knew, but I would've watched your six regardless because you were under my command. You were my responsibility. For what it's worth, you were my family."

"You fucked up," Patrick said, choking on a laugh that tasted like bile in the back of his throat.

"I know, and I am *sorry*."

Patrick looked away, the ache in Gerard's voice something he didn't want to acknowledge. Jono touched his hip, fingers squeezing gently, and Patrick glanced over his shoulder.

"He's telling the truth," Jono said.

"Doesn't make his lies any better."

"I thought the fae couldn't lie?"

"I have never lied to you, Patrick." Gerard held up his hand in a pleading manner when Patrick opened his mouth. "We fae deal in half-truths and twist words all the time. That's how we have always existed, but we can't outright lie."

"You told me your name was Gerard when it isn't," Patrick shot back.

"I've gone by many names over the centuries, and every single one was a truth I answered to. What else would you have me say to make this right?"

"I don't know if you can."

Knowing that he'd been lied to for so long by someone he

considered a friend—someone who was the family he'd picked
—*hurt*. It made Patrick want to scream, to punch something or
someone, and while he thought Gerard might let him, he had a
feeling Jono would hold him back.

"I would have told you who I was at the end of the Thirty-Day
War when we learned your truth, but you weren't in a place to
hear it, and I couldn't risk showing who I was in the middle of that
fight. I didn't want Ethan to steal my godhead for that spell of his.
Maybe that makes me selfish, but I like to think it makes me
human," Gerard said quietly.

Patrick glared at him, his jaw sore from how hard he was
clenching his teeth. "You still should have told me. I shouldn't have
had to learn who you really were like *this*."

Gerard nodded, his shoulders slumping a little as he rubbed at
his eyes with one hand. "I know. I'm sorry."

"You've already said that. I don't fucking care that you're sorry."

Because it hurt that he'd been lied to by someone he considered
a close friend who turned out to be a god. Patrick didn't care about
what Gerard had to say, because all his words were just noise right
now. They didn't mean anything, and Patrick wasn't sure they ever
would again. He couldn't trust whatever Gerard said, because he
knew he would always wonder if the other man was telling the
truth.

Gerard stared at him with an unreadable look in his silver eyes,
a weight to his gaze—to his aura—that Patrick wondered how he
could have ever missed the signs of a god over the years. Halflings
were one thing, but immortals were something else entirely, and
Patrick used to think he knew what to look for when gods
appeared in front of him.

Maybe he didn't. Maybe he'd been fooling himself all along.

"I've stood vigil for every man and woman who has ever fought
with me over the years, and I will stand vigil for you when your
time comes to pass on, whether you like it or not. Because I owe it
to you as your captain, and as your friend, even if you never think

of me as either again after this," Gerard said into the tense silence that had fallen between them.

"I don't want your prayers."

Gerard smiled sadly. "I never gave them to you."

Patrick rocked backward, bumping against Jono as he did so. A strong arm wrapped around his waist, steadying him, and Patrick leaned into that support because if he didn't, he knew he'd bruise his knuckles on Gerard's face.

"Keith still pissed at you?"

"They all are."

"Good."

"You can stay behind for this fight if you want. You don't owe me Órlaith's life."

"Shut the fuck up. We have a mission."

Patrick drew in a deep breath and squeezed his eyes shut. He gave himself one goddamn minute to let the anger wash over him before he gathered it all up and shoved it down deep into a corner of his mind. Patrick was excellent at compartmentalizing his life when he had to, and he needed to do that now.

Later, he would hole up somewhere with a bottle of whiskey to drink himself stupid. Right now, there were more important things to worry about. He opened his eyes, anger still a bitter taste on his tongue. He swallowed it down until he couldn't taste anything at all.

"The rider of the Wild Hunt was a woman. Tiarnán said we had it wrong, that the Wild Hunt was led by Gwyn ap Nudd," Patrick said, steering the conversation away from the shattered pieces of a friendship he wasn't sure could ever be rebuilt.

"I didn't see him that night outside the bar," Gerard said after a moment, willing to concede the conversation to Patrick's stubborn insistence.

"Tiarnán made it seem as if Gwyn ap Nudd would never relinquish his position."

Gerard made a face. "He'd be right. For once."

"You don't seem to care for the bloke. Why is that?" Jono asked.

"I exiled myself to the mortal plane. Tiarnán never got that choice."

"What did he do?"

"Does it matter? He's been trying to get back into Brigid's good graces for centuries. Finding Órlaith would do that. I don't think he would have asked for your help if he knew your association with me at the time."

"Bargain still stands. He owes us if we find Órlaith."

"Make sure he keeps it."

Patrick scowled. "Fucking fae lawyers."

Jono tightened his arm a little before pulling away. Patrick instantly missed his warmth. "If Gwyn ap Nudd leads the Wild Hunt, who leads the Sluagh?"

"The Sluagh hunt on Medb's order, but they have no defined leader," Gerard said.

"They went after the changeling. What's so special about a changeling they left behind?"

Patrick frowned, thinking back on that night in the Wisterias' nursery. "Maybe she wasn't left behind at all. Maybe someone hid her."

Gerard frowned thoughtfully. "If that's the case, then why?"

"Marek could probably tell us if I wasn't in the way of his visions."

"Is the child safe wherever she's at?" Jono asked.

"Setsuna would let me know if anything had happened to her. She never left a voicemail to that effect while we were past the veil. All she told me was that the State Department is getting stonewalled by the fae ambassador in DC. The SOA can't get a straight answer out of them about the missing Wisteria child, the Wild Hunt, or the Sluagh," Patrick said.

"Brilliant."

"If your changeling case and Órlaith are actually linked, then we need answers," Gerard said.

"No fucking shit," Patrick said derisively as he picked up his coffee cup and took a sip. It had cooled in the cold winter air while they argued, but he drank it anyway.

"We need to go to the source. I can take us to Gwyn ap Nudd."

"Because you're a god?"

Jono sighed. "Patrick."

Patrick ignored him. "You really want us to cross the veil again? We've already lost too much time already. You want us to risk losing more? You want to risk Órlaith that way?"

Gerard's jaw tightened, and Patrick recognized the determined look in his eyes. Patrick wished he didn't—wished he didn't know Gerard like this at all anymore, if only to save himself from the hurt.

"We have no other choice," Gerard said.

Patrick gulped down what remained of his coffee and crunched the empty cup between his fingers. He snapped the fingers of his other hand, and his mageglobe faded away, taking the silence ward with it. The sounds of the city rushed back between them all, the howling of the wind a counterpoint he didn't like.

"Your funeral," Patrick said as he headed for the street.

"Where are you going?" Jono asked.

"To get the rest of our pack."

Because at least Patrick had them while the memory of his old team felt tainted now. He wasn't burying the dead in Arlington that morning, but there were ghosts that would never rest between himself and Gerard now.

That realization hurt more than the gunshot wound he'd taken in the field years ago, the scar on his body nothing like the ones in his head now, in his heart.

16

Emma hugged Patrick, then shook him hard enough his teeth clacked together, then hugged him again. "I'm glad you're okay, but you need to stop this self-sacrificing bullshit."

Patrick glared over her shoulder at Gerard. "Wasn't my idea this time."

Marek's apartment was crowded, the front door propped open for people to come and go from the apartments below in the building. Patrick wrenched his gaze away from Gerard to scan the crowd, not recognizing anyone except for Keith, Arthur Russell, and Darren Thompson, the latter two the only other survivors of the original Hellraisers team they'd all been on.

Those two looked more pissed than the rest of the team that Patrick hadn't been introduced to yet, and right now didn't care to know. All he cared about was the pack of cigarettes that Keith held up and shook at him.

"We're taking a smoke break," Keith said.

Jono shook his head. "Patrick."

"Nope," Patrick said, holding up a hand in his direction. "Save it. We'll call this backsliding, and I'll mention it to my therapist, but don't even try to fucking stop me from smoking right now."

Patrick ignored the eyes that followed him deeper through the apartment. Keith, Darren, and Arthur followed after him, the four of them trekking up the narrow set of stairs that led to the snow-covered roof of the building. The wind was icy in a way Patrick didn't trust. Ducking his head, he conjured up a mageglobe and erected a shield to block the wind, even if he couldn't block the cold.

He erected another layer around the mageglobe, blending a silence ward in with the shield. Static washed over their small group, wrapping them in a bubble of quiet. Patrick glanced up at the gray sky and the snow that was falling in soft swirls.

"Right," Keith said, passing out cigarettes as they huddled together. "The team knows what happened in Tír na nÓg, and Gerard is hereby banned from poker night for the next year."

Patrick snapped his fingers, calling a bit of magefire into the air. They all took turns lighting up their cigarettes on the fire before he snuffed it out. The first hit of nicotine at the back of Patrick's throat nearly choked him, and he breathed it in deep through sheer muscle memory. It'd been months since his last cigarette, and this was a step backward he refused to feel guilty about.

"Only a year?" Patrick muttered around the cigarette in his mouth.

"He said he'd ask the Old Man about a transfer," Arthur said.

Patrick grimaced, not sure how he felt about that. "That's practically a blackmark on his jacket."

"Yeah, but he's basically immortal, so does it matter?"

Patrick drew in another lungful of smoke, looking over at the winter-white expanse of Central Park that stretched out before them. The slow, simmering anger from earlier was still present, making his skin itch, but had been overtaken by hurt betrayal that tasted sour on his tongue

"Gerard said he was made for war. I don't think he could leave this fight. He'd change his name, maybe change his face." Patrick pulled the cigarette out of his mouth and flicked ash onto the snow between his feet. "Glamour would hide who he was like it hid what he was all these years."

"He's a god, right? He has a stake in this fight with the Dominion Sect because of his rank. He wouldn't leave the fight, only the team," Darren said.

Keith scowled around his cigarette. "I'm pissed at Gerard, but I don't want him dead."

And that—yeah. Patrick could only nod silent agreement to that statement. He shoved his left hand into his jacket pocket, shifting on his feet. "He should've told us."

That was the crux of the whole situation, and Patrick was too angry to care about the hypocrisy of his statement. He'd lived his life as Patrick Collins for far longer than he'd ever been Patrick Greene. His life still paled in comparison to Gerard's as Cú Chulainn.

If it had only been lying about a name, he wouldn't be as angry, because he got that. He understood the need to hide. But Patrick had been at the mercy of too many gods over the years to immediately accept and forgive that one of his closest friends had been an immortal all this time.

"Would you want him to give up leading the Hellraisers?" Patrick asked.

Keith grimaced, taking another drag off his cigarette. "I've served with Gerard almost my entire career. Always wondered why he never got promoted after some of the missions we've done. Now I guess we know why."

Arthur nodded. "Because he's a god."

Patrick drew in another lungful of smoke, thinking about the argument he'd had with Gerard not even an hour ago. "Still immortal."

"Anyone told Spencer yet? Or Nadine?"

"Not the sort of information I'd trust to send in an email or over a phone, no matter the level of encryption."

Those two, while not Hellraisers, had worked with the old team enough times back in the day that this was a truth they should hear, especially since Spencer and Nadine were both read into the Morrígan's staff mission.

Darren leaned his head back so he could blow smoke toward the sky. "Not sure how I'd feel about breaking in another captain."

"You'd trust Gerard after this?" Keith asked.

"He got us home. Only right we do the same for his fiancée."

"That's not what I asked."

Darren shrugged, glancing at Patrick. "We got over it before and still trust Razzle Dazzle here."

Patrick winced, chewing on the end of his cigarette butt. "Fuck you."

There wasn't any heat in his words though, and the guys knew it. They stood in silence for another minute or two before Keith finally sighed, blowing out the last hit of smoke from between his lips.

"The Old Man gave us a mission. I'm not keen on changing up the status quo in the middle of a fight," Keith muttered, scuffing his foot against the snow.

That sounded a lot like they'd refuse to let Gerard leave the team. Patrick opened his mouth before snapping it shut. It was their choice to make, not Patrick's. He was no longer active duty, and the team needed to do what was best for it. If that meant keeping Gerard as their captain and keeping his secrets, then Patrick would only hope for the best outcome. He was mad, but not mad enough to wish ill will on his old friends.

Movement out of the corner of his eye had Patrick turning his head. Sage stepped onto the roof, squinting against the dull sunlight and the hard-blowing wind. Her hair was braided back, and she didn't wear the pendant that would hide her scent since she was home.

Patrick flicked his finger against the mageglobe, drawing down the silence ward and the shield. The howling of the wind and sound of traffic filtered over everyone again.

"We need all of you downstairs to plan what to do next, and Jono said we can't talk about it without a silence ward in place. The sorcerer on the team is willing to cast one, but Jono wants you to do it, Patrick," Sage said as she approached.

"Sure," Patrick said.

"Don't leave your trash on my roof."

Patrick drew one last drag off his cigarette before kneeling to put it out in the snow. The other guys did the same, and Keith was the one who gathered up the used cigarette butts to carry back downstairs and throw away in the trash.

Sage didn't move, and Keith was adept enough at reading a situation that he caught Arthur and Darren's eyes before jerking his head at the door. "We'll meet you downstairs."

The three left. Sage eyed Patrick for a moment before shaking her head. "You're still angry."

"You can't smell that," Patrick said, because he'd locked down his shields before they even arrived here.

"I don't need an enhanced sense of smell to know all of you are pissed off, even while your anger stinks up my home. Your body language speaks volumes."

Patrick scowled at her. "Me being pissed at Gerard doesn't concern you."

"It does if you're going to do stupid shit." Sage tucked her bare hands into the pockets of the too-large winter coat she wore. It looked like one of Marek's. "Jono wanted to come up and talk to you, but I told him I would. Jono will always side with you, but I'm your dire, and it's my job to tell you when something is wrong with the pack."

"Jono calls me out on my bullshit all the time."

"Not as often as you think."

"Why aren't you angry at Jono?"

Sage didn't blink at that accusation. "You may want to ward us again."

Patrick shrugged and did as she asked, conjuring up another mageglobe and filling it with a silence ward. Her request made him think the others who'd been with them across the veil hadn't revealed Jono carried Fenrir in his soul even as Gerard's true identity got picked apart.

"I was angry. I still am, to a small degree. But I know why Jono kept quiet about his patron, and I'm choosing to follow my alpha's lead because I trust him," Sage said.

Her words needled Patrick in a way he didn't like. "I have a therapist."

"I'm not here to psychoanalyze you. I'm here to tell you to stop thinking with your heart and start thinking with your head. We all got revelations thrown at us we didn't like, but you need to move past being pissed off."

"Wow. That sounds an awful lot like fuck you."

Sage didn't react to his veiled insult. "I'm your dire, Patrick. My job is to make sure the pack as a whole is safe. I know we won't be if we follow you into this fight when you're like this."

It stung being told she didn't trust his state of mind at the moment. Patrick's instinctive reaction was to argue that Sage was wrong, but he knew deep down she was right.

"Okay," Patrick said through gritted teeth. "You made your point."

Sage arched an eyebrow. "I'm not sure you listened."

"I'm not going to sabotage our side of the fight before we even make it into the field. I know better than to do that."

"You're still angry."

"I'm fucking allowed to be. Gerard was a friend."

And that's why this whole mess hurt so goddamned much. Being lied to like this hurt a hell of a lot more than the shit he'd gone through with Ethan in a way.

"You lied to us from the day we first met you until you had to come clean about your past. It's a little hypocritical for you to be pissed at Gerard for being in the exact same position you were once in," Sage said as she turned away.

"I hate lawyers," Patrick muttered, a curl of unexpected shame bleeding through the anger he still carried.

"Yes, I know, but you can't hate me. I'm pack, and your dire."

"Is this where you tell me it's a shitty job but someone has to do it?"

Sage didn't look back as she walked away. "It's an honor, despite the shitty pay. Now quit being an asshole looking for a fight. I'm not giving you one."

Patrick collapsed his mageglobe, letting the silence ward fall away. He hurried after Sage, managing to catch up with her in the stairwell. He grabbed her shoulder, keeping his touch light, and she paused where she stood with feet on different steps, looking back at him.

"You're right. I don't hate you," Patrick said, wanting to make sure she knew that.

Sage nodded. "I know."

"I'm still mad."

"Yes, I know, but be mad at the people who deserve it. Gerard never told you his real name, but he still gave you one that mattered. Most fae wouldn't give you anything at all to call them by. The fae can't lie, they never say thank you, and they never apologize."

Patrick's grip tightened a little before he let her go with a heavy sigh. "Gerard said he was sorry."

Sage reached for his hand, giving it a gentle squeeze. "Then he meant it."

"You don't know that."

"No, I don't. But the only one who can believe him is you."

Sage let his hand go and started back down the stairs, and

Patrick could only follow after her. They came back into the crowded apartment. The Hellraisers were huddled together in a group, with Gerard standing a little apart, no expression on his face. Wade was in the kitchen eating a sandwich. Jono stood with Emma, Leon, and Marek, though no one else in her pack was present.

Patrick caught Jono's eye before turning his head to look at Gerard. They stared at each other in silence for a long minute, everyone else waiting on them. Patrick wasn't ready yet to accept anything his old captain gave him—apologies or promises—but he wasn't about to let Gerard run off and fight alone.

Patrick was angry—and he knew enough about himself to accept he was being a hypocrite here—but emotion wasn't ever rational when it came to family.

"Are we doing this?" Gerard finally asked, breaking the silence.

Patrick nodded slowly. "Yeah. We're doing this."

"Great," Wade said from the kitchen. "What are we doing?"

Marek sighed deeply in a put-upon way as he pulled out his cell phone. "Funding terrorism again."

"Boys," Carmen practically purred from her spot where she sat on a stack of weapons crates. Standing to either side were two men who looked more affiliated with Lucien's Anahuac Cartel than his Night Court.

The sexual desire Carmen exuded warmed the cold warehouse in the Lower East Side better than any steam heat could. Patrick still cast shields over their small group, pushing back against Carmen's attempt to mess with everyone's heads.

Naheed closed the door behind the last of the Hellraisers and locked it, giving Patrick a silent nod in greeting. Despite the cold weather, she'd foregone a scarf, showing off the necklace of bite scars wrapped around her throat. As a favored human servant to

Lucien and one of Carmen's bodyguards during the day, Patrick wasn't surprised to see her.

"I thought you were joking when you said we had to deal with her again," Arthur muttered as he scowled in Carmen's direction.

"You know I don't joke about Lucien," Patrick replied.

"One of these days you should, if only to spare our sanity."

"No promises."

"If you want to waste time making deals with someone else, then you can leave," Carmen said.

She crossed one leg over the other, gently kicking her foot back and forth. The stilettos she wore were easily five inches in height. Patrick wondered how she managed to walk over the icy ground without breaking her neck. She'd opted for a pair of leather pants rather than a skirt and had passed on any form of shirt in favor of a suit jacket with a single button that gaped suggestively around her full breasts.

Her red pupils seemed to glow, the horns of her kind curled away from her skull. She'd left her thick black curls loose, and her hair fell around her body like a waterfall. Carmen would always be a seductive force they could never trust.

"We already told you we're willing to pay. Now show us the merchandise so we can be off," Jono said.

Carmen held out one hand to the guard on her left. He reached for her and carefully helped her off the stack of crates, his eyes lingering on the curve of her full breasts beneath the suit jacket.

"Your weapon choices are the same as before, as is the price, but a commission fee of one hundred grand is being added." Carmen flashed a smile at them, sharp teeth pricking her glossy red lips. "I need a new spring wardrobe."

Patrick winced but nodded at Jono when the other man looked over at him for confirmation. "Yeah. Not like we have a choice."

"Marek is going to whinge about this forever," Jono said.

"I'd say we can pay him back, but he's the billionaire, not us."

Technically, they were making this payment to Lucien from

pack tithes agreed to be paid by the Tempest pack. It didn't leave much left over for the next year, but Marek had flat out said he'd bankroll their god pack despite Jono's protest. They wanted to do things the right way, or as right as one possibly could when taking in what amounted as—legal—protection money.

It still left Patrick feeling uncomfortable, but not enough to stand back and go into the fight empty-handed.

He'd lost his tactical pistol across the veil and picked out a new one from one of the crates. It would have to do until he could report back to the SOA about his missing pistol and request a new one.

Gerard and Keith still had their rifles from the first weapons buy, but they grabbed more ammunition to be on the safe side. The rest of the Hellraisers picked out rifles, spelled bullets, and grenades as well, hiding their choices in black duffel bags after cartel members logged the purchases in an old bound book that reeked of magic.

At Patrick's questioning look, Carmen smirked at him. "Technology can be hacked. A warded record book spelled to burn if the wrong people try to access it is far more secure."

"I don't know about that," Patrick said.

"How we do business is not your concern."

Considering Lucien had been in the business of war and death for nearly a thousand years and had yet to be caught, Patrick figured the master vampire probably knew what he was doing. Patrick would never tell Lucien that to his face though.

They picked out their weapons, Jono contacted Marek to initiate payment, and as soon as Carmen nodded acceptance of the funds in their offshore account, Patrick texted Emma.

READY TO ROLL.

They weren't bringing the Tempest pack with them across the veil, but Emma's people were more than willing to chauffeur the Hellraisers and Jono's god pack around the city for however long they needed.

The three little dots on his screen finally morphed into a text bubble. *Two minutes. Cars are circling.*

"Our ride will be here in a couple of minutes," Patrick said.

Gerard hefted one of the bulging duffel bags onto his shoulder. "Then let's go."

They left the warehouse, and two minutes later, the convoy of cars pulled up in front of the warehouse. Most people didn't drive in Manhattan if they could help it, and many of the cars that braked to a halt on the street belonged to Marek and Emma. Their pack had unfettered access to most of the vehicles, and their collection came in handy on days like this.

Patrick and Jono climbed into the Maserati that Marek drove, Sage and Wade already in the back seat. Patrick squeezed into the back, giving Jono the front passenger seat to accommodate his longer legs.

"Ready?" Marek asked.

Patrick buckled up. "Yeah."

Marek's car was in the lead position, and he started driving. The plan was to drop everyone off in Central Park, and as soon as they were in the clear, Gerard would call for the Wild Hunt. He was a god of the Tuatha Dé Danann, a *duine sídhe* of the Seelie Court, and while he couldn't command the dead who belonged to a fellow immortal, he could still reach out to them.

Patrick figured that was why the Wild Hunt had fled the bar when Gerard confronted them at the beginning of the month. They must have known who Gerard truly was, and crossing an immortal was always a risk.

That whole fight seemed like it had happened only several days ago, but with the lost time they'd experienced past the veil, it was actually longer. He rubbed at his forehead. Going past the veil was worse than going past the International Date Line in terms of a body's circadian rhythm getting all fucked up.

"You sure you don't want our pack to go with you?" Marek asked, glancing at Patrick in the rearview mirror.

"We need you here for backup just in case," Patrick said. "Unless you've seen something?"

"No. You're still too close to whatever is going to happen, and the Norns can't see an end to it."

"That sucks," Wade said, chewing on a Pop-Tart.

"Can't say I enjoy the migraines my visions give me, but I wish I could be of more help."

"You've done enough. Paid quite a bit for what we needed today," Jono said.

"Guess it's a good thing I set up the offshore accounts all those years ago. The Norns never told me why, they just told me to do it."

Patrick snorted. "Gods never like giving straight answers."

Marek's smile in the rearview mirror held no humor. "Tell me about it."

The rest of the drive to Central Park was made in silence save for the quiet munching coming from Wade as he ate three packs of Pop-Tarts in a row.

"You're eating through all your snacks," Sage said.

"I'm hungry," Wade muttered.

"You had breakfast and lunch."

"Yeah, but...Pop-Tarts."

"If you eat another fae offering past the veil, you're grounded until next year," Jono said.

Wade shrugged. "Eh, not too bad."

"He never said until when next year," Sage said, raising an eyebrow at Wade.

He narrowed his eyes and shoved the last piece of brown sugar Pop-Tart into his mouth. "That's not fair."

"They're your alphas. Fair is what they decide."

Wade crossed his arms over his chest and sulked.

Early Friday afternoon traffic wasn't all that bad. Most people were at work or safe behind thresholds at home. Despite the approaching holidays and countless decorations, the city didn't have an air of festiveness to it.

"It's snowing," Marek said some time later when he turned left onto East Sixty-Sixth Street.

Patrick leaned against Sage so he could peer between the front seats at the snow drifting lightly onto the windshield. "Shit."

"Which one do you think is up there?" Jono asked, peering up at the sky. "Sluagh or the Wild Hunt?"

"Who the fuck knows, but let's hurry this up so Emma's pack can get home safely."

Marek sped up a little, aiming for Central Park. They crossed Fifth Avenue a couple of blocks later and drove onto the Sixty-Fifth Street Transverse, passing the stone wall boundaries of Central Park.

Snow-covered lawn and barren trees greeted them again as they followed the curve of the road. The stone walls on either side of them blocked much of the view, and Marek only stopped when they reached a point where the walls were low enough that they could be climbed.

Marek yanked up the emergency brake and put on the hazard lights. "Good luck."

"We'll contact you when we can," Patrick said as they got out of the car.

The Hellraisers piled out of the cars behind them, some grabbing the duffel bags from the trunks. Once they were on the sidewalk, the cars drove away. Patrick cast a look-away ward around everyone so they could climb the low wall in peace.

Patrick wasn't too out of practice and still managed to make it to the park level at the same time as most of the others. Jono, Sage, and Wade didn't bother climbing, the three of them leaping up to the snowy ground with preternatural strength.

"That's handy," Keith grunted as he straightened up. "You guys going to shift now or later?"

"Depends on what Gerard thinks our welcome will be like with the Wild Hunt," Jono said.

Gerard twisted his hand in the air, and the faint crack of displaced air made Patrick's ears pop. Gerard's spear appeared out of nowhere, the notched blade and bone pole glowing faintly. Looking at it now, Patrick wondered how he'd ever missed seeing the weapon for what it was—the *Gáe Bulg*, Cú Chulainn's legendary spear of death.

Fae glamour, he decided. *And a lot of misdirection.*

"Stay human for now. It'll be easier for the Wild Hunt to carry us if you are," Gerard said, nodding in the direction of the open expanse of the meadow before them. "We'll call for them over there."

There being Sheep Meadow, the open space ringed by trees, with the city rising up beyond the edges of the park. Patrick couldn't see anyone else in the park other than the few cars on the road they left behind them, and the emptiness was eerie.

"We aren't close to the hawthorn path," Sage said as they trekked to the middle of the meadow.

"That doesn't matter."

Patrick gripped his mageglobe with its look-away ward in one gloved hand and didn't draw down his magic until Gerard signaled him to. He let the mageglobe fade away as they all formed a loose circle in the snow.

The wind picked up, cold and sharp in Patrick's nose when he breathed it in. He blinked snow out of his eyes, gaze drawn to the golden bits of flame that sparked at the tip of Gerard's spear. Gerard raised the *Gáe Bulg* toward the sky, eyes on the churning clouds above that moved in a way Patrick didn't trust.

"Hear me, Wild Hunt," Gerard said, his voice ringing with a depth to it Patrick only ever heard when gods spoke, the smell of ozone warming the air. "You who carry the dead for eternity. I ask for safe passage for myself and my brethren to Annwn. I ask for an audience with your lord."

He slammed the butt of the spear to the ground, and Patrick was forced back a couple of steps by the magic that rolled away from the impact. Snow puffed up from the ground before being caught in the wind and spun into the sky. Patrick held on to his beanie, keeping it anchored to his head even as he dug his heels into the snowy ground. Jono snagged him by the elbow, holding him steady against the rising wind.

The clouds above them spun like a vortex, the roar of the wind turning into howls that made the hair on the back of Patrick's neck stand on end. In the depths of the clouds, a bright glow started to burn, like sheet lightning that never faded.

A sudden downdraft hit like a hammer driven by gods, throwing everyone but Gerard to the ground. Patrick spat out a mouthful of snow, trying to push back against the pressure that kept him pinned to the freezing ground.

"Don't fight them!" Gerard shouted.

"Easy for you to say!" Keith yelled.

Patrick turned his head, blinking up at the sky and the storm of lightning that exploded in the air as the Wild Hunt descended to earth.

The baying of hounds never faded as the dead drew near, riding spectral horses and stags through the air. Patrick tried to still the pounding of his heart even as he wrapped his right hand around the hilt of his dagger, the metal warm through his glove.

He didn't trust gods, and he sure as hell had never trusted the dead.

But some small part of him still trusted Gerard and maybe always would. Despite the hurt and betrayal, the lies and the bitter truth, Gerard was still the same captain who'd made sure Patrick had walked off the field of war when so many others never left it.

Patrick sucked in a steadying breath and let go of his dagger, steeling himself for whatever came next. The Wild Hunt filled his vision until nothing but the dead existed around them. Patrick didn't fight the heavy jaws of a hound that grabbed him by the back of his leather jacket and carried him into the air at a dizzying speed, the ground and New York City falling away from him.

The world spun sickeningly as the Wild Hunt gathered up Patrick's pack and the Hellraisers to ferry them across the veil, surrounded by the dead and stolen souls.

17

Jono fell through mist and landed on snow, the hard ground beneath him jarring every bone in his body. The pain rapidly receded, healed before he could even really notice it. He shoved himself to his hands and knees, blinking the world into view again.

"Status?" Gerard called out.

A chorus of voices responded back in the affirmative—*not dead* being a popular answer—but all Jono cared about was his pack. "Patrick?"

"And that little flight was *exactly* why I didn't become a mother-fucking pilot," Patrick groaned.

Jono got to his feet and would've gone to help Patrick, except when he turned, his attention was wholly taken up by the monument rising into the night sky before them. Jono froze, the full moon high in the dark sky bright enough to cast the hill they stood on in silvery light.

"What is *that*?" Wade asked, sounding a little uneasy.

"Glastonbury Tor," Jono said through numb lips.

His mouth went dry with the realization that he was standing on English soil for the first time in years. The sudden, unexpected longing for a home that had never wanted him felt exactly like the silver knife Theodore had stabbed him in the gut with the other week. Jono swallowed thickly against the tightness in his chest, night vision finally settling into something his brain could process.

St. Michael's Tower loomed above them, the Wild Hunt circling the stone parapets, as if waiting for the command to attack. They glowed with an unearthly light, while the full moon illuminated the terraced slopes of the ancient, snow-covered hill they stood atop. The mist hid the lower land where the city of Glastonbury should have been, but wasn't.

It was as if they were on an island in the middle of nowhere, with only the dead to keep them company.

"We're at the gates of Annwn," Gerard said.

"Looks like bloody Glastonbury Tor to me," Jono replied.

Gerard's spear crackled at the notched point with fire that gave off no warmth. "Because it has always existed as a crossroad for my people."

"One which you trespass upon at this moment, halfling. Annwn is not your territory."

The voice that echoed from the depths of the tower rang with the deep tone found only in cathedral bells. Patrick came to stand beside Jono, holding his dagger in one hand. The matte-black blade flickered with heavenly white fire along its sharp edges. His other hand brushed against Jono's in a silent show of support and comfort that steadied Jono.

Gerard's team scattered in a loose halfcircle around them, rifles at the ready. They stood in such a way that all angles of attack were covered, but Jono doubted the numerous spelled bullets they carried could do anything about the immortal who stepped out of the shadows.

Gerard's hand tightened on his spear before he dipped his head low in a sign of respect Jono wasn't sure he meant. "Gwyn ap Nudd."

"Cú Chulainn," the god replied, his Welsh accent thick in the syllables.

Jono eyed the new immortal, sizing him up. Gwyn ap Nudd was tall in his own right, but the antlers branching off the metal and leather helmet he wore over white-blond hair made him taller. The shirt and trousers he wore seemed made of dark leather, with symbols painted on them in a design that made no sense to Jono. The silver gauntlets the god wore glittered in the moonlight, and Jono could practically taste the metal on his tongue.

Gwyn ap Nudd carried a spear in his right hand, the metal of the spearhead burning red orange, as if it had been pulled from a forge's fire. The glow from it cast strange shadows on his face, revealing black eyes shot through with molten gold.

Beside the god strode a massive hound, its silver-white fur making it seem more like a ghost than something real. Which might've been the case, considering what circled above them. The Wild Hunt had yet to leave, and Jono, for all that he carried a god in his soul and the werevirus in his veins, still felt like prey.

"If we're in Annwn, we're losing time. This is a crossroad, right? Can't you put us back in the mortal world?" Patrick wanted to know.

The god ignored him. "I would know why a halfling thinks he has the right to request an audience with me."

Gerard took a step forward, drawing himself up to his full height. "We made a bargain with Medb. We came here looking for answers."

"I have nothing to give you."

"The Wild Hunt steals the living off the streets of New York City. You do not lead them through the storms that carry them on the mortal plane. Why?"

"That is not your concern."

"It's all our concern when the Morrígan's staff is in Medb's hands."

Gwyn ap Nudd said nothing to that, merely settled his left

hand on top of the hound's head to stroke the white fur between its ears. "If Medb truly had the staff in Tír na nÓg, then no power in any realm could keep the Morrígan from reclaiming what rightfully belongs to war. I cannot help you."

"I think you're lying," Jono said.

That molten gaze turned his way, and Jono found himself pinned by a regard that should have burned him. Gwyn ap Nudd's eyes narrowed, his head and the antlers he wore like a kind of crown tilting in a thoughtful manner. Fenrir stirred in Jono's soul, but he'd had enough of the god taking over his life in the last day or so, and firmly told the immortal *no*.

Fenrir growled in a way that told Jono he was being ignored.

"Cousin," Gwyn ap Nudd said after a long moment. "I was not aware you had given patronage."

"Just me, mate," Jono growled, ignoring the warning snarl that echoed in the back of his mind.

"Hey," Patrick said, drawing attention to himself. "We're running out of time standing around here arguing. Medb gave us until winter solstice to bring her the Summer Lady in exchange for the Morrígan's staff. If we don't make the exchange, then we're all fucked, because she made the same offer to the Dominion Sect first, and they have Órlaith."

Gerard shot him a quelling look. "Patrick."

"What? We don't have time to play the word games you fae are so fond of. We need to get moving."

"What does Medb hold over you, Gwyn ap Nudd?" Sage asked suddenly, her voice ringing through the cold air.

High above, the Wild Hunt keened, the sound reminding Jono of a dirge. Wade winced and clamped both hands over his ears, glaring up at where the spirits were in the sky. "All this over some kid?"

"Since when do you speak whatever the hell that was?" Sage asked, turning to look at Wade.

"Uh. Since I ate the not-apple? Maybe before?"

Gwyn ap Nudd's head jerked around, focusing on Wade with an intensity that had Jono moving to stand between the immortal and the youngest member of his pack. Some of Gerard's teammates pointed their rifles at the immortal, but Gerard quickly gestured at them to lower their weapons.

"For fuck's sake, don't shoot," Gerard snapped. "Our bullets can't kill a god."

"You sure about that?" Keith asked.

"*Yes.*"

"Well, shit. I think we wasted half a million dollars back at the warehouse."

"More like a million. Lucien drives a hard bargain," Sage said

"Kid," Patrick said as he lowered his dagger, sounding surprised. "Fucking hell, the *kid.*"

Sage looked over at him. "The Wisteria child?"

"No. The changeling they swapped her out with."

Gwyn ap Nudd moved, but Jono couldn't react fast enough to intercept the god when he went after Patrick, despite his own preternatural speed.

Gerard could—and did, like back at Emma's apartment when they'd faced off against Estelle and Youssef.

Gerard moved, a blur in Jono's eyesight, his spear coming down between Gwyn ap Nudd's and where Patrick stood. The clash of weapons made Jono's ears ring, skin prickling from heat instead of cold for a split second.

"Patrick is under *my* protection," Gerard snarled through clenched teeth, silver eyes blazing in the dimly lit darkness they stood in. "His soul doesn't belong to you."

"Yeah, it doesn't even belong to me, so get in line," Patrick muttered.

"Or not," Jono said testily.

Sage shoved Jono out of the way so she could guard Wade, eyebrows raised in a silent order. Jono left her to it and went to drag Patrick out of reach of Gwyn ap Nudd's spear, if not his murderous gaze. He shoved Patrick behind him, ignoring the mage's protest, not taking his eyes off the two immortals.

"Where is she?" Gwyn ap Nudd snarled.

He bore down on Gerard's weapon with enough strength to cause the tendons in Gerard's neck to stand out as he pushed back just as hard. The two were at a stalemate that would've broken any weapon made by mortal hands.

"Who?" Gerard demanded.

"My *daughter.*"

"Bloody hell," Jono said, eyes widening. "The changeling is your daughter?"

The tiny fae child the Sluagh had been after when the restless dead had attacked the Wisteria home—probably on Medb's orders, since she was the one who controlled them. Jono remembered that moment outside Tempest, when the Wild Hunt's lead rider had confronted him, asking about something he couldn't answer then, but could now.

"*Ble mae hi? Gallwn ei weld yn eich enaid,*" he said from memory, Fenrir shaping the words with his tongue.

Where is she? We can see her in your soul.

Gwyn ap Nudd slammed his spear point-first into the ground at an angle, trapping Gerard's weapon beneath it. He used the pole weapon as a crutch to hold his weight and kicked Gerard in the face hard enough to send the other god flying through the air. Blood splattered on the snowy ground, the scent of it hot in Jono's nose, but he couldn't worry about that, not when he had a furious immortal coming at him with murder in those molten eyes.

"*Enough!*"

The word was ripped from Jono's mouth, but the voice wasn't his. Between one heartbeat and the next, he gave in to Fenrir's demand for control so that Jono didn't die on the spear point that came to rest against his heart.

Gwyn ap Nudd was a frozen specter of death before him, holding back on murder only out of courtesy for another immortal. The god's mouth twisted into a snarl, the point of his spear burning through Jono's shirt to scorch his skin.

He never felt any pain.

"Cousin," Gwyn ap Nudd bit out. "You are not welcome in my domain."

Jono hated how his body no longer listened to him but knew giving up control to Fenrir was necessary in a situation like this. His mouth moved, but it wasn't him speaking, and that would never stop being strange.

"I think there is a bargain to be made between our sides. Will you listen to what this one has to say, cousin?" Fenrir asked with Jono's mouth.

Patrick's dagger pressed against the spear point digging into his skin, white heavenly fire crackling around the matte-black blade. Jono wrestled control back from Fenrir because the god allowed it, letting himself take a step back from the threat as Patrick knocked the spear-point aside.

"Back the *fuck* off," Patrick snarled, edging between Jono and the immortal who hadn't moved.

Jono shook his head as hard as he could, trying to clear it of Fenrir's presence. His thoughts were sticky, as if they weren't his own, but Patrick's hand gripping his arm was a steady, grounding touch he leaned into. Gwyn ap Nudd watched them with narrowed eyes before finally straightening up in a smooth movement, his spear leaving a trail of light in the air as he spun it around to rest the butt against the ground.

"If you kill them, then Ethan wins, and all our godheads are at risk, not just Órlaith's," Gerard said.

Jono spared him a glance, seeing that Gerard had gotten back to his feet with Keith's help. His mouth was a bloody mess, and even as Jono watched, Gerard spat out a tooth. Gwyn ap Nudd never even looked at him.

"My daughter," the immortal ground out. "Where is she?"

"Safe," Patrick said.

"I do not believe you."

Patrick dug his mobile out of his phone and unlocked it. Jono watched him scroll through his pictures until he came to one of the dark-haired changeling in puffy winter clothes and a jacket that made her look like a starfish. A different, older fae child held the girl, both of them staring at the camera with curious looks on their small faces.

Patrick turned the mobile around, shoving it toward Gwyn ap Nudd. "Is that her?"

Gwyn ap Nudd stared at the mobile without moving for so long Patrick had to tap the screen to keep it from locking up again. Finally, the god took the mobile in his hand, thumb hovering over the picture of the changeling.

A downdraft of cold air had Jono looking up at the sky as the Wild Hunt descended, settling in a circle around where his group stood on the hilltop overlooking a strange land. The lead rider he remembered from the bar guided her ghostly, undead horse forward. She only stopped when one of the Hellraisers refused to move, the man gripping his rifle with steady hands, even though it wasn't aimed at the dead.

Gwyn ap Nudd gripped his spear tight enough the silver gauntlet he wore scraped together at the delicate joints, the sound singing in Jono's ears. Then he rapped the butt of his spear against the ground three times, each hit making the ground shake as if an earthquake was happening, throwing everyone off balance.

"*Agorwch y ffordd*," Gwyn ap Nudd said, his voice ringing through the winter air.

A distant rumble grew louder, similar to how an approaching storm sounded as it neared shore. Jono's ears popped and his stomach swooped low in his gut. The full moon offered enough illumination for him to see the mist surrounding the hilltop they stood on rise into the air before suddenly sinking, as if someone had taken the earth in giant hands and dropped it.

The way Jono's brain rattled in his skull, it sure seemed like it.

Jono blinked away the spots in his vision, looking around at where they were—still at Glastonbury Tor, but the sky looked lighter at the horizon with the encroaching dawn light. The mist stretching out around the terraced hill wasn't so dense he couldn't make out the lights from a city in the distance. The wind howling over the hilltop sounded more like an element and not the screams of the dead. Snow crunched under his feet, though it wasn't falling as it had been in New York.

"The Wild Hunt is gone," Sage murmured.

Jono scanned their immediate area, seeing she was right. The Wild Hunt was indeed gone, even if their leader was still present and still a threat, his ghostly hound ever a faithful companion beside the god.

St. Michael's Tower was easier to see in the dawn's light, standing tall and ominous against the cloudy sky. The wind blowing over Glastonbury Tor was icy and cold enough to burn his lungs when Jono breathed it in.

"Where is she?" Gwyn ap Nudd asked in a low voice that rumbled between them.

"She's safe. I was given a case about a missing child and the changeling the family found in her place. The Sluagh tried to steal the changeling back, but I didn't let them. She's currently in a safe house run by my agency," Patrick replied.

"I want her returned to me."

"And Gerard—Cú Chulainn here—needs his fiancée back. Let's bargain, but I'll let our dire do the talking."

"Thank all the gods about that," Sage muttered.

Patrick extended his hand and made a grabbing motion at the mobile. "Can I have my phone back?"

Gwyn ap Nudd gave it back after staring at the screen for another minute or so, the longing in his eyes a type of pain that made Jono want to wince. Patrick looked at his mobile and swore.

"We lost two days while flying through the veil to get to Annwn. It's December Twentieth."

Which meant winter solstice was tomorrow, and they had barely any time left to complete the tasks required of them. Jono refused to believe they'd lose the race against time, because he wasn't going to lose Patrick to Medb.

Gerard approached, wiping blood off his face. The bruise on his jaw was stark against his skin, but it looked as if it was starting to fade. "I wasn't aware you had a daughter."

"She is not in my stories that are told, but Cadwyn is mine," Gwyn ap Nudd said flatly.

"Medb had your daughter, didn't she? Leverage is a bitch when we aren't the ones wielding it."

"The Queen of Air and Darkness knows many secrets, and I have spent too much time in the mortal realm in recent years. I had forgotten how secrets can become chains."

Gerard spat out a bit of blood and nodded, resting the side of his head against the pole of his spear. "Yeah, but your daughter is safe for now, and we need your help."

"I cannot aid you."

"Pretty sure you can."

Gwyn ap Nudd shook his head. "I heard whispers years ago of Medb coming into possession of the Morrígan's staff. I thought them rumors, for the staff has long been lost to the Morrígan since it was stolen from her on the battlefield. When I discovered the truth, Medb sought to buy my silence. When I refused, she stole my daughter. No harm was to come to Cadwyn so long as I remained in Annwn and called no attention to her plight."

"Medb sent someone to steal the staff from the United States' Repository a couple of years ago. You're saying she's had it for years and hasn't done anything with it yet?" Patrick asked. "I find that real hard to believe."

"Market could've been too hot to sell it," Jono said.

"Mortal money means nothing to her. That isn't what she's after," Gerard said slowly.

"Power is the only currency someone of Medb's stature

would care about," Sage said, causing both immortals to turn and look at her. "She demanded the life of the Summer Lady in exchange for the Morrígan's staff. You need to ask yourselves why."

Jono grimaced, an uneasy knot settling in his stomach as he remembered what Brigid had called Órlaith—*granddaughter*. Trust Sage to cut through the bullshit to the facts they all needed. "Is Órlaith next in line to the Seelie Court throne?"

Gerard grimaced before he let out a heavy sigh. "Yes, but she doesn't want to be queen. Not right now."

Patrick groaned and rubbed at his eyes. "Fucking hell. The second Medb gets Órlaith, she'll never give her up. That's leverage over Brigid anyone would kill to have."

"Maybe that's why the Dominion Sect hasn't given her up yet," Jono said.

"She still has a godhead Ethan would love to own."

"Yeah, but whose is more powerful? Órlaith's or Brigid's?"

"Brigid, by far," Gwyn ap Nudd said.

Jono looked at Patrick. "Maybe Ethan is trying to decide which one he wants more."

"Another godhead or the Morrígan's staff? I'd rather he not own either."

"Ethan will need to decide soon, especially if he's running on the same time frame as we are. We need to be quicker than him," Sage said.

Patrick scowled. "We don't even know where she's being held."

"Órlaith will not be in Tír na nÓg. Neither will the Morrígan's staff, and neither was my daughter. We can find our own and what belongs to us in the Otherworld. It is the mortal plane, full of iron, where we are lost. I sent my Wild Hunt to look for Cadwyn because I could not leave, but even the dead can become disoriented by your cities," Gwyn ap Nudd said.

"The Sluagh probably wanted to take Cadwyn back once Órlaith was taken. If your Wild Hunt had managed to find her, would you have left Annwn for the Seelie Court and warned Brigid of Medb's price?" Gerard asked.

Gwyn ap Nudd's molten eyes blazed in his face, the brightness of dawn behind him haloing his head like pale fire. "If I was free of my promise, Medb's Sluagh would not be enough to save her from my Wild Hunt."

"Would your Wild Hunt be able to find her?" Jono wanted to know.

Gwyn ap Nudd looked at him with an assessing gaze. "Is this the bargain you would make? My aid for my daughter's life?"

Jono shook his head. "We don't want your daughter. We have a teenager. He's more than enough of a headache."

"Hey!" Wade protested.

Jono ignored him, meeting the immortal's gaze with his own steady one. "Your daughter is safe because Patrick said she is, and I trust his word above everyone else's. You will get her back when this is over, no strings attached, because we aren't into kidnapping kids. But the Morrígan's staff is everyone's problem, gods and mortals alike."

"Will you help us?" Patrick asked.

Gwyn ap Nudd was silent for so long that the sun broke the horizon before he spoke again, the fiery curve spilling golden light across the changing sky above them.

"I am bound by a promise I already made to Medb. I cannot leave Annwn to aid you until I have my daughter again or Medb breaks her word," Gwyn ap Nudd said.

"War is no place for a child. If we bring Cadwyn to you now, then war will follow and we lose our chance at finding the Morrígan's staff," Gerard said quietly.

"Then I cannot help you, Cú Chulainn."

"My lord. Would you have me beg?"

"You have spent too long amongst mortals. We gods do not beg."

Gwyn ap Nudd rapped the butt of his spear against the ground, and the shock wave that reverberated outward from the blow made Jono's teeth rattle in his skull. Around them, in the early-morning light, the Wild Hunt appeared again, ghostly riders and hounds illuminated by the dawn.

"I must remain. My Wild Hunt is under no obligation to do so."

Jono watched as the lead rider came forward once more, and this time, none of Gerard's team got in her way. Her eyes stared at them from behind her leather mask with its painted symbols before she refocused on Gwyn ap Nudd. She bowed from the saddle, a gesture of obeisance that the immortal accepted with a simple nod.

"Nerys will aid you," Gwyn ap Nudd said.

"Your Wild Hunt can find Órlaith?" Jono asked.

"Not without guidance. If you wish to find the Summer Lady, then you must ask another to point the way."

"Who?" Gerard asked warily.

"It is winter. These are the long days of the Cailleach Bheur, and she has no love for the goddess who sits on her stolen throne. Ask her for a path forward, and she might aid you."

Jono didn't know who the Cailleach Bheur was, but Patrick seemed to, judging by the heavy sigh he let out. "Great. At least she's an immortal who bled for my dagger. She might be willing to help."

Jono looked at him. "And if she doesn't?"

Patrick shrugged. "Medb makes good on the bargain we made with her."

Jono reached for his hand and held on tight. "She can't have you."

The words were a promise in their own right that settled heavily between them, the soulbond humming in his soul. If Medb thought she could take Patrick from him, then Jono would show her how wrong she was, and damn anyone who got in his way.

"Where is the Cailleach Bheur?" Sage asked.

"Where she always is this time of year. At the Cliffs of Moher, in her home of *Ceann na Cailli*," Gwyn ap Nudd said.

"Where is that? Ireland?"

Gerard nodded. "Yes. She has abodes in the old lands of the Celts. Modern borders mean nothing to her."

"How are we supposed to get there? None of us have passports to get through any sort of Customs."

Gwyn ap Nudd arched an eyebrow and tilted his spear in Nerys' direction. "My Wild Hunt will take you."

"Not through the veil. We can't risk losing any more time. Winter solstice is tomorrow," Patrick said.

"Then we'll ride with the Wild Hunt through the storms west of here and stay on the mortal plane," Gerard said.

Jono looked at the Wild Hunt surrounding them before catching Patrick's eye. "It's been years since I was last in Ireland."

"Next time, we're taking a fucking plane," Patrick retorted. "Where they serve alcohol and have seat belts, and don't treat the goddamn sky like a roller coaster."

"Fair enough."

"Good hunting," Gwyn ap Nudd said before disappearing through the veil in the way only immortals could.

Jono squinted against the dawn and ran his tongue over too-sharp teeth in his mouth. As far as blessings from the gods went, that was one he could accept just fine.

18

It was snowing when they finally reached the Cliffs of Moher a couple of hours later, and not even Jono's higher core body temperature or Patrick's heat charms could warm him all the way through. Winter's chill had settled in his bones during the flight west, and he'd give anything to be home in bed and warm right about then.

Not how I thought we'd celebrate our first Christmas together.

The gray clouds—occasionally edged in lightning—that had surrounded them on the long flight west started to thin. Jono turned his head and looked down past the stag's moving hooves at the glimpse of blue he could barely make out through a break in the clouds. Then the stag opted to dive instead of fly, and Jono tried to remember to breathe.

The Wild Hunt broke free of the low-hanging clouds that had led the way west. Jono was glad to leave the escort storm behind in the sky, but the dizzying descent to the earth below was enough to make his stomach crawl up his throat. He held on tight to the strangely solid rider seated in front of him on the stag. The ghostly warrior ignored Jono as the Wild Hunt dove toward the sea where waves crashed against the cliffs rising out of the ocean.

Sea fog made it seem as if they were flying through the veil mists, but Jono knew that wasn't the case. The Wild Hunt flew above the sea waves, ghostly hooves and paws skimming the top of whitecaps as they passed the shores, heading south.

The Cliffs of Moher stood like ancient sentinels against the wrath of the Atlantic Ocean, their craggy faces dark from the damp sea air, the land above covered in snow. Jono squeezed his legs tighter against the stag as the Wild Hunt suddenly started to climb back into the air, breaking past the top of a cliff to finally touch down on solid ground.

Jono slid to the ground, feeling a bit wobbly on his legs from being a passenger on a dead flying stag as it rode the storm. It was an experience he hoped never to repeat, but he knew the possibility was still there. This fight wasn't over yet.

Patrick slid off of Nerys' ghostly steed close by, staggered a few steps, then flopped to the ground on his back, starfishing out. "I can't feel my face."

"I can't feel my dick," Keith whined from where he knelt on the ground beside the massive hound that had carried him west.

"I feel fine," Wade said, sounding smug as he patted down his coat, looking for a snack.

"You don't count," Patrick retorted.

Wade ignored him, making a pleased sound when he found a candy bar. He ripped it open and started to eat it.

Patrick flopped a hand at Wade. "Don't litter. It's rude, and the fae hate it."

Jono walked over to where Patrick lay on the ground, the snow settling on the shield that covered him rather than his body. Magic crackled in a line down the shield as it parted, his hand reaching for Jono's. He grabbed it, easily hauling Patrick to his feet. Jono wrapped his arms around the other man, feeling him shiver a little.

"Heat charms, Pat," Jono murmured, before pressing a kiss to the side of Patrick's head. "They need a refreshing."

"In a second," Patrick said, wrapping his arms around Jono's waist. He sounded tired.

Something warm uncoiled in Jono's chest at the way Patrick leaned into him without hesitation. Half a year of wearing down Patrick's sharp edges meant Jono appreciated these moments more than he could give voice to.

They stayed like that for a few more seconds, soaking in the nearness of each other even as the snow continued to fall. The sound of the sea crashing below was a dull roar in his ears as Jono breathed in Patrick's scent.

Fingers stroked over his back, and warmth bloomed at the touch, pushing through his clothes and down to his skin, chasing away the cold that had numbed his body well before they made it to the western shores of Ireland. When Patrick pulled away, pale blue magic crackled at his fingertips.

Between Patrick and William Desmond, the Hellraisers' sorcerer from the Caster Corps, everyone in their group once again had their clothes charmed for heat against the freezing winter weather they'd found themselves in.

Sage dipped her chin behind the high collar of her wool coat and rubbed her gloved hands together. "Now what?"

The Wild Hunt had yet to return to the sky and didn't seem in any hurry to leave. Patrick trekked back over to Jono after finishing up the last charm on a soldier's clothes. Everyone was dressed for winter in a city, not flying through the elements and ending up on what could have passed as the edge of the world.

"We ask the Cailleach Bheur for her help," Gerard said.

"Are you going to summon her how you summoned the Wild Hunt back in Central Park?" Keith asked.

"Gods aren't like demons. You don't summon them," Patrick replied.

"I don't know about that. Quite a few are on par with demons in my book," Jono said.

Gerard pointed his spear at the cliff jutting out to sea to the south of them, with the tower situated there half-obscured by drifting sea fog. "*Ceann na Cailli* is that way."

Keith made a face. "Kin-what now?"

"The Hag's Head."

Gerard led the way, but Jono stayed with Patrick as the group formed a single-file line. They took a well-worn path toward their destination, following the cliff's edge as the storm winds sought to bowl them all over. Jono tasted salt every time he breathed, ocean coating his tongue and the back of his throat.

Patrick marched ahead of him with a sureness to his stride that Jono attributed to his military career with the Mage Corps. It was the same sureness the other Hellraisers carried themselves with. Sage and Wade walked ahead of Patrick, both of them keeping their balance against the buffeting wind. Their pack was in the middle of the group, with the Hellraisers' sorcerer taking up the rear. Desmond seemed more than capable of shielding everyone if an attack happened.

Jono looked over his shoulder at the cliff they'd left behind them, seeing the Wild Hunt still burning bright against the snow. He turned back around and found Patrick watching him.

"Think the Dominion Sect knows where we are?" Jono asked.

"I really wouldn't put it past Medb to reach out to their emissary and warn them. Fae don't like to lose a game, much less a bargain. Gerard was shitty for days when he lost our poker games in the field."

The memory made Patrick scowl, but Jono couldn't smell what he was feeling. Patrick's shields were locked down tight, and all Jono could really smell was the ocean.

The cliff edge ran parallel to the path, close at times and farther away in other areas. The path was dangerous to traverse in weather like this, even with the low stone wall between them and the rocks below, but they didn't have a choice.

The Hag's Head grew larger on the horizon, the stone watchtower rising through the fog with every step they took. Jono's feet sank into the snow that had accumulated in the area, the soles of his shoes skidding on hidden ice. He caught his balance and wasn't the only one finding that little surprise underfoot.

The snow seemed thicker somehow on this cliff, falling heavier than it had on the one they'd arrived on. The winter cold was icier, eating through the heat charms that Patrick had layered over his clothes and shoes in a worrisome way. Up ahead, Gerard's notched spearhead was a beacon of fire, standing out against the gray sky and the falling snow.

When they finally made it to the area in front of the watchtower, the land was more ice than snow, the ground tinted blue, as if they walked on a glacier. Gerard carefully stepped on the ice, using his spear to keep his balance. Patrick followed after Gerard, which meant Jono stepped foot on the ice as well.

Gerard made a hand signal that had the rest of the Hellraisers staying put. Jono caught Sage's eye and jerked his head to the side. "Come along."

Sage tucked her hands into her coat pocket and leaned into the wind as she started walking. Wade joined her, unbothered by the cold, and Jono wondered if that was due to the high body temperature that sustained fire dragons. He brushed the thought aside, focusing on putting one foot in front of the other and not falling on his arse.

They rounded the watchtower, and the wind picked up with a viciousness that had Jono ducking his head against it. He wrapped an arm around Patrick's shoulders, steadying him. The cliff stretched out behind the tower for quite a ways before cutting downward to a pair of stone stacks that stood immovable against the storm on a lower section of the cliff.

A figure stood on top of the stone mound on the lip of rocky earth below, hunched over and clutching a staff. The gray cloak they wore fought the wind in a tangle of fabric that snapped behind their curled body. Jono took a deep breath, and beneath the ever-present ocean salt, he smelled the electric, ozone scent of a god.

"Maybe I should've waited with the guys," Wade muttered. Jono heard him easily enough, despite the howling wind coming off the ocean.

"You're pack. You stay," Jono said.

"Thought I was grounded?"

"Technically, that still means you stay," Sage said.

Gerard ground the butt of his spear against the ice, coming to a stop near the cliff's edge. "My lady."

The figure didn't move, not for a long few minutes. Jono heard her voice before he ever saw her face, like the crack of ice breaking on a frozen-over river in the middle of winter.

"Long has it been since this land felt your steps, Cú Chulainn," the Cailleach Bheur said.

Gerard ducked his head, whether out of respect or to ward off the wind, Jono didn't know. "Home is where my people are. I make of it what I can as the years pass me by, but *Éire* will always be the place of my birth."

"The wind still carries your name here."

"I hear it stronger on other shores these days."

The goddess straightened up to her full height, her stooped form larger than life in a way Jono couldn't explain. She turned away from the storm on the horizon to finally greet them face-to-face. Even from a distance, Jono could see she wore no clothes beneath her cloak, but the lack of coverage in the cold didn't affect her at all. The goddess' wrinkled skin was a dark blue, and her hair was as white as the snow around them. It took Jono a moment to realize that the large shape in the middle of her forehead was a single eye.

The Cailleach Bheur climbed off the rocks she stood on, using her staff for support as she came to meet them on the cliff. The closer she got, the colder it became, and Jono's breath puffed out of his nose and mouth in soft white clouds. When she finally stood before them on the same level of land, Jono could see her single eye was dark gray and streaked with white, like the waves pounding the shore below.

The Cailleach Bheur curled both gnarled hands around her staff and leaned her weight against the ancient wood. Jono's gaze dropped to where the end touched the ground, noticing how more ice spread around where the goddess stood.

"Brigid called you home," the Cailleach Bheur said.

Gerard's expression never changed. "You heard her."

"Pah. I always hear, whether I am stone or like this. Brigid rules her seasons, and I rule mine."

"Then you know the Summer Lady was taken to complete a bargain with Medb."

The Cailleach Bheur's mouth curled, revealing teeth smeared red with blood. Strangely, her lips remained pale, pale blue, with not a hint of red staining them. "There are war games and there are *war games*, and that one's trickery does her no favors."

"Gwyn ap Nudd said you could help us find where they are hiding Órlaith."

The Cailleach Bheur tapped her staff on the ground, sending more ice cascading outward. "I am capable of many things, Cú Chulainn. Capable does not mean willing."

"Let me guess. You want payment for your help," Patrick said.

The bitterness in his voice had Jono taking a step closer. In doing so, he drew the Cailleach Bheur's attention, and her regard was harder to face than Brigid's. That fact seemed to amuse her.

"I bled for his dagger, wolf. I chose my side. My payment in this fight was already given."

"Then what do you want?" Jono asked, carefully ignoring the way Fenrir roused at her pointed remark. The god stayed quiet though, content to listen rather than speak through Jono.

"What our kind all desire in this modern world." That single stormy eye cut back to Gerard, the shrewdness in her gaze that of the long-lived. "A life remembered."

The wind howled over them, the only sound for minutes on end. The tip of Jono's nose grew numb, as did his ears. His hair, damp from falling snow, sent droplets of water trickling down his neck to seep into the collar of his shirt. He tried not to shiver, knowing that he'd probably never stop if he started in this supernatural cold.

"If my father wants me home, tell him to ask me himself," Gerard finally said, the words coming out from between clenched teeth.

"You have tales that have yet to be told, carried on voices of the Irish diaspora. Come home and speak them to new ears."

"And if I don't?"

The Cailleach Bheur shrugged, her cloak twisting around her hunched, naked form. "Then you must live with the echo of silence as the years pass all of us by. Your life cannot escape our pantheon despite the bits of mortal blood that run through your veins. You are immortal in the eyes of our kind, in our stories. No amount of distance will change that. You go by many names, but only one has ever mattered."

"Órlaith matters to me."

"If you want her, then you will come home, Son of Lugh. You will bring the prayers that sustain you and the worshippers who remember you back to this land they left behind."

"It's not his fault none of you figured out how to be worshipped as the world changed," Patrick said.

"It is not our fault those of your blood seek our destruction, and yet, here we are." The Cailleach Bheur shuffled forward, ice paving the way for her. "Nothing of worth is ever free. There is a price for all things, and we gods are not excluded from that give-and-take."

"The Dominion Sect is after the Morrígan's staff, and we need all the help we can get to find it. Don't take Gerard out of this fight, lady," Jono said.

"Cú Chulainn knows the cost. If he wants my help stealing the Summer Lady back from his brother, then he will pay it."

A troubled look crossed Gerard's face. "Ferdiad is working with the Dominion Sect?"

One gnarled blue hand lifted to touch Gerard's cheek, his skin going white from the icy touch. "How else do you think they knew how to reach the Seelie Court? Mortals can never find the way without guidance. You have been gone a long, long time from these lands, Cú Chulainn. The old stories do not sustain us as they once did. Are you surprised Ferdiad is trying to write a new one for himself?"

"He'll lose his godhead," Patrick said flatly. "Whatever he thinks Ethan will give him, it's a fucking lie."

"Then do not give him a chance to live it." The Cailleach Bheur patted Gerard gently on the side of his face before letting him go. "What will it be? Your life or your lover's?"

"Gerard."

"Everything has a price, Patrick," Gerard said, never looking away from the Cailleach Bheur's face.

"I *know* you, Gerard. You can bargain better than this."

"Here I thought you didn't want to know me at all anymore."

Patrick scowled, taking a step closer, but Jono reached out to grab him by the elbow. Jono didn't want him anywhere near the immortal currently bending another god to her will. Fenrir growled approvingly of his choice of action.

Jono wondered just how powerful the Cailleach Bheur was that his own patron was wary enough to stay silent when Fenrir had been more than willing to chat to all the others of the Celtic pantheon.

"I'm allowed to be angry," Patrick said after a tense pause.

Gerard shrugged. "And I'm allowed to want to save the woman

I love and intend to marry. If Jono was in her place, wouldn't you do anything to save him?"

"What makes you think he hasn't already?" Jono asked in a low voice.

Gerard's silver eyes snapped up to meet Jono's gaze. "Patrick's soul debt is to Persephone, not to you or your patron."

Jono's lips curled. "And your fiancée isn't the only one who's ever been at Ethan's mercy. I was supposed to be the final sacrifice back in June, but Patrick saved me before Ethan could kill me and steal Zeus' godhead. Whatever is in that bloody dagger of Patrick's tied our souls together. Maybe you never saw that bond because you didn't put your blood or prayers into its making."

"What the fuck?" Sage bit out, staring at them in shock.

"Jono," Patrick said, shoulders gone tight beneath his leather jacket.

"You...what?" Gerard asked weakly. "Patrick, that's—"

"A death sentence if anyone found out. I *know*."

"We both know," Jono said quietly.

Gerard barked out a short, harsh laugh. "And you have the fucking nerve to be mad at *me* for keeping secrets?"

"Lying about what the gods did is a bit different than lying about being one, mate."

After a moment, Gerard tipped his head their way in silent acknowledgment of that careful distinction. "I apologized for that."

"I'm still mad," Patrick muttered.

"You always were a stubborn asshole." Gerard sighed. "And now you're soulbound."

"Yeah. I can tap a ley line again through Jono's soul." Patrick's mouth twisted in a sick parody of a smile as he looked at Jono. "The gods gave me another fucking weapon I never asked for, but he's mine now, and I'm keeping him."

The words warmed Jono from the inside out. He took Patrick's hand in his and raised it to his mouth, pressing a kiss over gloved knuckles. The leather was cold against his lips, but Jono didn't care.

"I'm not going anywhere," Jono promised.

Sage crossed her arms over her chest, glaring at them. "Any other secrets you two are hiding that you want to announce? First Fenrir, and now this?"

"You know why we couldn't talk about this," Patrick told her.

Wade raised his hand. "I don't."

"You don't mess with another person's soul. *Ever*. That's a law on the books in every country," Sage said, staring at them with troubled eyes.

"I didn't do it on *purpose*," Patrick said.

Sage sighed heavily and pressed her fingertips against her forehead, as if she had a headache and was trying to will it away. "What excuse are you telling people when you *do* tap a ley line?"

"Uh…I try not to tap it. I don't like what it does to Jono."

Jono nudged him with an elbow. "And I've told you I don't mind."

"How you feel about the situation isn't going to get you out of a federal death sentence. You said the dagger caused the soulbond? Then keep using the dagger as your excuse. Whatever magic you do that you shouldn't be able to do, it's because of the dagger from here on out," Sage said.

Patrick chewed on his bottom lip. "I never reported my dagger as an artifact to the government. They can't know how I got it, or how powerful it really is."

"How did you get it?"

"Ashanti delivered it to his hand after all the gods of heaven bled for it and forged it. She died for her efforts," the Cailleach Bheur said.

Sage's brow furrowed. "Ashanti?"

"The mother of all vampires, and a goddess in her own right," Gerard said.

"Ah." Sage shook her head. "The dagger is still your best excuse.

If anyone finds out about your soulbond, you're looking at capital punishment, Patrick."

Patrick grimaced and hunched his shoulders. "I *know*."

"Then take my advice. I'm your dire, that's what I'm here for."

"Yeah."

Sage arched an eyebrow at them. "Any other life-altering secrets I should know about?"

Jono and Patrick shared a glance. Jono shook his head. "No?"

"Great. It's been years since I was this cold. Can we finish up? We only have so much time left, and we shouldn't spend it arguing."

Gerard's mouth twitched at the corners. "You've made some good friends, Patrick."

"Pack," Jono corrected.

"That, too. But Sage is right. We're running out of time, and you're tied up in the bargain with Medb as well, Patrick. I'm not willing to lose you or Órlaith to Medb or your father," Gerard said.

"What about your brother?" Patrick asked.

Gerard grimaced before looking over at the Cailleach Bheur. "His myth is fading, isn't it? That's why Ferdiad believed whatever Ethan told him."

"We all do what we must when faced with being forgotten. Sometimes the lies are what we wish to hear because we believe they will become our truth," the Cailleach Bheur said.

"If I promise to return home, will you tell me where Órlaith is? I will bring what followers I have with me back to *Éire* to sing our stories again, but only after we find the Morrígan's staff and stop Ethan from turning himself into a new god. I gave my word to the dragon who commands me, and I refuse to break it."

The Cailleach Bheur eyed Wade. "Not this fledgling, I hope."

Wade waved his hands at her in a negative manner and rapidly shook his head. "Hell no. I'm not military."

Gerard drew himself up to his full height, the flicker of fire on the spearhead casting warm light over his face. "Will you accept my terms, my lady?"

"I will," the Cailleach Bheur said with a low cackle. "A bargain made is a bargain kept."

She extended her hand and Gerard shook it, ignoring the way ice formed over his fingers. When they broke apart, the ice cracked and fell off.

"Tell me where Órlaith is."

The Cailleach Bheur lifted her staff and pointed at the gray horizon southwest of them. "The seasons chase each other all year round. I always know where spring and summer thrive, as they know where the chill of winter sits. You will find the Summer Lady at the edge of our lands, in the sea. They hold her at *Na Scealaga*."

Gerard bowed to the Cailleach Bheur. "Your assistance is appreciated, my lady."

"Your word is binding, Cú Chulainn. Do not forget that."

The Cailleach Bheur hunkered down within her cloak, the color of her dark blue skin darkening to gray. Her movements became stiff and slow as her body hardened into stone limned in ice.

"Uh, so where exactly are we going?" Wade asked as Gerard turned on his heels and headed back up the cliff.

"The Skellig Islands," Gerard said.

Patrick jerked around, nearly falling as his feet slid over the ice. Jono grabbed him by the arm to keep him upright. "What? That place is a bunch of rocks and birds. It's gonna be freezing in this weather."

"Yes, and we'll bring the fight to the Dominion Sect."

"We need a plan that includes not falling into the ocean, Gerard."

"What sort of fight are we heading into?" Jono asked as they walked back to where the Hellraisers waited.

"Zachary Meyers is a heavy hitter, and who the fuck knows

who he has fighting with him. I don't know about this Ferdiad god," Patrick said.

"My foster brother will be a challenge. He always was," Gerard said.

"We need more firepower than just you, me, and Desmond."

Gerard glanced over his shoulder at them as he walked. "Who do you trust that can get here on such short notice? Because I'm not waiting any longer than I have to, Patrick. We can't afford inaction."

Patrick rocked to a halt, causing Jono to almost run into him. Jono grabbed him by the hips and urged him to keep walking.

Gerard sighed. "I remember that look. I already have a headache. Don't make it worse."

Patrick waved off Gerard's words and pulled out his mobile. "Fuck you, I have great ideas."

"Sometimes," Jono drawled. "Sometimes they're utterly terrible."

Patrick scowled, letting Jono guide him forward as he tapped at his screen before putting the mobile to his ear. "Fuck you, too, Jono."

"Later."

Wade made a gagging sound that turned into a squawk as Sage elbowed him in the side.

"Who are you calling?" Gerard wanted to know.

Patrick's smile was all teeth, and Jono wanted to kiss him. "Nadine."

19

SPECIAL AGENT NADINE MULRONEY, OF THE PRETERNATURAL Intelligence Agency, drummed the fingers of one hand against the wooden table before leaning forward to smack Patrick upside the head.

"*Ow*," Patrick exclaimed, glaring at her. "What was that for?"

"Because you're an idiot," Nadine replied coolly.

"How am I the idiot here?"

"Because you still haven't learned how to stop losing pieces of yourself for other people."

Nadine sat across from him at the wooden table tucked in the corner of the Bridge Bar they'd commandeered, a silence ward ensuring their privacy. The restaurant in Portmagee, County Kerry, had the Irish charm most tourists expected to find in a tiny coastal village a stone's throw from the Atlantic Ocean. Except it was the middle of winter, the tourist season was long over, and the only people in town were local.

The Wild Hunt had flown them from the Cliffs of Moher to the tiny village a few hours ago, riding a storm that had hidden their arrival on the streets. People still noticed them—it was difficult to hide a group of twenty or so people who suddenly appeared with no vehicles to speak of and the screams of the dead echoing in the air around them.

Currently, the Hellraisers and Patrick's pack had taken over many of the available tables, most of them foregoing drinks in favor of a light meal. No one wanted to fight drunk, but neither did any of them want to overeat. Wade was the exception. The teen had happily ordered four servings of fish 'n' chips during their time in the restaurant and was currently perusing the menu again. Since Gerard was paying for the food, Patrick wasn't about to tell Wade to stop ordering.

Patrick stole another fry off Jono's plate and popped it into his mouth, chewing angrily. Nadine stared him down, brown eyes unblinking as she rocked back in her chair, balancing it on two legs. Her brown hair was tied back in a tight braid, and her winter jacket hung haphazardly on a nearby hook. She was dressed for a fight in winter, her choice of tactical clothes similar to what the Hellraisers wore, even if the glamour covering everyone portrayed them as travelers to anyone looking.

Patrick was just glad she was here to fight with them.

Nadine had taken a direct flight from Paris to Dublin, then transferred onto a puddle jumper for the afternoon flight out to Kerry. She'd rented a car and driven an hour west to Portmagee to meet them. Her arrival on such short notice was allowed only due to the joint task force that General Noah Reed had spearheaded between the PIA, SOA, and the Department of the Preternatural. Otherwise, Patrick had a feeling she'd have been denied approval to help.

"What's the plan?" Nadine asked, glancing around the table. "Please, for the love of everything, tell me there is a plan."

Gerard scratched at his jaw and the hint of reddish-brown beard coming in there. "We ride the Wild Hunt to the Skellig Islands, free Órlaith, and take her back to the Unseelie Court to complete the bargain with Medb."

"Just like that?"

"You asked what the plan was. I never said it would be easy."

Nadine let her chair drop back to the floor with a dull thump. Her gaze swept over the group sitting at their table, and Patrick waited her out. They'd updated her on everything that had happened—Gerard's real name, Wade's background, and the confirmation of their god pack and all that entailed—but they needed her opinion on the hastily sketched-out plan. Nadine was a former combat mage, but her magic's affinity was heavily in the defensive area. She could build shields like no one else, and Patrick knew they would need that support. It's why he had called her.

That, and she was his best friend. Nadine would've kicked his ass if he didn't ask her for help and she found out after the fact about everything that had happened this month.

"Stop taking pointers from Patrick," Nadine said.

"No Christmas present for you," Patrick muttered under his breath.

Nadine kicked him in the shin under the table. "Yours is in the mail."

Patrick winced. "Admittedly, I haven't shopped for yours yet. I've been busy."

"Yes, busy making bargains with the fae when you know better." Nadine held up her hand when Patrick would've argued that point. "That argument is over, I won, moving on. We're going in blind, which I hate, so I'll be tapping a ley line on the flight over. If Ethan or Zachary are on the Skellig Islands, they'll feel it and know we're coming."

"Could you wait until we reach the island before tapping a ley line?" Gerard asked.

Nadine coolly stared him down. "You're asking us to fly over the Atlantic Ocean in a winter storm with the Wild Hunt. No, I'm not waiting to tap a ley line. You'll need my shields."

"I second that," Patrick said.

Nadine's gaze slid to him, one brow arching questioningly. "My use of a ley line?"

"*Our* use of a ley line." Nadine kicked him in the shin again, giving him a warning look. Patrick moved his legs away from her feet. "Gerard and my pack know about the soulbond."

"Do they now?" she asked in a dangerously silky voice. "Do they understand what's at risk by knowing?"

Nadine had found out about the soulbond after the fight in Central Park on summer solstice. She'd helped hide his soul and the damage done to it from the doctors and witches on staff at the hospital that had cared for him. By rights, she was an accessory to what had happened, and now so was everyone else who knew and didn't spill their guts to the authorities.

"Yes," Gerard replied calmly.

"If anyone asks about my magical reach, I'll blame it on the dagger," Patrick said.

Nadine leaned back in her chair and crossed her arms over her chest, staring at him with a worried look in her eyes. "Are you sure that's wise? You risk inviting oversight you don't need if people start questioning the level of spells you can do now when you shouldn't be able to."

Patrick shifted on his chair, absently rubbing at his chest. The scars there stemmed from childhood, but the deeper ones—the ones in his soul—a good chunk of those came from the end of the Thirty-Day War. His tainted soul had been broken by that sacrificial spell, the channels that allowed him to reach external magic burned out.

Being soulbound to Jono gave him a workaround provided by the gods, even if he hated the pain it caused Jono, and the lack of choice they'd both had in its making. Despite all that, it was a change Patrick was learning to accept, mostly because Jono was far more forgiving than he was.

"I can't hold back in a fight like this, Nadine. You're going to need my combat spells."

"One of the Skellig Islands is a UNESCO World Heritage Site. Please don't blow it up," Sage said.

"Both of them are rocky islands in the middle of an ocean. Not much flat ground to fight on," Jono said.

"We also don't know what backup the Dominion Sect has brought," Nadine said.

"We know Ferdiad will be there, and I will deal with him," Gerard said.

"Your Hellraisers have limited ammunition."

"Yes, but we know how to fight on land with limited coverage, and we have two mages, a sorcerer, werecreatures, and a dragon as our backup."

Patrick nodded. "Been years since I fought with you, but I haven't forgotten my training."

Gerard leaned forward, gesturing for the rest of his team to join them in the corner. Chairs scraped back as everyone stood and immediately came over. Patrick dragged his hand over the sigil he'd drawn on the underside of the table, wiping it away. The muffled sound of the wind beyond the walls and the soft conversation of the waitresses by the bar finally filtered through now that the bubble of white noise disappeared.

Gerard laid his phone on the table, the picture on its screen that of a rocky island with hints of green, the sea calm around it. Patrick knew that wasn't the sort of welcome they'd be getting.

"This is Skellig Michael, the island with the old monastery on it. It's the most logical place they're keeping Órlaith," he said.

"What's the plan?" Keith asked, crossing his arms over his chest, no hint of anger or distrust in his eyes or voice.

They all had a job to do, and while this fight was personal, their grievances had no place at the table.

Patrick settled his hand on Jono's thigh and leaned forward to listen.

PATRICK FELT the winter cold even through Nadine's shields.

The Wild Hunt flew through the clouds, the wind screaming around them while the sound of the ocean waves churning below was a promise of certain death if they fell. Patrick ducked his head behind Nerys' back, the dead fae rider immune to the elements. Nadine's personal shields were malleable protection that moved with them as they flew, blocking the wind, sleeting rain, and lightning that carried the Wild Hunt forward.

Patrick squinted through the space around them, the dark clouds speeding past but not completely capable of blocking out fellow riders. The Wild Hunt glowed faintly with an electric light, giving him enough illumination to see Gerard to his left. His old captain rode a stag, his spear bright like a bolt of lightning in his hand.

The rest of the Hellraisers were scattered passengers on horses, stags, or hounds of the Wild Hunt, as were Jono and Sage. Wade was the only one of their group flying to Skellig Island on his own merits. The teen had shifted mass in the hills outside Portmagee, hidden by a look-away ward.

Patrick had given Wade strict orders to stay high in the clouds until signaled to join the fight. They didn't know what long-range spells would be used, and Patrick didn't want Wade to get knocked out of the sky. He'd shifted to his dragon form half a dozen times since August, when they'd take him over to Marek's home in the Hamptons, but Wade didn't exactly know how to fight as a dragon. He might be mostly immune to magic, but Patrick wasn't willing to take any chances with Wade's life.

A heavy, cracking *boom* broke through the roar of the wind. Nerys' steed kicked into a dive that made Patrick's stomach crawl up his throat. Something huge and bright cut through the clouds where they'd been, the heat from the fireball hot enough Patrick could feel it on his face.

"They know we're here!" Gerard yelled with a battlefield loudness that was still difficult to hear over the wind. "Let's get to ground!"

The only ground within miles was Skellig Island, and the rocky islands were ground zero for the combat spells targeting them. Patrick held on to Nerys as tight as he could as she guided her horse into quicker flight, the dead beast more than willing to obey.

A glimmer of violet magic sparked at his peripheral vision. Patrick sensed Nadine's shields getting stronger, the amount of magic surrounding them powerful enough to make the damp hair on the back of his neck stand on end.

The next spell, when it hit, exploded like a supernova at the front of the Wild Hunt, cascading over Nadine's defenses without so much as a dent. The Wild Hunt reformed up, riding forward through the storm with a single destination in mind.

Between them and their destination came the Sluagh.

Patrick craned his head around, staring over his shoulder to search out Jono. Two riders over and flying lower in the crush of spirits, Jono locked eyes with him and nodded. If he said anything, Patrick couldn't hear it, but Jono had given permission to use the soulbond back when their feet were still on the ground.

Patrick sucked in a steadying breath and reached deep inside his soul for his magic and the bond that tied him to Jono. It was wide open between them, Jono's soul burning bright in his awareness. Patrick focused on the channels the dagger had carved into Jono's soul in June, tied to the soulbond, and only accessible to Patrick.

He sent his magic down through those channels for the ley line that snaked deep beneath the ocean floor. When he connected, it was as if a live wire had shocked every last nerve in his body, and Jono's soul was all that stood between him and severe electrocution. Patrick's teeth tingled from the excess magic as he drew it out from the ley line and conjured up a dozen mageglobes. The spheres of magic erupted around him and Nerys, spinning like the rocky rings of an outer planet in the solar system.

Patrick cast a fusillade spell in every single mageglobe, the command trigger held tight in his mind, on his tongue. He let go of Nerys long enough to twist one wrist and splay his fingers wide in a command gesture. The mageglobes shot forward, streaking through the night sky like comets.

Smaller in formation by far than the nova spell the Dominion Sect had lobbed their way in the initial attack, Patrick's spell was military grade and made for a sustained attack. The Sluagh, dead though they might be, were still susceptible to magic.

When Patrick snapped his fingers, mouthing the command word, the world lit up like fireworks on the Fourth of July. Raw magic poured through Jono's soul and into his, straight through to the fusillade spell still exploding in the midst of the Sluagh.

As in August, when he'd fought Santa Muerte, the fusillade spell didn't stop after the initial explosion. The sustained attack forced the Sluagh to scatter, sending some tumbling down to the waves below when they lost their orientation in the air, and the ocean swallowed them whole. Those that remained screamed their fury, the sound louder than the wind.

Down below amidst the black sea, pinpricks of light held steady against a solid darkness that didn't move—the Skellig Islands.

Nerys wrapped the reins around her hands to shorten them and guided her horse back into the clouds, with the rest of the Wild Hunt following in her wake. The clouds swallowed them back up, blocking out the world, and Patrick's spatial sense didn't know what way was up. He swallowed back the nausea and focused on drawing more magic out of the ley line.

The plan was to do an aerial drop on Skellig Michael.

The plan was to not die.

The plan got thrown out of the goddamn proverbial window when something huge, dark, sinewy, and full of *teeth* cut through the clouds from below.

The creature slammed against Nadine's shields, sending violet ripples through her defenses. But they held, because it'd take more than a sea monster out of some long-forgotten myth to make Nadine drop her shields.

Patrick caught a glimpse of an impossibly wide mouth full of layers of serrated teeth that disappeared down its throat, and large eyes the size of a semitruck tire before the sea creature gave in to gravity and crashed back to the sea.

"What the *fuck* was that?" Patrick yelled.

"An annoyance," Gerard shouted back, teeth bared in a hard smile.

Patrick rolled his eyes. *I don't get paid enough for this bullshit.*

Nerys dug her heels into her horse's side and pulled on the reins, guiding the Wild Hunt right. Patrick couldn't see where they were going, but he could feel the route in his stomach. Nerys led them higher into the sky before her horse gave a mighty kick into a spinning dive that made Patrick dizzy and reminded him of flying dark into a war zone to land under threat of fire.

And the fire did come.

Spells shot through the sky like ballistic missiles, slamming against Nadine's shields with enough force Patrick was momentarily blinded by flashes of violet light that curled back over the Wild Hunt.

Patrick gripped Nerys' belt tight in his left hand before leaning around her far enough to extend his right hand toward the ground. He opened himself up to the soulbond and the ley line, letting a flood of wild, raw magic pour out of him and through the stabilizing mageglobe spinning against the palm of his hand.

The shock-wave spell ripped out of Patrick like a tsunami, the arc of magic tailored for the living and the dead, but not the earth below, cognizant of the ancient structures they didn't want to destroy. His magic ripped through the spells coming their way, the air around them vibrating with power. Patrick made a fist, the mageglobe encasing his hand in burning pale blue light as he guided the spell.

Magic exploded over wet black stone, bathing Skellig Michael in bright light long enough for the Wild Hunt to shake off their passengers. Patrick launched himself off the ghostly horse and hit the ground hands-first. He rolled head over heels, getting his feet under him and pulling his dagger free of its sheath. The matte-black blade spat heavenly white fire, giving him light to see by but making him a prominent target on the storm-lashed rocky island.

The Wild Hunt launched back into the sky where the Sluagh was regrouping in the storm. Lightning exploded in the clouds, followed by the deafening sound of thunder and the screaming of the Sluagh. Automatic fire echoed in the air, the impact of bullets against Nadine's shield like tiny electric flares around them.

A large shape leaped out of the darkness toward him, and the only reason Patrick didn't go for the head was the soulbond. Jono landed beside him, a monstrous, hulking werewolf that looked ready to murder anyone or anything that got in his way.

Which was good, because the demon stalking toward them along the ancient stone wall below made Patrick freeze as recognition cut through his magic hot enough to make him forget about the cold. His mouth went dry, but that didn't stop him from shouting a warning, using an amplifying charm to pitch his voice loud enough to be heard over the storm.

"*Soultaker!*" Patrick shouted.

The demon in question screamed, the sound like tearing metal. It jumped off the stone wall and came up the wet slope of land to their position at a quick pace. Its bipedal body traversed the muddy dirt easily enough.

Mottled, leathery gray skin was split over joints, black bones like shadow in the after-flash of lightning and the flare of magic in the sky. Razor-sharp claws extended from the stumps of its palms while its long, pointed tongue flicked in and out of its mouth with prehensile strength. Its head had no eyes, no nose, and was filled only with a wide mouth filled with rows of jagged teeth.

Soultakers fed on souls and magic, and Patrick had hoped he'd seen the last of hell's version of a walking bottomless pit of hunger back in June.

"Everyone! Watch your six!" Gerard shouted.

The plan was for Patrick, Nadine, Gerard, Desmond, Jono, and Sage to pair up with the remaining Hellraisers, creating an even balance of preternatural, magical, and mundane human fighting teams. That would've worked before the soultakers hit the field. Now, the only ones with a chance at stopping the damned demons were Jono and Sage due to their enhanced strength, speed, and senses, and Patrick's dagger.

Patrick, well, he was still prey.

That didn't mean he couldn't become the hunter.

Jono snarled a warning and took a step forward, wolf-bright blue eyes never leaving the soultaker. Patrick conjured up a mageglobe, filling it with raw magic. He expanded his own personal shields and looked over his shoulder at where Nadine stood, a tiny, violet mageglobe hovering near her left shoulder.

Nadine's shields could withstand a lot, but the one thing she couldn't win against was a soultaker. The large shield she had around their group flickered at the first tearing bite from the demon.

"I need to take down my shield before it drains me," Nadine said, thumbing the safety off her tactical handgun.

Patrick nodded. "Do it."

"Get ready to scatter," Gerard ordered.

The mageglobe near her shoulder disintegrated. Her shield expanded outward, giving the Hellraisers a last bit of cover before it, too, faded away. Everyone scattered in search of cover, racing into the dark and toward who knew what threats. Patrick held his ground with Jono on the slope, pulling his magic out of the soulbond, because no way was he going to give the soultaker a chance to gorge on a ley line.

"You hungry?" Patrick asked, struggling to locate the soultaker in the dark.

Jono snorted once before racing forward, a massive, hulking beast that dwarfed the soultaker's body. It screamed again, the sound making Patrick's teeth hurt as he raced after Jono, not sure what cover was best on either side of the stone wall. Anything was better than out in the open at this point.

Illumination was a risk once they got boots on the ground, and the lack of it made it difficult to get one's bearings. Patrick could hear just fine though—the roar of the wind and sea, and Jono's pissed-off snarl. The soultaker's scream echoed in the air before abruptly cutting off. Lightning flashed above, and Patrick could just make out the stone wall ahead and Jono's hunched-over form not far away.

Patrick put his back to the wall and crouched down, blinking through the rain. Jono's eyes flashed into view. Patrick uncurled his fingers from around his mageglobe to cast some light between them as Jono approached.

"Oh, gross," Patrick said, making a face at what Jono carried in his mouth.

Jono spat out the soultaker's head, having torn it off the demon's body through sheer brute force. It rolled over the wet dirt, tongue flopping around, and would've touched Patrick's boots if he didn't move backward.

"What? You want me to say thanks? This is not the kind of Christmas present I wanted."

Jono's eyes narrowed, the brightness minimizing in the dark. Patrick couldn't stop himself from reaching out to pat Jono on the head.

"Fine. You're a good boy."

Jono growled, clearly unamused, before moving past Patrick. He turned to follow where Jono was headed, staying low against the wall. In the next flash of lightning, Patrick caught a glimpse of an arched opening in the stone up ahead and the stairs that led up to it. He didn't trust what might be found through that entrance and grabbed Jono's tail, giving it a tug.

"Let me shield you," Patrick said.

Jono whipped his tail out of Patrick's grip and waited long enough for Patrick to expand his shields so the defense covered them both. They weren't as powerful as Nadine's, but it was better than nothing.

They hurried through the rain, Patrick holding his mageglobe close to his body to minimize the light. He trusted in Jono to guide him as they came up against the rocky stairs and supporting wall that bracketed the entrance.

A sharp whistle made Patrick pause. Seconds later, Gerard scaled the opposite wall and flung himself to the ground beside them. The *Gáe Bulg* burned with magic in his hands, the notched spearhead a beacon Patrick didn't care for.

"You gonna put that fire out?" he asked.

Gerard straightened up, attention on the shadowy entrance they had yet to reach. "No, I don't think I will."

"You never did learn how to lay down your weapon, *dearthâir*," a new voice said.

Jono pressed against Patrick's side, angling his massive body so that he was between Patrick and the threat that walked out of the low arched entrance and straightened up to his full height.

Lightning crashed down to ocean at the rocky edge of the island, the blue-white light heating the air and casting shadows on Gerard's face. It was enough light for Patrick to make out the grim slant of his old captain's mouth.

"Ferdiad," Gerard said. He tossed Patrick his rifle and maneuvered the *Gáe Bulg* into a two-handed grip. "Where's Órlaith?"

As far as Patrick was concerned, family reunions were fucking *awful*.

20

Ferdiad's accent was nothing like Gerard's. He sounded as Irish as the fae they'd left behind in Tír na nÓg, but looked nothing like the last couple of gods Patrick had dealt with. Ferdiad was one who had embraced the modern world rather than live on the other side of the veil. In the glare of lightning and the illumination of the clashing Wild Hunt and Sluagh in the sky, Patrick could just make out the weirdly mottled skin on Ferdiad's face and hands.

The immortal wore black body armor and could've passed as any mercenary-for-hire if one ignored the spear he held. The weapon didn't burn with magic like Gerard's, but Patrick was going to treat the damned thing as an artifact and a threat unless proven otherwise.

"I won't ask again," Gerard said, pointing the *Gáe Bulg* at his brother.

"If you want her, get on your knees and beg," Ferdiad said, falling into a fighting stance.

"Gods don't beg."

Gwyn ap Nudd's words fell off of Gerard's lips, and all the rage he'd been holding back followed with a yell Patrick remembered from the battlefield. It echoed in the air like thunder as Gerard lunged forward, thrusting the *Gáe Bulg* forward to push Ferdiad back. The other immortal pushed Gerard's spear aside, but the defensive move was immediately countered by Gerard.

The two engaged in an arms dance that had them both leaping to scale the wall with a reach no human would have. They left the entrance wide open as they fought. Patrick ran through it with Jono, hunched over to clear the low ceiling. He kept his shields raised and clambered up a set of stone stairs. When he cleared the narrow passage, Patrick was nearly thrown off his feet by the coordinated attack led by Zachary Myers and other Dominion Sect acolytes.

Pale blue sparks burned away from his shields as multiple attack spells slammed into him. Jono braced him from behind, making sure he didn't tumble down the stairs. Patrick pressed his hand against the curve of his shield and added another layer, strengthening it as much as he could.

Witchlights flickered into existence above them, casting silvery light on the waterlogged courtyard. The beehive-shaped domes built out of rocks by long dead monks rose behind Zachary and some of his fighters. Patrick took in where they held the line with a couple of soultakers, blocking the path that led to the domes. He didn't see Ethan or Hannah, but that didn't mean they weren't here somewhere.

Gunfire and shouting echoed through the air from other areas of the island—the Hellraisers were taking the fight to other Dominion Sect mercenaries. Patrick hoped all the enemy magic users were standing in front of him and not making his old team's lives a living hell.

"Patrick," Zachary said, his hands raised, palms extended outward. Beneath the witchlights, Patrick could make out the black concentric circles tattooed onto the palms of his hands.

"Where's Órlaith?" Patrick demanded.

Zachary smiled, fingers spreading wider. "She's ours now."

The winter chill couldn't compete with the icy feeling that trickled down Patrick's spine. He'd survived being sacrificed to the hells as a child when his twin sister had not. Hannah's body contained Macaria's godhead now, a mistake that Ethan had yet to rectify. Ethan was tied to Hannah, and he used the power in her soul like his own personal nexus.

That power bolstered Ethan's efforts in the past to steal Ra and Zeus' godheads. Patrick hoped Ethan hadn't tried again with Órlaith, but he wouldn't know until he got eyes on the Summer Lady.

"She never belonged to *you* in the first place."

"We take what we want for the greater good."

"Is that what you're calling it these days?"

Patrick eyed the soultakers that paced on either side of Zachary. The bullets in the rifle Gerard had given him wouldn't pierce the demons' thick skin, and any magic he used on them threatened to be swallowed whole. Patrick hesitated a second before he ejected the magazine from the rifle and shoved it into his back pocket. He dropped the rifle to the ground, with the intention of retrieving it later if they survived this mess. He needed his hands free for this fight.

Patrick conjured up half a dozen mageglobes, lining them up in front of him. He unsheathed his dagger and gripped it tightly. White heavenly fire erupted from it, the silver words of prayers in languages he didn't speak drifting across the matte-black blade. Patrick extended his free hand toward Jono, fingers brushing over thick wet fur.

Across from him, the concentric tattooed circles on Zachary's palms split open in the center of each line. Blood dripped down the palm of his hands and off his skin to form murky, red-black mageglobes in the air. The recognition that shot through Patrick at the use of blood magic made him almost gag.

"Oh, it's that fucker."

Keith came up the stairs into the courtyard, and Patrick was quick to raise a shield between his friend and the enemy.

"Thought you had your orders?" Patrick asked, not taking his eyes off Zachary.

Keith braced his rifle against his shoulder and aimed the weapon at a sorcerer standing to Zachary's right. "And I'm following them."

"You and your team weren't enough back in the Thirty-Day War. What makes you think you'll be enough this time?" Zachary asked.

Patrick eyed the way Zachary's mageglobes scattered in a line to counter his own. "Because we're fucking stubborn."

Patrick let loose the strike spell at the same time Zachary released his. The two spells collided, the resulting explosion making Patrick shield his eyes from the light and dig his feet into the muddy ground. The blowback ran through his nerves, the strike spell tearing through Zachary's in a way that canceled each other out but still sent chunks of earth high into the sky. The stone wall to his right broke apart, ancient pieces of rock hurtling into the air.

"I thought we weren't supposed to destroy the heritage site?" Keith said.

"That was more of a suggestion," Patrick replied.

"I'll let you be the one to tell Sage that."

The sharp stretch of magic in Patrick's soul as the soultakers ate the last vestige of his spell made him grimace. Jono growled, as if he could feel what Patrick was going through and didn't like it.

Zachary hadn't moved, but his magic users had repositioned themselves to better cover the stone pathway leading to the beehive-shaped huts. Patrick sank his free hand into Jono's fur, giving him a little shake.

"Think you can find Órlaith?" Patrick asked.

Jono growled, and that was all the answer Patrick needed.

Patrick opened himself up to the soulbond again, sending his awareness through Jono's soul and down to the ley line burning below. Skellig Michael didn't have a nexus below, but the ley line that ran directly beneath it was powerful enough to make Patrick light-headed for a second when he tapped it.

Beside him, Jono didn't react, eyes on the enemy as Zachary conjured up several more mageglobes. Blood magic had a particular feel to it that made Patrick want a shower. Magic sparked at Patrick's fingertips as more mageglobes spun into existence in front of him. The soultakers stalked forward, their mouths opened wide as their tongues lashed out, tasting magic in the air.

An explosion of magic behind Zachary's position had some of the Dominion Sect magic users turning to face the new threat. The spells they tossed at the group of Hellraisers coming up behind them crashed harmlessly against Nadine's shields.

Zachary clenched both his hands into fists before jerking his arms to the side. The rolling wave of power that exploded their way was followed by the soultakers. The top layer of Patrick's shields sheared off, with the tearing pull in his soul starting up again. The glare of Zachary's spell faded, replaced by soultakers who'd closed the distance between them in the courtyard.

Teeth sank into Patrick's shields, the demons too close for comfort. Keith kept his finger off the trigger of his rifle, knowing that bullets were wasted on soultakers. Which left Patrick and Jono to take the lead.

"Get ready," Patrick said.

He lobbed another mageglobe at Zachary, filling it with raw magic meant for explosions and nothing else. Patrick set them off at the same instant he created a hole in his shields for Jono to pass through. Jono attacked the nearest soultaker, dragging it to the ground while Patrick sacrificed mageglobes to the other pair of soultakers to give Jono time to fight.

Screams erupted over them, and Patrick jerked his head back in time to see the Sluagh descending on their position. The restless dead crashed against his shields and the area around them, clawing at his shields. Jono snarled, dodging the clawed legs of a few spider fae while trying to force the soultaker onto the defensive.

Patrick shoved his shields past where Jono fought, which meant, while Jono was safe from the Sluagh, none of them were safe from the soultaker that came with him.

Keith dropped back down the stairs for cover. "Motherfucker!"

Patrick put himself between Keith and the soultaker, dagger at the ready. Half his attention was on how Jono was herding the demon his way, the rest was on the Sluagh struggling to tear through his shields and the other soultakers that were getting damned close.

"Get with the magic, Razzle Dazzle," Keith said.

"Oh, fuck you, it's not like I enjoy getting my soul sucked dry," Patrick yelled over his shoulder.

He didn't rely on his magic, but his dagger and Jono's ability to corral a demon most others ran from. Which would be the smart option, but Patrick had never been one for *smart* over getting the job done—not when lives were on the line.

One of Zachary's spells exploded against Patrick's shields right as he lunged for the soultaker's back. He drove his dagger through the demon's thick skin even as the backwash of the magical hit brought him to his knees. Patrick dragged the soultaker down with him, black spots flickering at the edge of his vision as heavenly magic burned through the demon quicker than Jono's teeth could sink into its body.

The soultaker burned to ash in his grip, the remnants of it sinking into the mud. The other soultakers eating their way through his shields screamed loud enough that the headache building in the back of Patrick's head exploded through his skull. He shoved the pain aside with long practice, getting to his feet. Jono turned to face the soultakers who had nearly eaten their way through Patrick's shields, lips pulled back in a snarl.

A storm of ghostly arrows fell from above, aimed by the Wild Hunt. The arrows slammed into the Sluagh and forced them away from the shields. The soultakers shook off the attack as if it were nothing.

"Take cover," Patrick ordered Keith, who ducked down the stairs without argument. "Nerys! We need a lift!"

The Wild Hunt flew over the courtyard, raining hell on the Dominion Sect magic users, forcing them to scatter. Patrick caught sight of Zachary sprinting for the beehive-shaped domes at the rear of the courtyard. Patrick tore down his shields in order to deny the soultakers more magical fuel for their insatiable needs.

Nerys descended on her horse like an avenging angel of war. She held out her hand, and Patrick grabbed for it as she rode past. She swung him up behind her, the fatal wound in her chest that had killed her long ago looking as if it would tear her torso in two as she moved. A pair of riders cast a golden net that scooped Jono up in a way Patrick would laugh about if the situation wasn't so life or death.

"Drop us on the next level!" Patrick yelled

The Wild Hunt flew low over the domes, dropping them both into a waterlogged courtyard. Patrick flung himself off Nerys' horse while Jono shook himself free of the net. They fell fifteen feet to the ground, ready for the hit. Patrick took the impact in his knees and ankles, stumbling through the momentum so he didn't break any bones. Jono landed beside him, digging all four paws into the ground to steady himself. The Wild Hunt rode back into the sky where the Sluagh was regrouping, screaming a challenge Nerys seemed intent on meeting.

Then Jono's head swung around, ears pricked forward as he zeroed in on the small dome at the end of the upper courtyard. Patrick followed where Jono looked, seeing the stone there practically glowing with wards he couldn't read, but he could feel the magic embedded there down to his bones, despite his shields. Those were wards set by an immortal, to hide something—or someone—of worth.

The heavy boom of an explosion directly above them nearly

deafened him, making Patrick hunch over instinctively. Patrick looked up at the violet shield stretching over their area of the courtyard and the hissing, burning blood magic that crawled over the impact site. Patrick didn't know where Nadine was, but he was grateful for the assist.

Patrick ran for the warded dome but skidded to a halt when a soultaker stepped out of the low opening, its whiplike tongue lashing the air. Jono didn't stop, barreling toward the soultaker with a single-minded focus that would worry Patrick if he knew the other man couldn't handle the threat.

The soultaker lunged at Jono, who twisted out of reach before headbutting the demon in the side hard enough to send it flying through the air. Jono went after it, and Patrick went after whatever it had been guarding in the dome.

The threshold wrapped around the stone entrance tasted like hell in the back of Patrick's throat. He swallowed against it, half listening to Jono's fight happening behind him. He didn't have time to undo whatever wards had been set on the rocky dome, so he went for the most direct approach.

Patrick switched up his grip on the dagger and stabbed at the low entrance with the blade. White fire flared around his hand, crackling through the air and fighting with the magic tangled across the way in. The wards flashed a violent red, and Patrick ripped the dagger downward, the heavenly magic in the blade breaking through mortal magic.

The wards broke apart in a cascading wave, the power erupting outward hot enough to burn. Patrick dove through the entrance, his dagger and a couple of mageglobes lighting the way. Heart pounding in his chest, Patrick didn't know what he was going to find inside and was prepared for the worst.

Something crashed over him, muffling his magic in a way that made him swear. His mageglobe winked out of existence, the shock of its disappearance making his head throb. Being inside the rocky dome gave him the exact same sensation as the binding ward Medb's iron bracelets had shackled him with back at the Unseelie Court. Patrick shook his head, tightening his grip on his dagger. At least this time, he had something to fall back on.

"Come any closer, and I will tear out your heart with my teeth."

The Irish lilt to a raspy voice had Patrick stepping closer to the person who spoke, no matter that it drew him to the center of the spell. Patrick extended his arm, letting the dagger's white light help him see.

Órlaith knelt in the center of concentric circles drawn with blood, stripped naked and held in place not by binding wards, but iron chains etched with bloody sigils that glowed. Heavy manacles were locked around her wrists, ankles, and throat, the chains connecting to the stone rocks that made up the dome.

Órlaith bared her teeth at him, the split lip and bruised cheek evidence that she hadn't succumbed to this quietly or easily. Her red-orange hair was a knotted mess, hanging down over her torso and hiding her full breasts from view. Her arms were raised behind her at an angle, the pressure in her shoulders probably excruciating.

Patrick raised his hands in a calming manner, eyes on the concentric circles he'd crossed over. "I'm with Gerard. Uh, I mean, Cú Chulainn."

Órlaith squinted up at him, the gold flecks in her summer-sky-blue eyes catching the light from his dagger. "I remember you. You fought with him some years back."

"Yeah. It's one big family and team reunion right now."

Órlaith leaned forward as far as she could, the bones in her shoulders rotating in a way that looked as if they were about to pop out of the joint. "Free me."

Patrick's heart pounded in his chest. Releasing her was the goal, but it felt a lot like letting loose a bomb in a crowded room, and he was standing at ground zero. Patrick stepped closer to Órlaith and knelt in front of her. The spell keeping her contained was built on blood magic, but he knew it took another immortal to contain an immortal. Zachary might have built the spell's circles, but Ferdiad was the one who had shackled her on this island in the middle of the ocean.

Patrick raised his left hand and let it hover over Órlaith's cheek. "Can I touch you?"

"Get me out."

He took that as permission granted and gently placed his hand against her face, tilting her head back as far as the thick iron collar would let him. A Celtic knot stamped into the iron of the collar glowed with an orange-red light that made it look like metal just taken out of a forge. Patrick pressed the tip of his dagger against the knotwork, the blade flaring with magic that cast strange shadows on Órlaith's face.

The dagger's magic cut through the spell cast by Ferdiad, with the sigils fading to nothing down every chain that held her in place. The concentric circles that acted as an anchor to the spell flickered but didn't fade out.

The collar fell away, and the air became electrified with power as Órlaith clenched her hands into fists and jerked her arms forward. The chains ripped free of the stone walls—and the circles beneath their feet exploded from power that backwashed through the spell which had imprisoned her.

Patrick ripped his shields wider, hoping to encase Órlaith in them, but they both still caught the brunt of the explosion as the spell deteriorated. The stone rocks that made up the ancient dome shattered and flew through the air like shrapnel. The impact of magical backlash against his shields nearly blinded Patrick as he and Órlaith were thrown through the air with enough force they cleared the courtyard and terraces below, flung far from the safety of earth.

Even Nadine's shields couldn't stand for long against the power of a god, and Patrick felt her defenses fall before they hit against it at a speed that would break bones. Gravity pulled them both toward the stormy ocean that lashed the base of Skellig Michael that Patrick couldn't see, his yell lost to the wind. His stomach twisted in a way it hadn't when flying with the Wild Hunt, arms windmilling hard as he struggled to orient himself in the dark.

I'm gonna die.

The frantic thought was cut off as fire flashed between the sharp teeth of a dragon, the light reflected in Wade's gold eyes.

Patrick nearly swallowed his tongue when Wade flew toward them from below, wings flapping hard to gain speed and altitude. Sharp talons snagged Patrick and Órlaith out of midair before they could hit the ocean. Patrick curled his arms around one black talon, his legs dangling in the air as rain pelted him in the face.

"Okay!" Patrick yelled, his voice a little high-pitched and heart pounding so hard in his chest he thought it might break a rib. "You're not grounded anymore!"

Wade snorted fire and smoke out of his nose. Patrick figured that was teenage dragon-speak for *no take backs.*

Wade flew over the monastery of Skellig Michael before banking hard on one wingtip. He spiraled down to land on the rocky area overlooking the courtyards and terraces. Wade folded his wings forward to cover Patrick and Órlaith as he set them on the ground. Patrick's feet slipped on the wet rock, but he got his balance back after a second or two.

Then Wade thrust his long neck forward, body shifting over them in a protective manner. Patrick was nearly knocked over, but he managed to stay on his feet. Wade raised his head toward the sky, powerful jaws chomping on what once was a soultaker. His long throat undulated as he swallowed the soultaker down in chunks.

When he finished eating the demon, Wade craned his long neck down toward them, his large wedge head tilted so he could stare down at Patrick with one golden eye. Fire flickered between his teeth, the warmth of it nearly drying the raindrops or cold sweat on Patrick's face—he wasn't sure which sort of wetness it was that trickled down his skin.

"We're good." Patrick reached up to pat Wade on the side of his scaly nose. Wade huffed out a breath that almost singed Patrick's hair. "Stop that. Don't make me ground you again."

Wade gape-grinned in a way that showed all his teeth, but Patrick had seen Wade passed out on the couch in a snack coma too many times before to ever think he was a threat in either form.

Patrick ducked under Wade's jaw, shoving his dagger into its sheath as he approached Órlaith. She stood on the rocky ground, head bent back to soak up the winter rain even as green moss spread around her feet like a blanket of summer. Patrick shrugged out of his leather jacket and offered it to her.

"Here," he said. "You must be cold."

Órlaith lowered her head and opened her eyes, the power in her gaze that of a goddess unleashed. "Your gift is appreciated."

She took his leather jacket and pulled it on. Now that she was no longer bound, Órlaith was healing. The bruises on her face were starting to fade, even if her rage still burned just as hot in her eyes.

"Ferdiad is mine," Órlaith said.

Wade parted his wings, offering her a way out of his protection. Patrick didn't get in her way as the Summer Lady walked away, moss and flowers cascading away from every step she took. The sudden change in atmospheric pressure made Patrick's headache worse. He stayed next to Wade, watching as Órlaith raised both arms to the sky and *screamed.*

Patrick clamped both hands over his ears, but that did nothing to block out the sound. He heard it deep in his skull, a resonance that made it difficult to think and slammed into him as if it were a physical blow. Órlaith never stopped screaming, the sound echoing over Skellig Michael with a concussive force strong enough to push aside the winter rain lashing the island. Patrick looked up as the clouds broke apart above them, spinning wider until he could see the clear night sky.

"*Órlaith!*"

Gerard's shout pierced her scream the way nothing else could. Órlaith snapped her mouth shut, her scream fading to echoes. Patrick carefully uncovered his ears, looking around as witchlights flickered into existence above where they stood, revealing all the green that had burst through the rocky crevices to cover every stone and patch of dirt as far as he could see in the dim light.

The one bright spot was Gerard's spear as the other man vaulted over the rocky wall and ran toward them. Jono wasn't far behind, with Sage hot on his heels, both of them clawing their way over the walls in their werecreature forms.

"Cú Chulainn," Órlaith said in a relieved voice.

She spread her arms wide and Gerard ran right into her, lifting Órlaith off her feet in a fierce hug as he clutched at her. Órlaith held on just as tightly, kissing him fiercely. The desperation in Gerard's face tempered into a relief so deep Patrick thought he'd start crying.

Jono skidded to a stop beside Patrick, headbutting him in concern. Patrick sank his hands into Jono's thick fur. "I'm fine."

More figures headed their way from down the hill. Patrick conjured up a mageglobe out of caution, but he recognized Keith when the other man got within sight. The Hellraisers and Nadine regrouped with his pack and the immortals on the rocky incline overlooking the monastery. Some of the soldiers needed assistance, but all of them were alive and not critically injured. That was all Patrick cared about.

Gerard finally set Órlaith on her feet and kissed her deeply, holding his spear at an angle away from her body so as not to harm her with it. When they finally separated, Gerard looked down at her and brushed some of her long, wet hair off her pale cheek.

"Are you all right?" he asked.

"Bruised, but nothing worse than that."

"They didn't try to remove your godhead?"

Órlaith shook her head. "No. I was to be part of a trade."

"They wanted Brigid," Patrick said grimly.

"Yes. They said her godhead was preferable to mine for what it carried and what she is known for as a goddess."

Gerard tucked wet strands of hair behind her ear. "They can't have either of you."

"An admirable dedication, but I would prefer you promise me something else."

"And that would be?"

"I want your brother's head," Órlaith replied, her voice carrying with it the fury of a summer storm.

Gerard raised her hand to his lips and kissed her knuckles. "Then it will be yours."

"Speaking of that asshole, what happened to him?" Patrick asked.

"They retreated through the veil. The Sluagh went with them. Fucking cowards," Keith said, spitting on the ground.

"We need to do the same. I don't think Medb is expecting us to keep our side of the bargain, and I wouldn't put it past her to weasel out of the terms."

Órlaith looked at Gerard. "You made a bargain with that bitch?"

Gerard shrugged one shoulder. "Your life and Patrick's for the Morrígan's staff."

"Clearly you make terrible decisions when I am not around. Medb will never give that artifact up."

"I wasn't prepared to give *you* up."

"A bargain is still a bargain, and we need to keep it," Patrick said.

"How the hell do we get through the veil? Are we taking the Wild Hunt again?" Keith wanted to know. "Not all of us can ride, Captain."

Gerard straightened up. "Status?"

Keith jerked his thumb toward the team's sorcerer. Desmond looked a little worse for wear. "Those Dominion Sect assholes kept trying to knock him off the island."

"Nothing broken, just a few bruised ribs. I can still fight," Desmond said.

The rest of the Hellraisers echoed his assertion. Patrick pressed a knuckle against his temple, digging it in against the throbbing in his skull. "Can you guarantee the Wild Hunt can get us to the Unseelie Court in time?"

"No need to call upon Gwyn ap Nudd's hunters," a familiar voice interrupted. "Medb's throne belonged to me long before the stories gave it to her. I will take you to the heart of winter."

Everyone turned toward the person who spoke. Walking up the incline, her staff creating pockets of ice over all the greenery Órlaith had summoned with her freedom, came the Cailleach Bheur. Her hunched form moved with a fluidity the old never had, and her single eye gleamed beneath the hovering witchlights.

"My lady," Órlaith said, dipping her chin in a respectful manner at the goddess.

"I see you still live, child. Cú Chulainn would not have found you without my aid."

Órlaith frowned at Gerard. "What does she speak of?"

"I'll explain later," Gerard said, staring at the Cailleach Bheur. "After we have brought you to the Unseelie Court to fulfill my bargain with Medb."

"No. You will tell me now."

Gerard looked at Órlaith, his expression softening. "The Cailleach Bheur asked for me to return home in exchange for bringing us to you. I could not say no, *mo chroí*."

Órlaith framed his face with both her hands and stood on her tiptoes to press a soft kiss to his mouth. "I will stand by your side on any land you choose, but I refuse to go back to Medb."

"You are not the only one whose life I bargained with."

"Gerard twisted words when he agreed to what Medb wanted. He'll bring you to her, but he's not giving you to her. That keeps his promise and keeps you and Patrick free," Nadine said.

Órlaith glanced at her. "Medb will not see it that way."

"She will have no choice," Gerard replied.

"Save your rage for her, then. We need to get there first without losing too much time," Patrick told him.

"As I said." The Cailleach Bheur banged her staff against the ground, causing the entire island to shake as a crack opened up in the rock between their group and where she stood. "I can take you there."

Ice grew out of the jagged tear in the stone, lining the space that had opened up. It wasn't a hawthorn path, but Patrick supposed an immortal could part the veil wherever they liked when the need arose.

"Wade," Patrick said. "You can't fit down there like this. You need to shift."

Wade folded his wings against his back and sat on his hind legs. Within moments, he started to shrink, his form getting smaller and smaller until his scales blended into human skin, and everything that made him a dragon disappeared as his human body took form. It wasn't like a werecreature shift, where the body broke apart and twisted into something new. This was smoother and quicker by far.

Wade still ended up standing naked on the rocky incline. He leaned over and gagged, spitting out a glob of saliva and making the most disgusted face.

"Oh, man, demons taste *gross*," he said.

Keith shrugged out of his jacket and tossed it at Wade. "Put that on."

Wade scrambled to tie it around his waist, looking a little red in the face. Patrick wasn't sure if that was left over from him shifting mass or out of embarrassment.

The Cailleach Bheur pointed her staff at the icy path through the earth that would lead them through the veil. "Shall we?"

Patrick caught Gerard's eye and nodded. "Let's go."

Gerard held Órlaith's hand and didn't let her go as he led the way back to Tír na nÓg.

JONO SLID OFF ICE AND STUMBLED INTO A BARREN GARDEN shrouded in mist at the edge of a cliff. What trees he could see around them were dead and covered in snow. Black stone walls surrounded the garden in a half circle, offering no way out except through three sets of double doors built with bones. The dull roar that filled the air wasn't his ears ringing from crossing the veil, but the pond that emptied itself over the side of the cliff in a small waterfall edged in ice.

Jono shook his wolf head hard, the faint disorientation from crossing the veil lasting only a second or two before it faded away. He sniffed at the air as he took in their surroundings. His enhanced sense of smell hit his brain with information that took a few seconds to sort out. Tír na nÓg smelled subtly different than every place he'd ever been on Earth, even here in the dead of winter where nothing seemed alive.

"Oh, hey," Wade said, pointing at a tower that rose high above them. "I think that was our prison cell."

Somehow, the Cailleach Bheur had brought them to the palace that sat on a mesa, in the middle of a canyon, in this world the stories told in the mortal realm had never remembered.

Birds shrieked overhead, and Jono's head snapped up to track their flight across the dark sky. A line of light edged the horizon in the far distance, the first hint of dawn barely arrived. His ears pricked forward at the skittering, clacking sound of *something* crawling over stone.

Patrick conjured up a mageglobe, the pale blue sphere casting shadows on his face. "Are those—"

He never finished the sentence.

The trees that seemed dead came alive. Spriggans peeled themselves off the trees to grab anyone in the group that they could. Jono lunged at the one going after Patrick, sinking his teeth into the branch that passed as an arm. With a sharp jerk of his head, he broke the limb in two. The spriggan howled, sap flowing thick and sticky from the stump left behind. Jono spat out the branch clamped between his teeth, bracing himself for another attack.

Violet light snaked between him and the two spriggans looking to help their wounded friend. Nadine's magic smelled like she did —clean, with hints of citrus and lilies. The underlying bitterness in Patrick's wasn't present in the shields that were raised between their side and the fae who guarded the palace that was home to the Unseelie Court.

"That is *quite* enough," the Cailleach Bheur called out.

Jono didn't hear her staff touch the ground, but he smelled the ice it called forth before he saw it. The snow beneath his paws was covered in a sheet of frozen ice that was so cold it burned. He watched as the ice slammed into the spriggans who realized too late what was coming their way. Every last one of the fae were frozen by winter where they stood, becoming ice statues that would break with the slightest touch.

Beyond the crackling sound of settling ice came the warning shouts of fae from inside the palace. The doors that three pathways led to were thrown open and out poured a contingent of guards who wore the same armor as those who had been in the throne room the last time Jono came here. Spider fae scuttled through the doors, crawling up the palace walls that surrounded the garden everywhere but the cliff side with its icy waterfall.

"Anyone know what day it is?" Patrick asked, his dagger in one hand and a mageglobe in the other.

"Winter solstice," Gerard replied.

"Fuck."

Jono's keen eyesight made it possible for him to see the figure who stepped through the doorway directly ahead. The fae in question was memorable only because he held some semblance of rank and power in the finicky ways the fae counted such things.

"Cairbre," Órlaith spat out with enough venom in her voice that several Hellraisers looked impressed. The scowl on her beautiful face promised a violence Jono was more than willing to help her indulge in.

"I see you found the Summer Lady, Cú Chulainn," Cairbre said, his words coming out clipped as he approached.

"I made a promise. I kept it," Gerard replied, glaring at the other fae through Nadine's faintly shimmering shield.

"You are late. The winter solstice is already upon us."

"We are here, on the shortest day of the year, as I *promised*."

"My queen said by winter solstice, which has already started."

"The sun has not risen, nor has it set. It is winter solstice when *I* say it is, Cairbre Nia Fer," the Cailleach Bheur said in a firm voice.

Cairbre rocked to a halt at the use of his entire name, a hint of unease crossing his too-beautiful face as he stared at the immortal. "Cailleach Bheur."

"Child," the Cailleach Bheur said with a smile that showed off her bloodstained teeth.

Jono wanted—*needed*—a voice for this conversation. He gave a full-body shake to get rid of some of the rainwater that had settled on the outer layer of his fur, ignoring Patrick's swearing as he did so. The lacerations Jono had acquired during his fights with the soultakers had healed, but the dried blood was still matted in his fur. The aches and pains had faded, courtesy of the werevirus and the side effect of accelerated healing that came with it.

Knowing what they'd be going into, and that he'd want to argue in favor of Patrick, Jono shifted back to human. The immediate flash of fiery agony lasted only a second or two before the nerves in his body blocked the pain. His body twisted and broke apart, fur sinking back into skin, muscles migrating to new joints. His vision faded from a werewolf sharpness to human colors.

Jono suppressed his senses until the shift was completed, breathing hard through his nose as his brain settled back into being in his human body. He flexed his hands against the ice before straightening up from his crouched position.

Keith leaned around Patrick to give Jono a once-over before nudging Patrick in the side. "I see why you're with the Brit."

Patrick rolled his eyes, a faint flush hitting his cheeks for a few seconds. "Can we focus on the mission and not Jono's dick?"

"Not sure he'll have much of one if he stays outside in this weather for too much longer."

Patrick shot Keith a murderous look that the other man shrugged off with ease. Keith flashed a hand signal at Arthur, who nodded and quickly divested himself of his jacket. It was tossed to Jono, who took it with a silent nod of thanks.

Jono tied the jacket around his waist, more to save everyone else's sense of modesty than for warmth. Jono didn't care about walking around in the nude. He'd ruined too many sets of clothes over the years due to shifting that he'd rather be naked in preparation for a fight than haul around extra clothes while on the run. Jono could handle the cold well enough, even in human form.

Once he was mostly decent, Jono scanned the area for the last member of his pack. Sage hadn't shifted back to human, her massive weretiger form standing guard next to Wade. The teen was holding on to the fur on her back with one hand covered in iridescent red scales.

"Don't shift," Jono said, knowing Wade would hear the order and know the warning was meant for him.

Wade's gaze flicked his way, a hint of gold in brown eyes. Sage shifted on her paws and sidled closer to Wade, reminding him she was there and he wasn't alone.

Jono's attention was dragged back to the silent staring contest going on between Cairbre and the Cailleach Bheur. Jono had his money on the goddess, and if that bet had been placed with a bookie, he'd have won a pretty prize.

"This land is no longer yours," Cairbre finally said.

The Cailleach Bheur pointed her staff at Cairbre. "I was old before you even existed on the lips of storytellers, child. The walls here remember the echo of my footsteps, and always will. Lead the way, or step aside."

Cairbre hesitated, but not even the backup he had in the form of Unseelie fae could make him stand his ground. Cairbre inclined his head to his elder and half-turned to gesture at the doorway he'd walked out of.

"Follow me," he said.

Nadine's shields didn't fall. Gerard looked over at where she stood with a halo of tiny mageglobes circling her head. "Stand down, Mulroney."

"Are you going to ask for hospitality so they don't stab us in the back?" Nadine asked.

"I made a bargain, and I'm here to keep it. That's hospitality enough."

"If you say so."

Nadine drew down her shields, enabling everyone to follow Cairbre into the palace. Jono knocked over a spriggan ice statue balanced on one foot when he jostled it while walking past it. The statue shattered when it hit the cold, ice-covered ground. Jono kicked a piece out of his way.

"You know what I want for Christmas?" Jono said quietly as they headed for the palace door.

"What?" Patrick asked.

"For us to be home and this bollocks over with."

Patrick reached for his hand, tangling their fingers together. "Me, too."

Their group entered the palace beneath dozens of eyes and weapons pointed their way. The Hellraisers kept their rifles in their hands but weren't aiming at anyone or anything in particular. Jono had no doubt that they'd be able to wreak havoc at the first order Gerard gave.

"I lost my gun in the fight," Nadine said quietly from behind them. "Requisitioning a new one is going to be annoying."

"Don't feel too bad. I left Gerard's really expensive rifle back on Skellig Michael," Patrick said.

"We're probably going to lose the rest of them to the guards at the Unseelie Court. It's what happened in the Seelie Court, only they gave the weapons back. I doubt Medb will be so generous here," Keith said.

Jono knew that would put them at a disadvantage. Only one of the Hellraisers was a magic user, and he wasn't certain a sorcerer could do much against fae magic. Everyone else would have to make sure Gerard's team survived the fight Jono knew they were walking into. It felt like a trap in the worst way, but Jono wasn't leaving Tír na nÓg without Patrick. If it meant fully giving over his body to Fenrir, then that was something Jono had no qualms doing. He didn't care if it came across as the Norse pantheon declaring war on the Celtic pantheon. What was one more battle line drawn in this fight anyway?

Cairbre led the way, and winter's chill followed them inside the palace. Patches of ice covered the hallway floors as they walked, courtesy of the Cailleach Bheur's staff.

Fae watched them as they passed—goblins, dwarves, spriggans, Red Caps, some too coldly beautiful to be real, and still others that seemed pulled straight out of a nightmare. None of them smelled right to Jono's nose, or maybe it was the palace itself. Jono was used to a world that smelled far more human than this.

Eventually, they were escorted into the throne room with its glass dome ceiling and onyx floor that felt oddly sharp beneath his feet. Jono ignored the discomfort, knowing his skin would heal mere seconds after every cut that was made.

A crowd of *daoine sidhe* filled the throne room. A sea of faces with strangely colored hair and eyes turned their way. Armored guards that carried weapons which smelled of magic stood in front of the throne itself. The barren tree with its grasping roots loomed over everyone, its branches reaching for the glass domed ceiling. The sky above had grown marginally lighter, and Jono wondered how much time they'd lost on the other side.

If we miss Christmas, I'm going to be bloody pissed.

Sitting on the vine-covered throne, watching them come forward, was Medb.

Her patchwork gown was made out of skin in various shades of blues this time, the color washing her out. Jono thought the color was a pointed jab at the Cailleach Bheur. Paired with Medb's ash-colored hair and dark eyes, the Queen of Air and Darkness looked like a corpse sitting upon her throne. Her crown made out of fingerbones sat firmly in place upon her head, and the necklace of eyes she wore around her throat watched them as they approached.

Medb's expression seemed carved from ice, and all her attention was reserved for the goddess who greeted her with a low, mocking laugh.

"My throne has never suited you," the Cailleach Bheur said, her staff making ice blossom over the onyx floor, cracking the stone.

"You have no throne here, hag," Medb replied in a chilly, unwelcoming voice. "The stories have forgotten you."

"So you say."

"So I *know*."

The Cailleach Bheur gripped her staff with both hands and planted it before her. The cloak she wore swirled around her hunched, naked body, ice crystals sticking to the cloth. "Your wisdom is misplaced. It always has been."

Medb pushed herself to her feet in a smooth motion, standing tall before them on the throne dais. "Do not insult me."

"You gambled, and you lost. A bargain was made, and it will be kept. You know what must be done."

The Cailleach Bheur rapped the end of her staff against the floor, sending ice cascading over the floor of the throne room in a blink of an eye. It slid beneath everyone's feet, the sudden cold making Jono flex his bare toes. The ice crashed against the edge of the dais and the roots that hung there but went no further, blocked by something Jono couldn't see. Magic glimmered at the tips of Medb's fingers, the scent of ozone getting stronger.

"The Cailleach Bheur is right," Gerard said as he stepped forward with Órlaith by his side. "It's winter solstice, and I've brought the Summer Lady to you, Medb."

Medb was too old, too powerful, to let whatever she was feeling show on her face. Jono couldn't get a hint of emotion off her through scent either, nothing but the taste of electricity in the back of his throat. Patrick stepped forward as well, and Jono went with him. At Patrick's warning look, Jono rolled his eyes.

"No way am I letting you talk your way out of this mess without help," Jono told him.

"Your faith in me needs a little work," Patrick muttered.

Jono's gaze slid to where Medb stood, her ancient eyes staring right back at him. Deep inside Jono's soul, Fenrir growled a warning. "I have faith, and it doesn't belong to her."

Medb extended her hand as she stepped down from the dais, and Cairbre was there to aid her down the steps. Jono watched as he escorted Medb to where they stood in the throne room, surrounded by fae and ice and a cold that made his breath fog in the air.

"You seem to think the terms of the bargain have been met," Medb said, her eerie gaze flicking over all of them.

"I kept my word. Now it's your turn. Give us the Morrígan's staff and grant Patrick his freedom. That was the bargain, after all," Gerard said.

"Was it? I offered the Morrígan's staff for a price. It has not been met yet." She pointed her finger at Órlaith. "That one belongs to me."

"I belong to no one," Órlaith said through gritted teeth. Jono rather thought the *bitch* was obvious in her tone. What Medb lacked in emotion, Órlaith carried enough to share. Her fury burned with a sharpness that almost made Jono's eyes water.

"Your life for the Morrígan's staff was the bargain we made. You will stay here in the Unseelie Court, Órlaith, Daughter of Ruadán."

At that demand, Órlaith lifted her chin high and took Gerard's hand in hers. "My life does not belong to you."

"I said I would bring Órlaith to you, Medb. I never said I would give her to you," Gerard said.

Words and their intent mattered, especially for the fae.

Medb went still in a way that would've made Jono's hackles rise if he were in his werewolf form. He stepped closer to Patrick, claws piercing the skin at the tips of his fingers. Fenrir rumbled through his soul, but didn't speak.

The Cailleach Bheur tilted her staff in Medb's direction. "You made a bargain. You will keep it, or your word will be worthless."

Medb's eyes narrowed to slits before she blinked them wide again and smiled in a way Jono didn't like.

"I am not one to break my word. Twist it, as Cú Chulainn has done, well. We all speak with twisted meanings these days. It is how the stories made us, after all. Our stories change with the generations. We are forgotten and remembered and *misremem-bered*, and death is never a guarantee for gods when our histories are written for the masses to worship," Medb replied.

Jono's ears picked up a distant, heavy *thump*. Then another, and another. He dialed up his hearing, trying to pinpoint the noise, but it was difficult to distinguish what it was through the rest of the sounds in the palace. The ice that coated the floor and which had numbed his toes carried the vibrations as the scent of ozone grew thicker in the air.

"Patrick," Jono growled, half turning toward the throne room entrance. He didn't want his back to Medb, but *something* was coming their way.

"You may bring Órlaith to my Court and not give her over. That is your right within the words we spoke and the bargain we made. You brought her here before winter solstice touched the sky, which means the mage is free to go. But I claim my price was not met in full."

"I kept my side of the bargain," Gerard snapped.

Medb shrugged one thin shoulder. "My price was Órlaith's life. It was not met."

"Yes, it fucking was."

The vibrations in the floor got heavier, the sound of what had to be footsteps getting louder in Jono's ears. Patrick unsheathed his dagger and gripped it tight. The heavenly fire that spilled from it gave off a warmth Jono could feel against his chilled skin.

"I was prepared for your half-truths. I have not lived this long without knowing the way words cut."

Gerard ground his teeth so hard Jono heard one break. "You accepted the terms."

"I did, under the assumption you would pay my price. And the bargain brought you both here, to my Court, as it was asked of me. Because you, Son of Lugh," Medb said with a hard glint in her eyes, "your family has *missed* you."

The entrance to the throne room seemed to grow in size, the walls around it shifting by way of magic to accommodate the space made to allow a giant to walk through.

"Oh, we are so fucked," Patrick muttered.

"So, *so* fucked," Nadine agreed with wide eyes as she raised her shields around their group.

Jono watched as Gerard rotated his weapon around to point the notched spearhead at the new threat, the expression on his face seemingly carved from stone.

"Balor," Gerard said, with all the loathing Jono heard in Patrick's voice when he spoke about Ethan.

Jono took a deep breath and shifted, letting Fenrir take control.

22

Balor brought with him the heat of a scorching sun that poured out of his body, melting the ice on the floor. The immortal's craggy face was dominated by a large closed eye in the center of his forehead that Patrick did not, in any way, want looking at them. The tyrant king of the Formorians was at least two stories tall, with a bald head and a protruding jaw. He wore a gold crown and carried a wooden club that looked as if it was made from an entire tree trunk trimmed of its branches and roots.

Patrick wasn't sure how Balor navigated the world around him while effectively blind, but the god moved with an uncanny knowledge of where everyone was.

"Cú Chulainn," Balor said, teeth gnashing together around the name.

"You know, I don't see the family resemblance, Gerard," Patrick said offhand as he took a couple of steps backward. "Your great-grandfather is kind of ugly."

"None of us get to choose the blood we carry in our veins," Gerard retorted.

"I'm gonna make a wild guess that spelled bullets won't cut it here," Keith said as he aimed down the barrel of his rifle.

Gerard scowled, gripping his spear tightly. "You'd be right."

"If you go into a berserker rage right now when we don't have an exit strategy, I will take you off my Christmas card list," Patrick told Gerard as the Unseelie fae courtiers started to scatter.

"You don't send cards. And I thought you were still mad at me?"

"Yes, yes, still furious as fuck. I'll think about forgiving you if you get us out of here alive and in one piece."

The sound of bones grinding together that came from Jono's body as he shifted finally stopped. Jono's massive werewolf form made Patrick breathe slightly easier. Sage had herded Wade closer to where they were, and Patrick reached out to grab the teen by the elbow, hauling him close.

"Should I shift?" Wade asked, staring up at Balor in trepidation. He swallowed thickly, both hands clutching at the jacket tied around his waist. The skin over his knuckles shimmered with red scales.

Patrick opened his mouth to reply, but the Cailleach Bheur cut him off without saying a word. The goddess slammed her staff onto the floor—

And the ice storm that erupted was beautiful in its deadliness.

Patrick's breath puffed out as fog in the sudden temperature change. Ice spread across the floor and up the walls, all the way to the glass dome ceiling. It frosted over immediately, hiding the sky, and started to crack in a way Patrick knew wasn't good. The sheet of ice that covered the floor was cold enough that Patrick could feel the chill through the soles of his boots.

Condensation settled over Nadine's shield from the cold, obscuring his line of sight. Jono growled in displeasure, but Patrick wasn't about to tell Nadine to drop her shields.

"Do *not*—" Medb said, sounding furious, but whatever order she was about to give never made it past her lips.

The ice beneath their feet cracked apart, along with the floor beneath it, the sound like ice shearing off a glacier to fall into the sea. It spoke of something deeper breaking—not just the ground, but the veil.

Tír na nÓg existed in the minds of mortals in a unique way. It had never been forgotten, not completely, and there was power in names and memory and belief, and a world that had always shared a border with the Old Country and the far-flung shores its children fled to.

The fae had carved hawthorn paths through the veil with the help of their gods for centuries upon centuries—passages where the veil was thin and easy for mortals to get lost in. Creating a path or a crossroad took a wealth of power that was only carried by those who possessed a godhead.

The Cailleach Bheur was the Queen of Winter, and the myths these days might have Medb sitting on her throne, but the core legends always remained where they were born.

Winter would always live in the heart of the Unseelie Court, and the Cailleach Bheur cut a new crossroad through the veil with a strength neither Medb, nor Balor, could counter.

Patrick's stomach did that hard swoop to his feet that only came from falling through the veil as he and everyone else inside Nadine's shields fell through the broken ice into a gray abyss.

"*Shit!*" Nadine cried out, drawing her magic back into her soul.

Patrick held on to Wade as they pitched down an icy hole in a freefall that made his heart beat fast in his chest. He winced at the scream Wade let out as they fell, the muscle in the teen's arm moving in a way no human's ever would.

"Don't shift!" Patrick yelled.

"I need to fly!" Wade shouted, the panic in his voice making him sound younger.

Patrick tightened his grip as they fell through a gray mist where it was impossible to tell up from down. "Trust me!"

They tumbled through the veil, and Patrick lost sight of everyone but Wade. He forced the panic down about being separated again, sending his awareness deep into his soul for the soul-bond. It burned as it always did, not stretched thin and feeling out of reach as it had when he'd worn Medb's shackles.

Jono was close by, and that was all that mattered.

Patrick's stomach crawled up his throat, the shift in gravity nearly making him sick. The gray mist thinned out, and he had just enough time to brace himself as the snowy ground rushed up to meet them. He landed in a way he'd learned long ago that wouldn't break any bones. Patrick still got a mouthful of snow, which he spat out with a curse.

"I lost my jacket," Wade said with a high-pitched giggle.

Patrick raised his head and blinked his eyes clear of snow, staring at the snow-covered mountains and land that stretched out before them. A large gap dipped between the two ranges, dawn's light shining weakly over the horizon's edge. It was brightest at the lowest point of the gap, sunlight reflecting off the hint of an iced-over lake in the far distance.

A shadow fell over him, and teeth gently nipped at his shoulder through his long-sleeved shirt. Patrick turned his head to blink up at Jono, his large wolf's head so close it blocked out the sky.

"I'm all right," Patrick promised.

Patrick picked himself off the ground, stumbling a little until he got his balance back. He reached for Wade, offering the teen a hand up. Wade was doing his best to hide his dick with his left hand, still not entirely comfortable being naked now that he had a choice about clothes. Once Wade was standing, Patrick wasn't surprised to see iridescent red scales push through Wade's skin in large patches to protect him from the elements and give him a semblance of cover.

Around him, the rest of the Hellraisers, Nadine, Sage, Gerard, and Órlaith were on their feet or getting there. Nadine raised another shield, a mageglobe spinning near her left shoulder. Patrick flexed his fingers around the hilt of his dagger, shivering from the cold. He cast a heat charm on his clothes, trying to get warm.

"Where are we?" Keith asked, scanning the area over the barrel of his rifle. He wasn't the only one on guard and covering their location.

Gerard ground the butt of his spear against the hard, cold ground. "The Gap of Dunloe. The Cailleach Bheur took us back to Ireland."

"Nice of her to leave us in the lurch. Where'd she go?"

"I don't know."

Patrick patted his pocket, pulling out his phone. The screen was cracked a little in the corner, but it still worked. He didn't have any signal though, and the phone still showed the wrong date.

"Is it still winter solstice?" he asked.

Órlaith nodded, tugging at the collar of Patrick's leather jacket that she still wore. "It is."

Patrick shoved his phone back into his pocket. "Now what?"

Before anyone could answer, the earth jerked beneath their feet hard enough to make Patrick lose his balance. He crashed against Jono's side, grabbing at Jono's thick fur with one flailing hand. The earthquake rumbled through the early morning air as mist rose from the ground, drifting between them and the Gap of Dunloe in the distance.

"You *had* to ask," Arthur yelled at Patrick.

Patrick hauled himself upright, bracing himself against Jono. He rode the shaking earth as best he could, the pressure in his head from an atmospheric change making him look up at the sky. High above, clouds began to swirl, and the distant screams of the Sluagh drifted on the rising wind.

Shadowy figures began to appear in the mist between them and the Gap of Dunloe. A downdraft of freezing wind blew the mist aside as the earth finally settled. Some of the mist twisted and solidified into a tall gray horse with fiery eyes and strangely sharp teeth.

Seated atop the Ceffyl Dŵr was Medb, the Queen of Air and Darkness looking ready for war in black armor that sucked up what little light the rising sun was giving off. Arrayed around her was a small army of Unseelie fae ranging from *daoine sídhe* to goblins to trolls. The Sluagh hovered overhead, waiting to attack.

Cairbre stood on Medb's right, while Balor was an imposing figure to her left, the giant's height and breadth nearly blocking the Gap of Dunloe from sight. The air smelled of ozone and the recognition burning through Patrick's magic was enough to nearly choke him.

"I would really like a tank right now," Patrick said to no one in particular. "Maybe an airstrike."

Sage snorted, her round, weretiger ears swiveling his way, as if agreeing with him.

"I second that assessment," Darren said.

Gerard spun his spear around, aiming the notched spearhead at Medb's Unseelie fae. The *Gáe Bulg* erupted in golden fire, twisting around the weapon in a menacing manner. *Something* shifted in Gerard's aura, and the punch of magic that poured out of him crashed against Patrick's shields. He didn't feel human to Patrick's senses anymore—he didn't *look* it in that moment, standing tall and proud and furious in the face of the enemy.

Beside him, Órlaith gripped the empty air in front of her with both hands and yanked her arms downward. When she lifted them again, she was holding two short swords, one in each hand. The steel blades were carved with runes that glowed with a soft blue light, the same color as her summer-sky-blue eyes. Her bright red-orange hair fell loose around her body, standing out against the black leather jacket.

Patrick shared a single glance with Nadine before they both conjured up mageglobes at the exact same time. Patrick threw his awareness into the soulbond, reaching through Jono's soul for the ley line that roared beneath the earth. His concentration was momentarily jolted when he realized the ley line wasn't the only external magic below.

Deep beneath the Gap of Dunloe was a nexus—and its magic carried a signature that spoke of belonging to the fae.

Patrick opened himself up to the nexus anyway, the connection shocking his nerves in a way that left his ears ringing. He drew that power through Jono's soul and into his own, filling his mageglobes with a multitude of combat spells while Nadine used hers to raise another shield over everyone. Her ward hung heavy in the air; the weight of her magic powered by the nexus.

"Spread out and pick your targets," Gerard ordered.

"Wade?" Patrick said, not taking his eyes off Medb.

"Yeah?" Wade said.

"Now would be a good time to shift."

Nadine retreated to the rear of the group, moving uphill to get a better vantage point in order to manipulate her shields. Jono and Patrick took up position at the front, and he passed his mageglobes through Nadine's shields, lining them up. Around them, the Hellraisers scattered to find what cover they could on the mostly open land, intending to rely on Nadine's shields for most of their protection for as long as possible.

Sage bounded over to where Desmond stood, the sorcerer leaning most of his weight against Arthur. Desmond had cast concentric circles on the ground beneath his feet to help anchor his magic. Sage planted herself by his side, intent on guarding him while Desmond worked his magic.

Jono's soul shifted in a way that made Patrick's mageglobes flicker. Patrick jerked his head around, noticing the white fire that flickered at the outer corner of Jono's bright blue eyes. When that huge wolf head turned to look at Patrick, the presence staring out of those wolf-bright eyes wasn't human in the least.

Patrick pointed his dagger at the god inhabiting Jono's body. "You get him hurt and we're going to have fucking *words*."

The growl that came out of Jono's mouth somehow twisted into words in Patrick's ears.

"*Focus on the kill, not on the wolf,*" Fenrir told him.

Patrick raised his middle finger at the god before turning his attention on the Unseelie fae and the gods who led them.

A large shadow drifted over where he stood. Patrick looked up in time to see Wade stretch out his leathery wings as wide as they would go before folding them down against his back. Wade sat back on his haunches in his fledging fire dragon form, smoke drifting out of his nostrils. His molten golden eyes with their black slit pupils glinted in the light of the rising sun. He gnashed his teeth, a hint of flame sparking on his tongue.

Gerard strode up to Nadine's shield and planted his feet wide, holding the *Gáe Bulg* at the ready. "Is this how you keep your word, Medb?"

Medb guided her steed forward, the rest of her fighters following in her wake. "I kept my word."

"Bullshit. Where is the Morrígan's staff?"

"Give me Órlaith and I will tell you."

"And use me to take the Seelie throne?" Órlaith retorted, holding up her short swords. "I would rather die than let you rule my people."

"Hey now," Patrick said. "Don't give her any ideas."

"Too late," Keith said as the Sluagh dove their way.

Fenrir let out a roar through Jono and easily passed through Nadine's shields, veering left and aiming for the horde of spider fae trying to flank them. His body was haloed in fiery white light, the god's aura burning bright around him.

Patrick swore and made a sweeping gesture with his left arm. He sent his mageglobes flying forward, filled with strike spells. He wasn't sure what fae defenses were like, but they were about to find out.

His mageglobes slammed into Medb's central fighters and exploded upon impact, sending dirt and snow and body parts flying into the air. The lesser fae couldn't counter his magic, but the *daoine sidhe* shielded against the attack easily enough.

Balor strode across the wintery field, every step the giant took shaking the earth. Wade launched himself into the sky through Nadine's shield with a fiery roar, clearing himself a way through the Sluagh as he flew toward the giant. Balor seemed to sense Wade's approach, the god's head turning to look at him.

"*Wade!*" Patrick yelled, heart pounding in his chest as he caught a glimpse of ugly fire peeking out from between Balor's eyelids.

That deadly eye opened, and a searing beam of light erupted from it. Wade let loose a burst of flame that met Balor's attack head-on, wings flapping hard. Patrick expected the worst—that Wade would be cut in two by the giant's eye of destruction—but Wade's dragon fire kept the god's power at bay.

"I like that kid," Keith said, taking careful aim at a horde of goblins racing their way. He switched his rifle to burst mode and pulled the trigger, letting off a couple rounds through Nadine's shields.

Patrick grabbed the magazine he'd saved from Gerard's rifle out of his back pocket and tossed it to Keith. "For when you need to reload."

Keith grabbed it with his left hand. "You give the best presents."

A boulder slammed into Nadine's shield overhead, making them both look up. The stone shattered, sending violet light rippling over the front expanse of the shield. Another boulder flew through the air, tossed by a troll. A third was tossed at Wade, who managed to dodge the attack but very nearly took a hit from Balor's eye while doing so. The Sluagh took advantage of his split attention and tried to force Wade to the ground.

Patrick let magic pour out of his soul and into a blast of raw magic that cut through some of the Sluagh harassing Wade. They scattered, allowing Wade to flap his wings and gain altitude, spewing fire as he went.

Balor turned his head their way, that eye of his opening once more. The light shining out of it was as bright as the sun and hot like a scorching day in the desert. Patrick knew Nadine's shields wouldn't be able to stop the god's attack, but she wasn't the only one working their defenses.

Órlaith raised one fist over her head, the short sword in her grip flashing with magic. The earth in front of Nadine's shields rose upward and turned to stone. Órlaith poured her magic into the stone wall she'd created as the destructive power of Balor's eye slammed against their defenses. The goddess pulled up more and more earth and turned it all to stone, one layer after another, as fast as she could, but it wasn't going to be enough.

Then Gerard vaulted into the air and threw his spear, the weapon burning bright as it passed harmlessly through Nadine's shield and flew toward Balor like a heat-seeking missile. The giant tried to twist out of its way but wasn't quick enough.

The *Gáe Bulg* slammed into Balor's right shoulder, and the god roared in agony as the notched spearhead exploded outward upon impact. Patrick could see bits of metal sticking out of the god's shoulder as thick blood flowed from the wound and down his arm. The god's destructive eye slammed shut, but not before carving a deep furrow in the land beyond them. Balor crashed to his knees, then to his side, the earth shaking from his fall—down but not out.

Medb let out a furious scream that was taken up as a rallying cry by the banshees with her, and it echoed in the early-morning air like a death knell.

It was challenged by the baying hounds and furious cries of the Wild Hunt.

A storm spun up over the mountains with a sudden ferocity, thunder and lightning crashing through the clouds that came out of nowhere. A heavy wind blew across the valley, making Patrick's teeth chatter. Breaking free of the clouds came the ghostly riders who had carried them west across Ireland. Patrick squinted at the lead rider, realizing it wasn't Nerys at the front, but Gwyn ap Nudd.

Seemed the god was done standing on the sidelines.

The Sluagh broke away from fighting Wade to meet the new threat, screaming all the while. Several got a face full of dragon fire that seared them black, whatever magic that existed in dragon kind capable of affecting the dead. Wade flapped his wings some more, gaining altitude. Then he flew after the Sluagh with a roar, fire flickering around his teeth. Part of Patrick wanted to yell at him to *get back here*, but he knew Wade would ignore him.

Fenrir came racing back their way, a spider leg held between Jono's teeth, half a fae's body dangling off the end. The god spat it out before vaulting through the shield to stand beside Patrick again. Jono's fur was covered in blood, some of it his own, most of it too black or green to be anything but fae.

"I told you not to hurt him," Patrick snapped.

Fenrir blinked once before deliberately turning his back on Patrick, his aura burning bright against Patrick's shields.

Fucking gods.

Mist exploded around them, drifting through Nadine's shields. The scent of spring was carried on the stormy wind—floral and full of green things that always made Patrick sneeze. Warmth settled around them, and Patrick watched as grass sprouted defiantly through the cold earth covered in snow.

The fae who came out of the mist this time burned bright, but none came close to the fiery light that surrounded Brigid like a halo. The Spring Queen of the Seelie Court rode a white horse that wore more armor than she did. Considering the power pouring out of her aura, Patrick figured armor wasn't really necessary for a goddess of her rank.

Snaking through the warmth of spring was a hint of winter as the Cailleach Bheur appeared out of the mist, her staff freezing the ground where she stood outside Nadine's shields.

Patrick looked around at the ranks of Seelie fae facing off with Medb's side, and the tightness in his chest loosened. He caught

Keith's eye and jerked a thumb at the group of spear wielders to their left.

"When you run out of bullets, maybe you can ask one of them to borrow a blade," he said.

Keith rolled his eyes. "Maybe next time we spend another million dollars for double the ammunition. Marek can afford it. He's a billionaire."

Gerard raised an arm and hand-signaled Nadine to take down her shield. This time she didn't argue and drew down her magic. The cold wind that smacked Patrick in the face made his teeth chatter. The heat charms on his clothes were turning out not to be enough in this supernatural weather.

Brigid stood at the front of her forces, her fiery hair falling around her, the crown on her head not jostling one bit. "You tried to steal my granddaughter from me, Medb."

"There is no stealing involved when a bargain is made, Brigid," Medb shot back.

"You sent mercenaries into my lands to kidnap Órlaith."

"I gave no such orders."

"You gave them aid in the form of Ferdiad, a *duine sídhe* who knows the hawthorn paths and crossroads. No mortals would have found her without his help."

"I offered that which they most desired for a price they were willing to pay."

"My granddaughter's life was not yours to bargain with."

The tension in the air between both sides was thick enough to cut. Overhead, the Sluagh and the Wild Hunt screamed as they fought, the sound hurting Patrick's ears. The earth shook a little as Balor got to one knee, the *Gáe Bulg* sticking out of his shoulder. The god tried to remove it with one huge hand, but the weapon wouldn't be dislodged. If anything, it carved itself deeper into bone, and fresh blood flowed from the wound.

Patrick wondered if the spear of death was powerful enough to kill a god.

He wouldn't find out that morning.

A murder of crows flew through the Gap of Dunloe, cawing all the while as the sun broke the horizon behind their beating wings. Weak winter sunlight spread across the sky and earth, casting a long shadow in front of the giant riding a huge white stag across the snowy field bristling with flowers. The seasons were out of place in the valley, with winter and spring fighting over summer. The stag gave no ground to snow or grass, walking steadily forward.

The huge, bearded, redheaded god wore tanned leather pants and a shirt that seemed woven from the leaves of trees. He carried the *lorg mór* in one hand, the great staff carved from ancient wood. The elaborate curved frame of a harp peeked over his shoulder, and Patrick thought he could hear music on the wind.

The Sluagh and Wild Hunt separated in the sky and settled on the ground, picking their sides. Wade roared one more time before gliding back to earth, his large wings sending up eddies of dirt and snow as he landed behind them. Wade brought the scent of fire with him, but it couldn't overtake the power of gods that made the air crackle with electricity all around them.

Keith lowered his rifle. "Who the fuck is that?"

Patrick watched as the stag and its rider drew closer, licking his lips. "The Dagda."

The king of the Tuatha Dé Danann, father of Brigid, and husband to the Morrígan. Patrick knew his history, and he knew his myths and legends. If anyone had a chance at stopping this fight, it was the Dagda.

"You give the mortals nightmares with these antics," the Dagda said, his deep, booming voice echoing in the valley. "I hear their prayers like bells in my ears. Cease this madness, my children."

No one moved, not even Balor, and Patrick wondered about that—wondered how little worshippers that god had left these days to not make a play at killing the king of his enemy. The Fomorians and Tuatha Dé Danann had never cared about anything but shedding each other's blood over the centuries. That he would not try now was telling.

Time changed all things, even the lives of immortals. It seemed whatever prayers Gerard had accumulated on the shores of America had made him stronger than his father's fabled enemy.

The Cailleach Bheur banged her staff against the ground, spreading ice all around her. "A bargain must be kept. I am here to see it done."

"As are we all," the Dagda said as he drew near.

The crunch of bone had Patrick looking over at Jono, seeing the other man shifting from wolf to human. When Jono turned to meet his gaze, no sign of Fenrir was left in his wolf-bright blue eyes.

Jono scratched at his bare chest, smearing blood over healed skin. "You all right?"

"I'm not the one wearing blood like I'm an extra in a documentary about Picts," Patrick retorted.

Jono rolled his eyes. "I'm fine."

"Your patron is an asshole."

"Yeah, not gonna fight you on that one."

Jono sidled closer and Patrick moved to stand in front of him. Jono was a line of heat against his back that Patrick wanted to sink into, but now wasn't the time.

They both turned to watch the Dagda heave himself off the white stag, who barely moved as the god dismounted. The stag's rack of antlers looked to be about as tall as Patrick, but that didn't stop the beast from bending his neck to nibble at the spring grass pushing through the snow.

"Medb," the Dagda said with a fierce smile as he planted his staff against the ground.

The Queen of Air and Darkness raised her chin defiantly. "Dagda."

"This fight ends now. You made a bargain. Words were spoken. Intent was given. Tasks were accepted and completed."

"My price was *not* met."

"You failed to mitigate Cú Chulainn's offer in an attempt to lure him and the followers he has gained home to *Éire*. You failed, and that does not discharge you of your debts." The Dagda pointed his staff at Medb. "I know what you stole. I know what you hide. Count your blessings it is I and not my wife who offers judgment here."

Patrick figured if the Morrígan was acting as judge, jury, and executioner, they'd all be six feet under right about now.

Gerard stepped forward and bowed to the Dagda. "I ask that mine and Medb's bargain be finished, *Eochaid Ollathair*."

"And it shall, Cú Chulainn."

The Dagda strode over to where Balor sprawled on the ground, blood still trickling from the wound in his shoulder. The giant turned his head at the Dagda's approach, but did not open his destructive eye.

"I would kill you," Balor rumbled.

"I am remembered far more deeply than you," the Dagda replied. "But there are greater threats afoot than the old wrongs between us."

Balor did not flinch when the Dagda grabbed the *Gáe Bulg* and poured his magic into the weapon. The notched spearhead snapped back together into a single piece of metal within the god's body, slicing through more flesh and bone. Blood gushed from the wound as the Dagda pulled the spear free.

Balor covered the wound with one big hand. "Will you take your vengeance, Dagda?"

"This is not where your story ends. You will fade, and my children will rise. That is an end I can live with. Vengeance pales before that sweetness."

The Dagda raised the *lorg mór* and tapped the staff against the wound. Balor wasn't dead, but the end of the staff that could bring the dead to life healed the wound whole again. Balor took in a deep breath, and Patrick seriously thought the Dagda would be blown off the face of the earth by that destructive eye.

"We are fading. We wanted those who remembered us to return," Balor said through gritted teeth.

"There are better ways to go about that than kidnapping children."

"We all do what we must to survive in this age."

"That we do." The Dagda walked away from the immortal, heading toward Medb. He pointed his staff at the goddess, staring her down. "Close out the bargain, or it will be known your word is worthless."

Even from the distance between them, Patrick could see the rage on Medb's face at being outmaneuvered. "Dagda—"

"Your word, Medb. Or I will call for war."

The only sound in the valley was the wind for a long few moments. No one spoke, and the one to finally break the silence was Medb.

The goddess turned her face away from the Dagda to look at Gerard. "My price was not met, but you paid what you promised. Our bargain was a life for the Morrígan's staff. You brought me Órlaith, but did not give her over. Fair enough, but you are not the only one who spins words into knots like tangled thread, Son of Lugh."

"Give us the Morrígan's staff," Gerard demanded.

Medb's smile was cold and vicious to behold. "You may have its location, for that is still something of worth within the bounds of the bargain we made. The staff resides here in the mortal world, and I will give it up only when I am satisfied of the price it fetches."

Patrick swore quietly, knowing that was all they would get out of her. Gerard had twisted his side of the bargain, and Medb had twisted hers. In the end, neither fully won, and neither fully lost, but the mission to retrieve the Morrígan's staff was not over yet.

Medb pulled on her horse's reins, turning the steed around. Her Unseelie Court moved as one to follow her, and the Sluagh rose into the sky, departing through mist. The Unseelie fae disappeared, taking their dead with them, leaving behind a scarred valley as the only hint they had walked the earth.

The Dagda tossed the *Gáe Bulg* to Gerard, who caught it in one hand. "Your bargain with Medb, such as it was, is complete, Cú Chulainn."

"Mine is still open," the Cailleach Bheur replied with a toothy grin. "Walk far, Son of Lugh. When your road ends on that other shore, carry your worshippers home for the good of us all."

The Cailleach Bheur hunched over, her blue form turning to stone. The earth opened up beneath her and swallowed the goddess whole, leaving behind a thick patch of ice as the only evidence of her memory.

Brigid dismounted from her horse and strode over to Órlaith, pulling her granddaughter into a hug that looked like it hurt. Gerard watched them with tired eyes, the relief on his face clear for all to see.

"What now?" Jono asked in a low voice.

Patrick blindly reached behind him for Jono's hand, grasping at air for a moment before their fingers met. "We go home."

The Dagda pulled the Daur da Bláo off his back, plucked at the strings, and coaxed music from the harp that put the seasons to right in the valley below the Gap of Dunloe.

The summer heat faded around them, spring went to sleep, and winter ruled the shortest day of the year once more, as it always had, and always would.

23

"Considering what Medb hinted at, the best route we can take is to look into the black market antiquities and artifact trade. We have contacts who have inroads in that area and will ask them to keep an ear out for word on the Morrígan's staff," Tiarnán said, looking at his laptop screen.

Patrick clenched his teeth against a yawn. "You mean you have thieves and fences on your payroll."

"I do not believe those words left my mouth."

Patrick rolled his eyes. "Yeah, whatever. I call it like I see it."

Beside him, Jono snorted very quietly. Sage sat at the head of the conference table, taking notes on a legal pad. The silence ward in the conference room was soft static in Patrick's ears.

Two days past winter solstice found them back in New York, trying to reorient themselves. Patrick's body had hit a wall of exhaustion around noon yesterday, but he still hadn't found time to rest. Going past the veil was like crossing the International Date Line a dozen times in a couple of days.

It sucked.

Meeting Medb's terms and completing the bargain hadn't

gotten rid of their problems. Sure, Patrick might be in the clear with the Queen of Air and Darkness under Gerard's bargain, and they might have a promised alliance with the fae to acknowledge their god pack, but that didn't fix the PR problem the fae had now.

The Morrígan's staff was still missing, the Wisteria child was never coming home, and the SOA was caught in the crossfire between the Wisteria Coven's lawyers and the State Department's inability to bring the fae to the discussion table. The fae's arrogance wasn't sitting well with the public, especially during the holidays. Margeaux Wisteria's crying face was as prominent in the media now as it had been at the beginning of the month. Public opinion was solidly in her favor, but that meant nothing to the fae.

Luckily, Casale and the PCB had managed to dodge most of the bad press since the SOA was in charge of the Wisteria case. Now that the Sluagh and Wild Hunt were no longer riding the storms over New York and the curfew had been lifted, the PCB wasn't stretched so thin on manpower. Patrick hoped that meant Casale wouldn't have to work overtime this week and could spend Christmas with his family.

Patrick wasn't so lucky. The case was still open, and he still had one last task to do before he could think about time off. Órlaith might have been returned to the Seelie Court, but Gerard still had a promise to keep to the Cailleach Bheur. Sometime in the future, Gerard would have to give up his commission to the United States military, hand over command of the Hellraisers to someone else, and go home.

Patrick knew change happened and that it always came with a cost, he just didn't like it.

Tiarnán looked across the table at them, his violet eyes revealing no emotion. Patrick met his gaze head-on, never one to flinch away from someone else's judgmental regard.

"Medb most likely spoke the truth to the Dagda about the location of the Morrígan's staff. I highly doubt she would remove it from the mortal realm," Tiarnán said.

"Why?" Jono asked.

"Its presence would be felt beyond the veil, and it would be hunted. It is easier to hide something powerful in a world where the population numbers in the billions and iron coats the earth."

"Which means we're back to square one," Patrick said.

Back to chasing down rumors, hoping to reach the prize before Ethan did. Patrick didn't know where Ethan was these days, but he knew enough from Zachary's presence on the Skellig Islands that his father was building up alliances the same way Patrick was. Ethan was still hunting for power and preparing for war.

He still wanted to be a god.

Macaria's twisted godhead in Hannah's soul was still at his disposal, because Patrick knew Ethan would never give up that power source. Patrick liked to think, in his darkest moments, that he'd know when his twin sister died for good.

"Medb bankrolls her mortal businesses through legal and illegal avenues. We will follow the money," Tiarnán said.

Patrick nodded, tapping at his phone to check the time before getting to his feet. "Great. You do that. Keep us updated."

"Where are you going?"

"We got a flight to catch."

Sage set down her pen. "I'll walk you out."

Patrick pulled on his wool coat, the fabric thick around him, and put on his gloves. Órlaith still had his leather jacket, because he hadn't been willing to ask for it back when that was the only clothes she'd been wearing after the fight. Jono grabbed the small carry-on from the corner that held what little clothes they were bringing for the quick trip.

"Will you be back in time for Christmas?" Sage asked once they reached the lobby of the building.

They paused by the glass doors leading to the street. The security barriers present at the beginning of the month had been taken down sometime during their travels back and forth across the veil. Patrick could still sense the wards in the building's foundation, fae magic subtle and powerful where it pressed against his shields.

"We'll be back tomorrow morning. The flight plans have already been filed for both trips. Tell Marek thank you for the jet. Trying to get a last-minute flight out was impossible when I looked at tickets," Patrick said.

Sage smiled slightly, absently playing with the turquoise pendant hanging from around her throat. She felt human to Patrick's magic now that she was back to wearing the artifact filled with fae glamour to hide her werecreature status.

"You're coming over for Christmas Eve dinner, right?"

"Wouldn't miss it, love," Jono said.

Patrick wasn't sure what consisted of a pack Christmas Eve dinner, but Jono was right. They wouldn't miss it, and Patrick was looking forward to it. He hadn't celebrated Christmas in a way that mattered since he was a kid growing up in Salem. Wade seemed particularly interested in the food and had been asking Leon questions about the dishes since they'd returned from Ireland through the veil.

"Marek will have your presents delivered to your apartment while you're gone. I've told Wade he's not supposed to touch them."

Patrick laughed. "Tell Marek we owe him for saving Christmas."

Sage stepped closer to hug Patrick. "Tell him yourself tomorrow. Safe travels, both of you."

Patrick hugged her tight, before letting go. Sage had been the one to organize last-minute Christmas gift shopping through Marek's personal assistant. Money definitely talked at a time like this, and that was something Patrick was definitely going to pay Marek back for.

Jono gave Sage a hug, discreetly scent-marking her. "You're in charge until we get back."

"Don't worry, I'll keep an eye on things," Sage promised.

Emma had given them a brief update yesterday about the goings-on in the werecreature community. Either Gerard's threat earlier in the month to Estelle and Youssef had been enough to make the pair momentarily stand down, or they were getting into the holiday spirit and saving murder for the new year.

Patrick didn't give it too much longer before Estelle and Youssef started up their harassment campaign again. He and Jono would wait for them to make the first move and go from there, whenever it would be.

Patrick waved goodbye before he and Jono exited the building. He shoved his hands into his coat pockets, bouncing a little on his feet. The weather seemed colder due to the fae's presence in the city from the last few weeks. The Dagda's harp had really only settled the seasons at the Gap of Dunloe. New York was resigned to a very cold and snowy winter.

"Ready?" Jono asked as he hailed a taxi, his distinctive eyes hidden behind sunglasses.

"Yeah. Let's go."

"I wish you had been able to find her," SOA Director Setsuna Abuku said over the phone, her voice cutting in and out a little due to the shoddy connection. He should've requested a satphone before leaving New York.

Patrick pressed his hand against the SUV's roof to better steady himself as Jono took a turn on a snowy, bumpy road with a little more speed than he would've liked. But the rugged vehicle had snow chains, and if they got stuck in a snow drift, Jono could lift them out of it.

"The Wisteria child isn't ever coming back. Medb stole her, and everyone knows children taken by the fae are never seen again," Patrick said.

"That has never stopped a parent from wanting their child back."

"Wanting something doesn't mean you'll get it."

He should know. Patrick had wanted the family he lost for years before he finally gave up on that dream turned nightmare. Sometimes you had to let go of the past and move on, otherwise it would consume you. Patrick had a feeling the Wisterias would never stop searching for what they'd lost.

"They will never stop looking for her."

"I'm sorry for their loss, but there's nothing we can do. They can sue us, but the SOA isn't the one who took their kid, and we exhausted every avenue we could. The lawsuit will get thrown out."

"Most likely, but it's negative exposure for the agency, and we've had enough of that this year."

"I don't think the new year will fix that."

Setsuna was quiet on the line. Patrick stared out the windshield at the snow-covered evergreen trees and high mountains that was all he could see. Montana in winter was mostly white, and the cold was different than the chill they'd left behind in New York and past the veil. Out here, in the mountains and the valleys where the preternatural world claimed more territory than mundane humans, everything felt different. Patrick wasn't sure if that was nature or magic, but either way, he missed the city streets.

"I'm giving you from tomorrow until January second off," Setsuna finally said.

"I didn't put in for time off."

"The paperwork has been handled."

Patrick leaned his head back against the seat, making a face. "You still owe me an actual vacation."

"I'll let you put in the paperwork for that." Setsuna paused before continuing with "Merry Christmas, Patrick. I'm glad you're home."

He blinked at that, some tiny part of him wondering if she was glad for his own sake or for whatever reasons drove the decisions she made. Setsuna had been his guardian while growing up, but the holidays had never been easy for them.

"Merry Christmas," Patrick echoed.

He ended the call, tucking his phone into the pocket of his leather jacket. Órlaith had given his jacket back with a smile and heavy protection wards written across the leather back at JFK hours ago. Nadine's magic was now overlaid with that of a goddess', and Patrick had accepted the gift without outright saying thank you, because it would've been rude.

Manners were sometimes backward when it came to the fae.

"I know this place," Gerard said suddenly from the far back seat where he sat with Órlaith.

Patrick peered over his shoulder, gaze skipping past where Gwyn ap Nudd sat alone on the center bench of the SUV. "How? We're going to a safe house not even the CIA knows about."

Gerard's silver eyes seemed almost too bright. "This is where I came after the Civil War."

Patrick blinked, tamping down on the riot of emotions those words hit him with. His anger toward Gerard had cooled a little after everything they'd gone through, but that didn't mean Patrick had completely forgiven his old captain for lying to him.

"Been over a hundred and fifty years since you were last here. It's snow and trees. How is it familiar?"

"There's fae magic out here."

Considering what the safe house held, that probably shouldn't have been surprising. Patrick turned back around, catching Jono's eye.

"How much longer?" Jono asked.

Patrick used the flashlight on his phone to illuminate the paper map unfolded across his lap. He didn't trust the signal out here in the mountains, and sometimes magic played havoc on electronics. Besides, the only person who knew where they were going was him, and the route wasn't—and couldn't be—written down.

They'd taken I-90 west out of Missoula, Montana, and turned south onto Petty Creek Road, driving through Lolo National Forest. Night fell early this far north, and the cold was getting to the point that even the SUV's heater wasn't enough.

"The turnoff is coming up."

The quiet in the vehicle lasted another five minutes before the particular recognition of fae magic pricked against Patrick's shields. The bright headlights illuminated a break in the trees up ahead that he knew most people would never see.

"Turn right in about ten meters."

To his credit, Jono didn't question him, despite it probably seeming like he was about to drive them into the nearest tree. Jono turned the steering wheel to the right, and the SUV passed harmlessly through a shroud of magic that glinted at the edge of Patrick's vision. Gerard sucked in a sharp breath from the rear seat but didn't say anything.

The headlights led the way over a bumpy path that couldn't be called a road and was barely wide enough for a modern vehicle. Tree branches scraped the sides and roof, and Patrick winced, thinking about the damage to the rental. At least he wouldn't be the one paying for it.

Jono slammed on the brakes ten minutes later as flickers of light erupted from the trees, dancing through the headlight beams. The seat belt dug into Patrick's chest, and he pulled at it to unlock it.

"Pixies," Órlaith said. "They're harmless."

"I don't know about that," Gerard muttered. "They're biting little fuckers."

Patrick snorted out a laugh. "Aren't they distant cousins of yours?"

"Shut your mouth."

Jono stepped on the gas again and drove forward. "I think I'd like them more if I wasn't afraid they'd splatter on the windshield."

The pixies led the way, more flying through the trees to dart ahead and illuminate the path. They came in a variety of colors, their wings leaving shimmering trails in the dark that slowly faded. Patrick squinted through the dark, watching as the pixies up ahead seemed to suddenly vanish.

"Keep driving," Patrick said.

Jono nodded and kept a firm grip on the wheel. Patrick folded up the paper map and shoved it in the glove compartment. They didn't need it anymore.

The SUV passed through the shielding encasing the safe house, and they drove into a winter wonderland.

Witchlights sparkled above, fighting the stars for the night sky. Three large wooden cabins were clustered in a small clear area on top of the low hill they drove up. The doors were closed, but warm light shone out the windows, the shine glimmering through icicles hanging from the siding.

A bonfire had been lit in the clearing the three cabins surrounded. Figures huddled around the fire, some small, some larger, many of them holding sticks in the fire. Patrick watched as one pulled their stick out of the flame, pulling at the glob of white at the end and stuffing it in their mouth.

The SUV's headlights cut across the bonfire, and heads snapped around. In the light, Patrick got a glimpse of strangely colored eyes, sharp-featured faces, and skin of various coloring that would never be normal for a human.

Jono carefully braked to a halt as some of the taller figures swiftly gathered up the smaller ones, ushering them toward the cabins.

"What is this place?" Jono asked.

"A safe house for changelings," Patrick said.

"It was our home," Gerard said quietly.

Jono killed the engine, and Patrick undid his seat belt. He pushed open the door and got out, boots sinking into the snow. He was dressed for winter, and the heat charms set into his clothes should have kept the cold at bay, but fae magic was tricky. Everywhere that wasn't covered by Órlaith's ward in his jacket started to lose warmth.

The changeling children running through the snow abruptly stopped as the door to the largest cabin opened on silent hinges. The woman who stood framed in the doorway was tall, with wide shoulders and hips, her thick, orange-red hair falling to her waist in a riot of messy curls. She wore snow pants and a parka, though the spear in her hand was anything but modern.

Gerard made a wounded sound in the back of his throat, silver eyes shocked wide in his face. "Scáthach."

"Welcome back, Cú Chulainn," Scáthach said, her Scottish accent so thick it was like walking down a street in Glasgow.

"What...how are you here?"

"Someone needed to look after the *bairns* that no one wanted."

The children had stopped running, with one or two creeping back toward the bonfire, sticks in hand. One of them clutched a half-empty bag of marshmallows, her companion carrying a bag of Hershey's chocolate bars. The lure of s'mores overtook escape now that it seemed Patrick and the others weren't the enemy.

Gerard took a hesitant step forward, eyes locked on the warrior woman of old. He shook his head before striding through the snow to where Scáthach stood. She leaned her spear against the wall of the cabin, stepping off the porch to meet him halfway.

They hugged in the light of the bonfire and floating witchlights overhead, old friends reunited. Patrick glanced at Órlaith, seeing a soft smile gracing the Summer Lady's lips as she watched them.

Scáthach put Gerard at arm's length, giving him a long, assessing look before finally nodding. "You look well."

Gerard let out a shaky laugh. "I've been better."

"You are still alive and remembered. That is enough, these days."

Gwyn ap Nudd pushed past Patrick, his footsteps not making a sound in the snow. Scáthach watched him come with an unblinking gaze, unconcerned about the Welsh god's presence in her domain.

"Scáthach," Gwyn ap Nudd said. "I understand you have something of mine."

"If you mean your daughter, then yes. I have kept her safe since the moment she was given to me," Scáthach replied.

Behind her, someone else walked out of the cabin, holding a child in his arms. It took a moment for Patrick to make out his face, backlit as the god was, but when he did, he wanted to strangle someone—preferably the trickster.

"Hello, Pattycakes," Hermes said with a smirk.

"What the fu—" Patrick began. Jono's hand covered his mouth before Patrick could get the rest of the word out.

"There are children about. Watch your language," Jono told him mildly.

Hermes cooed at the dark-eyed changeling Patrick had last seen when he'd handed her off to another SOA agent for safekeeping. Cadwyn patted Hermes on the face with one tiny hand stuffed into a mitten before waving her other hand at Gwyn ap Nudd and letting out an excited squeal that made Hermes wince.

"That is not what I call safe, Scáthach," Gwyn ap Nudd said tightly, glaring at Hermes.

"Relax. I'm not going to take your kid," Hermes replied.

"She is in your arms."

"And Patrick is free of Medb's strings. If he wasn't, you'd be dealing with Persephone, not me." Hermes made a kissy face at Cadwyn. "I'm just a messenger."

The reminder of who owned his soul debt made Patrick wince. Wondering what would have happened to Cadwyn if he hadn't gotten free of Medb's bargain wasn't worth thinking about.

Patrick pulled Jono's hand away from his mouth. "Give Gwyn ap Nudd his daughter."

Hermes saluted lazily with the hand not holding the changeling. "Whatever you say, Pattycakes."

Hermes walked over to Gwyn ap Nudd and handed over Cadwyn, the tiny fae child clinging to her father like a limpet once she was in his arms. The god held her close, his mouth pressed to the hood of her mini-parka, lips moving around silent words.

After a moment, Gwyn ap Nudd raised his head and looked at Patrick. "You kept your promise."

"I don't use kids as bargaining chips. She's all yours," Patrick said.

Gwyn ap Nudd cupped his daughter's head with one hand, eyes like molten fire in his face. "When you call for war, I will fight."

If the Welsh god thought he owed a debt, Patrick wasn't going to argue. He'd take all the promised help he could for future fights in this war. "Sure."

"Now I see why you let Sage do all the talking. You could've gotten anything out of him and he'd have paid it," Gerard mused.

"Shut up."

Patrick tucked his chin beneath his scarf as a cold wind blew up, carrying with it a mist that wrapped around Gwyn ap Nudd and his daughter like a shroud. They disappeared through the veil, free to be together again after who knew how many months apart.

A piece of wood in the fire cracked and popped from the heat, sending sparks into the air. A child giggled, most of them having returned to the bonfire to continue making s'mores. Their quiet voices drifted on the air in a few different languages.

"We hunted earlier. I have a venison and potato stew cooking on the stove." Scáthach eyed Gerard and Órlaith before nodding at the closest cabin. "You should stay and tell me the story of your life since last I saw you."

"We accept your hospitality," Gerard said with a faint smile.

"Dibs on the cornbread," Hermes said, heading back to the cabin.

Scáthach held out her hand to Órlaith, who took it with a smile on her face. The two goddesses followed after Hermes. Gerard watched them go for a few seconds before looking over at Patrick.

"Stay for dinner," Gerard said.

Patrick shook his head. "We really should get going. It's a long drive back to our hotel in Missoula, and our flight leaves pretty early tomorrow."

"Stay. Please."

They stared at each other in silence, the giggles and shrieks from the changeling children echoing in the crisp, cold air.

"You lied to me. But it's been brought to my attention that I've done a lot of lying myself."

"You had your reasons."

"So did you."

"I'm still sorry. I always will be." Gerard extended his hand, meeting Patrick's eyes. "Nothing that matters is ever easy, and you have always mattered, Patrick. I need you to know that. I never meant to hurt you."

Patrick could have ignored the gesture of peace, but Sage's words from the roof stairwell still resonated with him in the back of his mind. He reached out and grasped Gerard's hand, gripping it tight. "I don't care where you are when you get married, but you better fucking invite me, Smooth Dog."

Gerard's face split into a wide smile at the use of the field nickname. "Yeah. Of course I will. Yours will be the first invitation I send out when I write them up for the team."

A tight knot unfurled in Patrick's chest, making it easier to breathe. He could hold on to the feeling of betrayal that had been with him since Tír na nÓg or let it go. Nothing good came of a wound left to fester, and Patrick chose to believe that Gerard's apology was sincere, because that was the only way to move on. Gaining a pack over the last half a year had made it clear what Patrick had missed since leaving the Mage Corps.

Family.

Something Gerard would always be, because Patrick had always looked up to him like a brother. He wasn't willing to give that up simply because the gods had fucked with both of them in the end.

"Come on," Gerard said, gesturing at the cabin. "I want to introduce you to Scáthach and tell her all about you."

"She asked about your stories, not mine."

Gerard's smile tempered into something fond. "You are part of my stories, Patrick."

Patrick swallowed past a hard knot in his throat, not knowing what to say to that.

Gerard headed for the cabin, and Patrick watched him go.

"You all right?" Jono asked in a low voice, a warm presence beside him that would never leave.

"Yeah," Patrick said before taking a deep breath and reaching for Jono's hand.

For once, the answer didn't feel like a lie.

Together, they walked toward the cabin, where Gerard and all the names he went by waited for them.

24

PATRICK STEPPED INSIDE THE FLAT FIRST, TURNING ON THE LIGHTS. Jono squeezed past him and headed for the kitchen. Whoever had come by yesterday while they'd been out of state had left the heat on, so the place was cozily warm.

The stack of Tupperware containers in Jono's hands was heavy with leftovers. Considering the loads of food that had been cooked and brought by the Tempest pack for the Christmas Eve meal at Marek's place—enough to feed a small army or a pack of werecreatures—he hadn't thought any would be left.

Jono made room in the refrigerator for the leftovers, taking a moment to check that none of the herbs had fallen out of the goose where it sat in a pan on the bottom shelf. Jono needed to remember to ask Marek's assistant where she'd found the shop that produced the bird. He hadn't had roast goose for Christmas since leaving England, but Patrick had surprised him with the meal when their groceries had been delivered early that afternoon after arriving home from Montana.

He straightened up and closed the refrigerator door. Digging through the cabinets, he pulled out a bottle of Macallan and two glasses. After pouring a generous amount, he carried both out to the living room, where Patrick was sprawled on the couch, staring at the lit-up Christmas tree.

The overhead lights were off now, the only illumination coming from the colorful lights wrapped around the Christmas tree. It was still alive, thanks to Emma's pack, and the stack of neatly wrapped presents underneath looked nice.

Patrick had taken off his shoes and jacket, both tossed aside on the armchair, and was currently sprawled on the sofa. Jono set both glasses of whiskey down on the small coffee table before toeing off his own shoes. He pulled off his jumper and left it on the armchair as well, running a hand through his mussed hair as he stared at the Christmas tree. One of the ornaments was dangling precariously at the end of a branch, and he went to fix it.

"Not how I thought Christmas would go for us," Patrick said, sounding rueful.

Jono looked over at him, seeing he'd leaned forward to grab a glass and was holding out the other for Jono to take. Jono stepped closer to accept it, sipping at the whiskey and appreciating the warmth that slid down his throat from the drink.

Jono settled on the floor in front of the Christmas tree, watching how the colorful lights played over the drink in his hand. The curtains were drawn, and it was just the two of them for the night. Wade was staying over at Sage and Marek's flat; they'd come over tomorrow for late-morning present opening and the Christmas meal.

"We're alive, and you're here with me. I couldn't ask for anything more," Jono said.

Considering all the bargains and promises that been thrown about between gods lately, Jono wanted nothing more than a few days to themselves. Time spent on only them, and not running back and forth through the veil, skipping illegally through countries, trying to stay alive.

He took a sip of whiskey, studying Patrick. The other man

looked tired, but in a good way caused by lots of food and a crowd of friends. Jono had done his best to take Patrick's mind off of everything that had happened, even though the fight wasn't over.

"I got you presents. You'll have to accept those."

Jono smiled. "I'll take anything you want to give me. You know that."

Patrick took a long sip of his whiskey before setting the glass on the coffee table. Jono watched as Patrick slid off the sofa, crawling over to him. The Christmas lights turned his dark ginger hair into odd shades of red. Jono set his own glass down as Patrick crawled onto his lap, knees on either side of Jono's hips. His weight was a comfort after this past month and the time they'd lost past the veil.

Jono wrapped his arms around Patrick, pulling him close and breathing him in. He dipped his head, pressing an openmouthed kiss high on Patrick's neck. Breathing in his bitter scent soothed Jono in a way he never thought would be possible until they met.

Patrick tilted his head to the side, breath catching a little in his throat. Jono slid his hands beneath Patrick's shirt, fingers skimming over his back. Jono moved his head, biting at Patrick's earlobe and tugging at it with his teeth for a moment.

Patrick worked his hands between them and started to unbutton Jono's dress shirt, leaning back a little to give him space to work with. Jono wasn't on board with that and made an annoyed sound before pulling Patrick flush against his body. The pressure against his rapidly hardening cock made Jono groan, and he chased after Patrick's mouth for a kiss.

"You drive me absolutely mad sometimes," Jono muttered against his lips.

"Only sometimes?" Patrick said, grinding their hips together. "I should probably work on that."

"Please don't."

Patrick laughed, the sound full of humor and nothing else. He'd laughed a lot more now than when they'd first met, and Jono was glad for it. Teaching Patrick there was more to life than the job and his past that built him was less a struggle these days than it used to be.

"What would you do without me, hm?"

Jono kissed Patrick hard and deep, stealing his breath. "I don't want to find out."

Patrick tangled his fingers in Jono's hair, keeping a tight hold as he surged upward. Jono steadied him with firm hands, kissing him fiercely. Patrick was panting when he finally pulled back, green eyes dilated and a flush on his cheeks that was interrupted by splotches of colorful lights from the Christmas tree.

Jono reached out and smoothed his thumb over the sharp jut of Patrick's cheekbone, tracing a random path of freckles. Going past the veil had wreaked havoc on their bodies, leaving them all dragging over the last couple of days. Feeding Patrick had been high on Jono's list, along with making sure he had everything he needed.

Patrick shoved at Jono's shoulder, licking his lips. "Lie down."

Jono did as he was told, leaning back on his elbows and stretching out his legs. Patrick finished unbuttoning his dress shirt, the fabric falling away on either side of his torso. Patrick's hands were warm when he dragged them down Jono's torso, fingernails scraping over his abs. Jono twitched a little at the touch, arching a little against Patrick's fingers.

"Thought we promised Wade no sex in public spaces?"

Patrick snorted as he undid Jono's belt and tossed it aside. "He has his own apartment. Which we paid for."

"Technically, Marek did."

Patrick arched an eyebrow, his hands stilling on Jono's zipper. "You want me to go down on you or not? Because if you want to argue, I'm sure I can—"

Jono shut him up by grabbing him by the shirt and hauling him forward. Patrick sprawled over him as they kissed, and Jono slipped a hand between Patrick's legs to cup his cock and give it a good squeeze. Patrick rocked into his touch, moaning a little.

Desire and want was a heady scent rising off his body and filling Jono's nose.

"I'm sure I really want to see your mouth wrapped around my cock," Jono said, nipping at Patrick's bottom lip.

Patrick pulled back, breathing a little faster. Jono had to push down the desire to upend Patrick onto his back and ravish him.

"That all you want for Christmas?" Patrick asked, sitting back up again.

Jono dragged the heel of his palm over Patrick's cock before he got too far away. Then he propped himself up on his elbows once more. "Just you, every day of the year."

Patrick lifted a hand and ran his fingers through Jono's hair, stroking it out of his eyes. Patrick's gaze searched his, teeth biting at his bottom lip until the skin there went white from the pressure. Jono reached up to gently pry it free, skimming his thumb over the seam of Patrick's lips.

Patrick turned his head a little to press a kiss to his thumb. When he looked at Jono again, there was a weight to his gaze that made Jono go still, the rush of blood in his ears loud like thunder.

"If the gods had given us a choice on who they bound me to, I would have chosen you," Patrick said, the honesty in his words like honey that Jono could almost taste.

The confession made his heart skip a beat, and he stared at Patrick in wonder, thinking about how he wouldn't have any of this if he had walked away from Marek's offer all those years ago.

Jono thought of the accidents and decisions that had led them to each other, and the way nothing in their lives seemed to happen by chance, but by what the Fates decreed. Maybe they could've fought going down this twisted path, but Jono knew they couldn't win against gods. What was important was they were each other's in all the ways that mattered—lover, partner, weapon. It was enough.

Patrick would always be enough.

Jono curled one hand around the back of Patrick's head and

pulled him in for a kiss that stole the breath from both their lungs. They didn't stop until it hurt to breathe—then Patrick dug his fingers into the ticklish spot high on Jono's ribs. Jono jerked backward, swearing, his elbows sliding out beneath him as he landed on his back with a gasp.

"Bloody cheat," he said with a laugh, even as he helpfully lifted his hips so Patrick could divest him of his jeans and underwear until he was lying naked in front of the Christmas tree.

Patrick smiled at him, a hungry look in his gaze that went straight to Jono's cock. "If cheating gets me what I want, then I'm all for it."

Jono reached down and stroked his cock, the dry friction making his nipples harden. "This what you want?"

"Like you have to ask? Now lie back and think of England."

Jono laughed, body shaking with it. Patrick laughed with him, grinning in a carefree way that Jono rarely saw. He tucked one hand behind his head and helpfully spread his legs. Patrick took the invitation for what it was and slid down until his mouth hovered over Jono's rapidly hardening cock.

Patrick's fingers were warm when they wrapped around his cock, and Jono hissed at the touch. Nothing compared to Patrick's mouth, and Jono didn't blink as Patrick wrapped his lips around the crown to suck at it. Jono shivered at the first flick of Patrick's tongue against the head, teasing him.

Then Patrick swallowed his cock down in a messy, wet, and absolutely *filthy* slide, until he was choking on it. Jono groaned, the constricting tightness of Patrick's throat making Jono want to push deeper into his mouth.

"Fuck," Jono bit out, reaching for Patrick to get a grip on his hair.

Patrick hummed at the touch, the vibration making Jono bite the inside of his cheek. He pulled at Patrick's hair, guiding him all the way down until he could feel Patrick's lips and nose against his groin. Jono closed his eyes, cock throbbing deep in Patrick's throat, and he swallowed reflexively at the feeling.

Jono let his hair go, fingers stroking over Patrick's face. Patrick pulled back, using his hand to stroke up Jono's cock after his mouth. Then he swallowed Jono back down, head bobbing, eyes glimmering through his lashes. His face and Jono's body were bathed in colorful Christmas lights as he sucked Jono off, lips reddened and spit-slick where they were wrapped around his cock.

They hadn't had sex in what seemed like weeks, but Jono blamed that on the constant travel through the veil and the toll it had taken on their bodies. Lying here, with Patrick's mouth on his cock, was something Jono would always want.

Jono cupped Patrick's jaw, and pressed his thumb into the hollow of his cheek, feeling out the line of his own cock. "You look good like this."

Patrick's gaze flicked up to meet his, and Jono didn't look away. He hitched his hips up a little, thrusting shallowly into Patrick's mouth. When Patrick didn't stop him, he did it again, and again, a slow slide into heat that left him wanting more.

Then Patrick moaned, and Jono couldn't stop the jerk of his hips, pushing against Patrick's face. He would've apologized, but his tongue was stuck to the back of his teeth. Patrick only pulled back far enough to breathe before sucking Jono's cock back down his throat, working him to a hardness that hurt. It left Jono almost too warm, skin prickling at the scrape of the rug against his back and the scratch of Patrick's nails on his thighs.

Everything narrowed down to Patrick and his mouth—the slide of his tongue and the heat of his throat. Jono's cock throbbed between Patrick's lips, balls going high and tight with every second that passed, and he moaned.

When Jono came, his brain lit up like the Christmas tree, bright lights bursting across his vision. Patrick drew every last drop of cum out of him and swallowed it all. Jono blinked sweat out of his eyes as Patrick finally lifted his head, lips swollen and wet with spit and cum.

Jono pressed his palms against the floor and sat up, reaching for Patrick. Jono dragged him back onto his lap, deftly undoing Patrick's belt and zipper, palming at the hard bulge of his cock and the damp fabric of his underwear. Patrick bit back a whimper, arching into the touch, before kissing him. Jono could taste himself on Patrick's tongue, the hint of whiskey long since faded.

Jono pulled Patrick's hard cock free of his underwear, stroking him with dry, firm fingers. Patrick hissed at the touch, jerking his hips through the circle of Jono's fingers, but he never pulled away.

"I'll always want you," Jono muttered, dragging his mouth down Patrick's throat to bite at his collarbone through his shirt. He never stopped moving his hand, the sheer amount of *want* pouring off Patrick filling his nose and urging him on.

"Jono," Patrick said, voice a little rough, coming out a little desperately as he dragged his hands across Jono's shoulders.

Jono raised his head, meeting Patrick's gaze, staring at this man who'd been alone for too long and didn't know the first thing about pack until they'd gone down this road together. He kept stroking Patrick, knowing that it had to hurt a little, but also knowing Patrick was so close to coming that it probably didn't matter.

He dragged his other hand over Patrick's throat, pressing his scent into warm skin, wanting everyone to know that Patrick was *his*, and always would be, in every way that mattered.

"I love you," Jono said, meaning it with every part of him that didn't belong to a god.

Patrick's eyes half rolled up into his head, and his entire body jerked as he came with a cry that Jono kissed away to nothing. Patrick's tongue moved sluggishly against his for a few seconds as Jono stroked him through his climax, hand sticky with cum.

Jono leaned back, taking Patrick with him, until they were both sprawled on the floor in front of the Christmas tree. The living room smelled like sex and pine and *them*.

Jono gently ran his clean hand over Patrick's back, feeling him breathe. "You don't have to say it back."

"Shut up," Patrick mumbled, fingers pressing bruises into Jono's skin. "Say it again."

Jono settled his hand on the back of Patrick's neck, thumb curving around his throat to press against his pulse. He closed his eyes and breathed in Patrick all around him.

"I love you."

The way Patrick's grip tightened, as if he would never let go, was a wordless answer Jono heard loud and clear in the quiet that settled between them.

<hr />

"Did you *defile* my presents?" Wade asked in a scandalized voice, clutching a brightly wrapped package to his chest over by the Christmas tree. "It smells like sex in here!"

"Keep your nose to yourself," Jono said as he helped Sage out of her coat.

"Oh my god, my poor *presents*."

Marek rolled his eyes and held up a reusable bag straining at the straps. "I brought wine."

"Cheers, mate. You can put the bottles in the kitchen."

Jono ignored Wade's muttering as the teenager started to sort through the presents under the tree, stacking up the ones that had his name on them all around him.

"Don't open those," Patrick warned as he came out of the bedroom, dressed in jeans and a T-shirt, with socks instead of slippers on his feet.

"But they're mine," Wade whined. He patted the stack of presents in front of him with both hands. "*Mine*."

"Your hoarding tendencies are ridiculous. Jono is making you hot chocolate and the rest of us hot toddies, and there are a dozen cinnamon rolls in the oven. We'll open presents after drinks are passed out and the snacks are ready."

"You opened our presents to you at six this morning. You can wait a little longer for these ones," Sage said.

Patrick made a face. "Six? I'd have sent him back to bed."

Wade heaved out a loud sigh, projecting how unfair he thought that decision was. Then he ignored them all in favor of shaking his presents.

Jono didn't tell him to stop. This was Wade's first proper Christmas in years, and none of them wanted to take that from him. Everyone in their pack was alive, and together, and Jono wasn't going to complain about any of that, even if Wade would complain until he could open his presents.

"Merry Christmas," Sage said, giving Patrick a hug.

Patrick returned the hug with a smile. "Merry Christmas. How was getting over here through the parade?"

"Hellish, but we made it."

"Did you have fun at Emma's?"

"Always. We ate before we came over, but those cinnamon rolls smell good."

"Jono made bacon as well."

"Yeah," Marek said as he came out of the kitchen, munching on a piece. "I know. You should grab some before Wade inhales it all."

Patrick pinned Wade with a look, making the teenager freeze halfway to his feet. "He won't."

"But *bacon*," Wade said.

"It's for everyone. You'll have to share."

Wade pouted, but the lure of his presents overcame his desire to steal food. Jono headed into the kitchen to finish making everyone's drinks and pull the cinnamon rolls out of the oven a couple of minutes later. The platter of bagels, cream cheese, and lox was already on the coffee table in the living room.

Lunch was a mishmash, because the real meal would happen in

a few hours. Jono would put the goose in before they opened up the presents, and Sage had promised to help with the side dishes. Patrick was still terrible at cooking and was excused so none of them ended up poisoned and in the emergency room.

Someone turned on the television, switching it to the channel broadcasting the Macy's Christmas Day Parade. It was almost noon, so the parade was nearing the end. Considering the amount of snow New York had seen this month, Jono figured it had probably taken a fleet of snow plows to clear the parade route.

"Pat, can you come grab a tray?" Jono called out.

"Sure. Be right there," Patrick replied.

A few seconds later, Patrick came into the kitchen. Instead of grabbing a tray of drinks, Patrick wrapped his arms around Jono's waist and rose up onto his tiptoes to steal a kiss. Jono smiled against his lips, enjoying the easy looseness that had settled in Patrick since last night. When Jono tried to pull away, Patrick chased after his mouth, and they ended up spending nearly a minute kissing each other, the drinks forgotten.

But not for long.

"Stop making out in the kitchen! I have presents that need to be opened!" Wade yelled, sounding as if the world were ending.

Sage and Marek's laughter echoed loudly in the flat. Patrick broke the kiss with a snort, one hand still groping at Jono's arse. "He might kill us in our sleep if we wait any longer."

"I've money on before supper," Jono replied.

It took two trips to bring the drinks and food out to the living room where Jono had already set plates and napkins on the coffee table. Marek had already made himself half a bagel piled high with schmear, lox, and capers. Sage took it upon herself to pass out the hot toddies and the giant mug topped with a mountain of whipped cream and drizzled chocolate that was Wade's, who made grabby hands at it.

"Don't spill it," Patrick warned.

"You know cleaning charms," Wade replied, already taking a sip of the overly sweet drink. He got a dollop of whipped cream on his nose, which he wiped off with a finger that he then licked clean.

"Teenagers," Marek said with a laugh. "You guys know you're starting a little backward, right?"

Patrick threw a wadded-up napkin at his head. It bounced off Marek's curls and fell to the sofa. "Shut up."

"*Now* can we open the presents?" Wade asked.

Jono's mobile going off had Wade groaning loudly, a mournful look settling on his face. Jono dug his mobile out of his pocket and checked the number flashing across the screen. He frowned at it.

"Who is it?" Patrick asked, eyes narrowing a little.

"The callbox downstairs," Jono said.

"We got all our packages yesterday. No one delivers on Christmas."

Jono answered anyway. "Hello?"

He could hear a multitude of heartbeats through the staticky connection before someone cleared their throat. "Jono?"

It took him a moment to place the voice. He hadn't seen or spoken to Letitia since she had come to their home at the beginning of the month asking for territory advice with Marco's rival pack.

"Letitia? It's Christmas. Why aren't you with your pack?"

"Some of them came with me."

"Us too," Marco added, making Jono blink in surprise.

"And me," a new voice said that he didn't recognize.

Sage leaned forward, cradling her mug of hot toddy in both hands. "You should let them up."

Jono hit the numbered button on his phone screen that would buzz them through. Patrick grabbed a cinnamon roll off the platter and started to tear it into smaller pieces for hospitality purposes.

"Marek, can you grab a bottle of sparkling water from the fridge? We'll make them take turns drinking from it," Patrick said.

Sage muted the television while Marek went to do as he was asked. Jono went to unlock the front door and open it. The group's footsteps got louder on the stairs until nearly a dozen people were crowded into their flat. He looked over at Patrick, who was silently counting heads and ripping up a few more pieces of cinnamon roll. Wade had planted himself in front of his presents, scowling at everyone over his mug of hot chocolate.

"Got the water," Marek said, brandishing the bottle.

"All right, hospitality first before anything else," Patrick ordered. "Be welcome, all of you."

The new arrivals dutifully ate the bits of cinnamon roll and took turns sipping at the sparkling water. Jono stood before the two packs and the petite Mexican-American woman who smelled like a weregrizzly to his nose, meeting everyone's eyes.

"Why are you here?" he wanted to know.

Letitia raised her chin, jaw set. "We've come to pledge allegiance to your god pack."

"Us, too. We're prepared to tithe accordingly," Marco said with a nod that was echoed by the three members of his pack who'd come with him.

"And I'm here to ask about protection," the independent weregrizzly said.

Jono blinked, absolutely floored by that declaration. Gaining Emma's Tempest pack was one thing—he knew them, was friends with them, and she'd been quietly campaigning for him to take a stand for quite a while now. It was something else entirely for packs he'd had only a single interaction with and didn't know beyond that to come to him and declare they wanted to leave Estelle and Youssef's New York City god pack for his own.

Patrick came to stand by Jono's side, and Sage joined them seconds later. Jono rubbed at his jaw, scratching at smooth skin instead of the beard he'd shaved off that morning. He studied the group before him, trying to sort out his thoughts.

"It's going to get worse with all the other packs around you before it gets better," Jono finally warned.

Letitia shrugged, her mouth pressed into a thin line. "Can't be worse than what we went through when we were ordered before the other alphas for going to you in the first place."

Jono didn't ask, but the faint whiff of fear that drifted up from both packs was enough to tell him they'd been punished for coming to him, despite his threat to Nicholas.

"You said you thought they were yours," Patrick said, looking at him. "If that's the case, then you should do something about it."

Jono held his gaze, nodding slowly. "Yeah. I think I will."

Jono looked at the pack, holding the gaze of each alpha and the independent werecreature. Despite the lingering scent of fear brought about by bad memories, all of them looked determined in a way only the desperate were—as if they had nothing left to lose.

"Come forward," Jono said. Letitia, Marco, and the weregrizzly stepped closer and went to their knees. He nodded at each of them before smiling at the woman he didn't know. "What's your name?"

"Marisol." She blinked dark eyes up at him as she unzipped her coat and shrugged out of it. "Marisol Callejo."

"Nice to meet you, Marisol."

The three had gotten rid of their coats and scarves. Jono stepped closer and methodically dragged his hands and wrists over their throats, pressing his scent into them and taking on theirs the way he'd taken in Emma and Leon's.

His soul cracked open, nose burning with the smell of them—a mix of scents that somehow separated into individual recognition in his brain and nose. Jono would know these alphas—and the people who were part of their packs—by scent until they left his protection. He would know Marisol the same way.

Jono's nerves sang throughout his body, a buzzing high that left him feeling light-headed when he finally stepped back, holding the lives of two new packs and an independent werecreature in his hands. He stared at them, noting how their breathing matched his, as the overwhelming feel of them settled in his soul. Something shifted—some indefinable thing that Jono could only feel in his soul and taste in the back of his mouth.

There was no going back from this.

"I take on responsibility for your *Escorpión* pack, Marco, and your Gold pack, Letitia, and you as well, Marisol," Jono said.

Patrick and Sage stepped forward to help Marco and Marisol to their feet, while Jono helped Letitia. The three stared at him, looking a little dazed but happier, the fear in their scents before gone now and replaced with a calmness that smelled sweet to Jono.

Deep in his soul, Fenrir's presence rumbled in a satisfied way.

"Thank you," Letitia said, her words echoed by the other two.

"We'll talk tithes later this week. Give me a call and we'll set up a meeting at the Tempest bar," Sage said, picking up Marisol's jacket from the floor and helping her back into it. "It's Christmas. You guys should return to your packs."

None of them argued, and all of them left with smiles on their faces and a wonder in their eyes that Jono knew would always stay with him. Sage closed the door behind the group and locked it.

Patrick stood in front of Jono and wrapped his arms around Jono's neck, green eyes searching his. "How do you feel?"

Jono took in a breath, his hands steady when he gripped Patrick by the hips to keep him there. "Like I'm about to dive off a cliff."

"That's life for you." Patrick arched an eyebrow, a faint smile quirking at the corners of his mouth. "We'll catch you though, you know that, right? Well, Sage will catch us. I'll be throwing myself off with you."

Jono kissed him fiercely, until the only thing he could taste was Patrick. "I know."

"*Now* can we open presents?" Wade asked loudly.

Jono wrapped his arms around Patrick and muffled his laugher against the top of Patrick's head. "Sure. Have at it, Wade."

Wade's gleeful cackle was drowned out by the sound of ripping paper. Jono kissed Patrick one more time before leading him back to the armchair. Sage was already curled up with Marek on the sofa once more, a smile on her face that Jono had never seen before.

He sat down on the armchair, tugging Patrick onto his lap only after the mage had grabbed their hot toddies. Patrick slung one leg over the armrest and settled against him, his heartbeat calm and steady in Jono's ears. Jono tucked his fingers beneath Patrick's shirt, rubbing them gently against warm skin.

"Did you get me fucking *socks?*" Wade exclaimed in an affronted voice, holding up a large pack of them, having opened the practical present first by accident rather than the new game console they'd bought him.

Patrick laughed so hard he almost spilled his drink. Jono held him tight so he wouldn't fall off, laughing as well. Surrounded by his pack, Jono felt lighter than he had in a long, long while.

This, right here, was home.

Jono never wanted to leave it.

If you like science fiction romance and are a fan of comics and their movie counterparts, check out Hailey Turner's Metahuman Files series, starting with In The Wreckage.

Don't want to miss out on any Hailey Turner news?
Sign up for her newsletter and download some free short stories while you're there!

GLOSSARY

Short descriptions of words, acronyms, and phrases used in the story that weren't readily explained in text. Included as well are character names.

Abuku, Setsuna: Witch. Director who oversees and leads the Supernatural Operations Agency.

Academy: K-12 school that teaches magic to practitioners of all affinities and designations. All provide boarding options to students.

Aífe: (Pronunciation: ah-FEH) Immortal. A warrior woman and Cú Chulainn's first wife.

Annwn: (Pronunciation: an-noon) Welsh name for the Otherworld.

Ashanti: Immortal. Goddess and mother of all vampires. Takes the shape of an Asanbosam vampire out of West African myths.

Balor: Immortal. Tyrant king of the Fomorians. Personification of drought, blight, and the scorching sun.

Beacot, Sage: Weretiger. A Diné lawyer who works for the fae law firm Gentry & Thyme. Dire to Jono and Patrick's god pack.

Breckenridge, Gerard (Captain): Immortal. Current identity of Cú Chulainn. *See,* Cú Chulainn.

Brigid: Immortal. Celtic goddess associated with fertility, spring, healing, smithing, and poetry. Spring Queen of the Seelie Court. Daughter of the Dagda and member of the Tuatha Dé Danann.

Cadwyn: Immortal. Goddess and daughter of Gwyn ap Nudd within the story.

Cailleach Bheur, the: (Pronunciation: KAI-lach burr) Immortal. Goddess and divine hag. Considered a creator deity and Queen of Winter. Has various Irish and Scottish origin stories.

Cairbre Nia Fer: (Pronunciation: KAHR-bre nia fer) Immortal. Unseelie fae out of the Ulster Cycle.

Carmen: Succubus. First known recorded appearance was in Venice, Italy.

Casale, Giovanni: Human. Chief of the NYPD's Preternatural Crimes Bureau.

Caster Corps: Military branch under the purview of the US Department of the Preternatural. Accepts all magic users except mages.

Ceffyl Dŵr: (Pronunciation: cef-fil dur) A water horse in Welsh folklore. Can evaporate into mist.

Changeling: Fae child left in place of a human child stolen by fae of either Court.

Citadel: United States military academy for magic users. Located in Maryland. All Academies across the nation feed into the Citadel. Mages get automatic inclusion. All other kinds of magic users need recommendations.

Cliffs of Moher: Location. Sea cliffs found in County Clare, Ireland.

Collins, Patrick: Mage. Former combat mage with the Mage Corps, currently an SOA special agent. Has a tainted soul and crippled magic. Is technically a mage in name only due to a soul wound. Co-leader of the god pack he shares with Jono.

Connla: Immortal. Deceased in the myths. Son of Cú Chulainn and Aífe.

Cú Chulainn: (Pronunciation: ku CULL-ann) Immortal. Celtic god and son of the god Lugh. Member of the Tuatha Dé Danann. Irish warrior. Carries the *Gáe Bulg* in fights. Currently hiding under a mortal identity by the name of Gerard Breckenridge.

Dagda, the: Immortal. Celtic god affiliated with life, death, crops, and seasons. Member and king of the Tuatha Dé Danann. Husband to the Morrígan.

Daoine Sídhe: (Pronunciation: dee-na SHEE) Irish term, plural for People of the Mounds. *See*, Tuatha Dé Danann.

Daur da Bláo: Artifact. The Dagda's harp that can put the seasons to right when played.

de Vere, Jonothon: God pack werewolf. Originally from London, England, currently resides in New York City. Alpha of a god pack he co-leads with Patrick.

DEA: Drug Enforcement Administration. A US federal law enforcement agency tasked with combating drug smuggling and distribution. It shares jurisdiction with the FBI and the SOA.

Dire: A rank held only within a god pack. The moniker is taken from the dire wolf but has been shortened to account for different werecreature species. Essentially a rank held by a loyal pack member who helps enforce the alphas' orders.

Dominion Sect: A shadowy terrorist group consisting of mundane humans, rogue magic users, immortals aligned with the hells, and other preternatural creatures intent on destroying the veil between worlds so that hell and its denizens can reign on earth. Some members are attempting to steal godheads in order to ensure their hold on power in the new world they hope to create.

Duine Sídhe: (Pronunciation: din-na SHEE) Irish term, singular form for fae reference. *See*, Tuatha Dé Danann.

Fae: Supernatural beings who reside in Tír na nÓg. There are lesser or higher fae depending on their status and species. *See also*, Tuatha Dé Danann.

Espinoza, Wade: Teenaged fledgling fire dragon. Part of Jono and Patrick's god pack.

Fenrir: Immortal. Wolf in the Norse pantheon. Patron to a god pack.

Ferdiad: (Pronunciation: fer-DEE-a) Immortal. Cú Chulainn's foster brother.

Formorians: Race of supernatural beings who were the enemies of the Tuatha Dé Danann.

Gáe Bulg: Artifact. Cú Chulainn's spear. Translated as "spear of mortal death."

Gap of Dunloe: Location. Narrow mountain pass in County Kerry, Ireland.

Ginnungagap: Primordial void. Belongs to the Norse myths.

Glastonbury Tor: Location. Hill near Glastonbury, England, where St. Michael's Tower sits. Linked to Gwyn ap Nudd in the myths.

Goblin: Lesser fae.

Godhead: Primordial power belonging to immortals that gives them life. The strength of their power can be altered by worship, or lack thereof.

God pack: A pack of werecreatures infected with the god strain of the werevirus. They act as spokespeople for hidden werecreature packs in their territory. They are supported by monetary tithes from the packs under their protection. Very few retain a connection to their animal-god patrons.

Greene, Ethan: Mage. Was a double agent formally employed by the SOA. Is currently a mercenary and allied with the Dominion Sect.

Greene, Hannah: Mage. Currently a vessel. Spiritually deceased.

Gwyn ap Nudd: Immortal. Welsh god and ruler of Annwn. Leads the Wild Hunt.

Hades: Immortal. Greek god of the dead and the Underworld.

Hag's Head, the: Location. In Irish called *Ceann na Cailli*. The name given to the southernmost point of the Cliffs of Moher in County Clare, Ireland. This portion of the cliffs is a rock formation that resembles a woman's head looking out to sea. It is an abode of the Cailleach Bheur.

Hellraisers: A US Department of the Preternatural Special Forces team Patrick once belonged to.

Hermes: Immortal. Greek messenger god and god of trade, thieves, travelers, sports, athletes, border crossings, and guide to the Underworld.

Hernandez, Leon: Werewolf. Partner to Emma Zhang and co-leader of the Tempest pack.

Huginn: Immortal. One of Odin's ravens in the Norse pantheon, whose name means "thought."

Kappa: Japanese folklore water demon.

Kavanaugh, Nicholas: God pack werewolf. Dire of the New York City god pack.

Khan, Youssef: God pack werewolf. Alpha of the New York City god pack.

Ley lines: Metaphysical rivers of powers that drain into nexuses.

Lorg mór: Artifact. The Dagda's great staff.

Lucien: Master vampire. Was a soldier in William the Conqueror's army before being turned by Ashanti. Currently a weapons and magic trafficker. Is wanted by many governments.

Lugh: (Pronunciation: LOO) Immortal. Celtic god and warrior.

Macaria: Immortal. Greek goddess of the blessed death and Hades' daughter.

Mage: Highest rank of magic users and the only practitioners who can tap external power from ley lines and nexuses.

Mage Corps: Military branch under the purview of the US Department of the Preternatural. Accepts only mages.

Magic: Emanating from and powered by a person's soul. Roughly one-quarter of the world's population has magic. Strength varies, with different titles being bestowed depending on a person's magical reach. Casting is divided into defensive wards and offensive spells.

Medb: (Pronunciation: may-ve) Immortal. Celtic goddess. Queen of Air and Darkness. Ruler of the Unseelie Court. Member of the Tuatha Dé Danann.

Morrígan: Immortal. Sometimes depicted as an individual Celtic goddess, or more commonly as a triple goddess, of war and fate. She is particularly affiliated with foretelling of death or victory in battle. Often described as a trio of sisters sometimes given the names of Badb, Macha, and Nemain.

Muginn: Immortal. One of Odin's ravens in the Norse pantheon, whose name means "memory" or "mind."

Mulroney, Nadine: Mage. Works counterintelligence for the PIA. Is fluent in French and based out of Paris, France.

Necromancer: A magic user who can be of any rank. Their magic has an affinity for the dead, allowing them to raise the dead, control zombies, and manipulate the lingering souls of the deceased. Their kind of magic is heavily restricted in use in the United States and in most countries.

Necromancy: A family of magic that deals with the dead, usually involving blood magic and sacrifices. Predominately illegal or restricted in most countries.

Nerys: Spirit. Second rider of the Wild Hunt.

Nexus: Metaphysical lake of power beneath the earth. Usually located in sacred areas or beneath major cities.

Night Court: Vampire group that oversees claimed territory. Headed by a single master vampire. Several Night Courts can exist in the same major city.

Norns: Immortals. Norse Fates.

Odin: Immortal. Norse god of wisdom, healing, death, knowledge, battle, and the gallows, and is the titular king of the Aesir.

Ogre: Lesser fae.

Otherworld: Land of the Celtic pantheon deities, as well as land of the dead, located past the veil. Is more tightly connected to the mortal plane than other mythological worlds. Goes by many different names, and those names can be interpreted as places within it. *See*, Annwn, Underhill, and Tír na nÓg.

Órlaith: (Pronunciation: OR-lah) Immortal. Daughter of Ruadán. The Summer Lady of the Seelie Court and heir to Brigid. Cú Chulainn's fiancée within the story.

Pearson, Keith (Sergeant): Human. Soldier in the Hellraisers.

Persephone: Immortal. Greek goddess of the Underworld and springtime.

PCB: Preternatural Crimes Bureau. A PCB is usually found only in the police departments of major metropolitan areas in the United States. The PCB in New York City is headed up by a bureau chief. The five detective boroughs within the NYPD all field detectives specializing in preternatural crimes through the PCB. The PCB has jurisdiction throughout the five boroughs and its own detachment of cops that work in homicide, narcotics, major crimes, and CSU. The PCB is one of the least manned departments in the NYPD due to the type of cases it handles.

PIA: Preternatural Intelligence Agency. PIA is a national-level foreign intelligence organization overseen by the Secretary of Defense directly through the USDI. The PIA's intelligence operations extend beyond the zones of combat, and approximately half of its employees serve overseas at hundreds of locations and US Embassies in many countries. The agency specializes in collection and analysis of preternatural-source intelligence, both overt and clandestine, while also handling American military-diplomatic relations abroad. The agency has no law enforcement authority. (Equivalent to CIA)

Reed, Noah: Fire dragon. Currently hiding in human form as a three-star Army general who oversees the US Department of the Preternatural.

Red Cap: Lesser fae.

Ruadán: (Pronunciation: ROO-adh-ahn) Immortal. Celtic god and son of Brigid. Father of Órlaith in the story.

Santa Muerte: Immortal. *Nuestra Señora de la Santa Muerte* (English translation: Our Lady of Holy Death), commonly shortened and referred to as Santa Muerte. A personification of death associated with healing, protection, and safe passage to the afterlife.

Scáthach: (Pronunciation: SCAW-thach) Immortal. Scottish warrior woman who taught Cú Chulainn how to fight.

Seelie Court: Court of the spring and summer fae.

SERE: Survival, Evasion, Resistance, and Escape. A military program that provides US military personnel, Department of Defense civilians, private military contractors, and other at-risk agents and personnel with training on how to evade the enemy, survive and resist the enemy if captured, and to escape.

Shields: Ward. Defensive magic used for protection on a large or small scale.

Skellig Islands, the: Location. Irish translation: *Na Scealaga.* Rocky islands in the Atlantic Ocean off the west coast of Ireland.

Sluagh: (Pronunciation: SLOO-ah) Spirits of the restless dead. Aligned with the Unseelie Court.

SOA: Supernatural Operations Agency. SOA is the domestic intelligence and security service of the United States that focuses on magical and preternatural crimes and terrorism. Employs human, preternatural, and magically affiliated people to field positions for domestic defense. (Equivalent to FBI)

Sorcerer/Sorceress: Second-highest rank of magic users and moderately more common than mages but are outnumbered by witches and wizards.

Soulbond: A binding of two or more souls to tie people together for magical needs. Illegal under the laws of all governments.

Spells: Offensive magic.

Spriggan: Lesser fae.

St. Michael's Tower: Location. Tower that sits atop Glastonbury Tor in England. Linked to Gwyn ap Nudd in the myths.

Taylor, Marek: Seer. CEO of PreterWorld, a social media platform geared toward the preternatural and supernatural community. His patrons are the Norns.

Tezcatlipoca: Immortal. Aztec god of obsidian, jaguars, war, strife, night sky, and the night winds.

Threshold: Ward. Applied to a hearth and home for protection to keep out negative magic, spirits, and demons.

Tiarnán: Member of the Tuatha Dé Danann. Carries the title Lord of Ivy and Gold.

Tír na nÓg: (Pronunciation: TEER-na-nog) English translation: Land of the Young. A place in the Otherworld past the veil where the Tuatha Dé Danann and lesser fae reside.

Tremaine: Master vampire. Headed up the Manhattan Night Court. His maker was Lucien.

Troll: Lesser fae.

Tuatha Dé Danann: (Pronunciation: TOO-ah de-danan) Celtic pantheon of gods. They are considered high status fae.

US Department of the Preternatural: Employs all manner of magically affiliated and preternatural people for military service. Active duty combat mages are seconded to the Army, Navy, Air Force, and Marines and are required to go through BTC and joint training.

Underhill: Another name for the Otherworld.

Unseelie Court: Court of the autumn and winter fae.

Veil: The metaphysical barrier between Earth/mundane plane and other worlds/dimensions/planes, and versions of hell and heaven derived from myths.

Walker, Estelle: God pack werewolf. Alpha of the New York City god pack.

Wards: Defensive magic.

Warlock: Most common rank of magic users. On par with witches.

Werecreatures: Humans who are infected with the werevirus.

Can change form into various animalistic shapes. Werecreatures are either infected later on in life or are born with the disease.

Werevirus: An incurable disease that makes those who are infected change into monstrous beasts. Created by an ancient Roman mage, the werevirus was one of the first recorded instances of magically created biological warfare introduced into society. People are born with the werevirus or become infected through intercourse or blood. Two strains exist: a normal strain and a god strain. The god strain has stronger magical properties which can cause the infected to be susceptible to an immortal patron.

Wild Hunt: Supernatural and ghostly hunters who steal souls. Aligned with Gwyn ap Nudd.

Witch: Most common rank of magic users. On par with warlocks.

Yggdrasil: Norse world tree that connects the Nine Realms.

Zeus: Immortal. Greek god of thunder and titular king of the Greek pantheon.

Zhang, Emma: Werewolf. Alpha of the Tempest pack.

AUTHOR'S NOTES

This book was one of the hardest to write because real life got in the way in every possible way it could. A huge thank you to the friends who kept me sane and were there for me during some really hard times.

Nora Sakavic for all her support and friendship.

Leslie Copeland continues to be the best beta reader in the world, and aside from that, she's just an amazingly generous friend.

Lily Morton might live halfway across the world from me, but there are days it's like she's right by my side, and I'm forever grateful for that.

May Archer, my one and only bae, who alpha read this beast over the course of five months and told me to keep going when real life wanted me to stop.

Sheena J. Himes took time out of her busy schedule to read this monster, and I'm always grateful for her generosity.

Bear is forever and always on the other side of a text, and I'm so glad to call her my friend.

Toward the end of writing this book, I lost my fur baby of ten years. Bones was my writing kitty, who would always be on my lap or on my desk as I wrote. I miss him so much, but a whole host of friends were there for me while I grieved, and I'm forever thankful for their support during that tough time: Lucy Lennox, Sloane Kennedy, Aimee Nicole Walker, Jex Lane, Lynn Van Dorn, Piper Scott, Macy Blake, Layla Reyne, along with everyone above. Bones was loved, and I felt that love and support from everyone during the days of his passing.

Last but not least, to my readers. Thank you so much for enjoying the worlds I get to write about so that I can write more. You guys are amazing, and I wouldn't get to do this without you.

I took liberties with police work and federal agencies in this story. I don't work in either field, and I tried to blend both into the world I created as best as possible. My fluency in Irish and Welsh is zero. I did my best to find the correct pronunciations for the names and phrases used in the story. Any mistakes belong to me.

I would be thrilled and grateful if you would consider reviewing *A Crown of Iron & Silver* on Amazon or Goodreads. I appreciate all honest reviews, positive or negative. Reviews definitely help my books get seen, so thank you!

CONNECT WITH HAILEY

Keep up with my book news by signing up for my newsletter and get the free Soulbound prequel short story *Down A Twisted Path* and several free Metahuman Files short stories while you're at it.

Join the reader group on Facebook: Hailey's Hellions

Like Hailey's author page on Facebook

Visit Hailey's website: www.HaileyTurner.com

OTHER WORKS BY HAILEY TURNER

M/M Science Fiction Military Romance:
Captain Jamie Callahan, son of a wealthy senator and socialite mother, is a survivor.

Staff Sergeant Kyle Brannigan, a Special Forces operative, is a man with secrets.

Alpha Team, the Metahuman Defense Force's top-ranked field team, is where the two collide and their lives will never be the same.

Metahuman Files
01 – In the Wreckage
02 – In the Ruins
03 – In the Shadows
04 – In The Blood
05 – In The Requiem

A Metahuman Files: Classified Novella
01 – Out of the Ashes
02 – New Horizons

03 – Fire In The Heart

M/M Urban Fantasy

<u>Soulbound</u>
A Ferry of Bones & Gold – 1
All Souls Near & Nigh – 2
A Crown of Iron & Silver – 3

Thanks for reading!

Printed in Great Britain
by Amazon

32596364R00218